Afternoon Tea

Afternoon Tea

J. R. LaGreca

Copyright © 2008 by J.R. LaGreca.

Library of Congress Control Number: 2007908224
ISBN: Hardcover 978-1-4257-9112-4
       Softcover 978-1-4257-9098-1

All rights reserved. No part of this book may be reproduced or transmitted in any form or by any means, electronic or mechanical, including photocopying, recording, or by any information storage and retrieval system, without permission in writing from the copyright owner.

This is a work of fiction. Names, characters, places and incidents either are the product of the author's imagination or are used fictitiously, and any resemblance to any actual persons, living or dead, events, or locales is entirely coincidental.

This book was printed in the United States of America

You may visit the author's website at www.jrlagreca.com or you may email her at afternoontea@jrlagreca.com.

To order additional copies of this book, contact:
Xlibris Corporation
1-888-795-4274
www.Xlibris.com
Orders@Xlibris.com
43362

3 1327 00488 9572

Contents

PART ONE

Chapter One:	The Roses	13
Chapter Two:	The Debutante Ball	21
Chapter Three:	The Leyden Jar	29
Chapter Four:	The Gift	36
Chapter Five:	Rosewood	42
Chapter Six:	The Portrait	50
Chapter Seven:	The Old Church	57
Chapter Eight:	The Clandestine Kiss	64
Chapter Nine:	Dinner For Two	67
Chapter Ten:	Sweets For My Sweetheart	75
Chapter Eleven:	Cry In the Night	79
Chapter Twelve:	Woman's Woes	85
Chapter Thirteen:	The Red Lady	92
Chapter Fourteen:	The Black Widow	95
Chapter Fifteen:	The Tired Plumes	104
Chapter Sixteen:	With Child	108
Chapter Seventeen:	The Business Excursion	113
Chapter Eighteen:	The Red Devil	117
Chapter Nineteen:	The Banishment	127

PART TWO

Chapter Twenty:	The Witch Hunt	133
Chapter Twenty-One:	The Bridal Gown	141
Chapter Twenty-Two:	The Wedding	145
Chapter Twenty-Three:	The Witches of Salem	152
Chapter Twenty-Four:	Fishermen Fly South	157

Chapter Twenty-Five:	The Magic Potion	163
Chapter Twenty-Six:	Fulton Apothecary	166
Chapter Twenty-Seven:	Key to Your Heart	171
Chapter Twenty-Eight:	Home Sweet Home	176
Chapter Twenty-Nine:	The Ides of March	182
Chapter Thirty:	The Telegram	187
Chapter Thirty-One:	Family Heirloom	193
Chapter Thirty-Two:	The Reception	199
Chapter Thirty-Three:	The Jealous Wife	204
Chapter Thirty-Four:	Turn of the Century	212
Chapter Thirty-Five:	Act of Charity	218
Chapter Thirty-Six:	The Children	222
Chapter Thirty-Seven:	Maggie's Wish	227
Chapter Thirty-Eight:	The Bad Penny	231
Chapter Thirty-Nine:	The Bitter Dispute	238
Chapter Forty:	Head Over Heels	242
Chapter Forty-One:	Church on the Hill	249
Chapter Forty-Two:	The Easter Bonnet	253
Chapter Forty-Three:	The Governess	258
Chapter Forty-Four:	Spring of 1959	263

Bibliography of Afternoon Tea by J. R. LaGreca 271

A GRAIN OF SAND by Jody Riva LaGreca 273

To my darling daughter Sabrina

Cover Victorian Lady by whimzytreasures.com
Author Photograph by *Imran Ahmad*
Photo Presentation by *Nicole Perez* and *Jessica Mileto*
Hair by *Dennis Walter*
Styling and Make up by *Cheryl Bartow*
Special Thanks to the Consultants at Xlibris *Sarah Arizala,*
Sherwin Soy, Kate Philips, Kathrina Garcia, Pierre Pobre,
and *Anthony Corominas*
Also, Special Thanks to *Brooke Curtis* and *Angela Carrillo*
Heartfelt Appreciation for my husband *James*

Part One

Chapter One

The Roses

The town of Clinton, Connecticut lay beneath mounds of freshly fallen snow. A lone shadow against the New England landscape, Lawrence Gray's gnarled form veered alongside the cathedral to the Saint James Cemetery. The skeleton trees exaggerated the old man's pallor while the bouquet of roses he clutched contrasted to the winter and season of his life. Steadied by his cane with his head bowed in remorse, Lawrence struggled as his footsteps imprinted a path in the snow.

Lawrence visited the same gravesite everyday, the granite one adjacent to a twisted oak. The gravesite looked oddly picturesque, smothered with roses and glittering snow.

Meg Bailey spied him as she rushed off to church. This silhouette of a man stirred her heart, and Meg vowed she would pray for him. The mourner with the red roses, the bent old man with the cane, the pathetic romantic, whatever his motivations were, Meg wondered, "Why had the graveyard become his *daily* salvation?"

After the Sunday sermon ended, Meg engaged the priest, Father Dale, in their usual pleasantries as they walked out of Saint James Church side by side. "Father Dale, I've been meaning to ask you, do you know the old man with the cane who visits the cemetery every morning?"

"Yes, he's Lawrence Gray." Father Dale's jovial expression in the aftermath of prayer became somber. "I have often referred to him as 'a lover of graveyard stone'. His wife has been laid out by the sanctuary for forty years now. I buried her myself. What a pitiful day that was. It was the dead of winter, coldest day I could ever remember."

Father Dale's blue eyes became clouded as he struggled to gain his composure. "Lawrence is in his eighties by now. A poor old soul he is. Maybe if he would walk inside the church to pray every now and then it might bring him back to the Lord and give him faith; but not Lawrence Gray, oh no, he'd rather be out in the cemetery, consorting with the devil to try and bring his beloved wife back."

"That's so sad. Do you know where he lives?"

"He lives by himself in the old Tudor on the corner of Haines Street. Lawrence lives for his memories. I have never seen a man so devoted to a woman, let alone one who is deceased."

At that juncture Fanny Brund, the town historian, slipped in-between the two as another congregant diverted Father Dale's attention. "Fanny, do you happen to know Lawrence Gray?" asked Meg.

"Lawrence Gray and his red roses," Fanny's blue eyes twinkled. "I would venture to say Lawrence is the last of the true romantics."

"Fanny, I hate to admit I'm envying the dead," Meg chuckled wryly. "But at twenty-one years old I've never even received flowers from a sweetheart. As much as I'd love getting roses I'm not willing to die for them."

"Be patient, Meg, with your good looks and charm love will come."

Meg smoothed away a dark lock of hair as she smiled hopefully. "It's ironic how people often receive more flowers after they die than when they're alive. I watch Lawrence Gray from my kitchen window every morning and like clockwork, he brings his wife a new bouquet before the old one even has a chance to wither, no matter what the weather. I've often wondered about him. Does he have any family?"

"Yes, his daughter Emma often stops by to see me whenever she's in town. She threatened to take away the keys to his car after his crash up when he plowed into a tree on his way to the cemetery, and broke his leg. He was incapacitated for quite some time."

"It's no wonder it looks like he has trouble making it down the street. Haines Street is quite a distance from here . . . Not to mention forty years is a long time for a man to grieve."

"Forty years is nothing when a man is wracked with guilt. The truth is Lawrence felt responsible for his wife's death. His daughter Emma told me he moved back to Connecticut because he felt he owed it to her." Fanny divulged in a shaky voice.

"What on earth would ever make him feel responsible for his wife's death?" The whites of Meg's eyes illuminated curiously.

Fanny placed her arm on Meg's shoulder. "I'm one of the few people in Clinton who knows the real story. Stop by my house on your way home, and I'll tell you all about it. I live right around the corner on Brentwood. I could certainly use a cup of hot tea."

"So could I, the cold goes right through you. I can't even imagine how Lawrence Gray has the constitution to bear up under these brutal New England winters at his age." Meg's teeth began to chatter as the icy winds stung her cheeks.

There in the living room of Fanny's Victorian house beamed a fireplace. "Oh good, my husband has put on a fresh log. Come Meg, sit by the fire where it's nice and warm."

Meg took a seat on the velvet couch facing the incandescent flames. Fanny disappeared into the kitchen and returned with a silver tray of afternoon tea and crumpets. She placed the tea on the coffee table, and poured Meg a cup before she served the crumpets.

"Meg, I'm about to divulge a mystery to you which has perplexed the entire town of Clinton ever since Lawrence Gray moved back here a year ago." Fanny's silver hair glistened by the light of the fire as she began the saga.

* * *

In the spring of 1895, the young Lawrence Gray and his father William were traveling through the New England countryside in search of work. In their aimless wandering, they came upon the Reed Estate of Fairway.

William's face became enlivened. "This place looks like a palace! Believe it or not, Philip Reed and I were boyhood buddies. Do I dare ask for him looking like this?" William brushed off his seedy black overcoat, and readjusted his hat over his windblown, salt, and pepper hair.

"Father, true friends aren't concerned about appearances. If the way you look bothers Philip Reed then nothing is lost anyway."

"Well, I suppose you're right. It's certainly worth a try, and with an estate like this there must be plenty of work." Weary from travel the men settled their horses and buggy, before William sounded the brass knocker of Fairway.

Philip Reed's eldest son, fifteen-year-old Hal, opened the door. He stood nearly six feet tall with a shock of blonde hair. "Can I help you?" he inquired in a cold, flat tone.

"May I speak to Mr. Reed?" William sheepishly asked.

"Whom shall I say is calling on the master of this estate?" Hal shot back, glaring at father and son in disdain.

"I'm William Gray and this is my son, Lawrence. Are you Mr. Reed's son?"

"Yes, I am. And may I ask why you request to see my father?"

"I'm an old friend of your father's from boarding school," William meekly answered as he absentmindedly straightened his lapel.

Much to their surprise, excitement stirred as the name William Gray echoed throughout the mansion. Philip Reed quickly came forth. He resembled a Viking, impeccably dressed with blonde, sun-streaked hair, and broad shoulders. In contrast, William looked like a beggar in shabby work clothes with an unshaven face. The two men shared a gregarious greeting, full of backslapping and sentiment. It seemed as if a day had not passed between the men even though it had been thirty years since they had last seen each other.

Just then a beautiful creature with golden curls and blue eyes as ethereal as the sky gracefully stepped down the winding staircase. Her minuscule waist was cinched into an ecru gown full of ruffles and ribbons. The cameo brooch fastened onto the top of her bodice could not compete with her porcelain complexion.

As she reached the bottom of the stairs, Philip gently slipped her arm into his and led her over to his guests. "Emily, I would like you to make the acquaintance of an old friend of mine from boarding school, Mr. William Gray. William, this is my daughter Emily."

William tipped his worn hat, "Pleased to meet you, Miss Emily."

Emily curtsied while she and Lawrence's eyes became locked, as a magnet drew them inward. Electricity sparked in the air as they each felt the unexpected shock of the other. Lawrence was an impressive sight with thick black hair, an olive complexion, and an ironclad physique. A welcome change from the upper echelon of society; there before Emily stood a rugged man who smelled like the good earth intermingled with the wind.

Emily coquettishly turned her shoulders toward Lawrence as William Gray interjected, "Miss Emily Reed, allow me to introduce you to my son, Lawrence Gray."

Emily's dainty hand melted beneath Lawrence's strong grasp, and lingered in a sweet aftermath. "How do you do, Miss Emily?" Lawrence emanated in a powerful vibrato before he tipped his riding hat with finesse.

"I'm pleased to make your acquaintance, Lawrence." Their eyes linked in the magic; their thoughts concealed.

"How old are you, Lawrence, my boy?" Philip inquired with a piercing glance.

"I'll be eighteen on June 23, Mr. Reed."

"You and Emily are only two months apart; she will turn eighteen in April." Philip's eyes narrowed in scrutiny. "If I may ask, what brings you gentlemen to this part of town?"

"My boy and I were looking for work when we chanced upon your estate. We were forced to sell our farm after my wife Henrietta passed away, God rest her soul. I don't mean to put you in an awkward position, Philip, if you have no work for us, we'll just be on our way and move on." William sighed despondently.

"No need to look any further, my old friend, William. There is plenty of work for you and your son out in the fields. I will send for the stable boys to turn in your horses at once, and show you to the guest quarters." Philip gave William's burdened shoulders another back slapping welcome.

Emily looked delighted by the arrangement as she trailed behind the men. Her father led Lawrence to his chamber down t' hall from her damask room. On the marble table outside his chamber, Lawrence spied the book *The Mystery of Love Courtship and Marriage Explained*, published by Wehman Brothers in 1890.

Lawrence lifted the book tentatively, as he stifled a smile. He had the identical volume inside his trunk, though he dared not to admit it in mixed company.

"That is the precious possession of Miss Emily," Philip chuckled lightheartedly. "Young girls are all alike with their heads in the clouds."

"My head is not in the clouds, Father," Emily blushed. "We ladies of marriageable age must acquaint ourselves with proper protocol."

"It seems one day they're playing with dolls, and the next they're looking for a husband. I still cannot believe my little girl will be having her Debutante Ball next month. My wife Margaret has been counting the days before Emily will get scooped up by one of New England's most eligible bachelors." Philip Reed gushed with pride.

Philip opened the door to Lawrence's handsome quarters. "Here is your chamber, Lawrence, my boy. Your father and I used to be like brothers, so settle down and relax before I send up a tray with supper."

"The library is at the end of the hallway, if you're not too tired, Lawrence, maybe we could read poetry later," Emily suggested with a shy smile.

Philip chuckled. "Oh, Emily and her poetry, girls are such fanciful creatures!"

"Actually I'm fond of poetry, especially Shakespeare and Lord Byron," Lawrence divulged with a smile while his forlorn eyes made him resemble a stray cat in a pleasing new environment.

"You're a better man than me, Lawrence." Philip smirked. "I have absolutely no patience for abstract images, put me in front of a history book and I'm content."

"Well, you were always a history buff," William interjected as he shuffled his worn out shoes down the pristine hallway of ivory walls.

Philip showed William to his handsome chamber. It had a Chippendale poster bed and a nice view of the garden. "William, old boy, it's great to see you after all these years."

Philip's hard angled face softened as he smiled. "My wife Margaret and I spend a lot of time in Europe buying and selling rare treasures. My sons Hal and Charles are usually away at private school so it's pretty quiet around here. Maggie's sister Lilly stays to look after Emily when we travel. Girls are a lot more trouble than the boys." Philip rolled his eyes in amusement.

"Your daughter Emily is perfectly charming. There's no doubt she will get snatched up by one of New England's finest." William's face became sullen in self-reflection. "You're a lucky man, Philip. Henrietta and I had always wanted a daughter."

"You have luck as well. Lawrence is a fine young man, William. He reminds me a lot of you. Well, I'll have Miss Lydia bring up supper so you can unwind and get a good night's sleep. The men start working in the fields at the crack of dawn, so be prepared."

After supper, Lawrence found Emily at the mahogany table in the library mulling over a pile of books. Emily looked delighted as he entered the room. "Good evening, Lawrence," she greeted in a soft voice.

"Good evening, Miss Emily, I was hoping I might find you here when I noticed the light on." Lawrence gave her an awkward half-smile.

"You can find me here every evening. I would much rather sit and read than stay in the parlor with my mother and entertain whoever happens to stop by. It's always the same meaningless chatter. Shakespeare has said it all ages ago. Nothing in human nature or life has changed one iota, yet these highfalutin members of high society think they own the world." Emily laughed as Lawrence sat across from her and their eyes locked.

"That's the cycle of life. It's like when parents have a baby, they feel like it's the first baby ever born. Humor them." Lawrence's dazzling smile lit up his face.

"You figured that out fast for a newcomer," Emily quipped. "All I ever do is humor everyone, that's why my father says, 'My head is in the clouds.'"

"Well, I wouldn't exactly call myself a newcomer in the true sense of the word. If anyone's head is in the clouds it's mine, from working out in the fields before we sold our farm, and now thanks to your father, I'll be working in the fields with my head in the clouds once again." Lawrence chuckled lustily.

"Well, I see we have a lot in common," Emily's blue eyes gazed deeply into his. "We both have our heads in the clouds while everyone else is eating themselves into oblivion."

Unable to contain her laughter, Emily whispered, "Just between you and me, my mother cannot even fit into the dress she intends to wear to my Debutante Ball. She had it released two times already, which is another reason I prefer the library to the parlor where every imaginable dessert is set out."

"I've never known that life, Miss Emily. I'm practically self-taught. After working on the farm all day, I used to either read or set up an easel and paint. My specialty is painting portraits."

"I bet you're a fine artist, Lawrence," Emily enthused. "I can tell by your hands; they look very strong and capable. They reveal you're a hardworking man who has character and heart. I always look at a man's hands; they tell me a lot about him."

"And if I was to say I always look at a lady's hands, and then tried to steal a peak at yours; I'm sure I would be slapped," Lawrence teased with a playful grin.

"Not by me." Emily lifted her tiny hands from her lap and placed them on the table. "So what do my hands tell you, Lawrence?" Emily coyly asked.

"You've been protecting them with white gloves your entire life. They're perfect." Lawrence's voice deepened from the pit of his chest. "You're a delicate creature, Miss Emily, and I wouldn't want to say anything out of line. I have a distinct feeling your father would not appreciate me admiring your hands."

"Maybe, but then again, my father doesn't have the slightest understanding of what makes me happy. That's why I drown myself in Shakespeare and Jane Austen . . . Lawrence, listen to the first line of Jane Austen's *Pride and Prejudice*," Emily opened up the Jane Austen novel on the table.

"It is a truth universally acknowledged that a single man in possession of a good fortune must be in want of a wife." Emily grimaced. "Does that mean if a man doesn't have a good fortune he does *not* want a wife? The title sums it up; high society is all about 'Pride and Prejudice.' Not me, I look at a man for who he is, and how his circumstance has shaped him. I admire how resourceful a man is, and what's inside his soul, not what's inside his bank account. The truth is money can make men boring and arrogant."

"That's a provocative outlook. I suppose it explains why you're treating me so cordially. It's quite unexpected, Miss Emily, and I must thank you for that."

"And I thank my lucky stars I finally have someone to talk to, Lawrence, and please call me Emily." Her eyes softened to his penetrating gaze.

Lawrence's face flushed. "Emily, I have traveled a long, hard road before arriving at Fairway. I often wonder about the people who come into my life. I believe it's Divine providence. I hope I'm not offending you, but when I saw you walk down the stairs today you reminded me of an angel. Everything about you is light and airy." Lawrence sighed as he bent his head downward, "While everything about me is dark and brooding."

"No, Lawrence, a son is a barometer of his father, and my father attests to your father's kind heart and flawless character. I'm sure my father will become as fond of you as he is of your father," Emily exclaimed with conviction.

"As long as I know my place, and do my job well, hopefully your father will find favor in me," Lawrence replied as his eyes became downcast.

"Just so you know I have found favor in you, Lawrence." Emily beamed. "I feel like I'm in another world sitting here with you. It's as if I know you for my entire life."

Chapter Two

The Debutante Ball

Morning came up like a golden dome, glittering upon the horizon. The winding stairway in the center hallway had a succession of white bows tied onto the banister. An entourage of servants scrambled about.

Emily rose out of bed to her everyday accompaniments of lace, bustle, and petticoat. She and Lawrence met by the staircase on their way down to the breakfast parlor. "Tonight is your big night, Emily, are you excited?"

"Please, Lawrence, all of this fuss is far too ostentatious for me. I would be much more content to sit in the library with you and read poetry."

"You say that now, Emily, but just wait until you're the star of the evening. Every girl deserves her moment in the spotlight just like all the Jane Austen novels you revere. Why should you be any less the heroine with all your attributes?"

Emily's cheeks blushed in a delicate hue of pink. "I have no need to be a heroine, Lawrence, or in the limelight. All I want is to be understood. You're the only one around this stuffy place who I can really talk to. Who else in this entire house has an appreciation for poetry?"

"You, my dear Emily," Lawrence tenderly replied while his dark eyes smoldered with passion.

"Lawrence, the truth is I was going crazy from boredom before you came along." Emily grazed her delicate hand on his. "What I wouldn't do just to take a long walk with you today and feel the wind in my hair, and lay out a blanket by the apple tree to relax and read poetry together in the sunshine."

Lawrence smiled hopefully. "Maybe I could read you some Shakespeare tomorrow night."

Emily pouted. "That is if we're not bombarded with unexpected company. I feel like I'm being auctioned off to the highest bidder. It's sickening, and I want no part of it!"

Lawrence sighed as he looked at her longingly. The fragrance of honeysuckle and freshly cut grass eased in through the window as the pair descended down to the breakfast parlor. A bounty of home baked muffins, croissants, and meat pie had been set out.

Emily's mother Margaret Reed sat as sedate as usual, sipping on her morning tonic. The neat bun, pulled tightly at the nape of her neck, accentuated her stern features. Emily entered the room first and greeted her mother cordially.

Smiling, her mother beckoned Emily. "Come join me, Emily, we need to discuss last minute details of tonight's festivities."

When Lawrence stepped into the room, Mrs. Reed's expression quickly changed to disdain to see him trailing behind Emily like a dark shadow. She gave Lawrence a piercing glance.

"After breakfast, Lawrence," Mrs. Reed ordered curtly, "I need your help tidying the gardens. The expanse over to the left needs sprucing. The weeds must be uprooted, and the debris on the veranda needs to be removed at once."

"Yes, Ma'am, I will gladly take care of everything," Lawrence assured in a compliant tone.

Emily stole a peak at Lawrence's humbled countenance. "Lawrence, I hope you will be joining us tonight in the Red Ballroom."

"Emily, it would not be fitting for me to join in with your high society," Lawrence politely replied as he kept his eyes focused on his plate.

"Nonsense, if you would care to join in on the celebration, you are more than welcome," Emily insisted as Margaret Reed winced in displeasure.

Breaking the strained silence, Lawrence graciously replied, "Thank you for the invitation, Emily, but I must confess I don't have the suitable attire for such an occasion," Lawrence admitted in distress as he sunk into his seat.

"Well you're in luck!" Emily beamed. "You and my father are around the same height and build. I bet the two of you wear the same size clothing," Emily interjected as Margaret Reed's lips became terse.

"My father has a closet full of suits he hasn't worn in years. I know one of them will do you justice, Lawrence. I'll have one of the chambermaids set one out for you." Emily smiled reassuringly.

Mrs. Reed shot Emily an angry look as she urged Lawrence to hurry up with his breakfast so he could get right to work. Lawrence ate as quickly as he could, and gave Emily one final glance before he left.

Lawrence came upon his father working in the garden in preparation for the ball. "This has been one hectic morning," William echoed as he kept his head bent down to the ground.

"Mrs. Reed has given me my own list of instructions as well," Lawrence said with a frown as he started to clear the verandah.

"You know Emily has invited me to her Debutante Ball tonight," Lawrence divulged with reservation.

William laughed beneath his breath. "Trust me, son, the only place we're truly welcome when it comes to their high society is out here working. Besides you'll be so tired later you'll probably pass out from exhaustion. These balls start late, and go on until the wee hours of the night."

"Believe me, Father, if I could be there with Emily, I would get a second wind," Lawrence professed.

"Reading poetry with Emily in the library is one thing, son. If you decide to go, Mr. Reed will end up putting you to work, trust me." William lifted his brows knowingly.

Lawrence toiled straight through the day without taking a break for lunch. Despite his efforts to complete his tasks in a timely manner, dusk had begun to drench the sky with the glamour of stars. Such would be the setting for the grand occasion where Emily Reed would avail herself to a bevy of suitors, all vying for her attention. This realization shot through Lawrence like a wave of doom.

Lawrence pondered how in the one month he had been at Fairway, he had taken an irresistible fancy to the charms of Miss Emily Reed. Lawrence asked himself, "Could it be the slight curl of her upper lip when she *speaks?* Or is it the sweet scent of her *cologne* which she concocts by adding rose petals to oil? Then again, maybe it's the way her *eyes* catch the light before she lavishes me with her serene gaze."

Wearily, Lawrence climbed the long staircase to his chamber, and sighed with resignation as he switched on the light. Much to his surprise, he found a white shirt, a black linen suit with a collared vest, and a satin bow tie waiting for him on his bed.

Another delight awaited, someone had drawn a bath for him. Lawrence immersed his aching body in the soothing, hot water, and scrubbed himself clean. He wrapped a towel around his refreshed body, and combed his hair back. Lawrence then put on the ensemble which transformed him into a gentleman, a feeling he was unaccustomed to. Lawrence looked in the beveled mirror of his chamber and found the change striking.

The hour had struck at half past nine; dapper guests began to drift into the ballroom known as "Grand Red." The walls were covered in red brocade wallpaper. Gold moldings framed high ceilings, and woodcut scenes of cherubs were displayed above the doorways. Stately oil paintings from the early 1800s graced the walls in heavy gold frames.

Margaret Reed stood by the entranceway dressed in a coral, bead encrusted chiffon gown. She had tried to camouflage her thick middle to no avail. Nonetheless, a strand of heirloom pearls adorned her alabaster skin with the glory of the olden days. Margaret greeted her guests with friendly handshaking and joviality.

Emily was still upstairs fussing over last minute details with her ladies' maid. "Miss Agnes, please make sure the bustle in the back is evenly spread." Miss Agnes' nimble fingers dutifully arranged the bustle to precision.

Lawrence stalled in the center hallway anticipating Emily's grand entrance. Finally, a vision of perfection, Emily emerged. Her peaches and cream complexion glowed. Golden tendrils framed her face. She epitomized an emerging woman wearing a white chiffon gown with a scooped neckline softened by a ruffle. Her milky white breasts peeked over the top while her cinched waist appeared to be no more than eighteen inches.

Lawrence watched spellbound as Emily floated down the stairway looking as beautiful as a goddess. Emily smiled shyly at Lawrence before she walked into the grand ballroom. No less than a bride, a gasp of awe overtook the room as she entered.

Lawrence followed behind her, and blended into the myriad of suitors. All the available men were dressed in formal symmetry making Lawrence feel like just one of many. Lawrence's heart became wrenched as Emily demurely took her place beside her mother.

Lawrence eavesdropped as Mrs. Reed introduced Emily to Sir Walter Huntley, a doctor of well respected lineage who wore wire rimmed eyeglasses. "My Emily plays the piano beautifully, and I dare say she has a delightful voice as well. She's fluent in both Italian and Spanish, and of course, English, we must not forget that small detail, Sir Walter." Mrs. Reed chuckled, as did Sir Walter Huntley. "The way some of the young ladies converse nowadays I'm not so sure of their familiarity with their native tongue." Their conversation trailed off into gay laughter as Emily looked embarrassed by her mother's boasting.

Lawrence could not take his eyes off Emily, even while the butlers went around offering delicacies. He ate looking sideways, and watched as Emily was about to be dispersed to her high society. Before long the piano and instrumentation began, melting melody into the magic of night. The dance floor became a whirlwind of fancy footwork as a stampede of suitors exchanged dances and words.

Lawrence remained on the outskirts, and without the courage to ask Emily for a spin on the dance floor. He felt diminished amongst the finest men New England had to offer. Lawrence proceeded to walk out onto the veranda in defeat. He hoped some fresh air might do him good.

As he turned his back to exit, Hope Chancler, a bubbly blonde, giddily grabbed onto his arm. "Come on and join the fun; I haven't seen you dance once yet."

They exchanged introductions before they shared in a dance. Lawrence's eyes averted from Emily's furtive glance. He felt out of place to be dancing at all. In the meantime, Hope Chancler could not entice Lawrence in the slightest, even considering the feminine trimmings of her perfume and lace dress.

The music stopped for a brief pause, and Miss Cha 'r disengaged herself. "I'll be right back, Lawrence; now don't let anyone else sweep you off your feet while I'm powdering my nose." Hope twirled one of her curls as she giggled flirtatiously.

Emily broke away from Sir Walter Huntley, and approached Lawrence. "Are you enjoying yourself, Lawrence?" she asked in a clipped tone.

Lawrence nodded in a subdued affirmation when Emily continued with a displeased expression, "I see you've taken a fancy to Hope Chancler. Well, a word of advice, Lawrence, always look down at a girl's boots before dancing with her. If you had, you would have noticed Hope is careless with her buttons."

Emily continued indignantly, "My Aunt Lilly taught me all proper young ladies must have their boots and gloves in perfect order. See for yourself."

Emily suggestively lifted her petticoat, and offered Lawrence the sight of one of her boots with its mother of pearl buttons all intact.

"Most impressive to my sights," Lawrence replied as their eyes melded. "I would much rather dance with you, Emily. I was afraid to ask. I couldn't help notice you've been swamped all evening while I feel like I'm out of place here."

"Are you kidding, Lawrence? I've been waiting for you to rescue me from all those pompous men who have egos bigger than their hearts ever since I walked in here." Lawrence reached for her arm, and they began the two-step.

"Emily, you're the most beautiful girl in the room, not to mention the one with the most perfect boots." They shared an intimate laugh as Lawrence noticed from his peripheral vision Hope Chancler had returned, and looked crestfallen to see he was occupied. He glanced down at her boots, only to see they were scruffy and careless of a few buttons. He realized Miss Chancler was less the lady than he had first thought.

Lawrence became lost in Emily's fragrant hair. He floated weightless on a cloud, and felt the music in his feet which moved irrespective of him. At that juncture Clive Barron, a blonde headed gentleman with a sprinkling of sunny freckles approached, "May I break in, Miss Emily?"

"No thank you, Sir Clive, I have made my choice for the rest of the evening." Emily veered away.

"Emily, as much as I would love to be your choice for not only the rest of the evening, but for the rest of my life as your devoted husband," Lawrence gazed down at her with tender emotion. "But Emily, my sweetheart, we both already know your parents would certainly not want you to marry a man who doesn't even own a suit. I might as well be at a masquerade ball for all my appearance is worth, and yet my love for you is immeasurable, my sweet Emily." Lawrence vowed with a pained expression.

"Lawrence, how could I ever marry one of these pretentious men when it's you I've fallen in love with? You're the one I want to spend my life with?" Emily woefully professed. "I intend to tell my father how we feel about each other, and hope he'll understand. After all he's so fond of your father, and treats him like a brother. It's not like he put you in the servants' quarters or anything."

In the meantime, Philip and Margaret Reed looked at the dancing couple in disdain. "Philip, how I wish you had not welcomed William Gray and his son Lawrence into our family. Now look what has become! I warned you the Grays were men of inferior status," Margaret reprimanded with a stern countenance. "If only you would have listened to me, Philip, and had them stay in the servants' quarters where they belong. But to have welcomed them as a part of our family has no doubt given Emily the wrong message."

"Having my old, best friend sleeping in the servants' quarters, I will not hear of it, Margaret, however, I will break up their dance in no uncertain terms! The Grays might inhabit the guest quarters, but they are still merely field hands!"

"Well, for a start, please have the Grays eat their meals with the servants in the hallway. They do not belong with us in the dining room, Philip; once in a while fine, but not every night like you have been doing for the past month!"

"Let us not waste anymore time about what will be in the future, Margaret. I must break them up at once!" Philip Reed hurriedly cut into their dance, leaving Lawrence dazed in his borrowed suit.

"You must dance with the other gentlemen, Emily dear. I realize you find comfort in Lawrence's friendship, but our privileged society has a whole world waiting for you."

"Father, the only privilege I want is to be true to my heart. I have already danced with nearly every man in the entire room, now including even you." Emily sighed in frustration. "I'm technically a woman now, and I can make my own decisions on which gentlemen I fancy. Lawrence and I want to get married. I have fallen in love with him, Father, and he feels the same way about me."

"You love Lawrence," Philip cried out, "How preposterous! Where does a field hand come to an heiress? Don't turn this Debutante Ball into a sham! Mother and I have gone through a lot of effort for you to find a suitable husband. Lawrence might be a nice young man, and granted his father is a dear old friend of mine whose relationship I value; however, due to their present circumstance, Lawrence is not a proper match for you, Emily. A gentleman from a prominent family is the only man who will suit my standards, and Mother is just as adamant about your marrying well."

"Father, since when does the acquisition of wealth mean more than feelings? I have always been one to follow my heart. There is not one eligible bachelor in this entire room who can come even close to the rapport I have with Lawrence. We're soul mates; it's written in the stars, and nothing can ever change that!" Emily tearfully professed. "It's Divine providence. Lawrence has said so himself."

"Divine lunacy is a more appropriate description! Follow your heart against my approval will grant you disinheritance from your birthright! Emily, you must not pursue this folly any longer!" Philip Reed warned.

Emily indignantly broke from their dance as soon as the song ended. She went to find Lawrence when her father intercepted, "Lawrence, I need your help out yonder in the yard."

Startled and broken from the stardust of the evening, Lawrence followed Philip Reed outside. The scent of honeysuckle swelled up from the earth in the sweet, solitude of disappointment. The full moon, which beamed effervescently in the sky, now slung down like a shot of torment. On the threshold of rhapsody, where just moments before he had held Emily close, Lawrence became overcome by the throngs of the elite sipping champagne on the veranda, and chattering amongst each other.

Philip Reed led Lawrence over to a long table, where ample bottles of champagne were set out in silver canisters. "Lawrence, I need you to help if anyone's drinks need refreshing," Philip demanded with an uncompromising expression.

"Yes Sir, at your service." Lawrence feigned enthusiasm as Philip Reed presented him with a pair of white gloves which immediately changed Lawrence's status from eligible bachelor to anonymous servant.

Lawrence begrudgingly retreated behind the barricade which divided him from Emily while a line began to form in front of him. He overturned tumbler after tumbler of effervescence, while he succumbed to the fizzle of his own fate.

Lawrence glanced up at the doorway as Emily stood for one fleeting moment before her father took her arm, and led her back inside. Devoured in bondage, Sir Dexter Lund, the redheaded son of the famed Rosewood estate, whose ancestry could be traced back to British royalty, entrapped Emily for the rest of the evening. She made small, unimportant chatter with him while bemoaning Lawrence's exile along the outskirts.

When the sumptuous trays of desserts began to abound, Lawrence held the tray their way with thwarted emotion. "These look good, Emily." Sir Dexter pointed to a blueberry tart while Emily remained motionless. It was difficult for her to reach for any selection.

"Why not try the butter creams, Miss Emily," Lawrence suggested.

Emily took a butter cream as the colloquial "Miss Emily" hung over them like a dark cloud. It was at that rendering the differential of their ranks was drawn. It was so fine a line. Lawrence looked over at Emily, and recalled the incense of her flaxen hair as Sir Dexter absentmindedly scurried her away. The slight Sir Dexter walked so light on his toes it looked like he was about to burst into a pirouette.

Chapter Three

The Leyden Jar

While out on the fields harvesting the corn, William Gray chided. "Get a moving, Lawrence, Philip Reed has been generous to us, but sometimes I fear we're hanging on by a thread. The work we do doesn't even make a dent in this field, just look at it." Lawrence scanned the expansive farmlands, and dreaded his labor. Yet deep inside he knew it could have been far worse had Mr. Reed not taken them in.

"Will we be eating dinner with the Reeds in the dining room on Sunday?" Lawrence asked with anticipation.

"Yes, but then it's back to the main hallway with the servants," William echoed through the distance that divided them as he struggled to keep his footing on the unsteady terrain.

"Water always seeks its own level, son."

"Don't remind me; it's been that way ever since Emily's Debutante Ball. She never reads in the library anymore, how I miss sitting with her and chatting." Lawrence's eyes became filled with yearning.

"I know you've become fond of Emily, but you certainly can't expect the Reeds to have us as their in-laws in our present circumstance."

"I don't mean to be rude or ungrateful, Father, but I just can't bring myself to socialize with the servants in the Pug's Parlor after dinner. They're loud and boisterous, not to mention uneducated. I would much rather spend my time in the library with Emily, but unfortunately I have barely had the chance to even speak to her since her Debutante Ball."

"Things have changed since then, Lawrence, perhaps Emily's parents have forbidden her to be alone with you now that she's of marrying age."

Come Sunday, William and Lawrence Gray joined the Reed family in the main dining room. Hands were held as they got ready to recite grace. Lawrence cherished the chance to hold Emily's delicate palm in his. He believed the Almighty had pondered over Emily's flesh for longer than other mortals. He thought she had received her beauty at the price of others' neglect, with the multitudes of ordinary folk suffering for her perfection.

They all began grace in unison. "'Bless us, O Lord, and these thy gifts which we are about to receive from thy bounty, through Christ, our Lord. Amen.'"

Emily's younger blonde-haired brothers Hal and Charles were home for Easter vacation. They were seated together on the other side of her. They both had their hair combed in identical middle parts. Raucous laughter occurred amongst the brothers without warning while everyone else sat in formal mode at the long mahogany table with carved legs. Hand embroidered mats placed at each setting accentuated the polished wood. Bronze candelabra flanked opposite ends of the table while the last crest of sunshine streamed inward with the luminescence of sunset.

Everyone lifted their goblets as Philip Reed offered a toast in the Latin words, "Pax Introentibus-Salus Extentibus."

Philip then translated in a less dramatic tone, "Peace to those who enter; good health to those who depart."

Philip Reed made a motion to sip the rare vintage wine. Emily and Lawrence engaged in the consumption with the elders, while the younger boys drank grape juice. Lawrence pondered the latter part of Mr. Reed's toast. "Good health to those who depart." He feared perhaps he and his father were overstaying their welcome and should depart.

Lawrence tried to dismiss the thought when Miss Lydia brought in a sumptuous fare of roasted chicken with chestnut chutney, sweet potatoes, minced pie, and a rack of lamb. Large beefsteak tomatoes, ripened on the vine, accompanied garden greens.

"Delicious minced pie, Philip, this really brings me back to when Henrietta and I first purchased our farm. Minced pie was our staple. Of course, that was one of the only dishes Henrietta knew how to make back then." William and Lawrence Gray shared a sentimental smile.

"Don't worry it's not much different around here," Mr. Reed whispered in jest. "If it's not fresh cooked minced pie, then it's left over minced pie."

"I have no complaints. I would undoubtedly starve without it," Emily added lightheartedly. "So tell me, Mother, how long do you and Father plan to stay in France?"

"We are expected to return by the end of June, but with your father there is no guarantee." The aristocratic Margaret Reed's face was set in her trademark expression which made her look perpetually annoyed.

"What can I tell you, I'm a gypsy at heart?" Mr. Reed glowed with wanderlust.

"Here, Lawrence, you might as well join in on the family favorite." Emily passed the minced pie.

"It certainly tastes better then when I was a boy," Lawrence commented.

"Children are not keen enough to appreciate the delicacies in life," retorted Emily. "Why just take a look at my brothers." Everyone at the table chuckled to see the boys were still working on a piece of corn bread, spread with a generous layer of strawberry jam.

"Come on, boys, you don't want to stunt your growth. Here eat hearty!" Mrs. Reed passed the roasted chicken and potatoes their way while the brothers squirmed and grimaced like bookends with their look-alike cherub faces.

The sky began to dim when Miss Lydia, in her white bonnet and matching apron, came in to ignite the candles. "Too bad we can't set the fireplace ablaze, but they're out of commission ever since the spring cleaning," Emily said with a frown.

Lawrence glanced at the dwindling firewood. "Mr. Reed, you must have noticed the old oak tree out back is near dead. I will fell the tree for firewood."

"Cut the old oak tree down!" Emily protested. "That tree is like a good old friend. Maybe it can somehow be saved!"

"I hate to be the bearer of bad news, Emily, but its branches are in danger of breaking off and damaging the stables the next bad storm we have." Lawrence turned toward Emily. "I'll admit all good friends should be as steadfast as the old tree, but half the bark has crumbled to its death already."

The word "death" cast a somber tone as the bell rang, and Miss Lydia returned to set out another entree. The conversation then switched from the person sitting on the right to the person sitting on the left, and so forth.

For a finale, Miss Lydia returned with a tray full of home baked desserts and sweetbreads. The heavyset woman curtsied as she scurried off. It appeared as if she had already indulged in her fair share of sweets.

Mr. Reed got ready to recite the after meal grace. Emily and Lawrence received the bonus of a few extra moments of holding hands while everyone fumbled to catch up. Out of nowhere a jolt of electricity transmitted a shock, and the chain of prayer was relinquished in a frenzy.

Hal and Charles began to laugh beneath their breath as Mrs. Reed shrieked. She seemed faint from the shock to her system. "My smelling salts, get me my smelling salts, Miss Lydia!" She demanded in agitation.

Miss Lydia rushed off while Charles and Hal's faces reddened in suppressed laughter, and their turned up noses crinkled like accordions. Mr. Reed jumped up in anger to discover the two boys holding onto a jar.

"What is the meaning of this? Explain yourselves right this instant!" Mr. Reed demanded through clenched teeth.

Hal sheepishly admitted, "I followed the directions from the January issue of Harper's Young People on how to make a Leyden jar. I glued tinfoil along the inner and outer edges of the jar, and secured a piece of hardwood with a hole bored out on top, through which I attached a brass wire and chain, and fastened a brass ball. It creates electricity; an electrical current is transmitted when I hold my hand on the outer foil, and Charles holds the brass ball."

"I can see that!" Mr. Reed cried out.

Mrs. Reed inhaled her smelling salts in distress while Mr. Reed sucked in his terse lips until they almost disappeared completely. "Boys, this activity is not appropriate for a Sunday dinner!"

Mr. Reed angrily confiscated the jar. "All right boys, now enough of your shenanigans; you both are to go to your chambers without dessert. It is no laughing matter to startle people like that. Mother could have had one of her fainting spells, not to mention the disrespect of playing practical jokes before the reverence of prayer!"

Philip Reed's cheeks tensed inward and outward sporadically. The brothers looked deflated as they departed from the table in size order. Their clumsy black shoes dragged along the rug in submission.

At this inopportune moment Miss Lydia appeared all aglow. "You have a gentleman caller, Miss Emily. Shall I show him into the dining room?"

"Show who in?" Emily flinched in annoyance.

"Sir Dexter Lund." The name reverberated unkindly in Lawrence's head.

"By all means show the gentleman caller in," Philip Reed enthusiastically announced. It became apparent Sir Dexter Lund was a bachelor of good standing. Emily straightened her stature in obedience to her parents' preference while Lawrence slumped into his seat.

In walked the likes of Sir Dexter Lund, with his red hair combed backward. His freckles looked painted on with precision while the amber light of the candles exaggerated their overabundance. He was dressed in a dapper white jacket and brown riding pants with leather boots polished to a high gloss.

"I brought this for you, Emily." Sir Dexter handed Emily the April 1895 issue of Harper's Young People.

"Thank you, Sir Dexter." Emily seemed more pleased with the gift than the giver.

Mr. Reed showed Sir Dexter to the other side of Emily. "Do have dessert with us, Sir Dexter."

"How nice of you to join us, just feel free to stop by whenever you feel inclined," Mrs. Reed gushed, seeming to have miraculously recovered from her spell.

Lawrence's sweet bread turned sour in his mouth, while Emily clutched the Harper's newspaper. "Sir Dexter, as entertaining as this newspaper can be, if you would have walked in here just moments before you would have witnessed one of Harper's experiments in action." Emily chuckled as she caught Lawrence's eye in amusement.

"Enough said, Emily dear," Mr. Reed interrupted. "We would not want to burden Sir Dexter with minor details, before we say our after meal grace."

Everyone went to hold hands again. Lawrence became keenly aware how Emily's palm was tightly pressed into Sir Dexter's alabaster hand as well, while the prayer echoed.

Afterward, Sir Dexter asked Lawrence in a patronizing manner, "So tell me, Lawrence, how are the crops doing at this time of year?"

"The earth has been a bit dry, but we're counting on the springtime showers to see the crops through," Lawrence replied in a subdued tone.

"Talk of all this rain has got me in a fit for something cold to drink," Emily interjected with a giggle as she poured herself a glass of iced tea.

"How are your studies doing, Sir Dexter?" Margaret Reed inquired with sparkling eyes.

"I have just one more semester at Yale," Sir Dexter answered with a lilt of self-praise. "I will be graduating in June, and have made plans to join my father's law firm. Divorce law will be my specialty. I intend to offer good counsel to someone going through a divorce. If a man does not have a good lawyer, he can lose everything he has worked for, or visa-versa."

Margaret Reed beamed a smile. "This community needs to have more reputable lawyers. I hear many of them are scoundrels, and take advantage of poor widows. I commend you, Sir Dexter, for your honorable goals and accomplishments."

"To be assured, law school isn't easy. Then again, most things that require our utmost efforts are often as tedious as they are rewarding. I have received all honors, and plan on cracking down to the books after Easter vacation is over. Finals will not be long after that and I intend to maintain my position at the head of my class." Sir Dexter gloated immodestly while Emily stifled a yawn and poured herself another glass of iced tea.

William Gray, a bit woozy from ingesting wine, chimed in, "You're lucky, Sir Dexter, because not everyone in this day and age is privileged enough to have the opportunity to go to college and study law. There is nothing Lawrence would have wanted more than to become a doctor who specializes in apothecary, or even fine-tune his talents and become a professional portrait painter. Sometimes reaching your goals have to be cast aside due to circumstance."

"Well, if Lawrence is any good at painting portraits, he can make a good living working for my family. My parents have been waiting for over a year for the famed Herbert Lustick. They would be anxious to find a replacement."

"I will call your parents, and see if I can arrange it when I get back from France. An artist is more of a commodity than a field hand, Lawrence, my boy," Philip insisted with a lilt.

"Is your uncle, Dr. Mathis, still living with you at Rosewood?" asked Mrs. Reed.

"Oh yes, and as you know he is an expert in apothecary. He has a library full of textbooks with every possible combination," Sir Dexter added. "I'm sure my uncle would be more than happy to share his knowledge with Lawrence."

After dinner had concluded, Sir Dexter and Emily went out on the veranda. Miss Lydia carried out a tray of tea, and home baked cookies. Seated across from one another at a wrought iron table, the silhouette of stars and moon painted a picture of romance. Emily had no choice, but to submit to Sir Dexter's pleasantries since he had proven to be the most attentive out of all the eligible bachelors.

Lawrence retreated upstairs to his chamber. He felt devastated, especially at the prospect of being booted away to Sir Dexter's estate to paint portraits, and learn about apothecary. Nothing mattered now but being in close proximity to Emily.

He lit a candle while sitting on the antique rocker by the window, and peeked through a corner of glass behind the curtain. Lawrence listened to Emily and Sir Dexter's chatter, while watching their midnight silhouettes sitting amidst a lantern, with a stream of lights lit around the perimeter of the garden.

"When I graduate this June, Emily, I will be prepared to look for a bride," Sir Dexter stated as if in the midst of one of his stuffy old law books. "Would it be presumptuous of me to assume you might honor me with the fulfillment of this proposition, when I am appropriately situated?"

Lawrence cranked his ear to the slightly open window. "All things can only be said and done at their proper time, Sir Dexter."

Lawrence became aghast to realize Emily was leaving an open door which her position in society might force her through.

Chapter Four

The Gift

The Grays were working diligently out on the fields. Lawrence looked over the horizon which separated the farm from the estate. The farmlands burned hot through their lack of shelter. There in the distance he spied Emily walking toward him. She looked like a mirage even from afar.

William's expression became alarmed since Emily's associating with the workers on the fields was strictly prohibited. Nonetheless, Emily radiated in her ecru glory. She held up her hem in an effort to protect her petticoat. Lawrence arose from his planting. His dirt encrusted hands contrasted to the pure ivory of Emily's attire.

Within her grasp she held a present wrapped in blue and topped with a white bow. "This is for you, Lawrence." Emily spoke demurely. "I know my giving a gift to a man is a forward gesture, not appropriate for a young lady, but as you know I'm not one to adhere to tradition. I remembered you telling my father you would turn eighteen on June 23, and I wanted to surprise you."

"That is a surprise, Emily, and a welcome one at that! Who would have ever thought you would have remembered my birthday, let alone have the courage to bring a gift out here." Lawrence gazed at her lovingly.

Emily flashed a bittersweet smile. "Let's not sell your father short, Lawrence. I'm sure he must have remembered your birthday as well, right William?"

"I plum forgot, Lawrence, my boy, my apologies and have a very Happy Birthday. I know it's no excuse, but I lose track of time working out here. Everyday is the same to me," William replied with a note of regret as he buried himself back into tilling the soil before the planting of seed.

"Come, let me open the gift over there by the shade, Emily." Lawrence motioned to the large maple tree situated by an expanse of plush grass. "I wouldn't want you to soil your pretty garments. It's so muddy over here."

Together they walked looking incongruous in their combination of work cloth and lace. They found a spot in the shade beneath the tree. Lawrence removed his hat for Emily to plant her seat. She smiled at his chivalry before handing him the gift.

Emily's expression beamed like sunrise, luminous and full of golden grace. Around them the songbirds of summer chirped a lovely melody as the shade of the oak tree quelled the hot breeze to a soothing temperature.

"Your coming out here like this means a lot to me, Emily. I only hope Aunt Lilly doesn't find you here. It's obvious your parents gave her instructions to continue what they have been doing, in keeping us apart. It has been so unbearable for me to be kept away from you. I've missed you so much, Emily." A resigned expression became trapped on Lawrence's brow as he looked off into the distance.

"I've missed you so much also, Lawrence. Meeting you was like looking into a mirror. We're so alike, in spite of how my parents have forbidden our relationship," Emily said woefully.

"Mirror, mirror on the wall who is the fairest of them all? Why it's you, Emily, my beauty." Lawrence kissed her glove-clad hand with the respect of a proper gentleman.

"If Aunt Lilly was to see that, I'd be in big trouble." Emily sighed as her cheeks flushed. "She is even worse than my parents. She watches me like a hawk. I managed to sneak away when I saw her napping in the parlor. Now go ahead and open the gift before she wakes up and looks for me."

Lawrence removed the wrapping paper. Inside he found an inventive carrying case for shaving papers. Emily had constructed it by folding a bamboo place mat, and lining it with rose-colored paper with a ribbon slipped through the slats. She secured a ribbon at both sides, and tied it into a bow as a carrying strap. She hand-painted chrysanthemums, and a delicate spray of morning glories on the front.

"Thank you so much, this is beautiful, Emily. I'll treasure it forever!" Lawrence held it lovingly. "I have never been given anything as fanciful or precious to me."

Emily averted her gaze. "Lawrence, aside from today being your birthday I wanted you to have a little memento of me before I leave." Her voice trailed off painfully.

"Before you leave, to go where, Emily?" Lawrence's eyes darted in panic.

It was difficult for Emily to get the words out even though she had been practicing for days. "Lawrence, Sir Dexter has invited me to stay with his family for the summer at Rosewood, their Newport, Rhode Island Estate. Sir Dexter has graduated law school." Emily paused nearly choking on the words. "I don't know how to tell you this, Lawrence, but Sir Dexter has asked for my hand in marriage."

"Are you saying that you have accepted, then?" Lawrence blurted out wildly. A moment of silence exaggerated the hysteria of Lawrence's tone.

Emily bent her head while tears misted in her eyes. "I'm afraid I have, Lawrence. Our families have arranged the match. As you know, I have little choice when it comes to such matters. My parents have threatened to disown me if I don't marry Sir Dexter. My mother has worked diligently to impress Dexter's mother, Lady Sarah. As you can well imagine my mother has boasted of my affable nature and talents, and how I would be suitable as a 'wife of royalty.'" Emily's doleful eyes met his with a pang of sorrow.

"Lawrence, I know it's the right thing for me to do. We both already know my family is not romantic where marriage is concerned. Love bears little weight on their decision."

Lawrence's face paled as his lips drew tightly together. "So you have accepted Sir Dexter's offer for marriage only for the sake of your family," Lawrence reiterated mournfully, as he clutched onto her gift as if it was the last substance of Emily.

Emily's blue eyes merged with the airiness of the atmosphere. She remained silent, and unable to gather her composure.

"Do you think you can ever grow to love Sir Dexter?" Lawrence asked before he hung his head down. "I apologize, Emily, I know it's none of my business, forgive me. What can I do but wish you love and happiness in your new life with Sir Dexter?" Lawrence shrugged his shoulders in defeat.

"Lawrence," Emily cried out his name with gumption. "We both know I don't care one bit about Sir Dexter's status and wealth! He means nothing to me, absolutely nothing and he never will!" Emily's voice became pained with sentiment.

"Lawrence, you are the most fascinating human being I've ever met. You already know how I feel about you, but what good is it if I'm forced to marry Sir Dexter." Emily hesitated, near weeping, while her face became grave with woe.

"Let me at least have the memory of you saying you love me, even if it's for the last time! Please, Emily, let me have at least that much! Your words will have to be my heart's sustenance for a lifetime." Lawrence vowed despondently.

"You know I love you, Lawrence," Emily whispered with feeling. "But why should we torture ourselves over how we feel about each other? I'm getting married. I might not care for Sir Dexter, but my mother has assured me love will come." Emily wiped the corner of her eye with her lace handkerchief.

"But love has already come for us, Emily, and it cannot be turned off!" Lawrence proclaimed in frenzy as he uprooted a dandelion in rage. "I'm sorry, Emily. I mustn't speak like that now. You're about to be married."

Lawrence uprooted a second dandelion, and tore it into angry fragments which became dispersed to the wind like yellow dust. He then knelt on bent knee. "Emily," he cried. "Look at me, just look at me over here, dressed in these rags." He pulled onto his dirt encrusted outfit in self-depreciation. "Being out here on the fields day after day inside my thoughts, makes a man think long and hard. It's not always easy to face my thoughts, Emily."

Lawrence reached downward, and raised a handful of fertile earth before gently easing it back into the ground. "You see this earth, Emily . . . this moist earth is you. You see the sky, Emily." Together they looked at the blue over the horizon. "This bittersweet blue sky is you, Emily." He smiled sadly. "The very air I breathe is you. Everything I am is a part of you, my dear beloved, Emily."

Lawrence clasped her glove-clad hand tightly as he swallowed deeply. "I am you and you are me, Emily! Nothing can ever change that! If only I was worthy of you, I would propose right here on bent knee, but unfortunately I'm just a shadow of a man in your parents' eyes, a mere farmer."

Emily gently swept her hand across his stubbly cheek. "That's not true, Lawrence, what you do is not who you are. Besides, without your efforts, we would have no food. You are no less of a man for being a farmer, Lawrence." Emily insisted, as she gazed at him serenely.

Lawrence's mouth became downcast. "Damn it, Emily, I won't pretend I want you to grow to love Sir Dexter! The very thought of it destroys me!"

His face became pained as he looked into the distance of the endless farmlands and vowed. "For as long as I roam this earth, no matter where you are, I will feel your essence; the only hope I have is that my love will haunt you, and own you! When you are in Sir Dexter's arms, I hope you will feel my flesh and see my face. Look for me in the shadows; hear my voice in the silence. There is nowhere on this earth you can go where I won't be! It might sound cruel, but having you leave me is a far crueler fate." Lawrence crushed Emily in a strong embrace.

A delicate stream of tears spilled from Emily's eyes. "Lawrence, that night when we danced together at my Debutante Ball, and my father dragged you away, he destroyed the part of me that's free. He owns me, in the same way Sir Dexter will one day own me. Young women of marrying age are no more than a commodity, and revered for surface value only," Emily admitted somberly and with the acceptance of a martyr. "My feelings account for nothing, and yet I love you with all my heart, Lawrence," Emily whispered softly. "I have loved you from the moment I first saw you, and I will continue to love you in spite of this charade of having to marry Sir Dexter."

Emily's blue eyes glowed against the sky in a brilliant light, as if her very soul had been set aflame. Her voice became resonant as her lips trembled uneasily. "I want you to haunt me, Lawrence! We are one, and nothing can ever change that! To even think I must submit myself to another man is unbearable!" Emily professed dolefully.

Just then Aunt Lilly came scrambling over the hillside like a dark phantom in her black dress and parasol. She spied Lawrence in Emily's proximity with a displeased expression as she rushed to intervene.

"Miss Emily," Aunt Lilly reprimanded. "What in heaven's name are you doing out on the fields? I was going crazy looking for you, child."

Emily smoothed her dress in an effort to regain her composure as Lawrence reached forward and helped her upward. "I am no longer a child, Aunt Lilly. I came out here to wish Lawrence a Happy Birthday. He has turned eighteen today, and I don't feel I need permission to do so. I'm tired of being treated like a schoolgirl."

Aunt Lilly grabbed a hold of Emily's arm authoritatively. "Well, then don't act like a schoolgirl, Emily. You know it is just not fitting for a young lady to be walking out into these fields. Now come on back to the house this instant before you get sunburn. Just where is your parasol anyway? I warned you about that; you don't want to get nasty little freckles all over your cheeks now, do you?"

Emily's head hung downward as she averted both the sun and her sorrow. Lawrence watched as she drifted back over the purview that divided their hearts.

That evening Lawrence and his father dined in the servants' quarters once again. The clatter of the servants scurrying about, and preparing Emily's trunks for her excursion to Newport distracted him. Lawrence could barely touch his share of supper. His soul had a hollow spot where his heart had been.

Lawrence retired to his chamber early that evening. He sat on the rocking chair beneath the soft glow of his lamp, and examined the beautiful treasure Emily had given him. He felt an equal measure of comfort and heartache. He admired how her lovely hands had tied the generous bow, the hand-painted flowers, created by her delicate stroke of brush; the weaving of the ribbon, all woven by Emily's tender touch. Lawrence held it with the reverence of prayer, and regretted the hands that created his gift were going to be removed from his grasp. The sanctity of his spirit shattered into a grief larger than all his hope.

Lawrence reached inside the carrier, and took out every piece of shaving paper, as if they were sacred scrolls which beheld the secret of love. Tucked all the way in the bottom lining, he noticed a tiny note with the flowery penmanship of Emily's fountain pen.

It read, "Dearest Lawrence, *Love* is not always the answer to the passion of the heart. We must succumb to our fate in the sight of *dreams* torn apart. All My Deepest Respect, Emily Grace Reed."

Lawrence studied the sentiment until his vision blurred beneath the lamplight. How eloquently the stanza spoke of his emotions. Lawrence became reminded Emily's fate of marrying well had answered the question of the heart, not love! Lawrence tore one of the shaving papers into tiny shreds. Afterward, he scavenged for the pieces, and tried to find every bit of them. Once he did, he held them together in his hands in anguish.

Chapter Five

Rosewood

Lawrence came off the field early to say his farewell to Emily before she left for the Lund estate. There he spied the ghostly Sir Dexter who looked unnaturally pale from sitting inside for long hours immersed in law books. In broad daylight, Sir Dexter's red hair blared out harshly against his pale complexion.

"Lawrence, my friend, I have a proposition to make. I remember your father saying how you could paint portraits. Well, I have taken the liberty of speaking to my parents on your behalf. How would you like to work at my family estate of Rosewood for the summer painting family portraits? Be assured you will be paid handsomely for your efforts."

"I would be more than happy to take you up on your offer, Sir Dexter," Lawrence answered in ulterior motive to be near Emily.

"Excellent, then it's settled, Lawrence. You will do well to pack your things. We will be ready to adjourn within the hour . . . If you would not mind too much; perhaps you could first help load Emily's trunks onto the coach. The stable boys are out grooming the horses at present."

"I would be happy to oblige before I pack my things," Lawrence replied.

The book smart Dexter, and his pair of emaciated drivers had barely an ounce of muscle between the three of them.

William Gray stumbled in off the field. "Good day, William, just so you are aware, in accordance to our conversation that evening at dinner, I have spoken to my parents on behalf of Lawrence. They have decided to employ Lawrence at my family's estate to paint portraits for the summer, and Lawrence has agreed."

"That's wonderful." William raised his brows optimistically. "Well, Lawrence is a man now, and he's fit to make his own decisions." William came forward and gave Lawrence a heartwarming hug. "It's not easy for a father to part with his son, but it's for the best, Lawrence. It's a good opportunity for you to develop your talents."

Lawrence held his father to his chest in an emotional parting before he hurriedly gathered his belongings back into the same broken trunk he brought them in. He sentimentally packed the hand-painted gift Emily had given him, before he carried his things downstairs.

Last minute details detained Emily. "Miss Agnes," Emily fretted, "This dress will not do for travel. It's far too formal. I would prefer to wear the gingham one with the pink bow."

"Trust me that one is not special enough, and it will crease easily. When you get to Newport, you need to make a grand entrance. Your mother has advised me that Newport, Rhode Island is the resort place of the elite. Trust me, Miss Emily, it's the first impression that's made to last." Emily knew if anyone was up to the minute on the proper protocol, it was Miss Agnes.

"Very well, but hurry with all those buttons. I don't want to keep Sir Dexter waiting." Miss Agnes painstakingly pushed every satin button through the tiny-corded loops with a buttoning implement. Emily sucked her stomach inward as the dress cinched her waist even tighter than the corset had. As the finishing result Emily had attained a waist capable of fitting comfortably between the grasp of two hands.

Emily apprehensively found her way down the winding staircase. In the foyer, she could not help but notice Sir Dexter's lackluster contrasted unkindly to the sheer majesty of Lawrence Gray. Lawrence stood tall and proud by comparison to Sir Dexter who looked like a scarecrow the wind fitfully blew in. Lawrence's dark eyes melded into hers in a moment of wordless wonder.

"Good day, Emily." Sir Dexter tipped his black hat. "I have taken the liberty of asking Lawrence to come along on our journey. My parents have agreed to let him have a hand at painting portraits for my family."

"Lawrence will be an asset to Rosewood; he has done my father well." Emily's voice rose in spite of her trying to act nonchalant.

Sir Dexter grabbed a hold of Emily's arm with an air of chivalrous absurdity. He looked too awkward to be suave. "My family's estate of Rosewood is renowned for its prize winning roses and exotic trees imported from Europe. The ocean borders the property, and the air is so refreshing. I think you will love it, Emily."

"It sounds beautiful." Emily tried to sound enthusiastic when even nature's beauty at its best could not seduce her to care for Sir Dexter.

"Emily, I would like to say goodbye to Aunt Lilly before we depart," said Sir Dexter.

"I have already said our goodbyes to her; Aunt Lilly had to run out," Emily retorted with relief as her and Lawrence surreptitiously caught each other's eye.

Sir Dexter's coach was situated upon the front entranceway of Fairway, beside the marble pillars. One of the drivers dressed in a black top hat and riding jacket, opened the door for Emily. She found the opulence of rich burgundy velvet inside. She took a seat facing the drivers and their pair of well cared for horses, both white with patches of caramel and brown.

Sir Dexter took his place beside Emily, and seemed a bit awkward to be engaged. Emily sat as still as a statue looking untouchable, but graced with formidable style. Her sandy hair was tucked beneath a broad brimmed hat, and ornamented with a cluster of pale pink feathers. The plumes stood upward in a mound, high enough to rival the height of the stagecoach.

Lawrence positioned himself in the center of the opposite side. He looked out of place in his humble, yet clean attire. A straw fedora graced his head with tropical style, while his broad neck made him appear debonair without even trying. In contrast, Sir Dexter's tiny head looked lost beneath his stately top hat which overpowered his slight frame all the more.

The extra weight of the trunks in the back of the coach made the horses gallop a bit more slowly than they would have ordinarily. Small talk became awkward beneath the fortuitous turn of events, which enabled Lawrence and Emily to be in each other's presence. Their encounter beneath the maple tree seemed just a breath away in the summery air.

Long stretches of uninhabited woods wound in spirals on dry drifts of dirt which obscured the pathways. The drivers were well versed of their whereabouts since the journey was a challenging one. Thankfully, it was still early enough to enjoy the lavish sunshine which streamed in through the windows of the coach.

"The driver has secured the final part of our journey by waterway. If all goes as planned, we should arrive directly into Newport Harbor by tomorrow," Sir Dexter announced matter-of-fact.

Sir Dexter hardly even spoke to Emily during the carriage ride aside from details about her Welcoming Ball. It became obvious Sir Dexter was a man's man, who possessed an unsentimental nature. Emily sat rather motionless, being molded into a demure woman of refinement, who is "seen but not heard."

"So, Lawrence, Mr. Reed tells me your family used to own a farm in Westwood," Sir Dexter remarked with interest.

"I was born and bred in Westwood. We had a large farm, and grew all kinds of fruits and vegetables according to the season." Lawrence's face became bleak. "But then in the winter of 1892, my mother developed a mysterious illness. We traveled from town to town, but we could never find a cure. When my mother died, it broke my father's heart, and because of that, the fields were not properly tended. When the drought came about in the summer of '93, it sucked our lands dry. We had to sell the animals just to try to stay afloat, but we were too far behind on bills. We had no choice but to sell the farm. We lost everything by the time my poor mother died, rest her soul." Lawrence's voice weakened to a lull.

Sir Dexter's arrogant expression looked far removed. "Well, let me ask you, how did you come to work for Mr. Reed?"

"Philip Reed and my father were boyhood friends. Thankfully, Mr. Reed had been kind enough to offer us work in the fields when we showed up on his doorstep by chance," Lawrence divulged in a somber voice.

"Well, Lawrence, my friend, I remember your father telling me you had an interest in apothecary. As I was telling you that night at dinner, my uncle, Dr. Trey Mathis, has been living at Rosewood ever since he lost his wife two years ago. He brought a whole library of books on modern doctoring with him. I'm sure you could educate yourself enough to get started if you wanted to. It's not too late to pick up the pieces. You are five years younger than me. I just graduated so I would say there is still a chance for you." Sir Dexter smiled encouragingly.

"Well, I will most certainly look through the volumes when time allows." Lawrence's eyes enlivened with a spark of hope.

They arrived at Rosewood the following day just in time for a late lunch. Emily looked out of the stagecoach at her new habitat, and remarked on how "exquisite" the Bellaire Avenue estate was. The "cottage" that Sir Dexter had referred to, was in actuality a mansion which possessed the appearance of a stately castle. It was made out of stone with a myriad of balconies and fortresses with cathedral windows, and pointed spiral tips reaching up toward heaven. In fact, it dwarfed Emily's own claim into the upper echelon of society.

Gardens of impeccable flowers, blended into exotic motifs, surrounded the estate. There were droves of orange tiger lilies, intermingled with the sweet pink petals of Echinacea, Black-Eyed Susans, and daisies grew in clusters of quaint delight. On the outskirts, prize winning roses grew rampant, and enveloped the surrounding garden with their sweet fragrance. Red, pink, peach, white, and hybrid roses in full bloom were clustered into separate groupings.

Beyond the massive grounds, past the West Porch, the waves broke in the melody of the sea. Thrashing, crashing, and tumbling, while the shore nestled against a cluster of huge rocks, where one could sit and read, and lose themselves. The air refreshed itself with the swell of the ocean breeze in a winded paradise.

"Oh, how beautiful!" Emily exclaimed as the sea enchanted her with oblivion.

Sir Dexter broke off a dusty-pink rose fresh from the vine. "Here, Emily, see to it one of the servants puts this in water for you after I show you to your chamber. I cannot bottle the sea, so for now I hope this will do to content you."

Sir Dexter commanded Lawrence, "I would appreciate if you could carry Emily's belongings up to her chamber at once. It's the first room on the right hand side."

The center hallway of Rosewood had a high-vaulted ceiling. Within the perimeters were hand-painted roses. In the center of the ceiling hung a massive crystal chandelier which would be a feat for the footman to set ablaze. In spite of the fact it had been electrified, it still had spaces for candles. The blush walls were decorated with impressive artwork in somber tones with antique frames, while the winding staircase was even statelier than the one at Fairway.

Before Lawrence attempted to bring up Emily's last hatbox, Sir Dexter detained him by the drawing room where a most enchanting melody emitted. Lawrence became overcome by the opulence of the room. It was decorated with overstuffed sofas covered with floral tapestry.

A tea table, set with silver and an ornate teakettle, accompanied china cups waiting to be filled. The stark white walls added drama to the gold brocade draperies which hung from gilt cresting. A breathtaking view of the formal gardens in the back courtyard was visible while the borders of the property sung out in the rhapsody of waves. There in the corner was the side-angled view of a woman playing a soothing melody on the piano. The music stopped for an interval as Sir Dexter and Lawrence entered the drawing room.

The woman, who had been playing, gave Lawrence the impression of an "old maid" type. Her mousy brown hair was arranged in a careless bun. Wire rimmed spectacles made the whites of her eyes look fearsome, and over exaggerated. She was covered up to her chin by a dark fabric dress which looked too heavy and dismal for the summer. Her ordinary face bore an expression that was not pleasing. She possessed the aura of one who was not altogether *right*.

Lawrence became struck by the oddity of her demeanor while Sir Dexter greeted the woman amiably, "Lawrence, I would like for you to meet my sister. Sir Lawrence, this is my dear sister, Miss Mallory Lund. Mallory, this is, Sir Lawrence Gray."

"Pleased to have your acquaintance, Miss Mallory," Lawrence politely bowed.

It became apparent Sir Dexter's referring to him as the formal "Sir Lawrence" uplifted his rank equal to his sibling.

His sister's eyes illuminated like white lightning from beneath her spectacles. "The pleasure is equal to mine," Miss Mallory spoke in a melodic voice which made up slightly for her less than attractive appearance.

"Sir Lawrence will be staying at Rosewood for the summer season to try his hand at portrait painting."

"How commendable," Miss Mallory got up from her piano bench to greet Lawrence at a closer distance. It was then Lawrence noticed she walked with a lame gait. Her expression struggled in synchrony with her compromised dexterity.

"Where is Sir Lawrence from?" Mallory curiously inquired.

"His father William Gray was a boyhood friend of Emily's father, Philip Reed. Lawrence's folks used to own a large farm in Westwood, but it was sold and now he is on his own. Aside from being an aspiring artist, Lawrence has an interest in doctoring and apothecary. With all the books Uncle Trey has in the library, I was figuring Lawrence could set aside time each day to study after painting."

"Study for doctoring!" Miss Mallory sounded unduly impressed.

It was at that point in time Lawrence became aware he was being groomed into a respectable gentleman of status. His instinct told him there had to be a motive. Clearly it came to him; Sir Dexter's kindness had a cost, the price of marrying off his spinster sister to a future doctor, or to any willing man for that matter! It became obvious to Lawrence to marry Mallory would indeed require some compensation to make it palatable.

Lawrence became suspicious. He began to wonder if that had been the secret motive of Sir Dexter's invitation to Rosewood in the first place. The mere thought of it made Lawrence shutter. A sick, hollow feeling crept inside him, as he realized his sudden eligibility in securing such a bride.

Miss Mallory smiled a yellowed-tinge of teeth in welcoming Lawrence. She then excused herself to entertain them while the men reclined for tea. Her sweet voice, however, sounded in a soliloquy unsurpassed. If Lawrence had heard the voice in itself without the interference of Mallory's persona, he would have been charmed. It sounded no less than an angel. However now dread was the result, seeing that Mallory was older than him by years, but not by enough to make the match unsuitable.

After their tea, Sir Dexter showed Lawrence to his chamber right near Emily's. They walked through the ornate Victorian estate, true to elaborate details of the day. Sir Dexter spoke in a flat tone, "In case you were wondering, my sister Mallory was engaged to a fellow from Clinton when she was in her teens. But then she had a fall from her horse, and ended up with a badly mangled leg. Those were times of troubles . . . Her fiancé was unfortunately not one cut out for times of woe. All her plans of marriage dissolved after her spill off the horse." Sir Dexter paused optimistically.

"Mallory is a lot better now. She is only left with a lame gait. At twenty-two years old, it's high time for her to forget her old heartache, and move her sights to another. What she needs is a good husband. Mallory would make a fine wife, Lawrence. She is fit in every other way."

The prospect whirled menacingly through Lawrence's head, "A fine *wife.*" It became obvious to Lawrence; Sir Dexter had an undertone of suggestion in his voice, thus inviting Lawrence into the family through a possible love match.

The sight of Lawrence's chamber looked more like a master bedroom, than that of a guest quarter. He had his own private bathroom and dressing area along with an authentic Chippendale mahogany bed from the mid-1700s. His chamber was situated at the corner of the mansion with two windows which allowed for cross ventilation. The vision of the ocean swelled along the edges in a crest of restless waves, writhing against the shore. Lawrence inhaled deeply as the fresh air invigorated his senses.

He found a handsome chair, and a marble fireplace graced with a haunting portrait which looked at him with knowing eyes. On top of the mantle sat a hand-painted clock with a scene of heavenly cherubs, encircled by rhinestones with bronze angels atop.

Lawrence sunk into the chair. The scent of fresh-cut, red roses set adjacent in an antique vase greeted him. From his vantage point, Lawrence caught a catty-cornered glimpse of his face in the looking glass. There he saw the sunken hollows beneath his brooding eyes, and the underbrush of his day old stubble, which cast his face with a gray pallor.

There he sat a lost man, afloat; yet sinking into the misery of his gratitude for the man whose fiancée he coveted. His thoughts taunted him, while guilt for his secret feelings drenched him in deceit. There he sat a parody of an artist, a sham of an aspiring doctor, with nothing but falsity in his heart.

Lawrence got up to settle his meager belongings into the mahogany dresser, when he once again came upon the lovely memento Emily had bestowed him with that day beneath the maple tree. He held it in his hand for a moment of reflection, before he proceeded to take out his straight edge, and a piece of the shaving paper. He pulled it out, like an onionskin, ripping off a layer of heavy emotions with its removal. He went over to the pedestal sink to fill it with warm water, before making lather with a bar of tallow. After which he began to shave his face with the blade, wanting to look presentable for lunch.

In haste, Lawrence's hand slipped, and out shot a spurt of blood from a nick. Lawrence looked like a maddened creature to himself, and in the degradation of his own holy sacrifice. Lawrence felt strangely appeased, as if out through his broken flesh his passion had been momentarily released.

Chapter Six

The Portrait

Sir Dexter appeared at Lawrence's chamber in the latter part of the morning. "Breakfast is being served in the parlor, Lawrence. My parents arrived home late last night from the opera so we are running a bit off schedule today."

"Thank you, Sir Dexter, I will be down shortly." Lawrence felt apprehensive about meeting Sir Dexter's parents, and hoped to be well received.

The breakfast parlor had the flavor of a Victorian tearoom. Lawrence found Mr. and Mrs. Lund sitting at a circular table covered with a floral tablecloth. By their relaxed ambiance alone, the family group appeared more down-to-earth than Lawrence had anticipated.

Mr. Lund was on the lean side with red hair which had grayed to an odd shade of strawberry. He had the same freckled complexion as Sir Dexter. Dexter's mother, Lady Sarah, had an unusually youthful zest for a middle-aged woman. In fact, at a moment's glance, it could easily look like Mallory was the mother and Lady Sarah was the daughter. Lawrence surmised it must have been Lady Sarah's flaxen curls and rosy cheeks.

Sir Dexter made motion for Lawrence to sit beside him. "Good morning, Lawrence, do come in and join us. How did you find your chamber?" Sir Dexter inquired with a sense of camaraderie.

"I must say I enjoyed the lovely accommodations, Sir Dexter." Disoriented from how fast his life was changing, Lawrence stood for an awkward interlude before he took his place beside Sir Dexter.

"Mother and Father this is Lawrence Gray. Lawrence, this is my mother, Lady Sarah, and my father, Mr. Lund," introduced Sir Dexter.

"Welcome to Rosewood, Lawrence! Any friend of the Reed family is a friend of ours," Mr. Lund cheerfully announced as both he and Lady Sarah smiled in unison.

"Thank you," Lawrence replied, feeling grateful his connection to the Reeds had sparked such a warm reception.

The butler appeared with a hearty beef broth, shepherd's pie, and fresh cut fruit. Mr. Lund addressed Lawrence. "I'm sure Sir Dexter must have mentioned, we have been waiting over a year for Herbert Lustick to render our family portraits, and the soonest he can start is this spring. So when I found out Philip Reed had an artist living beneath his roof I jumped at the chance to snatch you away."

Lawrence radiated with a smile. "I have painted portraits of every member of my family as well as nature scenes before my father sold the farm. I find painting a fulfilling way of self-expression. Not to sound boastful, but I have a knack of being able to capture a subject's likeness."

Lady Sarah lifted Lawrence's work-worn hands. "Just look at these hands, they're strong and sensitive. "These are obviously the hands of an artist, and an artist must paint!"

Emily and Mallory entered the breakfast room in time to hear the tail end of the conversation. Mallory excitedly inquired, "Whose portrait is Sir Lawrence going to paint first, Father?"

"I'll let Mother decide, Mallory. Please get settled for your breakfast."

Both young women joined in at the table. Dressed in a blue calico dress, Mallory had a matching bonnet with a shawl draped around her shoulders. Her mousy hair was curled into tight ringlets, which rested flatly against her wire rimmed glasses.

Emily appeared well rested. She found a seat between Sir Dexter and Lady Sarah. Emily was wearing a pale pink dress with rosettes strategically sewn along the top of the bodice, and the same hat from the day before with the pale pink plumes.

Lady Sarah beamed enthusiastically. "Lawrence, why not begin with painting Emily, the new addition to our family . . . I would like to add Emily's portrait next to Mallory's in the drawing room. She is as pretty as a picture right now, just as she is. In fact you can get started right after breakfast. You will find all the supplies you need in the armoire of the study. There are smocks, as well as suitable clothing for painting in there. They are in pretty decent condition, and they should fit you adequately."

After breakfast Lawrence found the appropriate selection of wardrobe, which consisted of a relaxed pair of pants and shirt. His demeanor took on the look of a Bohemian artist with a cap tilted to the side of his head. Lawrence eagerly gathered the supplies of paints, canvas, and easel; having Emily as his model inspired him to great ambition.

Lawrence met up with Emily along the West Porch where the ocean breeze refreshed them with salted air. There set amongst the hemlock, and carefully manicured gardens, they came upon a secluded pasture. Lawrence found an ideal spot along the elm for Emily to situate herself, beneath a canopy of shade.

The sunlight streamed through the leaves in a beam of steadied light. Lawrence set up his easel, and peered at Emily intently. He watched how her pink plumes matched the tempo of the wind, swishing back and forth with feminine ease. Her face, shadowed by the grandiose brim, took on a coquettish mystery, while her blue eyes melded into the sky. Her delicate features looked demure, yet at the same time full of hidden passions.

The folds of her pink taffeta dress enveloped her like a rose in full bloom, while the scent of her perfume became one with the breeze. As a backdrop, the sea crashed against the shore in a rhythmic melody.

"Perfect, Emily, do you think you can stay like that?"

Emily nodded yes as she languidly leaned against the tree, and both their energies intercepted with nature. Within the silence of inner tidings, Lawrence became consumed by the concentration needed to capture Emily's likeness.

The paint became the medium Lawrence used to shape his love while his hands became the tool to unveil Emily's essence. She steadied her pose, and for the interlude of late morning well into afternoon, they remained as such.

Lawrence felt grateful for his stroke of luck, which enabled him to be alone in Emily's company. They were private, yet accessible to any member of the household who might want to sneak a peak at the work in progress.

However, it soon became apparent; the Lund family possessed an aesthetic respect of not disturbing an artist at work.

When the midday peak began to rise, and the afternoon sun cast a brighter play of light, Lawrence had accomplished enough for the first rendering. Emily stretched before she stood up in an effort to regain her mobility. She then began to twirl her parasol vehemently with a look of warning in her eyes signaling. "Be careful we are being watched!"

Lawrence was well versed on her sign from his copy of *The Mystery of Love Courtship and Marriage Explained.*

Out on the balcony Sir Dexter furtively peered downward at them. He took notice on the progress of Lawrence's session from afar before going back inside. Emily and Lawrence glanced at each other knowingly as Lawrence gathered his canvas and art supplies.

"Emily, I'm honored to have the opportunity to paint you. However no canvas can be a match for what nature has drawn so effortlessly." Lawrence's white teeth accentuated his swarthy complexion as he smiled.

"That's sweet of you to flatter me, Lawrence." Emily blushed. "I'm equally honored to have you paint me, but with that privilege is the disappointment for the way my life is unfolding. Sitting out here with you makes me realize all the more, my engagement to Sir Dexter is a complete farce. I will never love Sir Dexter . . . let alone even like him. What I feel for Sir Dexter is polite indifference."

Lawrence's face took on the shadows of sun which peeked through the leaves. "Emily, we both know fulfilling love is not always a reality. You are destined to be Sir Dexter's bride, and I must respect that now."

Lawrence's brow twisted in torment. "I have no choice other than to wish you happiness, Emily. Sir Dexter's family has taken me in, and given me the opportunity to paint and study doctoring. To think of my own personal happiness now would only be selfish and ungrateful. My sweet Emily, nothing can ever change my feelings for you, but what purpose will that serve us now?"

"Lawrence, I suppose I'll just have to go on, and live my life as if I'm in a charade, and not dwell on my happiness either," Emily sounded resigned yet embittered. "For now I'm thankful to still have you near me, Lawrence, but I'll be devastated when you complete the family portraits," she added ruefully.

"The Lund's initial offer for employment was for the summer, but it will take me longer to finish. Either way, we will be separated, since when the summer ends, you'll be going back to Clinton," Lawrence recounted sadly.

The pair entered the mansion to find a lunch spread awaited them in the formal dining room. The peach curtains breathed in and out with the breeze as the sunshine graced the room in an amber cast. Seated at the table was the family in full, including Dr. Mathis. Sir Dexter had saved a place for Lawrence between the doctor and Mallory, which granted Lawrence a remarkable view of the garden. As perfect as the scenery was, the underlying implications plagued Lawrence and Emily alike.

Sir Dexter looked over at Emily with the arrogance of ownership already. He then glanced at the canvas Lawrence had set in the foyer. "I see you have accomplished a nice beginning, Lawrence. I do say I see a likeness emerging already."

"Hopefully it will be like *The Picture of Dorian Gray*, and I shall stay young forever," Emily said in jest.

"Oh, but Oscar Wilde has his price for eternal youth, Emily," Lawrence teased. "You will have to eventually hide the portrait in a locked room for fear of anyone else seeing the real you, including yourself." All at the table had a gay laugh.

"Who needs Herbert Lustick when we have Lawrence Gray?" Lady Sarah exclaimed. "It's unlikely Herbert Lustick would have been able to do any better on his first sitting."

"Well, I can't very well cancel him, Sarah. I've already given Herbert Lustick a hefty deposit." Mr. Lund sighed. "If only I would have known Dexter would be bringing us such a talented artist."

Mallory smiled at Lawrence. "I look forward to when my turn comes to sit for Lawrence. It is due time I put the other portrait of me to rest."

"Yes; well don't be too overanxious, Mallory; an artist must take his time with each subject. It's a whole process of discovery," Lady Sarah said rather curtly.

Lawrence felt relieved, since he planned on milking every moment into his portrait of Emily.

Lunch was served in a formal, yet not overly stuffy manner. The long rectangular table was covered with a floral tablecloth, and set with whimsical china, patterned with fresh fruits. It made the food look even more enticing.

Mallory joyfully divulged, "I have started making a sign for the Welcoming Ball in celebration of Emily entering into our family. However, no one shall see it until the gala ball. I want it to be a surprise."

Lady Sarah interjected, "That reminds me, ladies, we must go into the parlor after breakfast and start our arrangements for Emily's Welcoming Ball. Then after that we have Dexter and Emily's Engagement Ball to plan. Everyone who is anyone in Newport will be invited."

Dr. Mathis addressed Lawrence, "So Dexter tells me you have an interest in doctoring and apothecary?"

"Yes I have always found apothecary fascinating."

"Well, I must say, Lawrence; you are a multifaceted young man. I have never had a son to pass down my tricks of the trade, so I would be happy to teach you. After all I don't want to take them to the grave with me . . ." Dr. Mathis paused in melancholy about his station in life. He epitomized a man past his prime with a paunchy middle, and a whitened wisp of hair.

"Lawrence, why don't we go to the library directly after lunch, and I will show you my medical volumes."

"I consider myself fortunate to have acquired a mentor, Dr. Mathis." Lawrence beamed. "Nothing fascinates me more than medicine. An uncle of mine was an apothecary. As a young boy, I used to watch him use his scales, and the mortar, and pestle for grinding his medicines."

"It looks like we might have a future doctor here." Mallory exclaimed gleefully.

Lawrence's eyes smoldered with ambition. "That has been my lifelong dream. But I would need four years of medical school, and unfortunately my father is unable to send me."

"Nonsense," Lady Sarah chimed in. "Any medical school will consider private study with a respected physician equal to schooling. You will probably only need a minimum of classes after Dr. Mathis is finished with you."

Sir Dexter shrugged his shoulders. "What are you worrying about, Lawrence, if a woman can become a doctor, you should have no trouble." Sir Dexter chuckled mockingly.

Mallory adjusted her spectacles before glaring at Sir Dexter. "You are no doubt referring to Dr. Elizabeth Blackwell, the first woman doctor in the United States. She is a credit and inspiration to women everywhere. I don't think you should be demeaning Dr. Blackwell's accomplishments, Dexter. We do live in modern times."

Dr. Mathis chimed in. "It was difficult for women back in the mid-1800s. Sixteen schools denied Dr. Blackwell's admission only because she was a woman. She eventually ended up studying at Geneva College, and after three years of private study with a physician, Dr. Blackwell came out at the top of her class in earning her M.D. She was a pioneer back in her day," Dr. Mathis added magnanimously.

Mallory held her head high in triumph. "Before Dr. Blackwell, the male doctors did not know enough to sterilize their instruments before each new patient. It took a woman to realize good sanitation helps to prevent the spread of disease. Dr. Blackwell won an honor for her great contribution."

Sir Dexter's eyes became vacant as he grimaced. "How preposterous to think her trite contribution could be considered a brainstorm. I would think the male doctors had common sense enough to know to wash their hands and sterilize their instruments back then."

On that note, Emily retreated with Lady Sarah and Mallory into the drawing room to go through the addresses for those invited to the balls. Sir Dexter and his father tended to their law practice where regular clientele arrived at their office. Lawrence had now fallen into his own niche, as he retreated into the library with Dr. Mathis.

That evening the Lund family retired to their chambers early as was their habit. Lawrence and Emily met outside by the West Porch to stroll the Cliff Walk, the picturesque path alongside the sea. Lawrence hooked his arm in Emily's while they strolled. Their steps became synchronized by the sounds of the sea.

Emily smiled at Lawrence. "Thankfully, the Lund family has no qualms against their guests or servants stepping out to enjoy the fresh air. I would go crazy cooped up in there all night."

"We're lucky, Emily, walking the Cliff Walk is a favorite pastime for the servants in the nearby mansions during the summer months. Thankfully, it's also an accepted activity for a man and woman to enjoy without the suspicion of others. After all, to be outside and to commune with the sea is what Newport, Rhode Island is all about. To have you by my side, Emily, makes it all the richer."

Chapter Seven

The Old Church

On Sunday mornings, Rosewood had an atmosphere of festivity with extra scrambling as the family got ready for church. Miss Julia was busy tending to Mallory and Lady Sarah's last minute calls for breakfast and tea in their chambers.

Lawrence lounged in his four-legged tub which had a generous sprinkling of bath salts. He stayed until the hot water turned cool, and his fingertips became shriveled. Afterward he put on the fresh attire laid out by one of the servants. Lawrence felt appreciative Mr. Lund had been generous enough to grant him clothing he no longer wore. The long-tailed jacket had a vent in the back which reached below his knee. It was paired with matching trousers, and a crisp white shirt and bow tie. A stovepipe hat crowned Lawrence with the elegance of a true gentleman.

At nine o'clock, the family adjourned out front by their opulent carriage. Sir Dexter, Emily, and Lady Sarah sat together facing the drivers, while Lawrence, Mallory, and Mr. Lund took seats across from them. It was a glorious spring day with everyone wearing his or her Sunday best.

The drivers prompted their horses forward as sunlight emanated through the vaporous clouds. Lawrence discreetly peered over at Emily, and noticed she too was taking a clandestine peek at him. Emily's blue eyes looked brilliant against the backdrop of sky. In the early morning light, Emily bloomed beneath her bonnet, embellished with peach flowers. Her upsweep had a few face framing tendrils tumbling downward. She wore a peach floral dress with ruffles strategically sewn onto the bodice, which cinched her slender waist admirably.

Mallory sat close enough for Lawrence to feel her body heat, intermingled with his own. Dressed in her usual drab attire, her rose dress had a gray undertone which saddened her overall aura. Her somber hat had a brooding of black net obscuring her spectacles. The veil looked like the crisscross of an unsightly spider web against a pane of glass where queer eyes peered outward. Lawrence felt thankful for her veiled mystique, and avoided direct eye contact with Mallory, made uncomfortable by their close proximity.

Mallory seemed in high spirits to be in Lawrence's company while Lawrence began to worry him and Mallory were going to be coupled-off out of convenience.

When they arrived at The Old Church circa 1749, Emily exclaimed, "The church is so beautiful! It looks like it's made entirely out of old stone."

Lawrence became overtaken by the antiquity of The Old Church as well. It hinted of ancestors rustling beneath the archway of the large old trees framing the perimeters.

Exiting out from the coach with the help of the coachman, Lady Sarah and Mr. Lund respectively linked their arms as did Sir Dexter and Emily. Mallory followed suit with Lawrence when they exited. The physical contact with Mallory intruded on Lawrence's sense of freedom, as they walked together down the ancient cobblestone path. Mallory's pronounced limp made her a bit unsteady. Lawrence hoped his surefootedness would compensate for Mallory's ungainliness.

The heavy wooden door of the church was left ajar as the congregants assembled into the pews. Mallory found seats for she and Lawrence in the center pew, while the other family members scrambled down the aisle to the side of them. The community appeared to be active in the church, yet intimate enough to know one another.

Lawrence looked up at the pulpit as the Priest, Father O'Leary, began the service. Lawrence admired the way the sunlight streamed through the stained glass windows in the radiance of prayer. The incense once lit, permeated the air with biblical secrets. Knees were knelt in submission to the Almighty. The sermon shed a light on Lawrence's forsaken heart. He recalled how his own family had not gone to church until after his mother became ill, and how vague moments of prayer had facilitated hope.

Lawrence's mind began to wander as he looked at the townsfolk, with their prim and proper attire, and judgmental demeanors. Lawrence could feel inquisitive eyes upon him. He hoped not to arouse any controversy by accompanying Miss Mallory as her Sunday companion. Lawrence dreaded the implications, and hoped Mallory might be mistaken for a relative.

He noticed out of the corner of his eye, a few younger girls were blatantly staring over at him. One of them, a dark beauty with a striking beauty mark turned her cheek toward Lawrence, and brazenly placed her forefinger upon her chin in an exaggerated manner signaling, "I desire an acquaintance," an obvert gesture of the day.

Lawrence tried to look oblivious. He instinctively knew Sunday church was not going to be a place for him to meet young ladies. Lawrence regretted he was Mallory's companion now, like it or not, it was an unspoken agreement. Lawrence then realized, even if given the opportunity, another young lady, no matter how beautiful, would only be a poor substitute for the affection he held for Emily.

At the close of the sermon, all the congregants assembled in a charming room to the side of the sanctuary. There were clusters of round tables covered with lacy tablecloths. Colorful bouquets of fresh flowers intermingled with baby's breath were set upon each table.

Lavish refreshments were temptingly arranged on a long table in the front of the room, consisting of baked goods, fresh fruit, coffee, and tea. Mallory sat down, seeming to be weary on her feet. "Lawrence, can you please get me some tea and fruit."

While standing on the line, the dark-haired beauty who had given Lawrence the signal of desiring his acquaintance approached, and addressed him in a flirtatious tone, "Hello, I've never seen you here before, otherwise I would have remembered. Are you new in town?"

Mr. Lund, who stood on line right behind Lawrence, interjected with an authoritative air, "Oh, allow me; if I remember correctly you are, Miss Suzette Cole, George and Clara's daughter."

The girl nodded yes while the tulle on her decorative hat obscured one eye in coquetry.

"Miss Suzette Cole, this is Lawrence Gray." Mr. Lund smiled at Lawrence in amusement. "I have known Suzette's family for many years now. In fact I have known Suzette ever since she was in diapers." Mr. Lund glanced over at Lawrence as he chuckled condescendingly.

By this point Suzette's crimson cheeks overshadowed her seductive eye.

"Mr. Gray has escorted my daughter, Miss Mallory, to church this morning, Miss Cole, and will be doing so every Sunday."

"It's a pleasure to meet you." Suzette half swallowed her words as she scurried away toward the fruit punch.

It was now out in the open; Lawrence's suspicion had been correct. Lawrence felt sick inside to realize he was a prisoner of the graciousness that had saved him from the bitter toils of the fields. He dutifully took his place beside Mallory, and presented her refreshments.

Mr. Belford, a dapper, middle-aged gentleman with a handlebar mustache curled with the help of wax, approached. "Hello and welcome to The Old Church. I'm Mr. Belford."

Mr. Belford reached forward to shake Lawrence's hand. "And may I ask what your name is?"

Mr. Lund replied for Lawrence, "Mr. Belford, this is Lawrence Gray; he is our in-house artist. He is currently painting a portrait of my future daughter-in-law, Miss Emily. She is the one with the peach dress."

Emily curtsied as Mr. Belford bowed. "Mr. Gray, I suggest you bring your portrait of Miss Emily to church when it's completed, a good artist is always in demand. I might like to have a portrait of my wife done."

Hector Lund interjected, "I have commissioned Lawrence Gray to complete portraits of my entire family; that will take considerable time. So as you can see, Mr. Belford, I'm sorry to say, but Mr. Gray has prior commitments."

"Very well, I wish you the best of luck with your endeavors, Mr. Gray." When Mr. Belford walked off, Lawrence felt like a piece of property.

Mr. Lund detained Lawrence outside the church where they were having a flower sale off to the side. "Lawrence, it's so nice for Mallory to have you as her Sunday companion. I haven't seen her look so happy in years."

Lawrence caught a glimpse of Mallory's somber silhouette standing by a wreath of garland. He noticed with dismay how her happiness had a sobering effect, even upon herself.

Hector Lund went on with his green eyes looking as lively as the leaves on the trees. "Lawrence, I think this is an opportune time for me to mention what Dexter and I have been discussing. We are both in agreement it would be to your advantage to consider taking Mallory for a wife. Mallory would make a fine wife."

Hector persuaded. "I can attest to that. Mallory has always had a pleasant disposition, and she excels at playing the piano. I'm sure you must have noticed Mallory has the voice of an angel." Mr. Lund patted Lawrence on the back. "Lawrence, I must say after seeing the two of you together in church, you make an excellent pair."

Lawrence became flustered to hear the very words he had feared spoken so plainly. "Mr. Lund, that's a gracious suggestion and I thank you for thinking of me so intimately. However, I am not in the position to offer security to Mallory or to any woman for that matter; I have put all thoughts of marriage aside for the time being."

"Nonsense," Hector Lund blurted out in rebuttal! "What do you think, I am some sort of an ingrate?"

Mr. Lund's choice of the word "ingrate" made Lawrence realize her father was well aware of Mallory's shortcomings.

"Any man who marries my Mallory will live in the East wing of Rosewood. It has been ready and waiting for quite some time now."

"East wing," Lawrence repeated in surprise as Mr. Lund continued.

"Yes, I have it roped off since it's not currently in use. There are two entire wings upstairs. The East wing is reserved for Mallory and her future husband, and the West wing is for Dexter and Emily after they marry."

"I wasn't aware. I thought the upstairs was all attic, or storage space." Lawrence's curiosity became enlivened.

Mr. Lund placed a fatherly arm on Lawrence's shoulder. "I will show you both wings after dinner tonight. I guarantee you will be pleasantly surprised. Mallory has decorated both wings all by herself, it's really quite fanciful. She has a good eye for detail, another one of her many talents."

As they headed back to the estate through the glorious countryside, Mallory commented, "This is the most enjoyable day I have ever had at church."

The reason became apparent. Mallory hovered by Lawrence's side, clutching onto his arm, and doting on his every word. Emily looked jealous as she inadvertently gave Mallory an icy stare. Lawrence laughed to himself at the absurdity. "Envious of me and Mallory, the emotion I have toward Emily's union with Sir Dexter is more like a *resignation* to my lot in life."

After dinner Mr. Lund brought Lawrence upstairs, and past the roped off barricade in a persuasive momentum. At the top of the landing was an entire floor, exquisitely decorated and as spacious as the main floor. The foyer had soft pink and moss green flowered pattern carpet.

"This is the East wing. It has two master chambers, and a room for a governess, God willing . . . The hand carved mahogany bed in Mallory's chamber is from the 1700s, and imported from France; the brocade curtains provide warmth when drawn shut. Each chamber has its own fireplace, private dressing area, and bathroom. As you can see Mallory's dressing table has lace tiers, another one of her feminine touches." Hector smirked.

"Now for the masculine chamber, Lawrence, Mallory has chosen dark woods and earthly artifacts. Here is the breakfast parlor. Meals can always be brought up by Miss Julia as she goes about her morning and evening rounds." Mr. Lund proceeded to show Lawrence to a sitting room, comprised of a handsome desk with feathered quills waiting to be used.

"The West wing has the same layout as the East, with equal sized rooms, and good views of the property as well. It's decorated with the same attention to detail." Lawrence admired the sentimental touches of photographs and memorabilia as Mr. Lund continued his tour.

"Each wing has a privacy door, with the exception of these two rooms which are to be shared. Here is the library with its wealth of books, and the drawing room."

The drawing room contained a piano, a Turkish rug, and overstuffed, velvet couches with lilac curtains drawn open by purple tassels. Mr. Lund planted himself on one of the chairs in the drawing room, while Lawrence sat himself on a couch, smothered by satin pillows.

"It's beautiful up here, Mr. Lund. It will be wonderful for you to have your married children living beneath the same roof with you. You are a lucky man, Mr. Lund."

"Indeed," agreed Mr. Lund. "Thankfully, Dexter has found his significant other, but as for Mallory, she worries me." Hector Lund paused. "I have noticed ever since you've arrived at Rosewood, Mallory has been in rather good spirits. I have a feeling you could be the one fellow to make Mallory reconsider marriage."

Mr. Lund continued solemnly, "I'm sure you're aware of Mallory's accident on the horse, and the misfortune which followed. After her ordeal, Mallory declared she would never wed, and has stayed in that train of thought ever since."

"Yes, Sir Dexter has told me all about her accident. I understand it was very rough, and a major heartbreak for Mallory, which clearly explains her shying away from marriage."

Mr. Lund looked pleased by Sir Dexter's priming. "As Mallory's father, I have my daughter's best interests at heart. Lawrence, I am offering you the privilege of asking Mallory for her hand in marriage. I'm not a fortuneteller, I don't know if you can persuade her. I am merely offering the suggestion."

"I will certainly consider what you've suggested, Mr. Lund. It's an honor to have a father suggest marriage to his daughter, and I appreciate your graciousness, and the possibility of our future connection." Lawrence pondered his own ulterior motive of having the chance to be in Emily's proximity.

Hector Lund's apple cheeks became ripe with color. "I will arrange for you and Mallory to dine alone this coming Saturday night while the rest of us go off to the opera. That will give you two a chance to become better acquainted."

"As you wish," Lawrence complied coolly.

"By the way, Dr. Mathis tells me your studies are doing quite well. Keep in mind, you are learning with the best. Dr. Mathis has an excellent reputation. Any protégé of his will no doubt find great respect in whatever field of medicine they choose."

"I'm very grateful for the opportunity, and I have hopes of going back to school to get a degree in medicine as soon as I save enough money."

"Money will come, Lawrence my boy, not to worry!" Mr. Lund opened his palms, making it clear having Mallory as his wife would buy Lawrence an education as well.

"Just so you know Dr. Mathis is closely associated with Herbert Smith, the dean of Yale Medical School. A college education is not a prerequisite. Dr. Mathis thinks you'll probably only be required to have less than three years of school with all the learning you've been doing. You can be a doctor by the time you are twenty-one, Lawrence. You have your whole life ahead of you. If you remain at Rosewood as Mallory's husband, we can always set up an office for your practice downstairs. It's always a good idea for a professional to have a home office."

Lawrence's dear Emily drew closer, and then farther away, dispersed by the wind of their scattered destinies.

Chapter Eight

The Clandestine Kiss

The morning sky was superb for continuing Emily's portrait. Lawrence set up his easel along the faithful trees while the sounds of the ocean soothed in the background. A keen likeness of Emily had taken form on the canvas. Lawrence had captured the caution in her eyes that saw without divulging their vision, as well as her secret passion.

Out on the veranda was a bird's eye view of Sir Dexter sipping tea with Mrs. Violet Reynolds, known as Lady Violet, a divorcee in need of legal advice. She was a straight-laced, no nonsense kind of gal, with jet-black hair in a French knot, and luminous brown eyes. Twenty-one and childless, Lady Violet had been coming to the law office quite often lately to discuss her affairs.

Emily spied the two of them sitting beneath an umbrella. Sir Dexter seemed thoroughly engrossed in the conversation, and oblivious to her and Lawrence along the garden's edge. Lawrence's painting had become merely an everyday event at Rosewood, which no one paid much attention to, least of all Sir Dexter.

In the meantime, Sir Dexter looked quite attentive, as he figured out details for the pretty and formidably wealthy Lady Violet. Emily watched the pair with a cautious eye, noticing Sir Dexter move in closer to her while they both mused over a single piece of paperwork.

"Emily, there's something curious I wanted to discuss with you," Lawrence said tentatively. "Mr. Lund and I had a heart to heart talk last Sunday after church. I don't know how you will react to his motive." Lawrence swallowed nervously. "But Mr. Lund has suggested I would do well to ask Mallory for her hand in marriage."

There was a pause of silence where even thoughts were wordless.

"After thinking about it I realized marrying Mallory would enable us to continue our friendship, Emily," Lawrence added in a flat tone.

Emily's serene gaze became wild with fury. "Oh Lawrence, you wouldn't dare to! You marry Mallory, that is positively absurd!"

"Emily, it matters little who I marry, if it's not you," Lawrence insisted softly.

"So you mean to tell me you're actually considering marrying Mallory!" Emily cried out. "What a crazy thing for you to even think about, Lawrence. The book I'm reading compares the worth of marriageable ladies as "two a penny;" now I see this comparison is far from fiction." Emily shook her head in disbelief. "Can Mr. Lund be so desperate to find a husband for his daughter that he would be presumptuous enough to suggest you marry her?"

Lawrence retorted, "Emily, I don't know that I'm considering taking Mr. Lund up on the suggestion, but I have been giving it some thought." Lawrence paused uncomfortably. "I did however agree to d   with Mallory after everyone has gone off to the opera this Saturday night. After all, I didn't want to insult Mr. Lund and refuse."

"Dine with her, you and Mallory alone?" Tears began to well in Emily's eyes as she jumped upward, and darted off in hysterics.

Lawrence rushed after her into the woods, dense in the thickets, and into a world of their own. There by a gnarly oak tree Lawrence grabbed a hold of Emily passionately, and slipped his hands around her waist. He embraced her close to his chest, and pressed his lips upon hers with a hunger that held them both powerless to the appetite. Their lips became the parched grass longing for the rain. Their fire became the sky smoldering with the heat of the molten sun. Their kiss encapsulated them in the hot larva which catapulted up from their earthly desires.

Emily caught her bearing as she breathlessly pushed him away from their delirium of danger and delight. "No, Lawrence, we mustn't!" Emily stepped backward and readjusted her dress.

Lawrence's pupils had become so enlarged the irises appeared near black. "Emily, I'm sorry, but it's all so unfair." His eyes burned their passion into ash as he cried. "If marrying Mallory is the only way I can be near you, Emily, so be it! How can I ever leave this house without it destroying me, knowing you will be living beneath this roof? I love you with all my heart and deepest soul, my sweet Emily," he whispered her name in supplication.

"I don't want you to ever leave me either, Lawrence." Emily's distraught gaze became hidden beneath her winded plumes. "But for you to marry Mallory! How can that be the right thing for you to do? It's preposterous! You can't possibly love her, or grow to love her, please tell me you can't, Lawrence!" Emily demanded in a harsh tone.

"Love her, of course not! There was never a mention of love; the match is out of convenience to be sure. Remember, Emily, I haven't yet asked Mallory, and she has not agreed."

"That doesn't make it any easier to bear." Emily went on mournfully. "Mallory will no doubt agree to marry you. Mr. Lund has suggested you propose based on the way Mallory hangs all over you, Lawrence. It's so inappropriate for a young lady to be as brazen as she, but then again Mallory is not such a young lady. She has to be at least twenty-two. It just kills me to see Mallory openly act the way I wish I could, of holding your arm, and sitting beside you."

Emily stifled a sob. "To think Mr. Lund would financially support his daughter's choice makes me all the more envious of her. I only regret my father had not possessed an equally generous disposition for my happiness."

"Emily." Lawrence touched her weeping face. "You have no more reason to be jealous of Mallory than I of Sir Dexter. Even if I was to marry Mallory, I will never love her! Ever since I first set eyes on you at Fairway, it was instant love for me, but love will not help us now. To marry Mallory would be a sacrifice, but at least we would be together beneath the same roof. Mr. Lund showed me the East and West wings, and it would give us the opportunity to have a lifelong friendship. Your friendship is the most important thing in my life, Emily, my dearest. I can see no other way if we want to have our lives intertwined."

Emily offered no rebuttal as they emerged out from the woods, and back to the canvas. Lawrence continued painting every ounce of sentiment onto the canvas, as colors bled the blood of all their heartache intermingled with their hopes.

Chapter Nine

Dinner For Two

Summer's heat enveloped the July evening in a balmy calm. Starry beams twinkled in the sky surrounded by a cast of midnight blue. Lawrence and Mallory were secluded in the opulent dining room with the candelabra set ablaze. They were formally seated at either end of the mahogany table, now less the two extra leaves. The long stretch of wood which separated them shined with a glossy sheen, reflecting the fiery flames.

One of the footmen, Mr. Henry approached the pair. In his hand he held the tiniest camera available on the market, one and a quarter by two inches in size, and small enough to fit inside a pocket.

Mr. Henry stood so tall and straight, he barely looked like a human being. He wore formal attire, and spoke while staring straight ahead, "Mr. Lund has instructed me to take your photographs. Shall I take them before the first course, Miss Mallory?"

"Certainly, by all means," replied Mallory seeming anxious for a memento of their first evening together.

Lawrence arose from his seat to pose together, unsure of the significance to the request while Mallory chuckled before she whispered, "I think it's best to remain where you are, Sir Lawrence. These photographs will only be one square inch in size. I fear we can't both fit inside the same frame."

Mallory posed first. Dressed in a mauve dress with embroidered trim, her waist was tightly cinched, having taken extra pains with the stays of her corset. Clusters of muted flowers adorned her black brimmed hat.

Mr. Henry squatted down to the proper level in preparation to take two photos of her. Mallory smiled readily, she looked a bit more vibrant than she had previously. Mr. Henry then proceeded to take two smiling photographs of Lawrence where his eyes remained cheerless.

"Mr. Henry, I was wondering, do you happen to know what company manufacturers that camera?" Lawrence asked with more interest in the camera than his companion.

"It's manufactured by Alfred C. Kemper, in Chicago, but they are manufactured abroad as well." Mr. Henry walked off with the first seedling of their connection.

"That's technology for you," Lawrence commented. "Mallory, the few times I have been photographed, I had to stand, and wait until all the equipment was ready which took forever. My family was more interested in painted portraits than photos. My mother insisted they could be passed down to be appreciated by future generations."

"Lawrence, do you think you would like to have children someday?" Mallory unabashedly asked.

"Perhaps someday," Lawrence tried to sound off the cuff as he laughed to himself.

"Marrying Mallory out of convenience is one thing, but having to actually be *lovers* with her is quite another. Perhaps I would be pleased to have *no* children after all; either that or become a slave to fantasy!"

Lawrence tried to conjure up Emily's fair face while he glanced over at Mallory. It was impossible even beneath the romance of evening. Mallory's complexion looked coarse, and like the rough hide of an animal, sallow and pitted with imperfection. The would be vision of Emily's blue eyes were lost to the reality of Mallory's dull, beady eyes, peering at him, ordinary and brown, from beneath the distortion of her spectacles.

The butler served a light but sumptuous fare, as was the custom of the day to have lunch as the main heavier meal. They conversed about impersonal topics, such as the weather, or on the details of the Welcoming Ball in Emily's honor, planned for next Saturday night.

"Emily is such a dear," Mallory sweetly said. "I think she and Dexter will be very happy together. It will be so nice to have a sister-in-law. Ever since

I was a little girl, I wished for a sister. Now, at last, I will have someone to sit by the fire with, and do needle work, take turns at the piano, or chat." Mallory smiled with gratitude at the cozy scenario she envisioned.

She then limped over to the china closet, and went inside the drawer. "Lawrence, I wanted to show you what I made for the Christmas tree last winter."

Mallory presented three handmade ornaments; a silk, magenta pincushion with a pink ruffle, and a circular disk of ruffled ribbons accented by an ecru bow. Lastly, was Mallory's prized creation, "the catch all." It was a brown denim pouch, decorated with bronze spangles and beads with a large ring at the top, and a smaller one at the bottom, tiny enough to secure items.

Mallory was full of pride as she pointed to the hand-painted gold lace on top. "It's tricky hand painting on lace. I had to be very careful with my zigzag motif." Mallory held "the catch all" lovingly. "Lawrence, this ornament is actually useful; it doubles as a whisk-holder. It would give me much pleasure if you would keep it."

"Oh no, Mallory, I couldn't take it from you, but thank you for the gesture. You enjoy decorating the Christmas tree with it."

"Nonsense," Mallory insisted. "I'm sure Emily and I will sit together and make many new ornaments for the tree this Christmas. I have already bought a fine India silk and a yard of Silesia, and the hoops, and matching ribbon to make another 'catch all.' I'm planning to start my ornaments early this year . . . Emily is excellent with embroidery and crochet, her beadwork shows such patience. I should only have half of Emily's patience. I do admire her; she is an exceptional girl."

Lawrence squirmed with deception at the mention of Emily. "Thank you for this beautiful gift, Mallory, but I feel guilty taking it. How thoughtless of me; I haven't even brought you as much as a rose." Lawrence looked downward in regret.

"Don't feel too badly, 'the catch all' can also be used as a receptacle for soiled hankies if you wish." Mallory laughed lightheartedly while her eyes registered disappointment at his oversight before she continued in earnest. "Lawrence, I have more than enough roses around here to keep me quite content. I'm more grateful to have your company than I would be for a token flower."

The word "grateful" spun around Lawrence's head as a humbled gesture. Lawrence studied Mallory in the semidarkness, and contemplated how tiny and vulnerable she looked. "Mallory, I consider you to be a friend of sweet companionship as well." Lawrence reciprocated in sympathy for her sincerity.

"Lawrence, many wonderful unions have been made from friendship," Mallory interjected without reserve. "My father wants me to marry while I'm still young enough to start a family. I'm sure you are aware he has arranged our dinner together as a prelude for this discussion."

Mallory's stature became tall, and her manner dignified. "Lawrence, my father has the utmost respect for your character. He finds you intelligent, and talented, and admires your ambition to have a career in medicine. My father has made it quite clear he recommends you as a suitable husband for me."

"Your father has spoken to me in your favor as well, Mallory. So let me ask you, Mallory, how do you feel about such a marriage?" Lawrence asked in obligation to the evening's agenda. Nonetheless he feared the answer.

Mallory inhaled with a smile while the words seemed to sing off her lips. "It would be a blessing for me to have you as my husband, Lawrence. I would be indebted to you. However, I must admit with reluctance, although I'm very fond of you, Lawrence, I can hardly say I'm in love with you after the heartache I've had in love." Mallory's eyes became deadened in painful remembrance.

"Love can be a bitter thing," Lawrence agreed without hesitation. He felt relieved the pretense of love was not involved in his charade. He looked at Mallory with repugnance, as he struggled to find the proper words.

Mallory had the gumption to speak for the two of them. "Well then, should I tell my father we've decided to honor his good advice, and get married?"

"If you find it suitable for yourself, Mallory, I will do my part in fulfilling my responsibility as your fiancé." Lawrence nearly choked on the words as his heart became full of dread.

Mallory got up from her seat, and approached Lawrence. Her limp seemed more pronounced than he had remembered. "Come," she said. "Let us go out into the fresh air, and relax a bit. All this talk of marriage is such a serious matter. I think it hangs a bit heavy for now, but with time I'm sure we will both adjust to the idea."

Mallory latched onto Lawrence's arm with familiarity. Lawrence steadied her across the expanse of dining room, and out onto the veranda. Together they sat on a wrought iron couch, cushioned for the outdoors, with a coffee table set in front of them. By appearance alone, it looked as if they had been together for years. Both of them acted a bit stoic in their commitment.

Miss Julia dutifully brought out a tray of after dinner tea and pastries for the pair. They sat beneath the swell of summer air, with apprehension around their thoughts, mingling like strangers in the mist. The moon stood out like a luminous sphere of faraway dreams, lost to Lawrence's reality. The crickets hummed their song out from the thickets while otherwise a spell of silence divided their togetherness.

The scent of Mallory's perfume wafted in a heavy floral note, interspersed with a musty tinge as it merged with her body chemistry. In the moonlight, Mallory's teeth looked a trite less yellow, and her complexion a bit less sallow.

"When I had my accident on the horse, my fiancé, Sir Theodore Wellington, could not find it in his heart to accept me as I am now, less than perfect. All my dreams crashed into a million fragments. You see, Lawrence, I loved Sir Theodore with every fiber of my being." Mallory's eyes twinkled with the stars by the mention of her past sweetheart while Lawrence thought.

"It's *ironic* how Mallory and I are more alike than I would have ever imagined. We're both holding a *torch* for another."

Lawrence asked with reservation, "Mallory, are you revealing to me you are still in love with Sir Theodore?"

"I want to be honest with you, Lawrence. The reason I have never looked for another husband is because I will probably love the memory of Sir Theodore for all of my days. Everything was so perfect between us before my unfortunate spill off my horse . . . But now life has showed me mercy, and you have unexpectedly appeared under my very own roof. I was resigned I would never wed, but then your friendship brought me hope." Mallory linked her arm on his, and held it tightly.

"Lawrence, you must promise me once our engagement becomes formal, you will stand true to your commitment, no matter what fate might befall," she added with a grave demeanor.

"Dear Mallory, let us be realistic. An engagement is a time for a couple to reflect on their compatibility. If any unforeseen tensions should arise between us, then we wouldn't be able to go forward. It could happen on your part as well, Mallory. I wouldn't want you to lock yourself into an engagement if you were to change your mind," Lawrence said feeling trapped.

"In that case I would like to keep our engagement as brief as possible, Lawrence. I could not bear any further disappointment after the way things have turned out for me. Dexter and Emily plan to marry in July of 1896. Perhaps we can make it a double wedding then." Mallory looked concerned but determined.

"A double wedding it shall be, if Sir Dexter and Emily agree," Lawrence sounded with false cheer.

"Lawrence, I just wanted to let you know about Sir Theodore Wellington and why my emotions are more dormant than I would like. I promise I won't make any further mention of his name from here on in," Mallory offered apologetically.

"Lawrence, I believe you're the one man who can help me find my heart again. Perhaps . . . in time I can also inspire that emotion in you. For now we're friends, and have a mutual respect for each other. We should be thankful, that's far more than many married couples can boast."

Through the solitude of their exchange, Miss Julia appeared with a silver tray with Miss Nellie Sand's calling card upon it, a dear friend of Mallory's. "Miss Nellie is waiting in the drawing room for you. I was not sure if you would be playing piano this evening, Miss Mallory."

"Of course I will be playing the piano and Nellie is welcome to stay for conversation and tea as always. There is no need to have her leave a calling card. Come, Lawrence, let's greet my friend Miss Nellie." Mallory and Lawrence walked arm in arm, to welcome Miss Nellie Sand in the drawing room.

Miss Nellie was a bit younger than Mallory. She was wearing a lavender dress with a soft shawl draped across her shoulders, which she kept fastened at the sight of Lawrence.

"Nellie, I shall just burst if I don't tell someone. You are the first to know, Lawrence and I are engaged to be married," Mallory excitedly announced.

"Married, the two of you?" The words sounded oddly on Nellie's lips. It seemed to be more of a shock than a comprehensible joy.

"Yes, we will probably get married next summer. The exact date has not been set, and there will be so much to plan. Nellie, I'm so happy you stopped by. Your timing couldn't be more perfect," Mallory said excitedly. "Nellie, it would honor me if you would agree to be my maid of honor. Without question, Nellie, you are my one and only choice."

"Maid of honor," Miss Nellie tried to regroup her thoughts as Mallory hung on for her reply. "Oh, of course, Mallory, nothing would give me more pleasure than being your maid of honor!"

Miss Nellie came forth to embrace Mallory in a tender moment of joy. Her young friend Miss Nellie seemed touched, as she choked back a tear.

"I wish you both much happiness . . . but I must be going now. I didn't mean to intrude on your special night."

"Nonsense, Nellie, stay for a cup of tea, I'll play for you and Lawrence. Come sit, you're always welcome at Rosewood."

Mallory motioned for Nellie to sit in her usual high back chair, positioned by the tray of tea and cookies, in case any guests should arrive. Nellie sat upright like a proper lady. Lawrence offered her a cushion, which Nellie in turn refused. Lawrence seated himself on one of the brocade couches. He felt happy for the interlude of music, and for the glimpse of how married life with Mallory might be.

Mallory's gifted hands played one of her old sentimental tunes, "Last Rose of Summer." Its melody added charm to an evening, on the verge of darkening to total blackness. Entranced by her music, Lawrence watched Mallory's silhouette beneath her lamp. It gave him a sense of solemn comfort. He was now in a place where wordless were the cords she played, in synchrony with the emotions that dwelled inward.

Deep feelings rose to the surface while Lawrence's eyes began to mist. However, tears of joy they were not. Lawrence squelched them back into his inner reservoir of bereavement. He grieved his odd lot of having to marry a girl he did not love, and who did not love him either. The duality of this marriage of convenience seemed quite inconvenient at this moment of pure thought.

The night went on as such until Nellie got up to leave, "Thank you very much for the tea and your piano playing, Mallory. I will leave the two of you to enjoy the rest of the evening, and congratulations!"

Shortly after Miss Nellie's departure, the Lund family stood in the center hallway, arriving home from the opera. One by one they entered into the drawing room with raucous joviality.

The men were a bit tipsy, Sir Dexter in particular. It became obvious they had ingested an improper amount of spirits. They all settled themselves to listen to Mallory's usual nightly performance of background music while they chatted amongst themselves. Mallory was now immersed in the tune, "Listen to the Mocking Bird."

Mallory arose from her piano bench as soon as the song was completed, with a joy that had been suppressed by the melody. "Everyone . . . I have an announcement to make. Lawrence and I have decided to get married. As of tonight we are formally engaged."

"Engaged," Lady Sarah cried out joyfully, as everyone else echoed cheerful exclamations of congratulations.

Mallory continued. "If Dexter and Emily wouldn't mind sharing the spotlight, we would be honored to make it a double wedding."

"A double wedding," exclaimed Sir Dexter! "Dear sister, nothing would give me more joy than to share my wedding day with you. I for one am truly delighted. That is if it's all right with Emily."

"I would be only too happy for them to share in the festivity." Emily emitted false cheer while her heart sunk.

The glimmer of Emily's eyes shined not from an inner joy, but with the same tinge of deceit that hid in the steel blackness of Lawrence's. Their eyes locked for a moment in a knowing conspiracy, bringing them deeper and deeper with the succession of each new event.

Dr. Mathis chimed in, "We had better make this a summer of extra hard study, Lawrence my boy, with the prospect of a new bride. In fact . . ." He got up from the couch to shake Lawrence's hand in congratulations. "Now that you're engaged to my dear niece, Mallory, I will give you all of my medical books as a gift. This way when you move upstairs into the East wing, you can put them in the library. I will call upon Herbert Smith, the dean of Yale Medical School as soon as the summer ends, and make the proper arrangements for you to attend school in the fall."

"Thank you very much, Dr. Mathis. I'm so grateful to you for all your generosity," Lawrence said with sincerity. He cherished both the medical volumes, and the opportunity to attend Yale Medical School.

Mr. Lund exclaimed, "This calls for a celebration."

Mr. Lund took a key out from the bureau drawer, and opened up a chest where a choice selection of quality wine and after dinner liquors were stored. He proceeded to take out a bottle of 1873 Chateau Briand, a cherished vintage.

Mr. Lund popped the cork with zest. "I have been saving this bottle for twenty-two years now, ever since my daughter Mallory was born. I have been waiting for a moment like this. I think it's high time we broke it open."

The women seemed a little concerned by the consumption of more alcohol when it was obvious the men had already surpassed their limits. Nonetheless, frivolity and excess continued way into the wee hours of the night. Emily and Mallory took turns in the spotlight at the piano, and entertained with the melodic overtures of their future sisterhood.

Chapter Ten

Sweets For My Sweetheart

𝕱ierce torrents of rain thrashed upon Rosewood. "It looks like there can be no further sessions of Emily's portrait today," Lady Sarah announced to the couple's mutual disappointment.

"Well, Lawrence," Lady Sarah continued. "Now is your chance to diagnose your first patient at the request of Dr. Mathis. Mallory has been feeling under the weather. Come, she's in the parlor with Dr. Mathis, and he'd like you to take a look at her."

Lawrence found Mallory lounging beside the fireside looking peaked, and in the midst of a coughing spell. Lawrence analyzed her symptoms. "Mallory, I recommend you take Roche's Herbal Embrocation. It will help alleviate your dry cough, and congestion . . . I will also have Miss Julia steep a strong kettle of chamomile tea to help soothe your nerves."

Dr. Mathis smiled with pride. "I see my protégé has recommended an appropriate course of treatment. I will instruct the head nurse to take a ride into town to purchase a bottle of Roche's at once. It's clear, Lawrence, you have a natural inclination for healing."

Indeed just the gentle touch of Lawrence's hand had a benevolent effect. "Don't despair, Mallory, I guarantee you will be well enough to attend Emily's Welcoming Ball on Saturday night." Lawrence comforted.

The rainy weather persisted through to the next week, and continued on in the morning of the Welcoming Ball. The day slowly cleared to oppressive heat. Mrs. Lund fretted as the servants began to set up the tables in the grand ballroom at her request. "Mallory, I had my heart set on having the affair beneath the summer sky, but the grounds will be too soggy to be used to full capacity. Well, at least the quartet will be able to play their tunes out on the veranda. The midday sun is slowly drying it, but the other instrumentation will have to be played in the grand ballroom. I suppose we can have dancing inside as well."

"Don't worry, Mother, it will be a beautiful affair inside or outside. I just want to run up, and give Lawrence the memento I made for him before I have Mr. Henry hang the sign I made for Emily."

Mallory found Lawrence in the library immersed in study. She appeared in her everyday blue calico with a white bonnet, pressed flat against her tight ringlets. She stood for a moment, and waited until Lawrence sensed her presence.

"Oh, I wasn't aware you were here, Mallory! Please come in," Lawrence welcomed from beneath his studies.

"I didn't want to disturb you, Lawrence, but thanks to your good advice I feel recuperated. I just know you will make a fine doctor one day," she said optimistically.

"Well, I'm happy to see my first patient has survived," Lawrence teased before they both chuckled.

"Lawrence, I have something I wanted to give you before the ball tonight. It's just a little something in appreciation for your medical advice." She handed Lawrence a wrapped gift with a crimson bow at the top.

Lawrence unraveled the paper to find an envelope photograph-frame Mallory had ingeniously created. She had cut squares into two envelopes, in order to display the mini photos Mr. Henry had taken of them. Mallory created a gold-washed effect around the openings with dabs of paint, and connected the envelopes by a daisy ribbon in blue "forget me not."

"Mallory, it's beautiful!" Lawrence put aside his textbook, and gazed at her handiwork in appreciation. "I must say you are most clever, Mallory."

"Well, I must admit, Lawrence, the idea is not original. I found the instructions on how to make it in the January Harper's Young People. I had clipped it out, and was saving it for the right occasion," Mallory admitted modestly.

"It doesn't matter one iota, you executed it so expertly, Mallory. I would not be at all surprised if yours was even prettier than the one Harper's made."

"Thank you, Lawrence, I hope you will grow to treasure it for years to come. I made one for myself, so we would both have a memento of the night we became engaged." Lawrence cringed at the unwelcome reminder as Mallory beamed joyfully. "I've also made a hairpin box for Emily, as a welcome into the family gift. Let me get it to show you."

Mallory hurriedly rushed back to her chamber. While she was gone Lawrence regretted the twin photos bonded them as an official couple. At a quick glance Lawrence thought Mallory could easily pass for his mother. He dreaded the obligation of having to hang the photographs in his chamber through the brass hoop connected to the ribbon.

Mallory returned with another one of her ingenious creations. "Here is Emily's hair-pin box. I constructed the box out of cardboard, covered with white linen. Look at the embroidered doilies I pasted on the front and on the sides. This tie on the top of the box is for opening and closing." She proudly opened it.

"I lined the inside with linen on top of a layer of perfume wadding." Mallory held the fragrance close to Lawrence's nose. "Smell what a beautiful scent the box has."

"It smells delicious! You did a great job, Mallory. I'm sure Emily will love the hair-pin box!"

"Thank you, I'm certain it will suit her needs. Emily has often complained to me how she is always misplacing her hairpins, so I thought this would be the perfect gift. I was wondering," Mallory hesitated, "Would you like me to sign your name on the card as well, Lawrence?"

"By all means no," insisted Lawrence. "I want you to take full credit for your beautiful handiwork, Mallory. What did I do other than admire the hairpin box? Besides, I bought Emily a selection of Walter Baker Chocolates."

"Walter Baker Chocolates are my all time favorites!" Mallory perked up. "Lawrence, I don't know if you're aware but Walter Baker received the highest awards from the Industrial and Food Expositions in both America and Europe for their superior quality."

"No, I had no idea, to me chocolate is chocolate." Lawrence shrugged his shoulders in surprise. "I asked the nursemaid to pick up a box of chocolate for Emily the day she went to the pharmacy for your medicine, and this is what she came back with."

Lawrence felt an uncomfortable energy in the air. "Now that I know you like Walter Baker Chocolate I will pick you up a box next time I'm in town." Lawrence offered somewhat awkwardly.

"Oh no, eating chocolate is not good for the waistline," Mallory insisted with pride, as she walked off flaunting her one physical attribute which was a step away from emaciation.

Chapter Eleven

Cry In the Night

Mallory's "Welcome to the Family," sign hung by the entrance of the grand ballroom. The massive chandelier in the center of the ceiling reflected prisms of light, glittering off the crystals. The cream curtains and silver moldings looked regal in combination with the antique white walls. Large circular tables covered by brocade tablecloths had centerpieces of pink roses intermingled with baby's breath.

Hector and Lady Sarah stood as the master of ceremonies with Emily and Sir Dexter standing by their side. Lady Sarah's lavender gown twirled as she moved. It had a ruffle effect framing her shoulders.

Emily wore a flowing, pink dress, so pale, it appeared like iced white. The delicate hue of the gown enhanced her complexion and golden curls. It gracefully grazed the glossy floor as she walked. Sir Dexter wore a long coat with tails, and slacks in a summer color. His red hair detracted from his wardrobe as the bright light of the ballroom exaggerated its intensity.

Lawrence escorted Mallory with reservation as the throngs of socialites began to assemble at half past ten. Mallory's gray satin dress made her look past the first blush of youth, and waiting for the providence of womanhood to take hold. As they walked in the ballroom arm in arm, Mallory tried to conceal her limp with the grace of her dress.

In the meantime, name-dropping chatter and formal conversation echoed in the background. Lawrence felt out of his league as Mr. Lund introduced him around the elite Newport society so fast his head began to spin.

"Dr. Denton and Lady Catherine, I would like you to meet, Sir Lawrence Gray. He is an accomplished artist who I have commissioned to do our family portraits. He is currently in private study with Dr. Mathis, and will be attending Yale this fall, with plans to take over Dr. Felder's clientele, a friend of Dr. Mathis."

"Pleased to have your acquaintance," Lawrence tipped his top hat feeling off kilter by his instant celebrity.

Lady Sarah excitedly told Emily, "My sister, Lady Chatsworth, has been holding several flawless diamond rings for whoever will be next in line. She has reserved an exquisite three-carat one for you. You will be receiving it at your Engagement Ball. I know you will be very pleased."

Lady Sarah whispered with a pompous expression, "Of course, there will be many more crown jewels, Emily, be assured. The ring you will receive was my grandmother's, and the one I'm saving for Mallory had been my great grandmother's. As far as diamonds go there is no shortage in the Lund family, and once you're bestowed with a Lund heirloom, it's yours to enjoy forever," Lady Sarah exaggerated her diamond laden hands with a flourish.

Dignified, aristocratic people wearing the latest Paris fashion swamped the ball. Many of the ladies were discussing their recent jaunts to Europe, and shopping sprees at The House of Worth.

William Gray arrived with the Reed family, dressed in the one black suit he owned. It still looked fairly new considering he had little opportunity to wear it. Nonetheless the exaggerated style of its collar made it look a bit dated.

"Lawrence, my son," William clasped Lawrence tightly to his weary chest, "Look at you! You have grown into a man of distinction. It would make your mother proud to see you looking so regal, and pursuing a career of painting portraits, as well as following your dream and studying to become a doctor. If only I could have done that for you, Lawrence." William looked downward in remorse. "But there were too many troubles after we lost the farm."

"Father, don't worry, you always did your best," Lawrence reassured with a pat on his shoulders. William Gray's eyes misted at the vision of his son, now taken under Hector Lund's wing as Mr. and Mrs. Reed offered a condescending smile Lawrence's way.

Mr. Lund walked over and Philip introduced William Gray to him. "You've raised an honorable young man, Mr. Gray, and what a gifted artist he is. Come let me take all of you into the drawing room to show you his portrait of Emily that he has nearly completed."

William Gray's tired eyes regained a spark. "Oh yes, I would love to see Miss Emily's portrait. Lawrence has always been a master at capturing likeness."

Emily's parents reluctantly smiled as Mr. Reed grabbed his wife's arm. "We will take a look at the portrait after we get something to drink."

Mrs. Reed gossiped quietly to her husband after the men walked off. "Can you imagine Hector and Lady Sarah being so desperate to marry off their daughter; that they have resorted to trying to groom Lawrence into a gentleman. Talk about making a silk purse out of a sow's ear!" Mrs. Reed sneered in disdain.

"Well, just look at Mallory," Mr. Reed murmured. "If Hector can save that poor creature from being an old maid he cannot afford to be too picky . . . But as for our beautiful Emily, only the cream of the crop will do for her." Mr. Reed smiled smugly.

Margaret Reed turned up her nose as well. "It's hard to believe Lawrence has been commissioned as an artist to do their family portraits? Can you imagine anyone wasting their good money on that, Philip?"

Philip chuckled. "Please, Maggie, don't make me laugh, family portraits are supposed to be a legacy that's passed down to future generations. I will happily wait my turn for the prestigious Herbert Lustick, so I can have something valuable to be remembered by." Mr. Reed rolled his eyes in scorn.

Mallory prompted Lawrence to dance out on the veranda beneath the stars. The night hung like a dark shadow over Lawrence. Other couples joined on the dance floor when the quartet played a waltz. Lawrence only felt the stifling of his free will through the festivity, until he danced like a marionette, pulled by the strings of his unlucky circumstance.

"I have to ask myself, how is it I'm *holding* a girl I do not care for, close to my heart beneath the moonlight?"

Mallory's floral cologne, even through the wind, invaded his nostrils like a sad flower. The scent immersed Lawrence with repugnance, and an austere melancholy. Lawrence could not even bear the sight of Mallory's face. With her glasses obscuring her gaze, she looked like an ordinary creature, a typical wallflower, saved from the sidelines at his expense.

Emily breezed past, and offered Lawrence a whiff of her trademark rose fragrance. Her luminous curls bounced beneath the glimmer of stars, shining upon her in mirth. Lawrence surreptitiously watched Emily as his heart set in despair. Mallory made a bit of mild conversation through the music, when just the sight of her face at that odd hour, looked far worse than usual. Mallory's pallor appeared an odd cast of gray, while her lips drained to purple, thin and craggy, against her tarnished teeth.

"Can I take even a moment longer of this *charade*? How can I actually go through with all this and *marry* Mallory?"

On top of that, Mallory danced lamely, being one or two steps offbeat. Lawrence sighed as he suggested they go in for a drink. Mallory sat down at one of the circular tables. She began fanning her moist flesh with the mauve fan she kept strung around her neck, at all times in the summer months. She was unable to fend off the heat very well. In fact, Mallory often opted to go without gloves in the summer, and her freckled hands showed the traces of overexposure to the elements.

Lawrence brought over two glasses of punch, with fruity wine mixed in. Mallory went to fan Lawrence in flirtation when Lawrence replied, "No thank you, Mallory, the fanning only makes me feel worse afterward."

"All you men say the same thing about fanning," Mallory smirked. "That's the difference between men and women. We women live in the present moment. So if it feels worse after, I'll fan myself again and again. Who cares, I can go on like this the entire evening if I like?"

Mallory continued the motion over her flushed cheeks while Lawrence thought the present moment was unbearable with or without a fan. "Mallory, I think it's harder for men to live in the moment because we carry more of the troubles of the world on our shoulders." Lawrence pondered the weight of his heartache.

Emily and Sir Dexter joined their table, looking overheated from all the activity. The warm night, and the cease of the rain had brought an oppressive humidity, with only an occasional breeze. Emily went to retrieve her fan which she had laid on another table before the dance.

With gloved clad hands, Emily gracefully breezed her ornamental fan, made out of long white feathers. It spread out like an exotic bird in flight. Emily, in turn, offered Sir Dexter a few welcomed motions of the fan, before making the same overture toward Lawrence.

With the flutter of Emily's feathers, Lawrence became mesmerized. It looked like Emily was in the midst of a magic act where she was about to pull out a white rabbit, nearly swiping Lawrence's top hat. Lawrence's dark lids swooned beneath Emily's attention, while Mallory became miffed.

"I thought you detested fanning, Lawrence!" Mallory cried out with annoyance.

"I took your advice; I'm living in the moment, Mallory." Lawrence quickly covered up.

"In that case," Mallory smiled eagerly as she joined in, and fanned Lawrence as well.

"Ladies, ladies over here," Sir Dexter motioned. Both Mallory and Emily giggled as Sir Dexter brought his face forward, and fluttered his eyelashes like a butterfly in flight.

A spirit of joviality emanated in the air. After the fanning, Sir Dexter stood up, "Excuse me, Emily, I'm going out onto the veranda for a smoke. My mother only allows smoking in the upstairs parlor, and who wants to trek all the way up there in this heat. Lawrence, why don't you come along with me?" Sir Dexter grabbed onto Lawrence's arm, giving him no choice in the matter.

The two men walked onto the veranda. Sir Dexter took a couple of drags from an oversized cigar, while the men cheered in congratulations on his engagement. The smoke caused Sir Dexter to cough, and rush back inside for another drink to soothe his irritated throat.

It became clear; Sir Dexter had a penchant for becoming inebriated. In fact he did not know his limits. Sir Dexter became downright sloppy, and a bit drunk, by the time the dessert came out.

The "Welcome to the Family" cake looked like a wedding cake, festooned with pale pink flowers over white icing, encircled with candied pearls. Emily blew out a single candle for good luck. She made a wish with all her might, while at least a hundred people watched her. Emily wished with all her spirit, and then she prayed with all her soul, that she would miraculously wed Lawrence instead of Sir Dexter. Afterward the hair on Emily's arms stood on end and her scalp tingled oddly.

Later in the evening, well after the ball ended, Lawrence was awoken out of a deep sleep. He heard weeping coming from the direction of Emily's chamber. Lawrence opened his door slightly, finding the hallway dimly illuminated from a nightlight. He wondered for a moment if he should summon for help as the weeping continued. He then remembered Mr. and Mrs. Lund had left with the Reeds on their jaunt to Italy directly after the ball.

Lawrence knew to awaken any of the servants on the lower level, would be cause for panic. Again in the silence, Lawrence heard a shriek of magnitude, which sent a shiver of fright through his being. Lawrence stepped outside his chamber, and stood adjacent to Emily's doorway noticing a sliver of light shine from beneath her door.

About to edge forward, but still afraid to intrude on perhaps the insignificance of a nightmare, Lawrence stood motionless in his stocking feet. There in the pit of the black night, Lawrence heard yet another cry which curdled his very blood.

Emily's door then swung open. Sir Dexter stumbled out hurriedly, while fumbling to fasten the waistband of his pants. He was completely disheveled with his shirttails hanging out of his trousers. Sir Dexter stumbled toward his chamber and down the hallway with the ungainliness of inebriation. In fact Sir Dexter nearly fell, and tripped on his own foot which awkwardly blocked the other one.

Sir Dexter remained oblivious to Lawrence's presence in the hallway. As Lawrence's eyes adjusted to the darkness, he watched dumbfounded as Sir Dexter disappeared behind his chamber door. Lawrence panicked for a moment, as he became wracked with anguish, and unprepared for what he had just witnessed.

Standing in the hallway, he could still hear Emily's sobbing. He then heard her get up, and bolt a chair against her door, before she continued to whimper. Lawrence wondered what he should do, as he stood in a frantic stalemate.

He did not want to make matters worse by confronting Sir Dexter, and then suffering any other consequence Sir Dexter might have in store. To try and speak to Emily seemed to him, not the proper overture, especially in the indecency of his nightclothes, and at that ungodly hour. Lawrence stood outside Emily's door as her crying subsided somewhat. All sorts of scenarios flashed through Lawrence's mind.

"Did Sir Dexter go into Emily's chamber to *comfort* her, after she screamed out in a bad dream? On the other hand, did Sir Dexter *force* himself unwillingly upon Emily in a drunken stupor?"

Just the thought of that scenario made Lawrence insane with anger and torture alike. He lay frozen, unsure of what he could do without making matters any worse. Lawrence decided it best to just wait until morning, and hoped he would perhaps have a clue to what had happened. Nonetheless the moments went as slow as molasses, and with a heavy weight.

Chapter Twelve

Woman's Woes

The next morning the rain had returned violently, thunderous lightning thrashed in white vengeance. A somber mood seemed to take hold at Rosewood in the aftermath of the Welcoming Ball. The gray sky was as dismal as Lawrence's spirit. Lawrence had been hoping for a lovely day to help erase his fears concerning Emily. He anticipated adding crucial details to her portrait. However to his dismay, Emily had not even left her chamber.

Lawrence overheard one of the chambermaids relaying the message. "Emily is unwell, with woman troubles."

The possibilities raged through Lawrence's head. He hoped all he had witnessed was a painful time of month. However, Lawrence doubted this new premise since he had been around Emily for long enough to know she was not prone to troubles of that magnitude. Lawrence worried it was something far worse, especially when he spied one of the chambermaids emerging from Emily's chamber with her sheets rolled up into a ball.

Lawrence snuck a peek, seeing the chambermaid was trying to conceal a large pool of blood which bled clear through the white cotton. A chill of terror raced through Lawrence as he contemplated knocking on Emily's chamber. To his further dread, he came upon Miss Julia carrying up a tray of tea and dry toast for Emily.

"Miss Emily does not want to be disturbed by anyone, anyone at all, including Sir Dexter!" Miss Julia sternly announced.

"Including Sir Dexter," Lawrence echoed, feeling on the outside as he became aghast with hateful imagination. His intuition told him Sir Dexter had plundered Emily's virginity in a drunken depravity as the vision of Emily's bloodstained sheets menaced with the unthinkable.

Lawrence proceeded down to the breakfast parlor. He hoped to size things up by Sir Dexter's demeanor, but to Lawrence's dismay all he found was Mallory quietly sipping tea with Dr. Mathis.

The doctor stoically told Lawrence, "Both Sir Dexter and Miss Emily are to remain in bed all day. Sir Dexter has a terrible hangover from overindulgence in spirits. Of Miss Emily," the doctor spoke with reservation. "Women's woes," was all he said having examined her that morning, and seeming free from suspicion.

After breakfast, Lawrence tried to tend to his studies, but not a single fact could permeate his brain. All he could think of were the memory of Emily's wails; he could still hear them inside his head. He repeatedly envisioned Sir Dexter scrambling out of her chamber with his shirttails out, and fumbling with the top of his trousers. The vision of this living nightmare would not leave Lawrence's sight; with his eyes open or shut.

Lawrence retired to his chamber after dinner, and dreaded another sleepless night. The deluge of rain chilled him to the core as Lawrence reviewed the scenario again. He knew it was inappropriate for a man to enter into a woman's chamber without a chaperone, and could not help fear what ravage had befallen Emily.

Lawrence decided to write a note to Emily, and slip it beneath her door. He found a piece of stationary inside the desk drawer, embossed with the letter L in fancy swirls. Thankfully, the L for Lund would be equally appropriate for Lawrence. He took the ink and quill in hand, and began to etch the words.

"Dear Emily, I offer my sincerest *concern* for your swift recovery. Yours Truly, Lawrence."

Lawrence slipped the note beneath her door, and lo and behold, a few moments afterward Emily slipped her own note beneath the bottom of her door. "Lawrence, your concern is my *courage*. Emily."

Come morning, the sun blazed litmus bright, over the horizon. Summer reclaimed the season in hot possession. Lawrence arose from his bed to find a tiny, nearly crumpled note beneath his door. He seized it hurriedly seeing it had been written by Emily's hand. "Lawrence, please don't *worry*. Emily."

Lawrence held the note, torn from an advertisement, and pressed it flat, before he put it inside the shaving-paper holder Emily had given him that day out on the fields at Fairway. How long ago those days now seemed.

Lawrence scrambled downstairs to the breakfast parlor where he found Emily looking like a shadow of the girl who had been welcomed into the Lund family just two nights before. By her appearance alone, Lawrence feared something grueling had befallen her in the interim. Her blue eyes had lost their sparkle as she stared straight ahead in a daze, and sipped on a tonic Dr. Mathis had prepared for her. The cast of blue-gray beneath her eyes marred her complexion. Dressed in her usual, portrait outfit, she looked considerably paler.

"Good morning, Emily. It's good to see you up and about." Lawrence tried to sound nonchalant. He did not want to illicit any attention from Mallory.

"Thank you, Lawrence," Emily replied, yet the way her eyes linked with his said more than words.

"It will do Emily good to pose today," Dr. Mathis advised. "She needs to breathe in the fresh air, and be outside in the sunshine."

After tea and the usual minced pie and fresh fruit, Lawrence retrieved his art supplies while Emily waited for him on the West Porch. She was fanning herself with her white feathered fan when Sir Dexter appeared from along the garden path, and tried to get past them. Emily closed her fan with deliberation, and then opened it again, only to slam it shut in an exaggerated motion. The obvert message of, "You are cruel!" confronted Sir Dexter.

The air stood still for a moment as Sir Dexter tried to sheepishly get past them. By his cowardly demeanor alone it became clear Sir Dexter could read the language of the fan. Emily said nothing as she moved aside, and granted Sir Dexter enough room to enter the porch.

"Good morning," Sir Dexter said in stilted words, in an awkward interlude of being half-inside, and half-outside.

"Good day, Sir Dexter," Lawrence said with reservation.

Before Emily walked off, she reached for her pink parasol, and struck it in her hand forcefully before she opened it. Her parasol gesture signaled, "I am very much displeased."

Lawrence and Emily walked over to the old oak tree beside the elm, and Lawrence set up his easel and art supplies. Lawrence looked over at his subject and the canvas, noticing how Emily looked like a different girl than the one he had painted the last time. Her lips were pressed together in tension with an angry expression on her face. Sorrowful waves of blue drowned her eyes in secret undercurrents, pulling her deeper and deeper into her private despair.

Lawrence began to paint, and hoped Emily might confide in him on her own accord. He feared any questions he might ask would only make her burst into tears.

After an hour had elapsed, Emily seemed settled in her thoughts. She began to speak with a pained countenance, "I don't know how I can marry Sir Dexter, Lawrence. When he drinks he becomes someone I don't know, someone cruel, and hateful!"

Lawrence put down his paintbrush. "Emily, I heard your screams the other night, and I have been crazed ever since. Did Sir Dexter hurt you?" Lawrence asked in rage.

"In every way," Emily cried out. "He's a hopeless drunk, who does not have the moral fiber to know disgrace. Decency forces me not to discuss matters such as these, Lawrence. I only want to forget. Paint, paint," she demanded impatiently.

"Emily, how can I paint when I know Sir Dexter has done something that has upset you? You are not obligated to go forth with the wedding if you find Sir Dexter's actions unsuitable."

"Unsuitable, ha, I assure you my parents will not find Sir Dexter anything but a prize! Guaranteed they will find my not safeguarding myself against such situations a cause for shame. I don't wish to delve any further into this topic; it will surely prove to be a fruitless one."

Lawrence's voice softened. "If you have found Sir Dexter cruel as you have just displayed before with your parasol and fanfare . . . Please pardon the pun, Emily, but I could not miss your gesture over by the West Porch, and neither did Sir Dexter. Has Sir Dexter dishonored you, Emily, please tell me?" Lawrence inquired with a grave expression.

"Dishonor, I have dishonored myself by my carelessness!" Emily shouted with tears. "Lawrence, I am no longer innocent be assured." Her lips began to tremble as her blue eyes filled with tears. "You tell me I have a choice about going on with this wedding. That's impossible now; I am married to Sir Dexter already! He has made certain to that, and has spoiled me for anyone else." Emily's face grimaced painfully.

"If there is anything I can do, please tell me, Emily! I feel just as powerless as you to this circumstance. That scoundrel, taking advantage of a woman! It infuriates me, how low can a man be! He does not deserve you, Emily. You are far too good for the likes of him!" Lawrence ranted in delirium.

"Thank you, Lawrence, I just want you to know you are the only true friend I have and I appreciate having someone I can talk to, especially when subjects are unspeakable. Now please go on with your painting. Sitting here posing is helping me to forget my troubles," Emily continued mournfully.

"Very well, Emily, I'll do as you please, but let me understand one thing first. Are you still sure you want to honor your engagement with Sir Dexter after how he has dishonored you?"

"There is no choice." Emily went on gravely. "My parents would not hear of it otherwise. I assure you the match of me and Sir Dexter is more about status, than character. Rarely can you find both in this day and age, with money breeds pride and decadence. To even think of going against my parents and refusing to marry Sir Dexter would be my ruination," Emily bitterly exclaimed.

"Go on, Lawrence, better you should paint, than for us to try to alter the society we live in. I will merely hold my head high, and go on as before. Perhaps I will be forced to live my whole life like this. Who am I to know my lot?"

Lawrence picked up his paintbrush again, and painted with the passion of their connection. He felt compelled to lure Emily into the forest again, and hold her in his arms. A tingling of passion for Emily, and anger at Sir Dexter, tormented Lawrence with an odd duality.

Lawrence continued to paint her perfect pout. He desperately tried to divert the topic. He did not want to defile Emily any further with improper thoughts, yet how proper they now seemed beneath the summer sun with the shade of the tree adding a shroud to the elements.

Once again, by mid-morning Sir Dexter and Lady Violet were seated outside, analyzing another pile of strewn papers. Lady Violet's summer clothing was far too tight and sheer while her jet-black hair made her look hardened at the age of twenty-one.

The shade of the umbrella shielded them from the sun, but not from Emily's suspicious eye. "There she is again, Lady Violet. Would you just look at how Sir Dexter is leaning into her so attentively! I don't put anything past Sir Dexter now. He's unscrupulous, and now on top of everything, he's becoming a ladies' man! Rumor has it Lady Violet is cold and calculating, and is capable of swindling whatever man she sets her sights on by using her feminine wiles to get whatever she wants."

"Don't pay attention to gossip, Emily," Lawrence retorted with paintbrush in hand.

"Are you kidding, Lady Violet is walking gossip!" Emily exclaimed. "Just look how tight and sheer her dress is. I know how to read people Lawrence, and Lady Violet is nothing more than a gold digger. Mallory was bragging to her mother the other day about how Sir Dexter has been able to wring every penny out of Lady Violet's millionaire husband, and how Mr. Reynolds was far too old for the beautiful Lady Violet in the first place. I overheard Sir Dexter telling Miss Julia this morning to expect Lady Violet for dinner tonight. Can you imagine the nerve of Sir Dexter inviting Lady Violet to dine with us?"

"Emily, with all the leftover food it's a wonder the Lunds don't have another grand ball to make a dent in it." Lawrence tried to comfort Emily. "Miss Julia has been busy canning the excess peaches and cherries, as well as tomatoes since the night of the Welcoming Ball."

"Welcoming Ball," Emily rolled her eyes. "If that's what a Welcoming Ball is all about, I would rather be unwelcome to the family!"

"Come, Emily, it's hard to paint when you chat, that's quite enough for today; the sun is about to peak soon anyway. I suggest we go back inside, before we get caught out in the midday heat."

"Lawrence, promise me all I have told you will remain just between us two." Emily urged poignantly.

"Of course, Emily, trusting me with a secret is an understatement. You could trust me with your life. I will never let you down." Lawrence gazed at Emily with loving regard.

Emily sobbed beneath her breath. "My mother warned me how a proper lady must protect herself against the indelicacy of a male . . . I should never have allowed Sir Dexter to enter my chamber at that hour of the evening, but he knocked and said he had to see me at once. I was half sleeping when I got out of bed . . . I had no idea he'd been drinking with a few of the men who had lagged on after the ball ended." Emily reached for her lace handkerchief, and wiped away a tear.

"It's not your fault, Emily! Don't blame yourself, how were you to know what would be?" Lawrence softly consoled.

"I should have known." Emily began to cry uncontrollably. "Proper ladies have to set respectable limits. Can't you see, Lawrence; I have disgraced myself by my negligence!"

"Shh, please don't cry, Emily." Lawrence soothed. "You're not to blame for what happened. How were you to ever expect something of that magnitude would occur? I heard you; at first I thought maybe you were having a nightmare, and didn't feel it was my place to intrude . . . All I can say is I'm so sorry; I wished I could have helped in some way," Lawrence whispered apologetically.

Emily lamented. "It all happened so fast, and now everything has already been planned. Our Engagement Ball is set for two weeks. I cannot and will not humiliate myself by doing otherwise. I will just have to go on, and pretend all this never occurred, and put it all behind me. That is the only way, Lawrence."

Chapter Thirteen

The Red Lady

Lady Violet arrived for dinner at half past six. She had changed into a snug fitting, crimson dress which complimented her dark coloring. Her blue-black hair had been parted in the center, and looked like it had been curled to no avail, with a red satin ribbon tied at the crown. Her appearance resembled a fortuneteller. Her large, cagey eyes looked apropos for peering into a crystal ball.

Sir Dexter sat at the head of the table next to Emily with Mallory sitting beside her. Lawrence sat across from Mallory and next to Lady Violet, while Dr. Mathis sat at the other head. The extra leaves were not utilized, making for a more intimate gathering.

Emily still looked rather pale from her ordeal, which did not pass Dr. Mathis' keen eye. "Emily dear, are you still drinking the tonic I recommended?"

"Yes, I had some again this morning," she weakly uttered.

"Emily, you must have the tonic morning and evening for the next week or so like I recommended. The brew contains a lot of iron which will help to build your strength." Dr. Mathis rang for Miss Julia to bring an evening dose.

Lady Violet peered at Emily curiously. "Emily dear, I must say you do look a little peaked. Do you have iron-poor blood?" she inquired in a condescending tone, before continuing when Emily's reply was not swift enough. "Emily, you must make sure to eat a lot of organ meats, particularly liver. I know it might not sound so palatable, but it can enrich the iron content of the blood in no time."

"Thank you for the advice, but I don't think I could stomach it." Emily grimaced with revulsion.

In the meantime, Sir Dexter remained quiet on the matter of Emily's wellbeing. In fact, he suddenly looked as pale as Emily. The chandelier shined on Sir Dexter at an awkward angle which exaggerated the fairness of his blonde eyelashes and white skin.

Sir Dexter reassured Emily with awkwardness, "Don't trouble, Emily. Dr. Mathis' tonic is a sure cure all."

Emily succumbed to the irony of not being able to cure her choice of fiancé. Emily began to wonder if Sir Dexter even remembered his savage behavior. She knew inebriated spells were often coupled with forgetfulness. Emily hoped it would be the case, and the memory would just vanish like a bad dream. She sat quietly in thought, eating the evening fare, while Lady Violet monopolized the conversation.

Lady Violet's voice sounded loud and boisterous, and devoid of feminine restraint. However with Lady Violet's nature, came a charismatic power, which clearly fascinated men. All the males at the table became riveted to her, and listened intently as she spoke of her recent vacation in the south of France. In-between her monologue, Lady Violet interspersed little quips of French words, which caused her lips to contort in a mesmerizing manner, which even captivated Mallory.

In fact, Mallory became drawn into the French spirit. "I would just love to go to the south of France, perhaps we can honeymoon there, Lawrence. It sounds like such a romantic place for newlyweds. Tell me, Lady Violet, is it frequented by many honeymooners?" Mallory asked blushingly.

"Oh yes, Mallory darling, you would do well in choosing France as your honeymoon destination. However, I suggest you learn enough of the language to get by. Mallory, I would be happy to teach you French if you're interested . . . I declare, Mallory, French is the most beautiful language." Lady Violet lowered her voice seductively while her long eyelashes swooned in suggestion. "It's the language of love, to be assured."

"Thank you for offering to teach me, Lady Violet, but I don't think I'd be brave enough to order in a restaurant, or to speak on behalf of myself. I'll leave that for Lawrence." Mallory gazed at Lawrence dutifully.

Lady Violet zeroed in on Lawrence, acting as if every man, available or not, was fair prey. "Lawrence, I'd be delighted to teach you French if you desire to learn."

An uncomfortable pause prompted Sir Dexter to interject, "Lady Violet, you haven't told me about your being a tutor in French. I would love to learn French in the event I honeymoon there. Please let us set up a schedule at once. After all, a double wedding surely calls for a double honeymoon. I will gladly be the spokesman for my party."

"A double honeymoon," Lady Violet exclaimed in surprise. "I've heard of a double wedding, but never of a double honeymoon. Isn't that going a bit too far? I do declare!"

Mallory laughed innocently. "Nonsense, we're like one happy family already. Lawrence and Emily's fathers were boyhood friends. The two of them are more like brother and sister than future in-laws. We all get along splendidly. I think it would be just wonderful for us to honeymoon together. Emily and I could run off shopping while the men play a friendly game of cards," Mallory said with a singsong lilt.

Emily smiled demurely. It pleased her to have one consolation in her imprisonment at Rosewood. Thankfully, her close relationship with Lawrence was accepted wholeheartedly and encouraged.

Lady Violet's eyes ignited with a new power. "Very well then, Dexter, we can begin Monday if you'd like, after we go over those documents you asked me to bring to your office. I'll gladly bring along my French supplies, just so you know I've been fluent in French ever since I was a child. I've been told my accent is perfect, and I speak just as eloquent as a native."

Dr. Mathis advised, "If you young people do decide to go to France, please be careful of the water. Sometimes the water in a foreign country can give you severe cramps. By all means, drink mostly fruit juice, it's much safer."

With all the excitement of discussing honeymooning in France, along with Lady Violet offering to teach Sir Dexter lessons in French, it seemed only fitting for Sir Dexter to invite Lady Violet to the Engagement Ball. Sir Dexter sat tall in his seat as he addressed her.

"Lady Violet, I hope you will give us the honor of your company next Saturday evening at ten o'clock. We are having a grand ball that shall be the talk of the town, I assure you."

"I'd be delighted to attend. I'll be there with bells on." Lady Violet accepted with an expression of conquest.

Chapter Fourteen

The Black Widow

On July 1, 1895, the gala Engagement Ball arrived. Lady Violet was one of the first guests to arrive, solo. However, it became obvious by her showy appearance Lady Violet did not plan on staying that way, even if it meant borrowing other women's dates to make up for the slack.

Lady Violet looked exceedingly radiant in a burgundy dress accented by ecru lace trim and red rosettes sewn along the top of the bodice. Her Mediterranean complexion had been sun-kissed to a bronze; in spite of the large hat she always wore to shield her face. Crowned by a jeweled tiara, Lady Violet's grandeur instantly overtook the room.

Emily feigned a polite hello while Sir Dexter became taken in by Lady Violet's charms. Sir Dexter graciously took a hold of the dainty gloved hand Lady Violet offered to him, seeming captivated by her coquetry.

"Good evening, Lady Violet, how lovely to see you have arrived." Sir Dexter said as he tipped his top hat.

While Sir Dexter and Lady Violet conversed, Miss Nellie Sand diverted Emily, the two young women veered off to a corner to chat. Miss Nellie gave a disapproving glance in Lady Violet's direction before she whispered.

"Emily, Lady Violet is a vulture. Her poor estranged husband, Mr. Vance Reynolds, was one of the most well-respected gentlemen in all of New England before Lady Violet ruined him. He was just a harmless older man, who incidentally was exceedingly wealthy, and I say *was* because he will no longer be after Lady Violet is through with him."

Nellie raised her eyebrows judgmentally. "Mr. Reynolds could have had his choice of any refined lady he desired. He was sadly misled to have chosen Lady Violet. She has no refinement at all, and is nothing but a money hungry fraud. Her accusations of Mr. Reynolds are completely fabricated. No offense, Emily, but Sir Dexter has been gullible to have taken them at face value."

Emily's face dropped. "Did you tell Mallory about this?"

"No, Emily, I tried to warn her, but Mallory is so proud of the way Sir Dexter has gotten Lady Violet financial compensation from Mr. Reynolds, she won't hear of it. It's best we don't upset Mallory with it. After all tonight is a special night for her being newly engaged, in fact Lawrence will make the formal announcement later."

"Oh." Emily sighed with agitation. "In that case, Sir Dexter certainly would not care to hear about it from me. If I told him I'm sure it wouldn't make one bit of difference. Let's face it, that's how lawyers earn money," Emily said in reproach.

Emily demurely resumed her place beside Sir Dexter. She looked beautiful in her aqua dress, but subtle compared to the striking Lady Violet.

Lady Violet commented flippantly upon Emily's return. "Well, well, look at the happy couple! Emily, I just wanted you to know Dexter is the most wonderful student. He has already learned the majority of the standard French phrases. Have you decided yet on making France your honeymoon destination?"

"Yes, as I'm sure you must have heard, Mr. and Mrs. Lund have purchased a villa in the French Riviera, and have agreed to allow us to occupy it after the wedding. It's quite large enough for all of us honeymooners," Emily said in a matter-of-fact manner. Nonetheless, she regretted no place on earth could enchant her heart with Sir Dexter as her groom.

"A villa in France, how positively delightful," Lady Violet sung out. "If I summer at my château in France next year, I'll certainly pay you newlyweds a visit," Lady Violet said smugly.

Emily smiled with difficulty; becoming incensed by Lady Violet's overbearing manner. Just then Emily's family entered the ballroom in their usual aristocratic style. "Mr. Reed and Lady Margaret of Fairway," a servant in tails and top hat announced.

"Excuse me, Lady Violet, but I must welcome my parents."

Lady Violet seized the moment. "Oh please be a dear, Emily, and allow me to borrow your fiancé. I barely know a soul here; besides, hardly any of the men would be inclined to dance with a recent divorcee." Lady Violet did not wait for a reply as she swept Sir Dexter onto the dance floor.

Emily became infuriated by Lady Violet's obvert overture only to realize it would be one less dance for her to contend with. Before Emily had a chance to greet her parents, Mallory approached with an expression of discomfort on her face as Lawrence stood by her side.

Mallory spoke quietly, "Emily, I see Sir Dexter is occupied. Would you be a dear, and dance with Lawrence. My back has been acting up, and I'm having difficulty merely standing."

Mallory then softly whispered in Emily's ear as Lawrence turned to give one of the servants his empty glass, "I can't very well have Lawrence dance with the unmarried ladies, especially not Miss Suzette Cole."

Emily looked over to see the dark hair beauty from The Old Church seductively looking over Lawrence's way. "Most assuredly, Mallory, it will be my distinct duty to keep Lawrence occupied. He will be quite safe from all the opportune females who seek to slip in when your guard is down. So go relax back on the couch, he shall be in good hands," Emily reassured.

Emily felt deceitful as she melted with favor into Lawrence's chivalrous arms. Dressed in a black ensemble of a long jacket and trousers with a white shirt, Emily deemed Lawrence had never looked as handsome. His leisurely lifestyle of doing artwork outdoors, and studying medicine agreed with him majestically. Lawrence held Emily close to his chest; her head reached just above the crux.

Lawrence felt a touch victorious when Mr. and Mrs. Reed looked in their direction. They appeared to be taken aback. However, there could be no reason for them to break up their friendly spin on the dance floor now, considering the pair was soon to be in-laws. Margaret and Philip Reed joined in with a dance and veered over to Emily, in good spirits.

Sir Dexter reclaimed Emily. They resumed their fancy footwork, while Lady Violet took possession of Lawrence's footloose charms. In fact, to Emily's despair, Lady Violet took turns dancing with Sir Dexter and Lawrence, getting cozy with the two young men. Sir Dexter appeared to enjoy the opportunity while Emily had the benefit of dancing with Lawrence in the interim.

Mallory sat the entire night out, and reclined on the couch. She was excused of such languishing because of her back problems which occasionally flared up since her accident on the horse. Mallory seemed only too grateful to have Lady Violet pick up the slack.

Margaret Reed hugged Emily with pride. "Emily, I'm delighted to see you being honored like this, entering into a fine family. There has been no expense spared."

Mrs. Reed then whispered in a disapproving tone, "I see Lawrence has taken a fancy to Lady Violet."

Emily looked over at the duo. "Oh, Mother dear, Lawrence is just dancing with Lady Violet out of courtesy. Her divorce just came through last month, and she's estranged in all of New England. Her husband, Mr. Reynolds, has said perfectly awful things about her character."

"Awful things about Lady Violet such as . . ." Mrs. Reed's piercing blue eyes became hungry for gossip.

"Oh, Mother, I shall not say. Lady Violet is an excellent paying client of Sir Dexter's. I certainly cannot partake in the spread of slander, especially since who is to know which side is true. I'm certain both she and her ex-husband each have their own gripes. Divorce is a messy thing."

Her mother looked appalled to notice Lady Violet had switched her sights over to Sir Dexter, now leaving Emily in the lurch. "Emily, I must ask you something. Do you find Lady Violet to be of an agreeable temperament?" Mrs. Reed questioned with a look of concern.

"Anyone who pays a handsome sum of money to Sir Dexter for services rendered, I had better find of an agreeable temperament. There is no choice, but for an affable association. That's the price of marrying into royalty, Mother," Emily said despairingly.

"But," Mrs. Reed said looking aghast. "Just look how that woman attaches herself to Sir Dexter. I'll say I have never seen anything quite like that. You say she's newly divorced?"

"Yes, Mother, I'm sure as soon as she comes into the grand fortune her divorce provides, she'll assuredly marry again. Women like that always set their sights on powerful men. Certainly, she'll be in the market to find another wealthy husband before long. After all I'm sure she will want to start a family, and have an heir to her fortune."

Her mother chuckled with triumph. "Well, luckily for you, you're already engaged to Sir Dexter, because it appears as if Lady Violet would have wasted no time had her lawyer been an available prospect. After all," Mrs. Reed continued haughtily, "There's no man on this side of town as wealthy as Sir Dexter and his family. Speaking of engagement, why, Emily, you haven't yet showed me your engagement ring?"

Emily took off her white kidskin glove exposing an exquisite three-carat diamond set in platinum. "Why my stars," raved Margaret Reed! "That stone is so dazzling it nearly blinded me. Wear it well, my daughter, and in good health. You deserve to be showered with diamonds, and I'm sure this is only the beginning. Rumor has it there are many other heirlooms waiting in the wings. You know, Sir Dexter's great grandmother married into royalty, noble family that they are."

"I don't care about jewelry, Mother, granted it's nice to look at, but there are other things that are more important to me." Emily lowered her tone considerably making sure no one could eavesdrop. "Mother, here I am engaged to Sir Dexter to fulfill your and Father's wishes. You assured me I would grow to love him with time. I must inform you I like him even less . . . I shall never love Sir Dexter, and I'm not happy. This whole engagement is nothing but a farce, and this ring doesn't make up for it one iota, nor any of the other crown jewels waiting in the wings!"

"Now, now, Emily dear, I can't say I know of any young lady who hasn't gone through similar doubts upon her engagement. Those feelings are natural, and will pass I assure you."

Her mother grabbed for Emily's bejeweled hand with reassurance. "Emily, being engaged and getting married is all a transition. It will become common nature to you in time." Margaret Reed smiled in vow of her advice.

"You were lucky, Mother. Father is a gem, but you cannot compare my relationship with Sir Dexter to yours and Father's in any way. Trust me when I tell you Sir Dexter does not know how to be a proper fiancé."

Sir Dexter approached, and stole Emily away to dance. Emily submitted to the obligation while regretting she could not renege on her word on the night of their Engagement Ball. Nonetheless, her mother looked on proudly.

Lawrence stood regally at the front of the ballroom, holding a glass of champagne. He bowed his head before he began to speak. "Attention, Ladies and Gentlemen, I have a formal announcement to make. I propose to make a toast in honor of the engagement of Sir Dexter Lund to Miss Emily Reed. May they have many years of happiness and fulfillment." Lawrence took a swig of champagne while the crowd followed his cue, and cheered.

Then Lawrence added with dread, "Ladies and Gentlemen, I have a little surprise for all of you, an added bonus to the evening's festivities. I would also like to announce my own engagement to Miss Mallory Lund. There will be a double wedding next summer," Lawrence echoed with false merriment.

Mallory, still in grave pain, walked stoically over to Lawrence's side, and tried to muster a smile. The crowd went wild with jubilation while the orchestra played a lively tune, and motioned for the couples to overtake the dance floor.

Emily and Sir Dexter danced majestically to the unsuspecting eye, looking as if all between them was agreeable. Mallory struggled with her injured back to get by, moving as little as possible. Lawrence began to worry he might appear like an opportunist. He then asked himself.

"After all, haven't I succumbed more to the Lund's *wealth* by overlooking Mallory's lack of beauty and charm? After all, didn't Hector Lund lure me to marry his homely daughter, by nothing short of *bribery*?"

In the meantime, Lady Violet stood on the sidelines with an ominous look in her eyes, while the supposed happy couples displayed their joy. She looked like an insidious vamp on the outskirts, waiting until Mallory was forced to sit out. Lady Violet then zoomed in on Lawrence, and took over where Mallory had left off.

Lady Violet was one of those rare women who could take on a less than wealthy husband if she desired. Compared to Miss Mallory, Lady Violet stole the center stage. In fact, there was a lot of whispering as to the divorced heiress zeroing in on the newly engaged Lawrence, in the face of his engagement announcement no less. By surface value alone, Lawrence and Lady Violet looked quite apropos as a couple with their matching black heads of hair.

Mrs. Reed whispered to her husband, "Can you imagine the nerve of this Lady Violet; just who does she think she is? I have never seen a woman so forward in my entire life. It's most unbecoming, especially being in the circumstance she's in, being a divorcee and all . . . To be openly dancing at the ball, and flaunting herself the way she's dressed. It's obvious Lady Violet is a woman without innocence, and has a devious tendency for securing wealth."

Mr. Reed hurriedly approached Emily as she and Sir Dexter stopped dancing with one another, and scooped her away for a quiet chat. "Emily, this Lady Violet, let me ask you, is she a good client of Sir Dexter's?" Mr. Reed's face contorted in concern.

"Oh yes," replied Emily. "Lady Violet is one of his best, and has paid him a handsome sum for all the success he has had in attaching her rights to her estranged husband's assets. Her ex-husband had an empire in the gold mining industry before Lady Violet finished with him."

"I see, just who is Lady Violet a guest of?" asked Mr. Reed with a disapproving expression.

"Why Father, Lady Violet is a guest of Sir Dexter's, she barely knows a soul in Newport. She lives by herself in Clinton, Connecticut."

"I find that quite unorthodox of Sir Dexter to have included Lady Violet in the festivities of your Engagement Ball. After all, who was she to dance with, a divorcee, no less? Few men would want to tangle with the likes of her."

"No doubt, it will not be easy for her to find another husband in these circles, but with all her money, I'm sure Lady Violet will fend for herself quite favorably in the future, Father," Emily said knowingly.

"Exactly my sentiment, my dear daughter, and this is obviously no place for her to circulate," Mr. Reed said with a stern brow before he went on. "Emily, your mother has informed me of your having premarital jitters."

"Oh, is that her version of our little chat?" Emily lowered her voice to a whisper. "Actually my premarital jitters stem from having to marry a man I'm not in love with in order to fulfill my parents' wishes. Did Mother tell you any of that?"

"No, dear heavens, Emily! You mustn't talk such nonsense. I assure you before I married your mother, we each had our reservations as to our parents' mutual suggestion we marry one another. However, time has proven our parents had more knowledge of our own selves than we did. Mother and I want only for your happiness, trust us." He placed a reassuring hand on her shoulders.

"Emily, there isn't a young lady of marriageable age in the entire country right now, who wouldn't trade places with you this instant, including Lady Violet." Her father glanced at the dancing couple before asking in distress. "Emily, don't you think you should reclaim your fiancé after this song comes to an end?"

"No Father, Sir Dexter can dance with whomever he pleases. His choice of partner does not faze me in the least. It's a courtesy of his business I presume. Being a part of high society does have its price, and we all have to pay one way or another," Emily said flippantly.

"Well, I for one don't approve of that type of liberty," Mr. Reed declared with a scowl.

Emily became reminded her father would certainly disapprove of her now being no more innocent than Lady Violet, and the *disgrace* it would bring to the family. Emily shuttered in shame at the recollection.

Mr. Reed held fast in disdain for Lady Violet, only to fall prey to her, as the temptress swaggered over to him. Lady Violet's dark hair and skin was drawn with a spindly exactness of the black widow spider. She smiled at the unsuspecting Mr. Reed as swirls of crimson fabric swished about her sensually, swathed in her pungent perfume.

"Well, well, Emily, you haven't introduced me to your handsome friend." Lady Violet's seductive demeanor caught Mr. Reed off guard.

"Lady Violet, this handsome friend happens to be my father, Mr. Philip Reed," Emily said impatiently seeing through her fraud.

"Your father, why no, he couldn't be," Lady Violet exclaimed! "He's far too young, I dare say."

In spite of his original reservation, Mr. Reed became flustered. He blushed; as her flattery diminished all resolve against her. In fact, within moments Mr. Reed found himself dancing amongst the generous swirls of Lady Violet's dress, and the incense of her intoxicating perfume.

"Why Mr. Reed, I do declare you're so light on your toes. I feel as if I'm floating on air."

Lady Violet batted her black eyelashes in flirtation before pursing her lips with the wiles of a temptress. "I must say, Mr. Reed, it's simply not fair that all the handsome men are either married or engaged. What is a girl to do? I myself was married, but my husband, Mr. Vance Reynolds, was such a heel. Why, do you know, he used to strike me when he was angry with me? He was violent and cruel and treated me like I was a child."

"Strike you, dear girl!" Mr. Reed reverberated. "That is no way to treat a lady. It's no wonder you're no longer married to him. Such a brute doesn't deserve a second chance." In spite of his ideals, Mr. Reed eyed her ardently as Lady Violet's girlish charms worked their magic.

"Exactly my sentiment, Mr. Reed, I guess that is why I find men such as you so appealing."

"Why Miss Violet," Mr. Reed smirked at her flattery. "I'm a married man, and even if I wasn't, I'm easily twice your age, old enough to be your father."

Lady Violet's sultry eyes became drenched in allure, while she puckered her lips as she spoke, "Well, I think it's only proper a girl should marry someone older and more mature than she is. Worldly men with experience, who know how to treat a lady, are the best combination with a young lady of twenty-one. Don't you agree, Philip?"

She looked into his eyes earnestly, making Mr. Reed believe Lady Violet only had eyes for him. Mr. Reed became taken in, and so flustered he could barely answer. Then out of the corner of his eye, Mr. Reed caught a sedate Mrs. Reed looking over at him with unabashed displeasure.

When the song ended, he regretfully disengaged from the dance, and dutifully found his way back over to his wife's side. Mr. Reed made a gesture for his wife to dance.

Mrs. Reed's expression remained stern. "Well," Mrs. Reed scolded, "I must say you certainly looked ludicrous out there dancing with Lady Violet. She's practically a child compared to you, how shocking for you to have such inappropriate behavior, at the engagement ball of your own daughter no less!" Mrs. Reed cried out with an angry cadence.

"A child," Mr. Reed retorted. "Lady Violet happens to be a twenty-one-year-old woman. The poor thing has just come out of a bad marriage with an abusive husband who used to strike her, and she is all alone in the world."

"Oh dear," Mrs. Reed exclaimed! "Is that the reason they have divorced?"

"It appears to be the case. He used to bully her around, and treat her like she was no more than a child."

"Well, that might be so," Mrs. Reed retorted with reservation. "But then again maybe Lady Violet angered her husband with all her antics, and he just lost control of his senses . . . I'm not saying resorting to violence is permissible or excusable. Heavens no, it's not something I approve of. But just look at the way she carries on, dancing with my own husband no less!"

Sir Dexter claimed Emily for the remainder of the evening, while the lone Lady Violet coerced Lawrence to be her dancing partner. Sir Dexter held Emily close to him, but she remained rigid.

"Emily, we are going to be married within the year. I think it's high time you get used to the demands a husband places upon a wife. It will do no good to push away from me like that." Sir Dexter forcefully pulled her closer as his face took on a chauvinistic edge. "You must learn to be more submissive. That's a wife's duty, Emily dear."

Emily became furious as her blood rose to an instant boil. "Sir Dexter, I realize a wife does have certain obligations to her husband, but then again an engaged lady must be treated with honor. I expect adherence to moral standards will be dutifully upheld in the future year."

"Most certainly, Emily," Sir Dexter agreed as his eyes became shady.

Chapter Fifteen

The Tired Plumes

Emily and Mallory returned from a swim at the exclusive Bailey's beach, the favorite for Newport's elite. They looked quite the pair in their modest black bathing suits, black stockings, and big black hats.

Emily breezed past Mallory as they entered Rosewood. "I must rush inside to change into my portrait ensemble. I'm scheduled to meet Lawrence by the oak tree."

Emily greeted Lawrence in her usual pink ensemble with her plume hat. He stood looking majestic with his eyes aglow with expectation. "Here I am, Lawrence." Emily resumed her pose against the old oak seeing Lawrence was anxious to continue his rendering.

"Very good, just move a little to the left, Emily." Lawrence directed as he examined his artistry against the arrival of his model. He could not help but notice Emily looked a bit downtrodden. In fact she appeared even paler than the last time, while the contours of her face looked swollen from either salt retention or weight gain. Lawrence found her semblance odd considering Emily had been complaining of little appetite from the heat, and had become finicky as of lately.

After only a short while, Emily yawned in exhaustion. "I'm sorry, Lawrence, I must have overdone it with my morning swim, but this will be enough posing for me today. I'm feeling a bit weary from the heat, and I must go in to lie down."

Emily opened her feathered fan to breeze her peaked face. "It feels like it has already reached ninety degrees. The weather has been impossible these past few days, and the heat is making me feel queasy." Her face contorted in discomfort.

"Why don't you have a little something to eat before you lie down? Lunch should be ready by now. Come, let's walk back so you can get out of this heat. It's far too hot to be painting outdoors in the first place." Lawrence placed a comforting hand on her shoulders.

Emily sighed in distress. "Please don't even mention food to me right now, Lawrence. I can't even think of eating a morsel this afternoon. I hate to sound indelicate, Lawrence, but for the past few days I've been having a problem keeping my food down."

"Have you spoken to Dr. Mathis about this?" Lawrence asked in alarm.

"Yes, in fact I mentioned it just the other day. Dr. Mathis has put me back on my tonic again, only this time he has made it stronger."

"Stronger, but you said it was quite intolerable before. Maybe that's the cause; herbs can be taxing to the system."

Emily attempted to raise herself upward, but she became so dizzy she was forced to sit back down again. She braced her chest with her palms as she struggled to catch her breath.

"What is it, Emily, you look faint? Shall I get Dr. Mathis?" Lawrence asked in panic.

Emily began to weep in a delirium of paleness and quandary as the tired plumes of her hat paused in the stagnant heat. "Lawrence," Emily murmured beneath her breath in a barely audible voice. "What I'm about to tell you is not good, in fact it's intolerable. I haven't discussed it with Dr. Mathis or another soul. I'm too distraught to breathe a word to anyone. I'll confide in you, Lawrence, if I may."

She continued in a weak voice, "A few weeks ago, I thought I was having woman troubles because my stomach had become very bloated, but then the nausea began . . . Lawrence," she whispered. "I'm quite certain, I am with child. I've already missed my cycle twice."

"With child Emily," Lawrence raised his voice in alarm.

"There can be no other explanation for my symptoms; the signs are all there, Lawrence." Emily stifled back a sob. "I just don't know what I should do. I'm so alone, Lawrence, with no one I can turn to at a time like this besides you," Emily professed as she began to weep.

"Emily, don't you think it would be best to summon Sir Dexter's good advice? After all, if you are to have a baby, then Sir Dexter is to be a father. He has a right to know." Lawrence's face changed to solicitude as Emily shook her head no.

"Emily, let's be reasonable here. I'm sure Sir Dexter would want to be the first to hear of such news," Lawrence said reassuringly.

"Speak to Sir Dexter about this!" Emily cried out inconsolably. "Lawrence, even the thought of it brings grief to my already stricken heart. Sir Dexter has caused me such humiliation I could not even express myself without falling apart. Believe me when I tell you, Sir Dexter will not save my good name for the desecration of his own."

Lawrence sat on the earth beside Emily, and looked deep into her misted blue eyes. "Emily, my sweet dearest, Emily, Sir Dexter has done you a great injustice. You must go to him at once. He has to know the consequence of his actions. You can't keep something of this magnitude to yourself, you mustn't!" Lawrence insisted obstinately.

Emily paused for a moment as her face became enlivened with courage. "Lawrence, I've heard of a doctor who lives in the countryside, who is known for taking care of matters like these. If I could just get away by myself for a little while, maybe I could go see him without bringing any suspicion."

"Emily, promise me you won't do anything of the sort!" Lawrence grabbed a hold of her arm. "That's not the kind of doctor you want to see. I have heard countless horror stories of young girls being left for dead after such butchering. A baby is a living thing, a part of you, not something you should seek to destroy! That's not the way God intended!" Lawrence preached with as much gumption as Father O'Leary. "You're engaged to Sir Dexter; surely he would not want to murder his own child!"

"I guess you're right, Lawrence." Emily sighed despondently.

"I'm just talking wildly, no I guess I couldn't really find the courage, or heart to kill my own baby. I'll just have to hide it in the meantime, until I get the courage to confront Sir Dexter. I've already had to loosen the stays of my corset."

Emily fretted as she pieced the details together. "My wedding to Sir Dexter is planned for next July; it's already the end of August. The way I have it figured out by March, I'll be at the end of my term. Whether I like it or not, there will be a baby. You as well as I know there cannot be a wedding to Sir Dexter Lund, if I'm to be an unwed mother first."

Emily's eyes became faraway and glazed with conjecture. "For all we know, Lawrence, you might be obligated to marry Mallory on your own. I fear I will undoubtedly be forced to return to Fairway in shame." Emily sobbed bitterly as her head hung low.

"Marry Mallory alone," thoughts of terror raced through Lawrence's head. "Without having a double wedding with you and Sir Dexter, no never!" Lawrence exclaimed in horror at the mere thought of it. "If not for you living beside me in the West wing I would not even have the gumption to marry Mallory at all."

Lawrence stared blankly into space as he continued mournfully, "I have already given Mallory my word of honor, and have made the formal announcement to all of Newport society. But, Emily, I cannot marry her on my own if you were to leave!" Lawrence attested in panic.

"Lawrence, I fear I'm not in control of my fate anymore than I am of yours." Emily managed to gather herself upward. "I must go inside to lie down, Lawrence. Perhaps I'll have a tall glass of lemonade. I will just try to think, but my thoughts are unbearable. The last two months have been terrible."

Lawrence insisted with determination, "Emily, you'll have to tell Sir Dexter and the sooner the better! I have faith Sir Dexter will not turn you out on your own, Emily. If there is indeed going to be a baby; it's Sir Dexter's responsibility to make good on what he's done. Then again let's not panic, your body might still surprise you. Maybe all this upset has thrown off your system. It's still rather early on to be absolutely certain."

Chapter Sixteen

With Child

By mid-September, it had become clear to Lawrence's watchful eye Emily was indeed "with child." Nonetheless, Dr. Mathis remained unaware as he advised. "Emily, you need to strengthen your constitution with plenty of fresh air and exercise. Maybe Lawrence wouldn't mind walking with you after we have breakfast."

"I would be happy to." Lawrence dutifully offered.

Emily and Lawrence walked side by side as the frothing waves crashed in the distance. "Emily, I hate to bring this up again, but have you discussed your condition with Sir Dexter yet?"

"No I haven't." Emily lamented. "I know I can't keep up this pretense for much longer. Even Miss Julia mentioned I've gained weight. She had to loosen the stays of my corset again, and each morning she struggles to close my buttons. Not to mention Lady Sarah warned me how I better start watching my portions because ladies sometimes spoil their shape before their wedding day, and are unable to fit into their gowns. I'm worried Lady Sarah might already be suspicious."

"I would be careful if I was you, Emily, and discuss it with Sir Dexter before it's too late," warned Lawrence.

"I'm planning to do so before I go back to Fairway," Emily somberly said.

"Don't remind me, Emily, it will be miserable here without you. Lady Sarah has commissioned me to do hand painting in Rosewood after my portraits are complete. She's in the process of deciding on my first project, and after that I assure you there will be another. Now that they've found a husband for Mallory, they will never let me out of their clutches," Lawrence said with dread. "The only thing that will keep me going is the fact you will be returning in the summer. Emily, all of this uncertainty is unbearable for me as well."

"Please let's not worry right now, Lawrence. The day is too beautiful for unhappiness." Emily held his arm tighter, as they enjoyed a tender moment of friendship.

The ocean trail was nearly deserted now that the cooler weather had set in. After a brisk walk, Emily and Lawrence stopped to rest upon a wooden bench across from the ocean, adjacent to the mansions. The sun shined a border of dusty pink over the horizon.

"Lawrence, just look how beautiful the sky is. I love this time of year when the air starts to get crisp. Before we know it autumn will be here, and the leaves will be changing. Here we are enjoying a perfect afternoon. What a contrast all this is to my condition. I feel so powerless by the changes of my body, Lawrence!"

"Emily, you're powerless to change your condition because you know it would be dangerous and sinful, but how you handle your situation still remains in your hands."

Emily watched the ocean skim over the rocks. "Lawrence, I've always been a good judge of character. Sir Dexter is a ruthless lawyer who goes by the letter of the law to the advantage of his clients. The law doesn't always focus on the truth. He will no doubt use this angle in dealing with me."

"Emily, Sir Dexter is to become a father. Give him a fair chance, and see what he's made of before you judge him so harshly. Who knows what will be? Maybe the two of you will elope. Think about it, Emily, no one will be all the wiser once the baby comes. They might whisper at first, but when they see the baby, all suspicion will be forgotten. Who doesn't celebrate the birth of a child?" Lawrence asked with a smile. "Think of Sir Dexter's parents, and how happy they'll be to become grandparents."

"Maybe you're right, Lawrence; I really should just tell Sir Dexter after our walk, and face it already. It won't be any easier if I wait another week, and who knows I might be even bigger then."

Just then Lawrence and Emily spied Mallory walking on the Cliff Walk, and toward them. Emily dutifully arose, and granted Mallory a seat beside her fiancé.

"Thank you, Emily dear." Mallory smiled graciously. "This is my favorite spot to sit as soon as the weather starts getting cooler. It has always been my secret hideaway, but now I see it has been discovered."

"Really this is your favorite spot," Emily said in dismay.

"Oh yes, I've been sitting on this bench ever since I was a child. I used to sit by the edge, and throw pebbles into the ocean, and watch the water ripple. I used to make wishes, which have now come true with my engagement to Lawrence." Mallory gushed as she glanced over at Lawrence moon-eyed while he forced a smile. Mallory then linked her arm in the crux of Lawrence's, where Emily had just had hers.

"I'd like to make a wish," Emily said while picking up a small rock along the embankment, and throwing it into the ocean. She watched as it spread in a rainbow shadow beneath the sunshine. Emily wished for everything to work out favorably, and for her to have the courage to confront Sir Dexter.

"Well, you'll probably be starting your session with Mallory's portrait soon. I guess I'll head back to the house now," Emily said with treachery in her heart.

As she walked off, she overheard Mallory say to Lawrence, "Lawrence, now that I know you like this spot, why don't we meet again tomorrow before you paint me. Sitting here with you is far better than my sitting out here alone."

Emily entered the West Porch, and headed toward the doorway. Just as she began to open the door she came upon Lady Violet leaving at the same moment. Dressed in a cocoa-colored dress with a chocolate-brown hat topped with black feathers, Lady Violet looked in synch with the coming season. Startled by crossing each other's path, the two women stepped back to avoid crashing.

"Why Emily," Lady Violet exclaimed. "I do declare I hardly recognized you. I heard you haven't been feeling well. I must say you do look rather pale."

"I feel fine," Emily rebuffed. "My morning walks are a bit tiring that's all."

"Oh, well do take care of yourself, dear. The end of summer is a peculiar time of year for illness with the season changing so rapidly. I suggest you wear a wrap across your shoulders, Emily," Lady Violet suggested condescendingly.

"I do appreciate your concern, but I assure you, Miss Violet, I'm more than comfortable in my present attire. Now if you shall just allow me to pass I would greatly appreciate it."

"Very well," Lady Violet retorted, giving Emily room to enter the house, while she walked off looking menacing with her black feathers blowing in the wind.

Emily found her way down the hallway to Sir Dexter's office, and knocked on his door with dread. "Come in," replied Sir Dexter.

"Oh Emily," Sir Dexter said in surprise. "Lady Violet just left and I thought maybe it was her since she forgot her parasol."

"I'm sure she'll take it next time," Emily retorted as she entered with slow, awkward steps.

"Emily, come sit down. Miss Julia has brought peppermint tea; it's still warm enough to pour yourself a cup."

Emily poured some into a china cup she found aside the two cups Sir Dexter and Lady Violet had used. She sweetened it with honey. The mint eased her queasiness for the moment.

"Sir Dexter, there's something urgent I must speak to you about. I hope I'm not distracting you from any important work, but it can't wait," Emily blurted out anxiously.

Sir Dexter put down his quill with a perplexed expression. "Emily, you are not one to disturb me in the office, please make yourself clear at once!" He impatiently ordered while Emily shuttered at his abruptness.

"Sir Dexter, I can't state it any simpler than this . . . You are about to become a father. I'm certain I am with child," Emily said simply as her mouth quivered unevenly.

Sir Dexter's brows scowled in an upheaval of red. "Me about to become a father, what in the world are you talking about, Emily? That's preposterous!"

Emily glared at him accusingly. "I hesitate to bring up the unspeakable night of my Welcoming Ball when you forced your way into my chamber. I have struggled to put that night behind me, Sir Dexter, hoping it would just go away. But I can no longer pretend nothing happened. I'm almost three months along already!" Emily cried out in anguish.

"Three months along, and you dare accuse me of this!" Sir Dexter's eyes raged like the sea on a stormy day. "Emily, I went into your chamber after the ball. I thought I heard you calling out for me. I thought you were unable to sleep from all the excitement so I brought you a flask of liquor to help put you to sleep."

"A flask of liquor, don't make me laugh. You had already drunk the contents when I found it on the floor!" Emily quipped.

Sir Dexter's nostrils flared angrily. "Emily, if you have gotten yourself into a predicament, it's certainly on your own accord I assure you!" He insisted unwaveringly.

"On my own accord!" Emily recoiled with consternation. "Sir Dexter, I know the difference between being drunk and being in reality! What's real, and my present condition attests to that! Your denying it doesn't help matters any. What should we do, Sir Dexter? I am going to have a baby in March! Nature has settled our differences for us! I know it must be a shock for you, as it was for me." Emily entreated in earnest. "Sir Dexter, I know it will take us some time getting used to, but we must for the sake of the baby."

"Emily, if there is to be a baby, and I don't doubt it, now that I study your ample waistline." Sir Dexter's face became calculating. "Emily, listen to me and hear what I say. There were over a dozen servants in the house on the evening of the Welcoming Ball; if indeed that was the night you got yourself into this predicament. Rosewood is not Fairway, I warned you about that!"

Sir Dexter's eyes became fierce as he shouted. "Our ballroom is twice the size as Fairway, and our servants are numerous. I cannot vouch for the character of every transient we hire. It's a known fact, Emily; you always leave your door unlocked!"

"Sir Dexter, how can you speak such nonsense? I know you want to deny all this, but it's not something that will just go away. It's real, and we must face it together," Emily shouted in outrage as Sir Dexter rolled his eyes with impatience.

"Sir Dexter, I can see there's no sense in discussing it any further right now. I'll speak to you after you've slept on it, hopefully tomorrow you will be more level headed. Let's not perpetrate this foolishness any longer, Sir Dexter!" Emily demanded as she struggled to lift herself from the chair. She noticed how Sir Dexter's face had become a mirror of his true character, both heartless and transparent.

Chapter Seventeen

The Business Excursion

When the morning came, there was no sign of Sir Dexter in the breakfast parlor. Lady Sarah alerted Miss Julia. "No need to set a place for Sir Dexter, Miss Julia. He has left unexpectedly early this morning on a business excursion."

Emily's heart fell to the floor in impending doom.

"Business excursion," Mallory echoed seeming surprised by the oddity of Sir Dexter's sudden departure.

"Yes, he rushed out on an emergency concerning Lady Violet," Lady Sarah revealed.

"I hope she's all right!" Mallory said in concern.

"Where does Lady Violet live?" Emily asked with a stone countenance.

"Your guess is as good as mine, Emily, as to where she might be at the present moment. Lady Violet and her family are from Massachusetts, and she visits there often. It's rumored she lives in a grand estate in Clinton on the water that had been Mr. Reynolds. It has been photographed in several magazines. She also has another estate in Charleston, her château in France as well as several other residences abroad. Sir Dexter would know those details better than me."

Emily's blood began to seethe. "Well, I don't understand why Lady Violet could not have just come here to speak with him. It seems out of character for Sir Dexter to leave Newport without even discussing it with me. After all I have come to summer here as a guest of his, more accurately as his future wife."

"Don't worry, Emily." Lady Sarah comforted as she poured Emily a cup of tea. "I'm sure Sir Dexter will explain everything when he returns. I have gone through similar situations with Hector when we were first engaged."

Lawrence dutifully waited by the West Porch for Emily to go on their morning walk. Emily had a woolen wrap draped around her shoulders just as Lady Violet had recommended. Lawrence held Emily's arm tightly, and warmed it with his overcoat. Together they walked into the winded paradise along the outskirts of the forest. The leaves rustled in the background as the singing of birds enchanted them.

Emily confided in a soft voice. "Lawrence, I finally told Sir Dexter about my condition yesterday after I left you and Mallory, and it is not good."

"Why, what happened?" Lawrence anxiously asked as they scurried along the path.

Emily sighed in anguish. "Lawrence, just as I predicted, Sir Dexter is in denial. He cannot deal with the consequence of his actions. He claimed he came into my chamber because I called out for him, and he thought I was having trouble falling asleep. He also told me he gave me a flask of liquor to help me fall asleep. He's obviously trying to cover his tracks since he dropped an empty flask on my floor. I threw it away the next morning because I was afraid Miss Julia would find it. He insists my condition could be from any one of the servants who were attending the ball on the evening in question. He then reprimanded me for being in the habit of leaving my door unlocked," Emily said tearfully, clutching her abdomen.

"Any one of the other servants to blame, nonsense, not with Sir Dexter leaving your chamber in a huff with his shirttails pulled out, and his waistband undone!" Lawrence angrily cried out.

Emily stopped dead in her tracks in a moment of clarity. "You mean to tell me you actually witnessed Sir Dexter coming out of my chamber like that?"

"Yes, Emily, with the nightlight shining on him when he left your chamber, disheveled and hopelessly drunk," Lawrence testified decidedly.

"Why haven't you told me until now? Exactly what did you see and hear?" Emily demanded wildly.

"Emily, listen to me." They looked into each other's eyes in earnest. "I didn't want to traumatize you any further. It's simply not respectable to speak of such depravity. Sir Dexter is even more debauched than I could have ever imagined. To run off this morning leaving you all alone with your worries, truly sickens me."

"I now worry less knowing you have firsthand witnessed Sir Dexter leaving my chamber in such a disheveled state. We all know no decent man would walk about in such a manner. Lawrence, what you have described attests to Sir Dexter's guilt, as much as my condition does." Emily began walking in a steady stride of courage. "Would you be willing to attest to what you've seen if Sir Dexter continues to be unreasonable, two accusers are no doubt better than one?" Emily asked triumphantly.

"Emily, I don't think it would be wise for me to go to Sir Dexter with that tidbit. If he has turned on you, he will surely turn against me, and I fear he'll have me turned out as expediently as he has left this morning. Then we'll have nothing, no means for us to even communicate. I'd be a broken man if that was to be. I have faith Sir Dexter will come to his senses, Emily. What gain would it be for him to do otherwise?"

"Come to his senses, conspiring with Lady Violet, nay! The two of them are probably comparing notes about that doctor I told you about who lives in the countryside. Who knows if Lady Violet hasn't been one of the doctor's patients herself? I wouldn't doubt it for a moment, the way she flaunts herself about, and carries on so."

"Emily, let's be rational. Lawyers encounter clients of questionable character all the time. That's the nature of their business. And as for emergencies, there are emergencies in every field. We can't lose sight of the fact Lady Violet and her estranged husband owned many estates. There must be quite a mess in dividing all their assets. From what I understand Lady Violet does not want to give up even one of her properties, and claims she deserves to keep all of them, as a consolation for all the abuse she claims Mr. Reynolds has put her through."

"I hope you're right about Sir Dexter. Perhaps he wouldn't be low enough to divulge his personal business to Lady Violet. After all Lady Violet could always use it against him if it was to her advantage. I only hope Sir Dexter is wise enough to realize what an ill choice of confidante Lady Violet would be."

"Emily, we both know Lady Violet is not spoken of highly. It's only her wealth that affords her any respect at all. It's a wonder she won't budge on relinquishing any of her properties. If she was to lose her wealth, Lady Violet would be nothing," Lawrence insisted.

"So then I'll assume my condition is safe from her. That gives me some consolation, since I certainly would not relish the idea of Lady Violet knowing my business."

By this point, they were approaching the wooden bench alongside the sea where Mallory sat waiting for Lawrence to return from his walk with Emily. Dressed in a brown velvet dress with lace trim, Mallory would have practically looked pretty if not for her spectacles. She had an ornate cameo pinned on her high collared neck, and her tight ringlets were arranged beneath a bronze hat with a feathered brim.

"Perfect timing," Mallory sung out with a happy lilt. "I cut my piano playing short this morning since I'm feeling eager to begin posing for my portrait. I must say, Emily, Lawrence's painting of you is truly a gem. I'm sure you must be delighted with it. When it's finally hung, it will do the drawing room proud. My father is having an ornate gold frame made for it. In fact, my mother was talking about having a ball to celebrate its completion."

"How wonderful, well Lawrence certainly deserves the honor. He's captured a remarkable likeness, and the painting is truly a masterpiece." Emily tried to sound exuberant while her dilemma consumed her.

Lawrence went off to begin his painting of the darkly clad Mallory, while Emily stayed to meditate by the sea.

Chapter Eighteen

The Red Devil

The following morning, stormy skies reigned over Rosewood. A cluster of black crows squawked as they flew over the mansion. In the distance, where the ocean met the clouds, Lawrence watched a dotting of birds fly across the gray sky in a V formation. Everything about the day had a morose quality. There would be no walk with Emily or further sessions on Mallory's portrait. The grounds were far too wet and slick with mud.

After breakfast, Lawrence retreated in the drawing room with Dr. Mathis. They encountered Emily doing needlework while Mallory played the piano. The combination of the rain and Mallory's droning music set a somber mood which disenchanted even Lady Sarah. "Mallory, could you perhaps play something a bit more cheerful, the rain is making the day all too dreary already."

"Lawrence," Dr. Mathis suggested. "You can go into the library in a little while to continue what you've been reading if you would like. Or perhaps you would rather put off learning for this morning and relax and enjoy the music."

Mrs. Lund interjected, "Lawrence, perhaps you would prefer to start painting the scene of cherubs I have commissioned you to do. I've purchased the canvas; it's in the study next to the desk. I would like the sky to be pale blue, with fluffy white clouds. I've decided to affix the painting to the ceiling of the grand ballroom. I know it will be quite an undertaking for you, but I have complete faith you can recapture the elegance of the Sistine Chapel."

"Wouldn't it be wise for Lawrence to complete the family portraits before he begins a new project?" Dr. Mathis asked with a scowl.

"Nonsense, with the way the weather has been there is no sense in completely wasting the day. By the time it's time for my portrait it will be too cold to pose outdoors. Maybe I should like to be painted by the fireplace," contemplated Lady Sarah with a twinkle in her eyes.

Lawrence remained in limbo as they chatted on how he could most effectively spend his time when he had little gusto for any of the suggestions.

Sir Dexter returned to Rosewood in a few days. His carriage arrived in the midst of the rain and haze. Lawrence noticed Sir Dexter's demeanor looked as sullen as the inclement weather he brought with him. Sir Dexter stood by the doorway while waiting for his valise to be carried in, with a stone-cold expression, standing as rigid as a soldier.

"Hello, Sir Dexter, I trust you've had an expedient journey." Lawrence greeted as Sir Dexter stomped his wet boots on the front mat.

"Yes, I have had a worthwhile journey. As much as I dislike being away from Rosewood on overnight excursions, it was most imperative that I went," Sir Dexter retorted evasively.

"Business no doubt," Lawrence said pryingly. "Your mother had mentioned there was an emergency concerning Lady Violet."

"I left for a combination of urgent reasons that were most pressing. Lawrence, I would appreciate discussing the nature of my journey with you at great length. However this is not an opportune moment, please come to my office tonight after dinner, and you and I could have a friendly chat. I will meet you there after Emily and I come in from our after dinner tea on the veranda."

"I'm looking forward to it, Sir Dexter," Lawrence retorted with compliance.

Lawrence proceeded upstairs to the library where a volume on *The Symptoms and Treatments of Common Ailments* awaited. For now the disease of deviousness remained foremost in Lawrence's curiosity. He had trouble concentrating, wondering what Sir Dexter intended to talk to him about in his office.

Before long Emily appeared in the library with a worried look over her face. She whispered, "Did you find out what the emergency with Lady Violet was?"

"Unfortunately not, but I'm working on it. Sir Dexter just rushed off to his chamber to get himself settled, but he asked me to go to his office tonight after dinner for a friendly chat. I'm a bit apprehensive about what he has to say, but I'm confident Sir Dexter has concern for your happiness as well as his sister's, and will do the right thing so we all can be together, as we have planned."

"Lawrence, this worries me! Why in the world would Sir Dexter want to speak to you when he has barely even said hello to me? I only hope he doesn't try to get you to turn against me as well. My position is so precarious, Lawrence; after all Sir Dexter is a powerful man, and a divorce lawyer to boot!" Emily cried out in distress.

"Emily, please don't let your imagination get carried away. When I'm finished talking to Sir Dexter I'll slip a note beneath your door, and we can meet out on the Cliff Walk."

Lawrence watched Sir Dexter and Emily at the dinner table. The strain between them was clearly detectable to his eyes. It remained uncertain if anyone else could sense the tension. After all, Sir Dexter was ordinarily cold and emotionally indifferent.

Lawrence noticed how neither Sir Dexter nor Emily turned their heads toward one another when Miss Julia rang the bell, and they were obligated to converse. Their exchange was sparse, and Sir Dexter seemed preoccupied.

Emily looked crestfallen when Miss Julia arranged her and Sir Dexter's nightly ritual of sitting outside on the veranda after supper had concluded. Lawrence went upstairs to peer down from his chamber.

From his vantage, he could see their conversation was clipped, and their body language showed their estrangement. Instead of sitting beside each other on the couch and having Miss Julia set up their refreshments on the coffee table as they ordinarily did, they both opted to sit on separate chairs to either side of the glass table. After a quick cup of tea they departed, both going in opposite directions.

Lawrence greeted Sir Dexter in his office, situated on the other side of the mansion. Not even the faintest hum of Mallory's piano playing, or singing in the drawing room could be audible from behind the heavy oak door. A pot of freshly brewed tea waited on the coffee table accompanied by an assortment of pastries. Lawrence poured himself a cup of tea, and situated himself across from Sir Dexter, who sat at a large mahogany desk with claw feet.

Sir Dexter got up and bolted the door with a skeleton key. Lawrence waited uneasily as Sir Dexter resumed his position at the desk. Sir Dexter looked powerful and tyrannical in his private domain. The deer head, complete with antlers which adorned the wall behind his desk, looked apropos.

Sir Dexter's face remained expressionless as he addressed Lawrence. "Lawrence, thank you for coming to speak with me this evening; what I must discuss with you is rather urgent."

Lawrence listened intently. "Lawrence, in spite of the fact that my wedding to Emily has been planned for next summer, it will be impossible for me to honor my vow." Sir Dexter paused solemnly. "Emily is no longer pure. She has informed me she is carrying a baby. For me to marry Emily now would bring shame to my family's good name. It is unheard of for the Lund family, to marry a lady who is not pure, let alone one who is having a baby out of wedlock. Under this unfortunate circumstance I shall be forced to turn Emily out," Sir Dexter divulged in a clipped tone.

"Turn Emily out, no you mustn't, you cannot!" Lawrence's dark eyes blazed with panic.

Lawrence felt like saying. "It's *your* baby she is carrying! You're the one who has *stolen* her purity." However his better judgment told him otherwise.

Sir Dexter continued, seeming cut and dried, as all his affairs concerning Emily were. "There's no question, Lawrence, I must . . . However, I have a proposition to make that might be of interest to you." Sir Dexter continued in calculating words, "I propose to give you a large sum of money if you take Emily away from here, and take responsibility for the baby as if it were your own."

Sir Dexter's voice became demanding. "Actually I'm not asking you, Lawrence, I'm telling you." Sir Dexter ordered in a cold tone. "You must bear the brunt in entirety. The baby will need a father, and so I've devised this plan to soften the blow for Emily."

Lawrence felt his blood become hot and then cold in his veins, while his appendages felt like fire, and then like ice. "Sir Dexter, I can't be bought into covering up what is your responsibility! The baby is clearly yours. Why else would you even propose such a scheme if it wasn't?" Lawrence glared knowingly. "I saw you coming out of Emily's chamber on the night of her Welcoming Ball, pitifully drunk and disheveled, with your shirttails out, struggling to fasten your trousers! You nearly fell over your own feet! I'm not blind to the present situation!" Lawrence shouted wildly while glaring at Sir Dexter.

Unfazed by Lawrence's accusation, Sir Dexter calmly went inside his desk drawer, and took out a huge stack of bills. He counted them carefully. "There, it's all here. This will be enough money for you and Emily to live on until you become situated. It's a handsome sum, Lawrence. It's all for the best, be assured."

Lawrence looked at the ample stack of green with stupefaction. "Sir Dexter, I mean no disrespect, but as you're well aware I have my own obligations to marry Miss Mallory next summer, and have given her my word of honor. I couldn't agree to ruin my good name, and shame Mallory's as well."

Lawrence raised his voice in disbelief, as Sir Dexter's demeanor remained unchanged. "She's your sister, Sir Dexter! Let's be reasonable, don't you at least care about Mallory's happiness?" Lawrence asked with anguish.

"You will not marry Mallory any more than I will marry Emily!" Sir Dexter exclaimed with certainty. "The weddings are both to be called off. I'm not asking you, Lawrence, I'm telling you! You have no choice but to accept responsibility for Emily's baby. You can either take the money, or leave penniless. That's entirely your choice. Furthermore . . ." Sir Dexter looked at him mockingly. "Lawrence, you're just as big a suspect as anyone as far as fathering Emily's baby is concerned." Sir Dexter cocked his head accusingly.

"Me a suspect," Lawrence echoed. "I'm a moral human being with a conscience! Your little charade is getting way out of hand, Sir Dexter! Let me just ask you, have you told any of this to Mallory?" Lawrence inquired pokerfaced.

"Just what I was about to get to, Lawrence, my friend." Sir Dexter smirked in victory. "Mallory has already come to me in great distress. It appears she had seen you and Emily kissing in the woods one morning from her window. Therefore, as you can see, this is the only way to salvage the situation."

Sir Dexter shook his head disdainfully. "At the time, I tried to console Mallory by persuading her that, perhaps it was not a romantic kiss, and merely a friendship kiss, if there is such a thing," Sir Dexter interjected a cynical chuckle. "However, now it will become clear to Mallory your affections for Emily were far from innocent, Lawrence."

Sir Dexter adjusted his shirt collar. "I assure you Mallory will survive the shock she has long suspected. I urged her not to tell my parents what she had seen, but you know Mallory has a mind of her own. I cannot vouch for how she handles her affairs, and now with Emily being in such a predicament, it shall be obvious to Mallory and my parents alike where the fault lies. It would be in your best interest, Lawrence, if you cooperate with my commands, and keep all this as civil as possible," Sir Dexter demanded sternly.

Lawrence recoiled in shame at his unbridled passion that day in the woods. He had assumed the trees had shielded them. As if in a game of chess, Sir Dexter had ingeniously trapped his opponent in a checkmate, saving his ammunition for the proper moment. Lawrence dared not to defend his honor in light of the blemish he had acquired.

Sir Dexter continued in a harsh voice. "I insist both you and Emily be out of Rosewood by Sunday afternoon before the family returns from church. I will make apologies for you and Emily being unable to attend church. I'll grant you one of my carriages, and coachmen for your travel. I suggest both you and Emily go far away from here where no one knows you . . . You must start over, Lawrence, my friend, but I trust you will find good fortune," Sir Dexter said with a little more heart.

"Leave Sunday, but today is already Friday. This is all so sudden!" Lawrence blurted out in panic without his own plan of action.

"There shall be no more discussion of it, Lawrence, either way both you and Emily must leave, together or apart!" Sir Dexter's red hair and unruly brows flamed in diabolical fury, resembling a red devil. "Lawrence, be advised there has been a change of plans . . . I have become engaged to Lady Violet, and have intentions to marry her next summer."

"You marry Lady Violet!" Lawrence exclaimed in shock, appalled by the added jinx to Emily's disgrace. "And do you think your parents will approve of your match with the notorious Miss Violet? Why Emily, even in her delicate condition, has far more merit than she."

"Don't fret, Lawrence, once my parents learn about Emily's circumstance, I assure you they will be only too happy to learn I have made other marriage arrangements to divert me from my grief. Don't distress too much, Lawrence."

Sir Dexter smiled triumphantly. "I know you don't love Mallory, and she will survive the blow. As for Emily, I trust you care a great deal for her . . . Here without any further ado, Lawrence, please take the money at once, and be gone with it, before I change my mind, and make you leave penniless," Sir Dexter ordered impatiently.

Lawrence looked at the stack of green still hesitating. He feared it would make him an accomplice to Sir Dexter's little scheme. Thus, adding further shame to his good name.

"Here take it! "Sir Dexter insisted with a bit more conscience. "Consider it a bonus for your oil painting of Emily if you will. In fact, I insist you take the portrait with you. Let it serve as an advertisement of your abilities. Your talent will provide you with work, and you are welcome to take the art supplies with you to help you get started. A good artist such as you, will never go hungry I assure you, Lawrence. Now here, let us get on with it!" Sir Dexter commanded.

Lawrence struggled for a moment before reaching for the stack of bills, and securing it in his trouser pocket. Sir Dexter got up with a look of triumph.

"Lawrence, I will leave it for you to explain it all to Emily. For the sake of Emily and the baby, I hope this transition will be as swift and smooth as possible. You can pack your things while we're all in church on Sunday morning. I will inform my family that you needed to add a few last minute touches to Emily's painting before the Portrait Ball next Saturday."

"What will become of the Portrait Ball?" Lawrence asked with remorse to have his night of honor forfeited.

"I assure you, there is always reason for a ball. My mother will undoubtedly find another one . . . The coach will be waiting for you by the front of the house at eleven-thirty Sunday morning. See to it you are both gone by then. I regret it had to turn out this way, Lawrence, but it's the only way I can see." Sir Dexter stood and unlatched the door for Lawrence.

Lawrence returned to his chamber feeling disoriented, and defeated. From the far side of his window overlooking the yard, he watched the angry sea, frothing up in billows of waves. Salted delirium drowned his senses in foreboding, as the sky darkened into evening. The hot air sweltered inward in a shroud of silence so still, Lawrence's thoughts became one with the waves. Violently crashing, pulling him farther out and deeper into Sir Dexter's deceit. The night stood still for a moment of reprieve.

Lawrence got the urge to stroll the Cliff Walk for one last time with Emily before their mutual banishment. The night would be a long one, and Lawrence vowed to himself he would try to temper it the best he could.

He had to speak to Emily at once, and alert her to what happened. Lawrence found a scrap of paper, and penned Emily a note in haste. It was still early evening, barely seven-thirty, and the time when many of the servants would walk the winding path alongside the ocean.

Lawrence frantically scrawled. "Emily, meet me by our spot along the Cliff Walk at once. I must speak to you, Lawrence." He tapped once on her door before slipping the note beneath, and waiting for Emily to retrieve his message.

The hot breeze of Indian summer enveloped Lawrence with the last of the season's fiery breath. The misty air beckoned Lawrence to surrender to the sea. The voice of the ocean swept his thoughts beyond earthly comprehension.

Out in the distance of night, Lawrence stood by an expanse of rocky terrain and watched breathlessly, as Emily appeared dressed all in black save the faded roses and gold glints of her hat, while a gold spider pin on her ruffled collar foreshadowed her quandary. She hurriedly approached as the white light from the stars shined over her head, like a wraith of unsure tidings. She shone out of the darkness of night with a luminosity which electrified the air, and enveloped Lawrence with the intangible substance of love.

Lawrence could see Emily's waist had expanded considerably against the confines of her already too tight dress. Emily's eyes were innocent spheres of blue, reflecting spiritual innocence, and purity of the soul. While her body had overtaken its girlishness against her will, in an inner sea of amniotic life, apart from her. The contrast was so divine Emily's duality resembled the Virgin Mary to Lawrence's keen eye.

"What is it, Lawrence?" Emily's face contorted with worry.

"Walk with me, Emily, let us go to a private spot where we can be alone and talk quietly."

Lawrence took her arm into his, and together they flanked the path with steady footsteps while nature bathed them in oblivion. Strolling together, they offered an occasional hello to a servant from one of the other mansions, getting their first breath of fresh air and freedom, after a day of tarried obligation.

Lawrence led Emily into an edge of woods, thick with the lush foliage of late summer. Emerald and green, the rustling of leaves fanned over their heads like a roof. There they stood a part of the trees, a part of the sea, a part of each other, together, yet each struggled with their own isolation.

Lawrence began as delicately as possible looking deeply into Emily's eyes with the darkness obliterating their sights, as shadows of night overtook them.

"Emily, my dearest Emily, I have met with Sir Dexter tonight on your behalf. Sir Dexter has informed me in clear terms that all our plans have been changed. There are to be no weddings between either you and Sir Dexter, or me and Mallory."

"What!" Emily shouted in alarm.

Lawrence took her trembling hands into his. "Sir Dexter has instructed me to inform you we are both to leave Rosewood by eleven-thirty Sunday morning with all of our belongings, and with only his apologies on behalf of our departure."

Emily seemed faint from the news, as she clutched onto Lawrence's arm to steady herself. "No weddings, are you saying Sir Dexter is turning us out, the both of us?" she asked in frenzy.

"Yes, I'm afraid he is, my dear Emily. He's paid me a handsome sum, and will supply us with a coachman and carriage to help us secure a new destination, far, far away from here, and the Newport society. Just so you know being with you, Emily, has always been my dream in spite of Sir Dexter's blackmailing us to leave with each other."

"You cannot be serious! We are to go away from here, just the two of us together in my delicate condition!" Emily exclaimed in hysteria as the shock made her body feel cold and damp.

"Yes, Sir Dexter has instructed me I must take full responsibility for the baby, as well as for your indelicate condition, without question, Sir Dexter will take no liability other than the conditions he has offered to us. We have no choice, Emily. We must leave at once without anyone's blessings. It's an impossible situation Sir Dexter has put us in, but I have faith everything will turn out for the best." Lawrence vowed with courage and composure.

After the initial impact wore off, Lawrence watched Emily's formidable will transform her demeanor. "Lawrence, if you would be kind enough to take me away from here and treat the baby as if it was yours, that would be the greatest mercy any man could show a woman. I only hope the gesture comes from your heart, and not from the money Sir Dexter has used to get his way. I have my pride, Lawrence," Emily admitted with a hurt expression. "A lady does not like to be jilted by one man, and then sold to another. I cannot be transferred from one owner to another, as if I were merely a chattel."

"Emily, my sweet dearest, Emily," Lawrence kissed her hand tenderly. "It is with no burden that I accept the position. I would have taken you away from here long ago, with only the laurels of my heart to sustain us. Now at least Sir Dexter's guilt has provided for us to get a new start. You must promise me something, Emily, I don't ever want Sir Dexter's name so much as mentioned when the baby is born. If I am to take full responsibility, then I intend to take full credit as well. I will gladly take the blame, Emily, if that's the price I must incur to have you for my wife."

Lawrence tenderly wiped the tears that trickled out from Emily's eyes. "Emily, I know it's not much of a proposal now, but in my humble way, I'm asking you, if you will take me as your husband?" Lawrence asked in a pleading voice.

They stood as two star-struck lovers on the verge of marriage in a tangled web of subjugation. "Yes, Lawrence, I'd be honored to marry you." Emily whispered with deep sentiment. "From the first moment I saw you at Fairway you moved something deep inside of me. Since that day it has always been my deepest hope, that we would someday get married." She half laughed through her tears. "In fact, I actually wished for it when I blew out the candles at my Welcoming Ball, and no matter how it has come about, I will cherish you as my husband forever, Lawrence."

They embraced beneath the moonlight, as a single silhouette of man against woman. They pressed their flesh, tightly together in a frantic anticipation of the unknown. It was all so crazed, and frenzied. In a reckless abandon, their souls celebrated how they would be together at last. The pair was still afraid of the uncertainty of their lives together, yet enthralled in one fell swoop.

Chapter Nineteen

The Banishment

On Sunday the Lund family left for church in spite of the overcast sky. By midmorning heavy rain began to thrash while the journey for Emily and Lawrence to leave Rosewood before noon remained forthcoming.

Lawrence and Emily hurriedly packed their bags as the morning quickly passed. Their driver James secured their belongings into the carriage; along with the stately oil painting of Emily, wrapped in a woolen blanket, the art supplies, and the volumes on modern medicine Dr. Mathis had given to Lawrence.

Lawrence scurried up to his chamber for one last time, to check if he had left anything behind. Emily followed him, and lingered in the opulent surroundings for a moment of contemplation.

"Lawrence, I'm tempted to leave a note behind that exposes the truth about Sir Dexter's despicable actions, and the desertion of his own baby. Why should he go about his life scot-free when we're forced to rush out of here like fugitives?"

"Emily," Lawrence insisted. "It's not worth it . . . You can never know what ramifications that type of note can bring. Sir Dexter's parents might search for your whereabouts and then force Sir Dexter to honor his marriage to you.

I'm sure you would have no tolerance for such a union, now that you know the true depravity of Sir Dexter's character. Emily we have to be careful."

Lawrence advised with a poker face. "On the other hand, Emily, Sir Dexter's parents might try to confiscate the baby from us to raise at Rosewood in the opulence we can't provide . . . No Emily, we must silence all controversy, and leave no trace of our trail. Hurry let's not waste any more time, Emily, it's getting late." Lawrence warned with haste.

Rushing against the clock, Emily and Lawrence were inside the carriage by the appointed time. The rain had simmered down to a mist, heavy upon the avenue. The weather caused the horses to tread cautiously, further hindered by the inconvenience of the muddy paths.

They looked at the opulent estates of Bellaire Avenue for one last time. On the right side of the avenue stood Woodlands, built in the Gothic revival style of asymmetrical lines with intricate gables, and dormers.

Farther down the block they passed the Chamber House, a Tudor, in Queen Anne Revival, with brick, clapboard, and shingles. On the left side of Sutton Avenue they drove past Birchwood, a stucco mansion with a breathtaking view of the ocean. Emily shuttered at the reminder of Birchwood's mistress, the formidable Mrs. Eleanor Winthrop, one of Newport's high priestesses, and an icon of American society.

"Lawrence, we'll no doubt be excluded from Mrs. Winthrop's list of desirables now that we're no longer associated with the Lunds. My unborn baby, who possesses the proper lineage, even according to Mrs. Winthrop's stringent standards, will be no bonus now."

"Emily," Lawrence scolded. "Remember your promise; your baby is no longer a Lund, and will be a Gray!"

One of the horses slid on the wet mud and let out a huge yelp. The driver James hurriedly got out to investigate, only to realize the stallion had gotten a cut on its shin. "It's a relatively minor bruise, but it will have to be cleaned and wrapped properly before we can continue on our journey. Unfortunately I will have to walk back to Rosewood while you two wait in the carriage with the horse. I need to get some antiseptic, and a cloth to bandage the wound."

The muddied road made the driver's walk down Bellaire Avenue and back to Rosewood a bit of a setback. The pair felt tension about being discovered in such a precarious predicament. Lawrence tried to comfort the distraught Emily. "Don't worry, if anyone sees us, they will be none the wiser of our intentions. After all we could just be out for a Sunday drive."

Nonetheless, the half hour wait felt like hours of agonizing anxiety. James finally arrived back with the proper first aid. However, some of the carriages were already returning from the morning service at The Old Church.

Mrs. Harris, one of the grand dames of Newport stopped her carriage to have her husband investigate Mr. Lund's coachman bandaging the horse's shin. Then seeing it was Lawrence and Emily who inhabited the carriage summoned a reaction of disdain. Mrs. Harris, dressed in her Sunday attire of a flowered hat, and a frilly lace dress, turned her nose up, and passed the couple by without a word.

Mrs. Harris made it apparent she no longer considered them fit for association. Lawrence and Emily knew that expression well, having seen it directed at others many times.

"Lawrence, Sir Dexter has spoken more than our apologies, there's no mistake in that! My guess is the word of my expected baby has spread all over Newport by now," Emily said in shaky words while her hands trembled.

"No doubt, Emily, and it's clear the elite society who had embraced us will now shun us with equal zeal." Lawrence shook his head with disgrace.

The fog began to lift, while the sun illuminated through the clouds, when another carriage spied the situation. This carriage contained none other than the Lund family. The Lunds stopped short in recognition, with an expression of detestation on their faces.

Mallory shouted out of the carriage with her eyes red from weeping. "Emily, you are nothing but a temptress, and a harlot!"

Sir Dexter remained silent as he stared at them blankly with a staged expression of grief, which alluded to him as being the jilted victim.

Mr. Lund in turn spat on the ground, at the mere sight of them as Mrs. Lund shouted out scathingly, "Sinners, sinners, the both of you!" before she prompted the driver to scurry the horses away.

Lawrence tried to still Emily's trembling hands into his. "Well, they're gone now, and hopefully that will be the last of them!"

Emily began to weep as she clutched her abdomen. "It's an unbearable cross to fathom, to go from being the favorites, to the scoundrels of Newport society literally overnight. I have now been branded as an immoral woman, and I must hang my head in shame. It's so unfair, Lawrence!"

"There's no loyalty in these circles, Emily . . . Worse than that, there is no honor."

Every carriage they passed turned their heads in scorn. Emily cried. "We have no choice but to flee Newport now. All this controversy will surely inspire my parents' disdain as well . . . I fear I could never go back to Fairway after being banished from Newport."

"I as well could not go back and face my father now. I wouldn't want to shame him when he had such hope for me. After all, the last time I saw him he was so proud of my portrait of you, and my studying to be a doctor . . . I only hope these awful rumors which are destined to travel to Fairway don't jeopardize the position my father has attained with your father."

James pulled over to the side of the road and suggested to the pair, "I think it would be a good idea for you two to settle in Salem, Massachusetts. I'm familiar with the area. I know the best route in facilitating the journey. I can call Mr. Joshua Martin, a former boss of mine who owns a house with rooms set aside for lodgers . . . Salem is a small town with a rich historical past. The townsfolk are welcoming to outsiders in an effort to redeem themselves from their notorious past of burning witches."

"That sounds like a good plan," Lawrence echoed, "As long as I'm far away from Newport that's good enough for me. Witches could be no worse than what we have just been through!"

Emily's condition made her excessively queasy as they tarried on their difficult journey. Thankfully, Lawrence had been astute enough to bring along a box of soda crackers. Emily nibbled on them sporadically, and rested her head upon Lawrence's shoulder, sleeping for a good part of the drive.

Part Two

Chapter Twenty

The Witch Hunt

James surveyed the seaport upon their arrival in Salem late the following day. "Mr. Martin should be here at any moment; you can count on that. I'll wait with you until I spot him."

James opened the carriage for the weary couple to get out and stretch their limbs. The majestic waters of the seaport refreshed Emily and Lawrence's senses while the cool breeze gave them hope.

"I just want to warn you a little about Mr. Joshua Martin. He's an impressive man, living in a rather unimpressive circumstance. He lives off his dwindling inheritance, has never married, has a tendency for drinking, and an eye for the saloon ladies. But Joshua has a heart of gold, and his doors are always open . . . There he is," James joyfully announced as Lawrence and Emily became taken aback by the vision of their new landlord.

Mr. Joshua Martin rode up in his somewhat worn carriage, driven by a pair of mismatched, tired looking horses. Approximately thirty-five, Mr. Martin looked pirate-like with windblown, sun-streaked brown hair, and a weather-beaten appearance. His scruffy eyebrows hung low, over slits of pale-blue eyes. An unruly mustache grazed over his top lip, and grew to the end of his face on the sides, framing a cleft chin. His casual manner of dress had the throwaway grace of a swashbuckler.

James and Mr. Joshua Martin shook hands with gusto. "Well hello there, James, good to see you old friend. These must be my new tenants. Welcome to Salem. I'm Joshua Martin," Joshua Martin exclaimed in a deep vibrato as his blue eyes mirrored the airiness of the sky.

Lawrence reached for Mr. Martin's strong hand, and they shook hands firmly. "I'm Lawrence Gray and this is Miss Emily Reed." Joshua Martin bowed gallantly to Emily while she did her best to curtsy in spite of her ungainliness.

"Step right in; you both must be weary from your journey. I'll drive us over to my house at once." They all waved farewell as James disappeared into the horizon, heaving up the dust of dry earth in his aftermath.

"I'm much obliged for your hospitality, Mr. Martin. The destination of Salem which James has suggested to us is one where we are strangers to all. Your consideration in coming to fetch us is well appreciated," Lawrence said with a grateful smile.

"I'm delighted to have the opportunity to be of help to strangers in a new town. You won't remain strangers long, I assure you," Joshua Martin retorted with a musical quality to his voice. "Now you both just sit tight and we shall be there shortly."

Mr. Martin drove them down the side roads of Salem, a town foreshadowed by intrigue. The antiquity of the Colonial era embraced Emily and Lawrence with a pronounced contrast from Newport. The houses on New Derby Street were box-shaped, modest, simple in style, and situated close to the roadways.

They soon reached the Joshua Martin House, located on Washington Street. The house was flat and squared, and covered in white clapboard in desperate need of painting with peeling black shutters. It had the faded remnants of Colonial splendor from the year 1767. Upon exiting from the carriage they were greeted by a tattered American flag blowing in the breeze.

"This house was originally my father's, the late Samuel Martin. My father was a patriot ship owner who attained a merchant empire . . . Well, I guess his grand aspirations skipped a generation." Joshua chuckled in a devil-may-care attitude.

"Step right into my humble abode." Joshua grinned in a sinister manner as he led the apprehensive pair through the center hallway.

Old oil paintings hung on antique-white walls which desperately needed to be painted. The portraits of family members painted in somber tones of sepia and Indian reds, displayed in tarnished frames, were obviously as timeworn as the house.

Flanked on both sides of the center hallway were six rooms, three on either side; a parlor, a library, and sitting room, on one side, and a study, a dining room, and living room on the other. The rooms were museum-like, and had been left in the same fashion of their glory days.

They followed Joshua Martin upstairs on an unsteady staircase which had settled unevenly, with the aid of his handheld lamp. Before he showed them to their perspective chambers, they passed a small bedroom. "This is where I lay my weary head at night." Joshua chuckled from the pit of his burly chest. "Feel free to take a peek."

Joshua's chamber was decorated with maritime symbols, looking fit for a bachelor. Next to his quarters, they came upon another modest chamber, which consisted of a sagging bed in desperate need to have its strings tightened, a simple pine dresser, and an antique rocking chair.

"This room is rented by Mr. Theodore Hensley. He's a fisherman who is often out at sea. You'll meet Mr. Hensley later; he's currently busy in the kitchen. He takes a fancy to cooking seafood, and doing everything himself; from the catching, cleaning, de-boning, to sautéing. You'll never go hungry in this house," Joshua said with a cagey grin.

"Sounds good," Emily perked up thinking at least there was some consolation to their meager surroundings.

"The chambers you'll be staying in are on the other side. These chambers were used by my parents before their ship, the ill-fated Lithuania, went down. My father was a hero who saved many lives at sea, women and children . . . Unfortunately," Joshua grimaced. "He couldn't save himself or my mother, and they both perished at sea." Joshua's voice trailed off into bitter emotion.

"I'm sorry to hear that, but to have your father die a hero must give you a sense of pride." Emily offered compassionately.

"Exactly my sentiments, Miss Emily, in those bygone days, men had more honor than the heroes of today. I try to be patriotic, and stand behind my country. However, being raised in this town has changed my perspective . . . I'm sure you both must be familiar with the Salem Witch Trials of 1682."

"I know about Salem's reputation for burning witches at the stake, but I'm not informed on the particulars," Lawrence retorted.

"Well, it was mass hysteria back then. All of the original documents and trials are over at the library. I've read them word for word. More than a hundred-fifty men and women were accused of witchcraft. As a result of The Salem Witch Trials, nineteen innocent people were sentenced to death. Thankfully, Governor William Phipps had appointed a new court that no longer allowed for 'spectral evidence.'" Mr. Martin spoke in a haunting tone while his eyes gleamed beneath his handheld lamp.

"Well, hopefully today people are more level headed," Emily interjected. "I shutter at the idea of false accusations, and of innocent people being used as scapegoats." Emily and Lawrence shot each other a knowing look.

"You can never be sure about people, Emily." Mr. Martin shook his head with suspicion. "If the government could allow for speculative evidence to rule the state then, who is to say what other dementia might arise in the future?"

"I couldn't agree with you more, Mr. Martin," Emily replied. "I have always believed, it's man's inhumanity to man that is the most brutal."

"Please call me Joshua. I've never been one for formality . . . Well, enough of my rambling on. Let me allow you to retreat to your rooms without further ado. Here is your chamber, Emily."

Emily's heart sunk upon viewing her quarters. The thin patchwork quilt covering the bed looked old and frail, and far too dusty to be fit for use. The cold wooden floors were worn, with nary a rug to warm their ancient wood. Her beat-up dresser had a mottled mirror atop, which distorted any reflections.

"And here, this is your chamber, Lawrence," Joshua announced. The chambers were both decorated in early American style, with predominately drab brown furniture and accents.

"My chamber is more than sufficient, Joshua," Lawrence mildly professed. Lawrence felt grateful to have found shelter at such a dire point in their lives. Nonetheless, he knew it would be difficult for Emily to adapt to the meager surroundings.

"Well, my house is a little on the rustic side. As you can see the house hasn't been modernized yet." Joshua snickered lightheartedly. "Last year I finally had a bathroom put in. You'll find it at the end of the hallway. However," Joshua confided while twirling the ends of his mustache, "I'd just like to mention I'm still trying to smooth out the glitches of modern plumbing. For now the tub runs only lukewarm water, I apologize for the inconvenience. What I do when I get around to finally taking a bath," Joshua chuckled like a mischievous child. "I have my servant girl Miss Bethany bring up a few buckets of water that she heats on the kitchen stove. It helps to take the chill out . . . Where were you two traveling from if you don't mind my asking? James didn't mention it."

"We just arrived from Newport, Rhode Island," Emily replied in wanderlust for the privileges of her former society.

"Newport, Rhode Island," Joshua repeated in surprise before laughing wryly. "Well, my friends, as you can see, Salem is a world apart from there."

Mr. Martin proceeded to help Lawrence carry up their trunks. "I'll leave you two to put away your belongings. When you're finished you can come down for supper."

Emily whispered with a worried expression while she held her swollen abdomen for a moment. "Lawrence, I don't know how I can bear it." She sighed inconsolably. "These accommodations are far worse than the servants' quarters at Fairway! I mean just look at this blar ͏ ͏t, it's ready for the trash." Emily lifted a corner when a huge explosion of dust dissolved into the dark air, illuminated only by candlelight.

"Emily, we can't complain, at least we have a roof over our head for now, and the promise of a new start. Let's hope for the best," Lawrence optimistically replied.

"You're a man, you can adapt to the rugged discomforts of this rundown old house. The house has not even been electrified yet," Emily exclaimed in dismay. "Look, there are no electrical outlets anywhere. We had better bring one of the candles on our way down; the steps are so crooked, it's treacherous, especially for me in my condition."

"Well, let's not fret, Emily, just walk down slowly, and hold onto the banister. What's important is that we're together and safe. Thankfully, Joshua has told us we won't go hungry in this house, considering you are eating for two, we have found luck already," Lawrence said with hopefulness. "Emily, let's try and concentrate on what's really important, and count our blessings the best we can."

The pair found their way down to the rustic kitchen, comprised of a heavy wooden table, marred by imperfections, with a metal lantern set to the side which emitted dim, amber light. The walls were dark, and the floors were oak. They showed the wear of over a century.

Joshua welcomed them with a broad smile. "Come and take a seat, make yourselves at home . . . The food will be served shortly. In the meantime, help yourself to some bread and ale. We also have iced tea, Emily might prefer that."

Emily and Lawrence each took a piece of crusty bread with great relish. It was still warm from the oven, and quite delectable to their gnawing stomachs.

"As you both might have guessed, I left the chambers you're staying in exactly as they had been in memory of my parents. However, when Emily told me you came from Newport, it got me thinking perhaps it's high time I stopped procrastinating and refurbished them."

Joshua sighed apologetically. "The problem is I'm often out at sea, and have had little time for restoring the old house, but I do intend to spruce it up. I have every intention to do so. In fact, I've already purchased the paint, and it has just been waiting in the cellar for some time now."

"Joshua, I'm handy around the house," interjected Lawrence. "I can do any kind of painting at a fair price. In fact, if you're interested, I can have the house in tiptop shape in no time . . . Perhaps we can incorporate any improvements in the rent I'll owe you," Lawrence said optimistically while Emily's eyes lit up.

"Say no more, my friend," Joshua interjected. "We can work out the particulars at a more apropos time. I'm easy, as you can see I care more for good company and food than money. Perhaps you can start with the little lady's chamber for which I have purchased light pink paint for the walls with rose trim. I hope you find that combination to your liking, Miss Emily."

"Oh yes, that sounds lovely, I'm very fond of pink." Emily felt pleased at the prospect of a fresh coat of paint, and for Lawrence to have secured work from the onset.

Joshua gave her a crooked smile and chuckled. "Emily, by the way your face dropped when you saw your chamber gave me a clue I had better spruce it up, and fast." They all had a laugh.

Mr. Theodore Hensley appeared with his fare. He possessed the casual appearance of a weatherworn fisherman with his gray hair looking a bit unkempt. Nonetheless, he proudly set out his freshly prepared platter of salmon, seasoned to perfection with a lemon wine sauce of onions and herbs.

Mr. Pierre Lamont, the French chef Joshua employed, followed behind him dressed with a French flair and a handlebar mustache. He presented a tray of scalloped potatoes, and sliced brisket with mushrooms and gravy.

Lawrence settled into the cozy kitchen with ease as Joshua Martin spoke about his travels.

"Well, Joshua," Lawrence interjected. "Now that I hear about all your adventures it's no wonder you have never married."

"Marry, ha," Joshua slugged down a waft of beer. "The only one I've ever had a real love affair with is drinking and the sea." Joshua laughed heartily.

"Actually," Lawrence said with a sheepish smile. "I have plans on marrying Emily as soon as we are settled. Would you happen to know a quaint place where we can get married, Joshua?"

"Marry one another, Lawrence, you're a braver man than me," chuckled Joshua. "As for a hall you are more than welcome to have the wedding right here if you'd like. There's a lovely garden out back, and I'd be much obliged to find you an official for the ceremony. I'd invite a few friends to help you celebrate. You've never been to a real party until you break bread with my friends," Joshua offered hospitably.

Emily smiled demurely as the excitement of getting married added merriment to the rural eating room. The plain oak table became transformed by the ample platters set upon it with the sounding of Joshua's bell. At least six courses were served, in a style which surpassed their expectations.

Miss Bethany, a scrap of a servant girl, who had a room in the basement, appeared to light the medieval candelabra as the evening sky turned black. She had an ordinary face with kind brown eyes, and thin, mousy-brown hair rolled into a bun. She was pale and slim with nimble fingers, and short stubby nails from engaging in heavy labor. Miss Bethany curtsied at the sight of the dinner guests before she helped clear the table, and wash the dishes.

"I intend to have the house electrified as well, especially now that there's a little lady from Newport staying in the house." Joshua rolled his eyes with a touch of humor.

"Everything in due time, my friends," Joshua toasted while everyone followed suit and sipped their ale.

"By all means, Joshua," Emily smiled with encouragement. "I agree it's time to modernize. Just think in five years from now it will be the turn of the century, and the year 1900. That's such a milestone for humanity. It gives me comfort to know my child will know more luxuries than we can even imagine at present." Emily pressed her hand gently over her protruding belly in unconscious recognition.

Theodore Hensley's piercing gray eyes noticed what he had suspected upon first sight of the blossoming Emily. "I see, so there's a baby on the way already." He smiled knowingly. "These days I never take the liberty of assuming that without being certain. With all the pastries the young ladies of today indulge in I've seen some look farther along than you appear, Miss Emily, and it's all an illusion to be sure." Mr. Hensley smiled warmly.

"Oh dear," Emily retorted. "I must make it my business to stay away from cake. I would not want to add on more than just the baby weight."

By and by, the divulgence of the premarital baby was not something they dwelled on in conversation or thought. Thankfully, that sort of thing was accepted as a fact of life in the Joshua Martin House.

Chapter Twenty-One

The Bridal Gown

Emily found lace curtains to replace the threadbare ones of her chamber while browsing in Sentiments, a novelty shop in Salem. She also found a hand-painted vase imported from Austria and an embroidered doily to place beneath it.

"I'll take these please," Emily told the saleslady who lived in the modest house connected to the shop.

The young lady carefully wrapped the exquisite vase in newspaper. "This vase will make any room special; it's one of a kind you know."

"That's a good thing, because my chamber is in desperate need of perking up. The vase is a little over my budget, but thankfully my fiancé just landed a job hand painting wallpaper, and he insisted I buy myself whatever I want."

"A generous fiancé is a prelude to a happy marriage. Best of luck to you, Miss, and I hope you enjoy the vase," the salesgirl echoed as Emily went out to the carriage.

A dapper dressed Mr. Lamont drove Emily back to the house. "I shall return after I get the ingredients for tonight's dinner. I was thinking of making leek soup, roasted chicken, and mushroom crepes. How does that sound to you, Emily?"

"That sounds wonderful, Pierre, just as all your menus always do."

Emily excitedly brought her purchases inside the house before she went into the yard. She eased herself on a hammock hung in-between two sturdy branches of a huge oak tree, and found shelter from the midday sun. The gentle wind fanned a bevy of leaves above her head as she became engrossed in Jane Austen's novel *The Three Sisters,* and enjoyed the leisure the Joshua Martin House offered.

In a while Miss Bethany came running excitedly into the yard with her kind, brown eyes ablaze. "Miss Emily, do come in right away. I've brought my sister's wedding gown, and have it laid out on your bed."

"That's wonderful. I cannot wait to see it!" Emily exclaimed, as she rushed to her chamber to find a gorgeous gown spread out upon her new satin blanket.

"It's so beautiful!" Emily gasped as her heart rejoiced.

"My sister has been saving the dress for me for five years now, but as you can well see, Miss Emily, I don't think I shall ever marry. My sister got married at eighteen, and I'm twenty-three already, besides who would have a servant girl as their bride?" Miss Bethany asked with a tone of acceptance.

"Miss Bethany, any man would be lucky to have you as their bride and in their household no matter what your age or profession is . . . I must say your sister is so generous to have lent me this breathtaking gown, and you have been so thoughtful to have asked her on my behalf." Emily's eyes began to tear; in awe of both the beauty of the gown, and sweet heart of Miss Bethany.

The servant girl dutifully helped Emily into the high-neck wedding gown. It was comprised of white satin with lace appliqués sewn onto the bodice, leg-o-mutton sleeves, and a full skirt which trailed the floor in the back. The tiny satin buttons had loops on both the front and back of the dress which added opulence.

The wedding dress fit Emily nearly perfect, being just a little snug along the midriff. Miss Bethany examined the dress with a keen eye. "I will release the gown slightly here, and ease out the back a little. That should give you plenty of room in the waist area where you need it. The length is perfect, plus the fullness of the skirt and high waistline are very flattering."

"Considering my present condition, Miss Bethany, I could not ask for more. My stomach is camouflaged as best as can be expected," Emily said with a reluctant smile.

"The beaded headpiece and the satin boots which still have all the pearl buttons intact and white kid gloves are in this box." Miss Bethany took out a glove, "Look, there is a seam slit to allow the bride to put on the wedding band without removing the gloves. Have you ever seen anything as clever?"

"No I have never seen gloves like that. Everything is beautiful, and perfectly preserved. Thank you so much, Miss Bethany, you and your sister have been so kind," Emily said with a tender smile.

Miss Bethany gently pressed her hand on Emily's emerging pregnancy, as she rearranged the gown. "I'm good with children. I practically raised my sister's twin boys when they were born."

"Well, that's good to know. I will definitely need your expertise, Miss Bethany. I'm a novice when it comes to babies."

"Rearing babies is difficult, especially without help, Miss Emily. After I helped my sister with the twins, I decided I wanted to be free from the constraints of marriage, and family," Miss Bethany revealed with a tinge of remorse.

"Well, on the one hand, Miss Emily, it gave me the motivation to find work, but on the other hand it sealed my fate of being a housemaid." Miss Bethany sighed.

"Miss Bethany, when the baby is born perhaps you could be the governess," Emily suggested cheerfully. "A baby brings joy to everyone's heart. Being a governess is a lot more rewarding than being a housemaid. I'm sure Joshua could easily find a new housemaid."

"Yes, I'm sure Mr. Martin would have no trouble replacing me, and he would gladly release me if I was to secure a more advantageous position. But if I was you, I wouldn't count on having a governess, Miss Emily, money is tight when a new baby comes," Miss Bethany said knowingly.

"That was the reason I helped my sister with her boys. But not to worry, Miss Emily, I will do whatever I can to help you. I know it hasn't been an easy road for you, to wind up here, without the blessing of your family. If anyone knows how rough life can be, it's me." Miss Bethany shrugged her shoulders. "Look at me, Miss Emily, I'm educated, and from a fine family from Lancaster, Pennsylvania, and here I am in the position where I have to work to make my own wages. It's not easy, and there are countless other women who would wait in line to fill my shoes."

"No one can fill your shoes, Miss Bethany." Emily, still wearing the wedding gown, embraced her close to her chest. "You are the most even-tempered and charitable soul I have ever known, Miss Bethany. You've been so good to me and such a dear friend from the moment we met . . . I would be honored if you would agree to be my maid of honor."

"It would be my honor, Emily, thank you so much for choosing me." Miss Bethany's face radiated with joy and goodness.

"You are the perfect choice. Lawrence has asked Joshua Martin to be his best man. So it'll be quite fitting for you to be a part of the bridal party as well, Miss Bethany."

Chapter Twenty-Two

The Wedding

On October 5, 1895, the wedding day of Lawrence Gray and Emily Reed had arrived. The crisp autumn air enveloped the night with a majestic quality. The golden leaves hung onto the branches by the fine line which separates one season from the next. Red roses, still in bloom, grew rampant on the vine.

Emily emerged into the yard looking breathtaking. She took her place before the petal strewn bridal path. Her white satin wedding gown trailed behind her in regal elegance. Her hair had been arranged in a crown of curls topped with the beaded headpiece which skimmed the ground in a fluff of white tulle as she walked.

The light from a succession of candles, set ablaze, lit up her angelic face while her eyes sparkled with luminosity equal to the stars. Emily held a bouquet of peach and pale pink roses intermingled with a spray of baby's breath within her white-gloved hands.

Joshua and Miss Bethany proceeded to walk down the aisle together in the formality of a true wedding. Miss Bethany had on the same pink satin dress she had worn when she had been her sister's maid of honor. In the background a quartet of Irishmen from O'Neil's, a saloon in town, played wedding music. Thankfully, the skilled musicians, renowned for their Irish jigs had a vast repertoire.

The mystery of night, bestowed a shadow of innocence upon Emily's face. Starry-eyed, Emily floated down the bridal path, as elegant as a princess. Lawrence walked down to greet her looking remarkable. He wore a claret frock coat with the carnation boutonniere pinned on his lapel which complimented Emily's bouquet. A dapper top hat accentuated his sleek black hair.

Even Mr. Joshua Martin looked the part of a gentleman in a blue frock coat with a pink carnation pinned to his lapel as well. The party of celebrants Joshua Martin had invited watched spellbound as Father Flanagan from Saint Catherine's Shrine of Our Lady, began the ceremony with lofty inspiration.

"Our sages say October is an auspicious time of year to get married since it signifies a bountiful harvest. May Lawrence and Emily's needs for sustenance always be met, but of equal importance is the need for them to nurture their love. May their love grow into a bountiful harvest to bloom and last for all of their days."

Father Flanagan's voice resonated powerfully. "I often ask myself what is the meaning of love. I have never heard it defined better than in the Corinthians 13:4-7."

"'Love is *patient*, love is *kind*. It does not *envy*, it does not *boast*. It is not *proud*. It is not *rude*, it is not self seeking. It is not easily angered. It keeps no record of wrongs. Love does not delight in evil, but rejoices in truth. It always protects, always trusts. Always *hopes*, always perseveres.'"

The priest continued in a moving voice, "We have all gathered here this evening to witness the love of a special couple who live by the word of the Corinthians. They have traveled far, and stand before us against all odds because they believe in love. Without any further ado let us begin. Please repeat after me, Miss Emily."

Emily echoed Father Flanagan's words with heartfelt soliloquy, "I Emily Grace Reed take thee, Lawrence Gray, to be my lawfully wedded husband, to have and to hold from this day forward, for better or for worse, for richer, for poorer, in sickness and in health, to love and cherish; I promise to obey you and be faithful to you until death parts us."

Lawrence repeated Father Flanagan's words with deep commitment, "I Lawrence Gray take thee, Emily Reed, to be my lawfully wedded wife, knowing in my heart, you will be my one true love. On this holy day, I affirm to you in the presence of God and these witnesses my sacred promise to be your faithful husband, in sickness and in health, in joy and sorrow. I further promise to love you without reservation, honor and respect you, provide your needs the best I can, protect you from harm, comfort you in times of distress, and cherish you for as long as we both shall live."

They proceeded to exchange gold wedding bands with their initials, and wedding date engraved inside. Lawrence reached forth; and slid the ring inside the slit of Emily's gloved hand. In the excitement, Emily clumsily dropped Lawrence's wedding band. She tried to hold back her laughter as she went to retrieve it, and her face reddened with embarrassment.

Father Flanagan interjected with a smile, "Don't despair, it's actually considered good luck to drop the ring during the ceremony, this means all the evil spirits have been shaken out."

The couple chuckled as Emily slid Lawrence's ring onto his wedding finger, and the sanctity of their sincere love and devotion for one another came to full fruition. There in the precious moment, of a tiny space in time, all the glory of their hopes had become a reality in spite of their circumstance.

Father Flanagan's voice reverberated with pride as he announced, "I now pronounce you husband and wife. You may now kiss the bride."

Lawrence grasped his wife Emily close to his heart, and pressed his lips lovingly onto hers. Their lips met with jubilation and longing. There in the crisp autumn air their spirits swept upward with the wind, floating, then soaring into infinity in a perfect moment, when impossible dreams become reality. The crowd threw generous handfuls of rice which landed joyfully upon the loving pair.

The wedding celebrants retreated into the dining room where a sumptuous table of fine china and cutlery had been set atop a yellow tablecloth with matching napkins. The white heirloom china had a motif of yellow and orange parrots, with gold edges. The house had been decorated by profusions of pale pink roses, adorning the doorways, balustrades, windows, and the fireplace.

Emily mentioned to Lawrence with an ironic laugh, how their present companions would have no doubt been considered the "vulgar of society," by her parents. The men were either servants or sailors of menial rank who were loud and bawdy. They were clearly becoming inebriated, with the same uncouth as the clientele of the local tavern. The women in attendance were servants of nearby houses; each being granted a night out on the town. They were a hearty, lusty bunch to say the least. The women were dressed in either gray or brown, in striking contrast to their rouge and red lipstick. The men wore clothing that looked fit for immigrants who were arriving to America as fourth-class stowaways, and having a merry time drinking beer and dancing wildly with the ladies. Nonetheless, Emily and Lawrence joined in, and danced with merriment while the quartet played a lively assortment of Irish Jigs.

Pierre served a sumptuous fare of garden greens, glazed duck with cherry sauce, flank steak smothered in roasted onions, asparagus with melted Gruyere, and sweet potato pie.

Lawrence rejoiced in victory. "Emily, I can still remember the fateful night of your Debutante Ball, when your father broke up our dance. Well, I hate to sound triumphant but your father cannot break up our dance now, we belong to each other legally. Love has won out!"

"Not to mention my father would never step foot in a place like this." Emily laughed lightheartedly. "But I guess he will never know what he's missing!"

"Yes and with a baby on the way. I suppose he will be missing out on becoming a grandfather too." Lawrence retorted with a bittersweet smile.

After dinner, three wedding cakes awaited, a small white one for Emily, a small dark one for Lawrence, and a large, dark fruitcake adorned with white-frosted scrolls and orange blossoms for their guests. The large wedding cake had long white ribbons fanning out from beneath the cake. All of the single girls gathered themselves around for the "cake pulling." Whichever charm they pulled out promised a special meaning for them.

"Miss Bethany, you shall be first to have your turn at the cake ceremony," Emily persuaded. Miss Bethany had a joyous smile until she saw she had pulled out a button.

"I told you, Emily, I'm to be an old maid, now my fate is sealed," she said half-laughing, holding onto the button superstitiously.

Next in line was Bessie McDonald, a plump blonde with glistening green eyes. She pulled on a ribbon and came upon a ring, which meant an engagement was imminent. Her cheeks radiated with joy as she grabbed onto her boyfriend Timothy McKinley to dance.

Next Cathy O'Conner tried her luck and pulled out the charm of a carriage. "I'm going to be blessed with children . . . Well, I hope I'll also be blessed with the means to take care of them, that would help."

Emily exposed the bottom of her petticoat to the ladies, where Miss Bethany's sister had fastened a small pouch containing a piece of cloth.

"Look, it's an old custom to fasten a small pouch to the wedding petticoat containing bread, cloth, wood, or a dollar. It's believed this will provide the new married couple with food, clothing, and shelter."

Becky Linden retorted in admiration, "Believe me, if I had been wearing such a fine white wedding gown when I got married, I wouldn't have to worry about food and shelter . . . I have three sisters, and we were all married within three years of each other. We all had to share the same lilac dress for our weddings. My mother would not hear of buying us a real wedding gown even considering we would have all used it."

"Well, I was lucky," Emily admitted. "Miss Bethany asked her sister if I could borrow her gown."

"The only reason why my sister didn't shorten it and scoop the neckline by now is because she has been saving the dress for me . . . But now I'm destined to be an old maid!" Miss Bethany exclaimed, while she twirled the infamous button in her hand.

The night went on in endless delirium. Bessie McDonald, the pale blonde with a lighthearted laugh, pulled Lawrence onto the dance floor, while her partner Timothy McKinley, a ruddy faced sailor, tried to sweep the weary Emily off her feet for one last spin.

"I'm afraid I must decline, Mr. McKinley, I'm about ready to turn in, but thank you anyway."

"Please call me Tim, I insist, come just one more dance for good luck." Mr. McKinley leaned forward, and accidentally stepped on Emily's toe without even realizing it. Emily, against her good reason obliged, even though she could barely even stand any longer.

At the end of the dance, Emily announced to the celebrants, "Ladies and Gentlemen, I have no qualms for all of you who have helped us celebrate our wedding, to go on dancing until the sun comes up. However, I regret I must retire to my chamber. I would like to thank all of you for coming to celebrate with us." Emily curtsied gracefully.

Lawrence chivalrously added, "Good night to one and all, and I thank everyone for enabling us to have a real wedding. Don't mind us, but I must see to it my new wife has a husband to escort her." Lawrence chuckled mischievously. "If I was to remain down here without her, it would clearly be my first blunder."

Lawrence about faced with a merry chuckle, and trailed Emily's footsteps. They each went up to their separate chambers. There was an unspoken awkwardness concerning the expectations of the wedding night.

Emily slipped into her floor length, white silk nightgown from the trousseau she had purchased in a bridal shop in town. The swell of her belly was clearly discernible through the thin fabric which she tried to camouflage with a matching bed jacket, trimmed in lace, to no reward.

Lawrence put on black silk pajamas, with a smoking jacket Mr. Reed had given him back at Fairway. Lawrence realized the gift contained a bit of irony now as he went to claim his bride. He knocked on the oak door connecting their chambers with an indescribable elation.

Emily spoke in a tiny, childlike voice, "Lawrence, please come in."

Lawrence opened the door to find Emily looking beautiful in spite of how her belly compromised her splendor. He embraced her in his strong arms, and nestled her flesh warmly inside his powerful chest. He leaned downward, and planted a loving kiss on her forehead, with sensitivity to her plight.

Emily looked up into his eyes as they melted in the first kiss in the privacy of marital bliss, while the lively celebration reverberated through the thin floor in an encore of jubilation. Emily then shed a tear of joy.

"Lawrence, I don't want to disappoint you on our wedding night. I apologize, but in my present condition, I don't feel ready to fulfill my role as your wife . . . If you would be so kind, and patient to wait until after the baby is born, I would be all the more enamored of you."

Lawrence felt his passion swell up from his chest, and then fall with a heavy weight as flat as a pancake. "Emily, my dearest, don't worry, sweetheart. I won't force myself upon you if you feel uncomfortable. I promise I will always try my best to be an understanding and sympathetic husband, and want only for your happiness. I just want to be near you, and hold you close to me, Emily. You are my heart and my soul . . . I love you."

"I love you too, Lawrence. Thank you so much for understanding how awkward I feel with this big stomach."

"Your stomach is beautiful." Lawrence gave her a tender look as he skimmed his hands over her abdomen with longing.

They kissed blissfully with the apprehension of intimacy removed from Emily's sights. Like innocents, they reveled in their affection, rising upward from the innermost depth of their souls. Their lips meshed in the ardent muse of lovers in synch with one another and connecting spiritually. The floral scent of Emily's tresses drowned Lawrence's senses, and awakened his primal urges.

The sound of the wind rustled with the crisp leaves, swishing in the frenzy of autumn. A cool breeze bathed them in refreshment, as it eased in through the lace curtains of Emily's chamber. The quiet provided the room with serenity as the loud celebrating finally came to an end, and the guests began to disperse one by one.

The newlyweds' hearts beat as one. Together in the tender calm of love, they lay side by side upon Emily's hay filled mattress which had been tightened comfortably. In a solace measured not by demands or expectation, Lawrence nestled Emily inside his brawny chest, and cradled her lovingly, as he kissed her lips and face endlessly. Smothering her at first with a burning passion, Lawrence then directed his fire to lighthearted tenderness, until Emily fell asleep blissfully in his arms.

Lawrence kissed her eyelids with tiny flutters, and reveled in her sleeping semblance inside his arms. Like a butterfly captured in flight, the cocoon of his caress possessed Emily's life. They both fell asleep in an intimacy as powerful as the exchange of their waking hours.

Chapter Twenty-Three

The Witches of Salem

Emily sat in the parlor sipping a cup of afternoon tea while she absentmindedly breezed through the local newspaper, the Salem Record. Her breath stood still as she came upon the nuptial section. There before her unsuspecting sights was the engagement announcement of Sir Dexter Lund to Lady Violet Reynolds, now going by her maiden name of Violet Wexler. Emily blinked her eyes, and then widened them with the same terror of one who has just seen a ghost. Emily's blood ran fast and then cold as she read the announcement in disbelief.

"Elizabeth and Sir Thomas Wexler of Salem are pleased to announce the engagement of their daughter Violet Ivy Wexler to Sir Dexter Lund, son of Sarah and Hector Lund of Newport, Rhode Island. Sir Dexter Lund is a lawyer with a private practice in Newport. Their spring wedding is planned for June 25, 1896, at The Old Church in Newport, Rhode Island."

Emily studied the photo of their smiling faces, posed cheek to cheek, and obviously matched dollar for dollar as anguish raged inside her.

Lawrence arrived home late in the evening from the job he had secured of painting fourteen-carat leaves on an emerald green silk wall covering for a local decorator. Emily bombarded Lawrence before he even had a chance to get both feet inside the door.

"Look at this!" Emily demanded, flailing the newspaper before his weary sights. "Salem and Newport are a lot closer than we would have ever imagined, Lawrence!" Emily cried out in misery.

Lawrence examined the announcement in mutual shock, to see it in their local paper no less. The whites of his dark eyes illuminated with ire as he tried to regain his reason. "Dearest," Lawrence reached for Emily's trembling hands to console her, noticing how tiny and cold they felt to his strong grasp.

"I must admit I already knew of Sir Dexter's intentions to marry Lady Violet. I'm truly sorry you had to find out this way, Emily." Lawrence looked deep into Emily's eyes with sympathy.

"You mean to tell me you knew all along, and didn't tell me!" Emily shouted inconsolably. "To realize Sir Dexter has used me on the night of the Welcoming Ball, and then just discarded me like refuse is degrading beyond belief! And to have been jilted for another woman on top of it; the idea he is now free to marry whomever he chooses infuriates me!" Emily wailed as she shook the newspaper clipping in rage.

"Lawrence, here it is right before my sights for the whole world to see. I'm sure they have their engagement advertised in every newspaper with all their money!" Emily's anger came to a new fruition, so intense she could practically taste it. Emily tried to swallow when her mouth became parched and the room spun around in dark circles.

"Lawrence, I can see Salem's reputation for witches is more accurate than we would have ever imagined. Lady Violet hails from Salem, and there's no doubt she has bedazzled Sir Dexter with her witchery. Sir Dexter was obviously an easy pawn for her." Emily pondered. "I should have guessed by how cozy the two of them always looked out on the veranda together. I didn't trust their connection from the start."

"Emily, listen to me my sweetheart, and please understand." Lawrence gave her a loving glance as the light of the fire made his dark eyes glisten. "Sir Dexter informed me of their plans to marry before he banished us from Rosewood, but I thought it would be best not to burden you with it, Emily, my sweetheart. Some things are best to be ignored. We have our own life now, and they have theirs. What difference does it all make now anyway?"

"Lawrence, the difference is we might run into them when they are in town visiting Lady Violet's parents. Mallory told me Lady Violet's family are from Massachusetts and how she visits her family often. But who knew it was Salem. Lawrence, this is not a good thing!" Emily cried out with worry.

Lawrence pulled the paper out of Emily's grasp, nearly tearing it. "Here let me have this. I will burn it in the fire at once!" Lawrence threw it in the fire, and they both watched spellbound as the newspaper exploded into a sphere of fiery red. The light it emitted illuminated the dimly lit room for a moment before it became reduced to ash and dust.

"There," Lawrence exclaimed with satisfaction. "There is no sense in having that around. What Sir Dexter and Lady Violet do with their lives does not affect our lives one iota. Who cares if they visit her family?" Lawrence insisted with a fixed gaze on the last remnants of smoldering ash.

"Maybe not, but I would have certainly liked to know the full spectrum of Sir Dexter's dishonesty . . . To realize in all that time he was conspiring to marry Lady Violet still has me in an uproar. Just think, the baby will be born before their wedding day. Sir Dexter is the most despicable man one could ever imagine, to be marrying in such a blatant fashion, after he has left us both to the wolves!" The veins of Emily's neck strained through her porcelain skin as she shouted.

"That we know already, Emily. Now no more thoughts of Sir Dexter or Lady Violet, we have our lives, let them have theirs," Lawrence reassured as the room darkened, and the air grew cold.

"If not for your honor, Lawrence, I would have every intention of going to their wedding at the Old Church and protesting their marriage. I would declare Sir Dexter is already a father, and take pleasure in telling everyone the truth. That would surely shake the town, and the bride and groom's smug satisfaction with each other." Emily snickered calculatingly.

"Lawrence, I feel I finally have my chance for revenge. I hate to say it, but I find it very tempting." Emily's face took on an incandescent ire as her lips turned up at the corners with cunning.

"That's the devil tempting you, Emily, trust me no good could become of it!" Lawrence warned in a steady voice.

Emily scowled. "Sir Dexter deserves to be confronted by me and the baby on his wedding day. Talk about scandal, even if the Newport society didn't believe me outright, there would always be that seed of doubt in their minds regarding Sir Dexter's character." Emily vowed self-righteously.

"You will do no such thing, Emily Grace Gray," Lawrence protested. "Now get any such thoughts out of your head . . . If you were to ever divulge the truth, there could be no telling what grief Sir Dexter's family would place upon us. Neither you or I, nor the baby would ever be safe from their interference. Best to let it be, my sweet Emily. No more talk of Sir Dexter being a father, you promised me! Sir Dexter has lost that privilege."

Lawrence chuckled from the pit of his strong chest. "I am to become a father, and Sir Dexter is to marry a woman who obviously has no heart. Emily, guaranteed Lady Violet is out to devour Sir Dexter, and all of his millions the same way she did to her ex-husband. Let's be honest, Lady Violet cannot possibly love Sir Dexter, and he is too blind to even realize he's being used, but he deserves it. That just goes to show Sir Dexter's evil actions can't possibly bring him good fortune." Lawrence smiled at Emily with closure.

"You honestly believe that, Lawrence?"

"I'm a firm believer everything you do in life comes back to you tenfold," Lawrence assured as he kissed her dank forehead.

"Well, by all means I don't wish to be vengeful. After all, Lawrence, Sir Dexter's wrongdoing has given us our freedom, and in retrospect, I'm quite content with my lot." Emily softened before she sighed with regret. "Just the same, Lawrence, it bothers me you have to work so hard, while Sir Dexter gets off scot-free. He should be the one financially responsible for me and the baby. The sum of money he has given you is pitiful compared to all his millions. The man is a lowly miser on top of everything else!"

"Emily, I'm not burdened by having to provide for you and the baby. What irks me most is that you have been removed from the lifestyle you're accustomed to. I feel certain your parents would welcome us at Fairway if you wrote to them, and told them the truth. Your family must be suffering terribly, Emily. Not to mention I worry for my father, and what my being disassociated from him will do. Don't you think you should at least send your family a note about your whereabouts and safety?"

"I will do no such thing, Lawrence!" Emily insisted obstinately. "Sir Dexter has no doubt poisoned my family against me with his lies. That was the deal; we left on Sir Dexter's terms! I couldn't even fathom the proportions of such a scandal, and the stigma it would have on us and the baby . . . My father already warned me the night of my Debutante Ball, if I was to pursue you I would be cut off. I'm sorry if that offends you, Lawrence, but believe me it was all based on financial status, nothing more."

Emily could not bear to meet Lawrence's eyes as she saw his expression sadden. "I don't hold it against him, Emily. I came to your father's estate as a poor man with my father a poor man as well. I can't blame your father's viewpoint in hindsight . . . Perhaps now that I'm to become a father myself I'll understand just what it entails."

Lawrence regained his spark. "However, your father sold me short. I intend to become a doctor, Emily. If things keep going in this direction it won't be long before I can afford to go to medical school."

"Lawrence, won't that be too much for you to bear? You slave all day hand painting wallpaper, and then each night you study beneath the dim light of a candle." Emily shook her head with frustration. "You would think with all the money we pay Joshua Martin for rent he would be able to afford to electrify the house. We are living in a primitive environment. I'm afraid it's just too much for one man to withstand. I worry for you, Lawrence."

"I'm quite all right," Lawrence assured with a kiss on her cheek. "When a man has a purpose, nothing is too much to bear. I worry for your happiness, Emily. I don't like to see you so upset."

They both assured each other it was only for each other's happiness they worried. As for themselves, both Lawrence and Emily proclaimed they were quite content. Emily then grasped her stomach in a moment of discomfort as the weight of the baby pressed heavily on her petite frame, and pain shot down her legs. Lawrence clutched her close to his heart, as he looked down into her troubled eyes.

Emily's worry over Lawrence's hardship wore her constitution down as did the cooler weather. "Lawrence, I have such a chill. Could you please get me another blanket, and put a fresh log on the fire. Look, my words are full of frost. It's freezing in here!"

Lawrence dutifully put another woolen blanket over his shivering wife. He dreaded the coming of winter if autumn could feel so raw. The first edge of cold had already arrived, and the leaves were growing restless on the branch. Lawrence watched as the golden leaves sacrificed themselves to the wind, falling one by one.

Chapter Twenty-Four

Fishermen Fly South

Joshua Martin entered the center hall holding a small satchel; it looked as if its contents were his only belongings. His windblown hair resembled the ruffled feathers of a bird in flight.

"It's off to Florida for me; they'll be no fishing here now that the cold has set in. Mr. Hensley got a head start on me, and left early this morning."

"Are you sure you don't mind us staying on without you?" Lawrence asked with concern.

"No, not at all, if you can bear the cold," Joshua grinned menacingly. "It's easier for me, Lawrence, now I don't have to board up the whole house. Miss Bethany and Mr. Lamont have both agreed to stay on, but like I've already told you, Lawrence, you'll be responsible to pay their wages while I'm gone. You're responsible for any repairs on the house as well while I'm away . . . But don't worry it shouldn't be too bad, this old house has seen many winters." Joshua reassured as he braced Lawrence's shoulders.

"Well, thanks for letting us stay on, we appreciate it, Joshua. I'd rather not move Emily now in her condition if I don't have to." Lawrence put a comforting arm around his expectant wife who had grown quite large.

Joshua flashed his brilliant blue eyes before he shook Lawrence's hand firmly, and bowed to Emily. "Well, good luck, my friends. I'll see you in the spring. I hope everything will have turned out well for you and the new baby. Lawrence, we can smoke a cigar together in the parlor, and celebrate when I return." Lawrence and Emily bid Joshua farewell.

Emily sighed with Joshua's departure. "Lawrence, I feel we've been misled. I had assumed the improvements Joshua had mentioned to us would be made in a timely fashion, especially with a baby on the way. It's obvious to me Joshua never intended to modernize this old house with heat and electricity. It has all been talk, and now we're left on our own, with an absentee landlord no less. I fear we are at the mercy of the impending New England winter, Lawrence," Emily droned.

"Trust me we will bear the winter, Emily, we'll manage somehow. My main concern now is Mrs. Rand, the decorator who commissioned me to do the hand-painted leaves. She asked to speak to me tomorrow morning, but has made no mention of another project."

"Don't jump to negative conclusions, Lawrence; maybe she assumes you know there's more work in store. After all you did such a great job. It probably takes her time in-between to get the new work together," encouraged Emily with a worried expression.

The following morning Lawrence apprehensively took a seat across from Mrs. Rand's desk. She rearranged her paper strewn desk before she addressed him in a sober voice, "Lawrence, I just want you to know I appreciate what a great job you have done hand-painting the wallpaper, but unfortunately business is slow in the winter. Orders on the leafy pattern you've become a pro at have come to an end temporarily."

"Will there be any other work?" Lawrence asked in panic.

Mrs. Rand raised her arched brows apologetically. "I'm sorry, Lawrence, but I'm going to have to let you go for now. Mr. Rand and I have decided to close up the shop for the winter, and go down to our house in Palm Beach . . . Please feel free to contact me in the spring; I should have plenty of work for you then."

Lawrence left her office feeling out of sorts with his life in Salem. It seemed everything had become a blur overnight.

Lawrence found Emily resting by the fireplace chilled to the bone. Her obtrusive stomach made it difficult for her to find a comfortable position.

"Lawrence, I've had terrible discomfort with cramping today when I stand. I've just been sleeping on the couch all day. When I stood I felt faint."

"Please, Emily, I insist on calling Dr. Kraus, he's an elderly gentleman who is one of the last old-fashioned country doctors. From what I hear his advice is well respected. Please let him at least look at you, Emily." Lawrence pleaded in a husky voice. "I don't want to play around, Emily. There is a baby at stake."

"Well, if you insist, but I tell you I'm fine, Lawrence. I just need to rest," Emily murmured weakly.

The silver-haired Doctor Kraus found the bedraggled Emily, shivering by the fireside. "Well, my stars," exclaimed Dr. Kraus. "I never knew Joshua Martin took in boarders in the colder seasons. These New England winters are brutal I tell you. This is just the beginning, it's still only fall. I warn you it will be a bitter cold, difficult winter, Mr. Gray. Without modernization this house will be an icebox."

Dr. Kraus examined Emily by the light of a handheld lamp. "You must get rest young lady; I don't want you out of bed until after the baby is born. Some women have a difficult time with the last few months, and unfortunately you are one of them, Mrs. Gray. You must make sure to keep up your strength with plenty of beef broth and hearty stews."

"But I have been queasy from the start, and my appetite has not been good," Emily whispered weakly.

"Try your best to have a lot of hearty broth. It has nutrients which are beneficial for you and the baby, and make sure to include whatever fruits and vegetables you have on hand . . . By all means, Mr. Gray, this old house is terribly drafty. It's advisable for you to seal it up at once, and look for other lodging. When the winter comes, it will be impossible the way it is." Dr. Kraus grimaced with concern.

"As for finding other lodging, it will be difficult at the present moment, Dr. Kraus. But I will certainly do my best to seal the drafts, and make sure Emily follows your suggestions." Lawrence showed the doctor out as the weight of the world hung on his shoulders.

"Emily, I think it would be best if you contacted your family. I don't care what becomes of me. I just want you to be safe. Maybe it would be wise for you to return to Fairway. I'll stay on here alone if need be, and when I secure adequate accommodations I will send for you." Lawrence insisted selflessly.

"I'm quite safe here with you, Lawrence. I'll be fine," Emily professed in a murmur as Lawrence exhaled in distress.

"Emily, we can't go on this way for much longer. I hate to bring this up and add further worry, but I've already spent my earnings, and the sum of money Sir Dexter has given me is nearly depleted."

"We'll manage," Emily mumbled before dozing off.

A brutal storm swamped the streets mercilessly. Lawrence awoke to buckets of rain pouring in through the ceiling of Emily's chamber. He situated a giant bucket beneath the leak which began to fill in no time.

Emily stirred as the storm reverberated inside her chamber. "Don't worry, Emily, I've been up for hours, everything is under control," Lawrence echoed.

Emily looked at the rain filling into the bucket in mortification. "Lawrence, to have to pay to fix this leak will be our ruination. This house is completely unmanageable!"

"Emily, it can't possibly be more than what we spent to fix the plumbing glitch. We'll get by don't worry," Lawrence reassured as he changed the bucket. "The roofer has already examined the roof, and is presently outside fixing it before it rains again. Let me go check to see how he's doing."

Lawrence returned after the roofer had finished with a somber expression on his face. Emily asked through chattering teeth, "I see the leak has stopped so how did it go?"

"Emily, I hate to tell you this in your condition, but the roofer has charged us three times the amount of the plumbing, and we're in deeper than I have ever anticipated," Lawrence said in distress.

"Well then, why didn't you argue with the amount he charged you?" Emily asked in anguish. "His prices are obviously way out of hand!"

"Emily, it's freezing out. The poor man had to climb onto the roof, and repair the leak that was frozen with ice . . . Do you have any idea how treacherous it is up there? Consider yourself lucky I even found anyone willing to fix it in this weather."

"I guess you're right, Lawrence, if it's this freezing inside, I can only imagine how unbearable it is outside."

Lawrence positioned Emily's bed as close to the fireplace as safety would allow before he added more coal. He then added a generous shovel of coal to the stove. Emily reprimanded weakly, "Please, Lawrence, remember Joshua has left no provisions for coal, aside from the meager amount he left in the basement. When it runs out that's it, and you've been burning both the stove and fireplace twenty-four hours a day!"

"Emily, I don't want you to catch another chill, you're still recuperating. Don't worry; we will somehow get through this." Lawrence's face blazed like the fire as his eyes sunk deeper into his troubled brow.

Lawrence went to the lower level to check on the supply of coal just as Mr. Lamont walked in from the servants' entrance. Mr. Lamont carried in bundles of the finest cuts of meat, and the most expensive ingredients necessary for his French fare.

"Lawrence, tonight will be porterhouse steaks with scalloped potatoes, and mushrooms," Pierre boasted as he placed the groceries in the kitchen.

Lawrence examined the expensive receipt Pierre handed him. He dreaded the debt he had already incurred with Mr. Schmitt, the town grocer, only to have this added onto his bill. "Mr. Lamont," Lawrence said in an apologetic tone. "Do you think you could purchase a less expensive cut of meat next time?"

"Nonsense, I need to buy only the best for my authentic French fare. If you are so worried, eat a smaller portion, Lawrence. I will not compromise the quality of my food," Mr. Lamont insisted as his pompous accent aggravated Lawrence further.

Miss Bethany appeared just as Pierre got ready to prepare Emily's lunch tray, looking quite pale herself. "Are you feeling all right, Miss Bethany?" Pierre inquired with a keen eye.

"It's not easy doing the work of two servants for the pay of barely one, but I do the best I can." Miss Bethany sighed as she dutifully carried the tray upstairs for Emily.

"Here you are, Emily. Pierre has prepared a hearty broth with the bones from the stew, and some freshly baked French bread."

Emily brought a spoonful to her pale lips before she pushed it aside and grimaced. "I can't eat this soup it's awful; it tastes like dishwater!"

Lawrence did whatever he could to render the old house airtight. Afterward he near collapsed on the armchair which faced the fire across from Emily's bed. "I will think of something, Emily," Lawrence vowed. "Things will get better, trust me. If we can just manage to tough it out this winter, we will be gone from here before next, I promise you, my sweetheart."

"Don't worry about me, Lawrence," Emily insisted courageously. "It matters little if I lay on this bed or another. I am quite comfortable enough beneath the blankets with the warmth of the fire."

"Luckily I've found two old stoves down in the basement. I'll carry them up, and place them to their best advantage. I've tested them, and they're both in proper working order."

"No Lawrence, they will require more coal than we can afford. We're spending money like water, and now you're without a job." Emily fretted while Lawrence tried to hide his anguish.

"Rest Emily, don't worry."

Lawrence got up and stood before the window, and contemplated the spirit of winter. The old oak tree looked like a skeleton without its leaves. Lawrence listened as the wind wailed through its bare branches without mercy. Lawrence looked off in the distance as the sky became edged in gray. On the horizon, a mist became visible from Lawrence's vantage. He watched as the first few snowflakes began to flurry, and then fall quickly, adhering to the earth.

It was at that instant Lawrence looked at his hands, and remembered the words of Lady Sarah with a faraway premonition. "These are obviously the hands of an artist, and an *artist* must paint!"

Lawrence turned toward Emily with a glint of determination in his eyes. "Emily, I know how much you have enjoyed having my portrait of you hanging in the parlor, but perhaps the owner of Rosamond's Gallery will allow me to hang your portrait there to help me get work for a commission. I was hoping you could be an advertisement for my work. But now that Dr. Kraus has told us you must stay home and rest, I will have to depend on the merit of your loveliness alone. I only hope I've done your beauty justice, Emily."

"You will undoubtedly gain both work and recognition, Lawrence. I have faith in your artistry. Besides you can always bring a photograph of me that shows the resemblance. Here take the one of me on my dresser."

"Perhaps I will; that is a brilliant idea," Lawrence exclaimed before leaving Emily to rest.

Chapter Twenty-Five

The Magic Potion

The New England winter arrived to full fruition with the bitterness of cold breath. White and sterile, snow scrambled to the earth, while the winds blew fierce and frigid. Emily sat huddled beneath her blanket, absentmindedly watching the grounds arise to cottony heights from her chamber window.

Lawrence brought up more coal to put in the fireplace from the dwindling supply in the basement. He resumed reading one of his medical books, as his mind wandered with worry and his brow became furrowed.

"What's the matter, Lawrence?" Emily asked.

"I still feel discouraged Rosamond's Gallery was not accepting the work of any new artists at present."

"Don't fret, Lawrence, I'm sure there must be other galleries," Emily bellowed out a succession of deep coughs.

Lawrence sighed. "I know you don't want me to be concerned, Emily, but I don't like the sound of your chest cough. Are you still taking the cough medicine Dr. Kraus prescribed?"

Emily could barely find enough breath to answer, still in the midst of coughing incessantly. "I have already finished with the second bottle of the cough tonic, and it has not helped at all," she weakly uttered as her face appeared bloodless, and her eyes became heavy lidded.

"So much for Dr. Kraus's antiquated cough syrup! I have it in my mind to combine my own herbal remedy for you, considering his didn't do a thing to help."

Emily let out another succession of coughs, which reverberated deeply in her chest. "That's it, I'm going down to the basement to see if I can conjure up a remedy for you! I have to do something positive around here, before I go out of my mind. As for Dr. Kraus he, can retire for all I care!" Lawrence cried out as he stormed off.

Lawrence retreated downstairs, and began to mix herbs he had purchased for brewing tea along with cherry bark. He combined ephedrine, chamomile, and lobelia, each according to their strength and healing properties. Lawrence added a small amount of alcohol which would evaporate considerably by the time the tonic was ready for ingestion.

After his remedy had cured, Lawrence administered the strongly brewed tincture to Emily. "You must take four drops of this five times a day," Lawrence said hopefully. "I will tell Miss Bethany to make certain you take it."

In a matter of days, Emily's blue eyes were twinkling again, and her strength had become renewed. Lawrence became relieved to see Emily was in good spirits, and her condition had improved.

Miss Bethany appeared with a bowl of beef broth, full of potatoes and carrots, with a hunk of crusty bread. Emily devoured the meal with new vigor. Miss Bethany smiled. "That's wonderful, I see you have gotten your appetite back, Emily. It's clear you are on the mend. Your color looks much better as well."

"Thankfully, I'm able to enjoy my food again. Pierre makes the best beef broth I've ever had."

"Is this the same Emily who said it tasted like dishwater a few days ago?" Miss Bethany laughed lightheartedly.

"Please, Miss Bethany, whatever you do, don't repeat that to Pierre, I fear he'll get even with me, and make me eat my words, literally." The girls shared a friendly laugh.

"Thank goodness for your tincture, Lawrence. Your blend of herbs has a calming effect that helped me to sleep through the night. So much for Dr. Kraus! He should be taking lessons from you."

"You know, Emily," Lawrence's face became enlivened with ambition. "The last time I was in town I noticed a sign in the window of Fulton Apothecary. They're looking for an apothecary, and you got me thinking, maybe I should apply for the position. I still remember many of my uncle's age old formulas, and right off the top of my head I can think of new combinations. What do you think, Emily?"

"I think you're a genius, Lawrence. I'm a living proof of your expertise. You'll never know unless you take a chance and try. My grandfather always told my brothers how important it was for them to have a trade. He used to say, 'Do what you know, and before you know it you'll know even more.'"

Chapter Twenty-Six

Fulton Apothecary

As soon as the streets were safe for travel, Lawrence ventured over to Fulton Apothecary. Outside the shop hung a hand-painted sign, "Fulton Apothecary, Established in 1785," with an image of the mortar and pestle beneath it.

Lawrence entered the quaint store, finding the owner Mr. Fulton standing behind a wooden counter. Mr. Fulton was a nice looking gentleman, in his mid fifties, with a full head of black hair, parted in the middle, and combed straight. His posture was erect with strong features; most notable were his eyes, which were intense and as black as coal. The walls behind him were covered with shelves rising up to the ceiling with colorful apothecary bottles artfully displayed.

"Can I help you, Sir?" Mr. Fulton inquired as Lawrence approached with sure steps.

"Hello, my name is Lawrence Gray. I'm applying for the position of an apothecary you're advertising." Lawrence portrayed a demeanor of confidence as he met Mr. Fulton's gaze.

"You seem rather young to be skilled in apothecary," Mr. Fulton remarked as he narrowed his eyes.

"I have had no formal training, Sir. However, an uncle of mine taught me the basics years ago, and the knowledge has stayed with me. I have also studied with a physician for a while. He has given me an entire collection of medical books which I study diligently every day."

"Remarkable, a young man such as you would have an interest in apothecary. I would think it might be too old world for the new generation." Mr. Fulton tilted his head curiously.

"Not at all, I believe strongly in the effectiveness of old world formulas . . . In fact, I have brought a sample of a tonic I devised for my wife for her chest cough when she didn't respond to ordinary measures."

Lawrence handed Mr. Fulton the tincture, and a handwritten formula a common layman could not fathom which contained the exact measurements, and specification for devising it. Mr. Fulton studied the formula with much interest. "Fascinating combination, Mr. Gray, I see you have adhered to all the proper medical standards, and you say this tincture has helped your wife?"

"Oh yes, she is doing wonderfully now, which is a good thing since she is going to have a baby in March."

"I'm impressed with your combination and know-how, Mr. Gray." Mr. Fulton opened his eyes with interest. "Do you think you would be knowledgeable enough to devise an apothecary line for common ailments, as that was my intention in advertising?"

"I have no doubt I can accomplish anything I put my mind on. Nothing motivates me more than medicine, and helping people. In fact, it's my dream to one day become a doctor," Lawrence professed. "I intend to go to medical school as soon as I can afford it."

"Well then, perhaps apothecary could be a good stepping stone. You know apothecaries are considered doctors already for many who cannot afford medical help. In fact many of us perform surgeries, and serve as man midwives, including myself. There is nothing like bringing a baby into the world."

Mr. Fulton walked out from behind the counter to stand beside Lawrence, and speak intimately. "My customers depend on my expertise. That's the reason I want to offer custom-made remedies. Do you think you would be able to alter your formulas to suit particular circumstances, if need be, Mr. Gray?"

"Certainly," Lawrence said full of conviction. "That's the secret to healing people. I believe I'm a natural healer. I have many formulas stored in my memory from my uncle, as well as my own ideas from research, and the instinct of being able to blend healing ingredients in novel ways."

"I have a proposition to make." Mr. Fulton contemplated for a moment. "Mr. Gray, if you come back here next week with a list of the herbs, and the combinations you intend to combine, I will look it over. If you can provide the formulas, you can begin as an apprentice, and you will be generously compensated, Mr. Gray. If your tinctures are effective, there will be no limit on the money you could earn."

"I will get started right away, Mr. Fulton." Lawrence's face glowed with purpose. "I'm willing to stand behind my formulas." The two men shook hands with the cordiality of gentleman.

"Emily." Lawrence beamed on arriving home. "I'm happy to see you looking so well. Just relax by the fireplace. I have found a possible opportunity to work with Fulton Apothecary as a result of the tincture I devised for you. Who would have thought your awful cough could have such a benevolent influence? Mr. Fulton has asked me to make an entire line for every ailment to stock on their shelves if it's to his liking."

"That's wonderful!" Emily beamed. "If my cough has been the seed of your success so be it!" Her rosy cheeks became enlivened.

"I will be a busy man, Emily. Please understand what this entails. I must begin right away while the ambition has me fired up."

Lawrence wasted no time getting started. With quill in hand, and a stack of books, Lawrence devised a variety of combinations for every common ailment from the newborn, to the elderly, from A to Z. He barely came up for air until he had completed the line.

The following week Lawrence arrived at Fulton Apothecary well prepared and versed in the creation of the Fulton Tincture. Mr. Fulton shook his head with satisfaction as he examined Lawrence's handiwork. "I must say I'm impressed, the combinations look good. Why don't we get started, Mr. Gray, and see how it goes. Come in the back, and I will introduce you to my son, Robert Fulton, he is to be your mentor."

Mr. Fulton brought Lawrence into a large room where his son was engaged in weighing herbs on the scale. In his early thirties, Robert Fulton had inherited the same strong looks as his father, with a similar intensity burning in his black eyes.

"Robert, meet Lawrence Gray, he will be under your apprentice for the formulation of the Fulton Tincture. Take a look at the intricate formulas he has penned out."

Robert shook Lawrence's hand enthusiastically. "Welcome to Fulton Apothecary, Lawrence. My father told me all about you, and I'm looking forward to working with you . . . Let me take a look at what you have devised." Robert's eyes lit up with hopeful expectation at the sight of Lawrence's expertise.

Over the next few weeks, the men worked diligently, and with precision on each formula. They hand labeled, and then stocked the shelves as ready.

It was a bad winter for the croup, and mothers began to come in droves in need of relief for their children. Mrs. Anna Kingston, a young mother walked in with worry all over her worn-out face. "Mr. Fulton, can you please recommend something to help my son's cough. Listen to him, he's wheezing, and then he goes into coughing fits that keep him awake all night."

"My new assistant, Lawrence Gray, will custom-blend you a formula. Let him look at the child, and give you his recommendation," Mr. Fulton advised.

Lawrence examined the listless child who was four or five, at most, and altered his original formula for cough by adding rose hips, and a touch of golden seal. "Here Ma'am, give this to your son, four drops, three times a day. In around two days or so he should be doing much better."

Anna Kingston walked in three days later. "As far as the last doctor I saw was concerned my son Ward was on the brink of pneumonia, and he said there was not much he could do to prevent it at this point."

Her soulful eyes welled with gratitude. "The formula you have devised was nothing short of a miracle, Mr. Gray! I can't begin to tell you how many remedies I had already tried. I just had to come in and thank you personally."

Mr. Fulton took Lawrence aside and whispered, "Lawrence, word of mouth is the best advertisement! I know success when I see it. This is the beginning of the most innovative apothecary in all of Salem and the neighboring town of Peabody."

A few days later Mrs. Sophie Woods, a young mother, came into Fulton Apothecary. "Mr. Gray, I was recommended to come here by Mrs. Anna Kingston. She insisted you would be able to recommend a remedy for my twin boys. One has grown so weak he's barely able to eat or drink."

Lawrence examined the sickly pair of twins. The two boys, barely three, were bundled beneath a tattered blanket. Harrison, the younger twin, looked on the brink of death. His eyes were faraway and listless, and in a lethargic trance.

"I'm a widow," Mrs. Woods said despairingly. "I have already spent countless money on my children's care. Nobody has been able to help them. If I spend any more, we will be forced to go hungry, and then I fear I will lose my babies." Tears streamed down the poor woman's face as she tried to silence her desperate sobs.

Mr. Fulton whispered to Lawrence, "Give the woman what she needs without charge."

It was at that juncture Lawrence realized he and Mr. Fulton were kindred spirits. Each possessed empathy, more powerful than the mighty dollar. Filled with gratitude for Mr. Fulton's generosity, Lawrence felt his emotions swell up in his chest.

"Here, Mrs. Woods, take these two bottles for your boys, compliments of Mr. Fulton. Administer two drops of the strengthening tincture in the morning and three drops of the healing tincture in the evening. The combination will work wonders, trust me, and please keep the boys warm and dry."

Within a week's time, the twins were miraculously on the mend. Mrs. Sophie Woods came into the apothecary with her rosy-cheeked children. "Just look at what you have done for these boys, Mr. Gray." She beamed appreciatively.

Lawrence patted Harrison on his curly head. "I see you're doing much better, little fellow."

"Mr. Gray, I just want you to know I have gone straight to the Salem Record in gratitude and praise of Fulton Tincture. They were kind enough to print a testimony on behalf of Fulton Apothecary and their new line of in house tinctures." Mrs. Woods handed Lawrence a clipping of her statement in the Salem Record before she left.

"That's splendid, and a feather in your cap, Lawrence," exclaimed Mr. Fulton as he examined the newspaper.

"Lawrence, nothing could be more effective in terms of advertising. It's no wonder apothecaries and pharmacies throughout New England have been calling the shop all morning, and ordering the line in full. Lawrence, we are going to need a real factory soon to fill all these orders. Fulton Tincture is destined for greatness!"

"All I can say, Mr. Fulton, is thank you so much for giving me the opportunity."

"Thank me!" Mr. Fulton laughed. "Why you are the one who is the genius, Lawrence. All I did was to recognize it and hire you."

Chapter Twenty-Seven

Key to Your Heart

On Christmas day, the tree will be ablaze with a hundred tiny red, white, and blue candles." Lawrence exclaimed as he decorated the evergreen tree positioned by the fireplace.

Miss Bethany carefully removed a selection of ornaments from a dust-covered box. "Mr. Lamont has found these ornaments in the basement. They're from Dresden, Germany."

"They're beautiful, Miss Bethany. Here's a good spot for them." Lawrence strategically positioned the geometric tin stars on the top tier. "I will leave room for your handmade decorations over here."

Miss Bethany began to hang her little nets, cut out of colored paper, and filled with sweetmeats. She added golden apples and walnuts from red bows, which appeared as if they were growing from the tree. Afterward she hung paper faces trimmed with wool and buttons. As a finishing touch, Miss Bethany garnished the tree with gold painted popcorn which gleamed out like shiny copper.

Lawrence was busy hanging waxed angels with fluted wings. "Miss Bethany, I just read in the paper how President Cleveland has added electric lights on the White House Christmas tree. I can only imagine how gorgeous that will look!"

Miss Bethany retorted, "I much prefer a traditional Victorian Christmas. Once we light this tree tomorrow it will be just as beautiful, believe me. Electricity does not hold a candle to these candles."

Lawrence laughed at her play of words. "Miss Bethany, please don't forget to put the bucket of sand behind the tree. I always worry about fire."

"Thankfully I have never had a problem, Lawrence. Now I'll hang the 'sugar plums', cookies, and sweets over here. Lawrence, just think we get to eat all these goodies on the twelfth day. Our tree is no doubt more delicious than the one in the White House. We have the advantage; they don't have Pierre as their baker."

On Christmas day, Emily pushed herself to join the festivities in spite of Dr. Kraus' advice. She wore a burgundy brocade dress with lace trim and rosettes edged along the neckline which Miss Bethany had let out. Her stomach was somewhat camouflaged beneath the generous swirls of fabric. While her golden hair shone out like tinsel from beneath a peacock-feathered hat, which swayed gracefully with her every move.

Emily was seated at the piano playing Christmas hymns. She had just finished playing, "Little Town of Bethlehem," and had begun playing, "We Three Kings." Her lovely voice enlivened the house with good cheer.

Lawrence enjoyed the festivity of Emily's song, pleased to see she was feeling better than usual. The fireplace was set ablaze and draped in garland. Lawrence had diligently sealed off the drafts, and thankfully the day was an unusually temperate one.

After Emily's repertoire ended, Lawrence sat down beside her on the piano bench. "Here, Emily, this is for you, Merry Christmas darling." Lawrence presented two gifts, both beautifully wrapped in gold, and adorned with red and green holiday tinsel.

Emily's face beamed with the dewy radiance of approaching motherhood, intermingled with joy. "Thank you so much, Lawrence. I feel terrible I was not able to make you a gift, since things have been difficult for me lately. It's a miracle I'm up and about. Well, I guess that's the miracle of the Christmas spirit."

"Don't worry, Emily; I'm happy to see you looking so well, and feeling good. Besides giving you a gift is enough of a present for me. Now go ahead open them." Lawrence demanded excitedly.

Emily's nimble fingers undid the wrapping paper of the first gift. She came upon The Opera Bar. "Sweets for my sweetheart, you are about to experience the first candy bar ever manufactured, welcome to the new craze, Emily."

"Am I supposed to sing opera now, or can I taste it?" Emily teased while singing an exaggerated high-pitched note.

"Well, I suppose just a taste won't spoil your appetite . . . While if you continue singing in that key, you might shatter the champagne glasses," joked Lawrence.

Emily undid the wrapper to find three delectable layers of cream filling, consisting of chocolate, vanilla, and strawberry. She took a generous bite. "Delicious, Lawrence, now that is a new sensation! Who makes them?"

"They are manufactured by the Startup Candy Company. Mr. Fulton sells them in the apothecary. They're manufactured in America, but they are becoming popular in other countries as well. In fact, Mr. Fulton can't stock enough of them."

Emily took another bite. "Mmm, delicious, you know how I am around chocolate. Well, I'm eating for two now, so at least I have an excuse!"

"Don't worry; Pierre will have you eating for ten men. He has been down in the kitchen since early morning preparing a traditional holiday turkey, with all the trimmings. I can just imagine the spread he's getting ready for us."

"And poor Miss Bethany has been down there right alongside him polishing the silver and washing the Christmas china. That woman works so hard, and never complains."

"Housework is her job and she's grateful for it . . . Here Emily, now open this one."

Emily opened the tiny box, and found a skeleton key inside. "But, Lawrence, I already have the key to your heart." Emily chuckled. "Tell me, am I supposed to string it on a chain, and wear it around my neck as a memento?" Emily asked with a bright smile.

"Emily, that key holds our future. With the help of Mr. Fulton, I have exciting news. I've found a house for us! We will be out of this hovel by the end of the month," Lawrence excitedly announced.

"Are you serious?" Emily asked joyfully. "That's wonderful, so then it's safe for me to move in my condition?" Emily's eyes gleamed as brightly as the candles illuminating the Christmas tree.

"Dear wife, I don't care if I have to lift and carry you bodily. The new house is completely modernized and furnished. You can redecorate later on if you like, but who knows you might delight in the house just as it is. It has a nursery, and it's situated on a nice piece of property with two giant maple trees in the yard. I have a feeling you're going to just love it, Emily!" Lawrence beamed.

"Lawrence, I'm sure I will adore the house, a house of our own I can barely believe it! This is the best Christmas of my entire life!" Emily radiated with jubilance as she held the key tightly to her chest.

"Emily, I know back at Fairway you were accustomed to living in grand style. Well, as much as I love the new house you certainly can't compare this house to your parents'. They need space to accommodate the servants, and their gala lifestyle. Things are different nowadays . . . Mr. Fulton has informed me the caterer trade has become enormous in the past few years. With all the competition, prices are even lower than they were back in the seventies. People have begun to leave everything to the caterers, and are having their affairs outside of the house. We no longer need a grand ballroom to entertain. Welcome to the modern age, Emily."

"I won't mind one bit not having a grand ballroom. My mother used to get exhausted by all the detail; she would be wracked with fatigue before the ball even began. I certainly don't need that!"

"Don't get the wrong idea, Emily. Our dining room table can easily accommodate over twenty people if need be," Lawrence proudly divulged with a gleam in his eyes.

"Are you sure we can afford a house of that size, especially with a new baby on the way?" Emily asked in apprehension.

"Everything will be fine, don't worry. Mr. Fulton has been very generous in lending me money for the down payment. Fulton Tinctures are growing at a faster pace than we would have ever imagined, so it will be no problem for me to repay him . . . Well, Emily, take your last look at this old house. We will soon be gone."

"Lawrence, not that I'm ungrateful to Joshua Martin, he has been very kind, especially to let us stay for the winter, but just to move into a house that has heat and hot running water, would be more than enough for me. I have been humbled, but that can be a good thing. I have learned to appreciate the many blessings I used to take for granted."

"As for myself, Emily, I have been a nomad ever since the day we lost our farm, moving from place to place, and living on the generosity of others to survive. Now at last we will be settled with a house of our own. Salem is a fine town."

Miss Bethany called out with a tone of holiday cheer, "Dinner is being served."

Lawrence helped Emily up from the piano bench, and led her toward the dining room. The medieval candelabra set ablaze illuminated the room. The flames danced in crimson red, and cast shadows of brilliance in the dimmed room. The ecru tablecloth was embellished with intricate handwork and scalloped edges. Handmade garland generously trimmed the table along the edges, while a wreath made from dried greenery interspersed with roses hung from the mantle.

The Christmas turkey had been roasted to perfection and waited to be carved. It was accompanied by chestnut stuffing, cranberry garnish, sweet potatoes, a fresh ham, apple-stuffed acorn squash, and a spinach-bacon soufflé.

"The best part is I actually have an appetite for once. Just look at this spread. It's too perfect to even touch." Emily raved after their Thanksgiving prayer.

"I have no problem being sentimental when it comes to food. Shall we begin?" Lawrence urged.

"I'm sentimental about everything, Lawrence. I'm even sentimental about being sentimental." Emily gave Lawrence a coquettish smile before indulging in the delicacies.

Chapter Twenty-Eight

Home Sweet Home

Lawrence put out the final embers of the fire at The Joshua Martin House. "I've boarded up the windows for Joshua, so at least the house will be secure . . . We are about to remove ourselves from a way of life known by our forefathers. I hope everyone is ready for the transition because Mr. Fulton's stagecoach has just arrived."

"I know I am, and I will never look back at this old house, trust me," Emily said as she bundled herself in the heaviest attire she could find, while Miss Bethany and Mr. Lamont followed suit.

The fierce winter weather greeted them, frothing up in circles of snowy frost. Lawrence held his blossoming wife close to his side and helped her steady herself along the winter terrain. Emily's winter coat could not close across her distended stomach.

"Step right in," Samuel Fulton's coachman announced as he lent Emily a helping hand. She slowly entered the stagecoach, burdened by the breadth and width of her expanding waistline. Miss Bethany and Pierre Lamont eased their way in afterward.

The blur of the snowstorm made the horses tarry slowly down the ice-laden pathway. "It has been a rough week, as soon as one storm ends, another one begins," Lawrence echoed as he covered Emily with the same shabby woolen blankets Joshua Martin had provided when they first arrived to Salem.

The holiday season heralded Christmas wreathes and decorations on all the houses they drove past. "Bitter cold night," Samuel Fulton droned. "But better Emily should move now before the baby comes. The way Joshua Martin keeps that house." Mr. Fulton shook his head in derision. "I tell you, Lawrence, the man is a gypsy. Having the nerve to rent rooms in that dilapidated house. I hate to imagine what those rooms looked like before you painted them. It's my bet that house had not been painted since his parents had revamped it thirty years ago."

"My painting the rooms was one thing, and it helped make the house livable. But when the cold weather came, it became impossible. It's no wonder Joshua Martin runs down south every winter. When he returns, he will be disappointed to have lost both his tenants and servants, but it was barely inhabitable even for me, let alone a lady, and a newborn."

"I'm a lady too," Miss Bethany exclaimed, "In spite of the fact Joshua Martin never noticed . . . Just the same I hope to never set foot in there again even if he did."

"You can't be serious, Miss Bethany," Emily retorted. "To get involved with a man like Joshua Martin would be worse than being on your own. He must have a lady in every port."

"That just goes to show; sometimes being an old maid is the best option of all." Miss Bethany shrugged her shoulders. "Well, at least I'm moving to better quarters. I usually stay with my sister for the winter, and it's even worse there with all the kids, not to mention I end up doing all the same work, only I don't get paid. I can't thank you and Lawrence enough for offering me employment."

"Are you kidding, Miss Bethany? You are the one doing us a favor. We would be lost without you and Pierre," Emily replied with appreciation.

After a treacherous drive they reached a quaint block, framed by oaks, bare before the darkening sky. Their ancient tree trunks were gnarled and laden with gleaming snow.

"Look up, Emily, this is our new house," exclaimed Lawrence with a lilt.

There, atop of a small hill with a fortress of cobblestone set around the perimeters, stood a pink Victorian. The "painted lady" had a large screened in front porch. Emily pictured lazy summer days sipping lemonade, and fanning her face.

"Lawrence, it's magnificent, I love it!" Emily gushed as they got out of the stagecoach, and Mr. Fulton drove off into the night.

"Emily, this is where my Christmas gift to you comes in handy. Now I will allow you the honor of opening the front door with the skeleton key."

Emily excitedly turned the barrel ajar. The warmth of a real home, chock full of sentimental details welcomed her. There were overstuffed couches with fanciful pillows, and assorted Oriental rugs on the wooden floors. The walls were freshly painted in peach with blush trim, and the fireplace had decorations of Christmas bows and garland.

"Lawrence, I love how it's decorated, it couldn't be more perfect just as it is," Emily exclaimed breathlessly. "I never thought it would be this beautiful!"

"It's wonderful and warm!" Miss Bethany said with a smile as Mr. Lamont stood awestruck, and the house enveloped them all with belonging.

The stately dining room contained a cherry wood table capable of fitting fifteen or more, without the extra leaves. The room had stained glass windows in rich tones of amber and topaz, intermingled with magenta and robin egg blue. It would no doubt look even more exquisite with sunlight streaming in. There were impressive oil paintings with heavy bronze frames displayed on the cream walls. The high ceilings had gilt crested moldings, and an ornate crystal chandelier lit up the room in glittering light.

"Come." Lawrence motioned to Miss Bethany and Mr. Lamont. "Wait until you see the lower level. The quarters down there are quite ample, and I think you will both be very comfortable. Each room has its own theme which coordinates with the overall decorating scheme."

When they arrived to the basement Lawrence pointed out, "Look the separate entrance for bringing in the groceries is conveniently next to the kitchen right down there, and as you can see the servants' quarters are quite spacious and cheerful."

They passed a chamber with a beautiful patchwork quilt on the bed with feminine touches of lace pillows. "I think this chamber will suit Miss Bethany," Lawrence cheerfully announced.

"It's beautiful," Miss Bethany exclaimed as she hung her coat in the closet, and set out to retire for the evening.

Farther down the servants' quarters they came upon a cozy chamber decorated in a hunting motif, with dark furniture against pale walls. The bear head gracing above the brass headboard looked apropos for the male gender.

"And this chamber will suit Mr. Lamont," said Lawrence. "It's right next to the kitchen which is complete with all the cooking utensils he will need."

"A handsome chamber indeed, it couldn't be more perfect. Well, I see Miss Bethany is settled in her chamber. I shall retire to my own, it has been a long day, goodnight," said Pierre.

"Come Emily, now that Pierre and Miss Bethany have settled into their chambers, let me show you around. As you can see it's not a mansion like you are accustomed to, but it's quite ample for a family and a few servants."

"It's more than I ever envisioned, Lawrence! I feel like I'm in the middle of a dream."

Lawrence began his tour through the house that spun in circles. It had hidden fortresses, circular shaped rooms, and balconies with three floors. Emily became overwhelmed when Lawrence gently took her hand into the comfort of his own.

"This might be too much excitement for you in your delicate condition, Emily. I have prepared your chamber, perhaps you would like to go to sleep. There will be plenty of time for you to add your own decorating touches here and there if you like after the baby comes. The main thing now is for you to stay warm and dry, and take care of yourself, Emily . . . Come, I'll show you to your chamber. The master suites are what sold me on the house, they're both very luxurious."

Emily's eyes became enlivened to see her quarters were complete with its own bathroom, fireplace, and dressing area. It had all the comforts she had left behind at Fairway. "Lawrence, being in such splendid style brings to mind my family. If only they could see what a wonderful provider you have become, perhaps they would have had a change of heart about our marriage after all."

"Emily." Lawrence scowled. "Let's be real, our new house would not be sufficient by your parents' standards. Remember it's not a castle, or even a mansion. We have no property to speak of besides the yard which is by no means large. To your parents it would be just an ordinary house."

"Call it what you will, Lawrence. I'll tell you one thing; this house is the grandest Christmas gift I have ever received. The one thing our house has is love, and love is the most extraordinary gift of all."

Emily smiled with gratitude. "Before I go to sleep I wanted to give you a little something I made you for Christmas, come let's sit by the fireplace together."

Emily went into her suitcase to retrieve a memento wrapped in tissue paper. Lawrence carefully unveiled a piece of cardboard with a beautifully scripted poem glued on with tiny cupids painted in gold in each corner. "Lawrence, the best I could offer you is a poem I've written, but it comes from my heart."

Lawrence read it silently with joy in his soul. "*Destiny*, Lilacs smell the sweetest when graced with your breath. Waters are the *deepest* when drenched with your depth. Skies are endless when raised to your height. My heart is filled forever with the *gift* of your delight. Love always, your devoted wife, Emily."

Lawrence held the sentiment lovingly. "How wonderful of you to write such a touching poem for me, Emily, thank you, I intend to frame it, and put it over the mantle in my chamber. It will be a daily reminder of this special moment."

Together they admired the hand carved fireplace as the echo of church bells chimed in the distance. Then they looked into each other's eyes for a soulful moment. Lawrence pressed his lips to Emily's hand before squeezing it joyfully. "Emily, just think we will be ringing in the New Year soon; a new house, with my new wife, and a baby on the way, such wondrous dreams are coming to fruition. Life has a way of taking us on a journey we are not even aware of. The roads can be treacherous at times, especially when you're waiting in a carriage with an injured horse."

Lawrence smiled wryly," Now our path is finally clear. Who would have ever thought we had this in store when we were like fugitives on the run?"

"Lawrence, just the thought of how close I came to marrying Sir Dexter, an immoral man I had no feelings for makes me cringe inside. It's strange how one man's transgression can become another man's future. Life is so unpredictable. Fate comes in many disguises." Emily held Lawrence's hand tightly with the power it emitted giving her hope and strength.

"Emily, my sweet angel, we have found happiness, and I'm grateful for that. It didn't come easy, and it's not unblemished . . . When I think of how our leaving must have hurt Mallory, my heart breaks for her. Sir Dexter is a despicable excuse for a man, but Mallory was a gentle soul. I feel certain she'll never get married now after this final blow. I feel badly about that, but even so, I would not want to sacrifice my life just so Mallory could have a husband."

"Lawrence, Sir Dexter has betrayed us all. You, me and Mallory, only Mallory doesn't know it. To think she actually believes we've betrayed her haunts me as well. I try to put it behind me, but I must admit I think about it often. The horrible things she screamed out to me from her carriage the day we fled Newport will never leave my mind! But Dexter poisoned her with his lies, and there's nothing we can do about it without making things worse for us. Lawrence, in spite of the fact Mallory had plans to marry you, I loved her like a sister, and it saddens me to know I will never have her friendship again . . . I can only hope one day Mallory will find it in her heart to forgive us for what we are innocent of. But we had no choice except to live a lie, and now we must look ahead."

Chapter Twenty-Nine

The Ides of March

Emily screamed out in the middle of the night in excruciating pain as she went into labor. Miss Bethany scrambled for the hot water, and towels to assist Miss Hillary Dunn, the midwife Lawrence had on standby.

"Come on, Emily, start pushing." Miss Dunn urged.

Emily's pale face contorted as she bore down, while clutching onto Miss Bethany's hand. After several hours of grueling labor, Emily pushed down with every ounce of strength her fatigued body could muster. Finally out came the redheaded crown before the emergence of a healthy eight-pound boy.

As soon as the baby was washed off, Emily held the infant close to her breast and began to nurse. "He's beautiful!" Emily gushed proudly, as she overlooked the reminder of his redheaded inheritance in a moment of supreme joy.

"The baby has come. It's a boy!" Miss Bethany rushed down the dark hallway, and knocked elatedly on Lawrence's chamber.

Bleary-eyed from sleeping, Lawrence rushed to see the baby. Upon his entry into Emily's chamber Miss Hillary Dunn proudly announced, "Congratulations! Mr. Gray, you are the father of a healthy baby boy. Mother and child are doing splendid."

Lawrence rushed over to Emily and the infant, setting his sights upon the mirror image of Sir Dexter Lund already. From the newborn's fair skin down to his inclination toward freckles and flaming red hair, even the newborn's features had the same irregularity as Sir Dexter Lund's.

"The baby is a beautiful boy, Emily. Have you made a decision on the name yet?" Lawrence said in spite of the likeness he displayed.

"I'm still torn. I definitely would have named him after my father, if things were different. I was thinking maybe we should name him Jake after my grandfather? He looks like a Jake. You can decide the middle name."

"I think Jake would suit the little fellow well." Lawrence smiled full of pride. "I propose we use William for the middle name after my father, so there we have it, Jake William Gray, a noble sounding name!"

"Miss Emily, you must rest now and nap whenever you can," advised Miss Dunn. "Motherhood can be very trying. Come, let us leave her in peace." Hillary Dunn handed the baby over to the governess Miss Fanny Ray, a mature, dowdy type who was naturally maternal.

Lawrence kissed Emily's flushed forehead in exhilaration before leaving her to slumber. As soon as her eyes were shut, she fell sound asleep.

The season changed from winter into the first sweet stirrings of spring. The temperature had become warmer. Tulips began to slowly lift their weary heads up from the incubating earth. The trees had sprouted their first shoots of green and inkling of fruits while birds flew through the air with tunes of merriment.

Lawrence looked outside the parlor, and watched as a red robin perched on the maple tree out back. He contemplated the baby's birth in unison with the renewal of springtime. All was at peace when Miss Bethany walked into the parlor with the Salem Record in hand, and a big smile on her homespun face.

"Here, Lawrence, I have a surprise for you and Emily."

Lawrence grasped the paper only to see a formal announcement of the baby's birth which Miss Bethany had placed into the Salem Record. "Miss Bethany, why would you put this in here without asking us first?" Lawrence inquired in a hysterical tone.

"I didn't mean any harm, Mr. Gray. I apologize if I was out of line. I just thought it would be a nice memento for you and Emily to save for the future," Miss Bethany timidly answered, averting Lawrence's penetrating gaze.

"Very well," Lawrence tore the page out emphatically. "I know you meant no ill intent, but not a word about this to Emily. New mothers don't always like to advertise their creations. To Emily, childbirth is a private matter."

Lawrence shook his head in despair as he read the birth announcement. "Look what the *stork* brought in! Jake William Gray, the eight-pound son of proud parents Lawrence and Emily Gray, of Salem." Accompanying the announcement was a photograph of the baby from his baptism at the Lady of Our Lord Church.

On her way over to Sir Dexter's office, Lady Violet neatly folded the Salem Record inside her attaché in addition to last minute paperwork which needed to be finalized before their June wedding. She sat down with Sir Dexter when out tumbled the newspaper turned to the birth announcement. It immediately caught Dexter's keen eye.

"What's this?" Sir Dexter inquired in shock.

"The Salem Record, I've had this subscription since my college days. I like keeping abreast with the small town news. Why don't you take a look?" Lady Violet retorted in a clipped tone.

Sir Dexter became spellbound by the birth announcement and the baby's photo. Jake's singular face looked just like his own when he had been an infant, along with the same shock of red hair, discernable even through the black and white photo.

Lady Violet exclaimed in contempt, "Can you imagine Lawrence and Emily having the nerve to announce their out of wedlock conception? This baby would have been illegitimate, if Lawrence had not jilted Mallory and married Emily. For heaven's sake, they're capitalizing on their shotgun wedding!" Lady Violet cried out. "Dexter, can you believe they're brazen enough to try to make a respectable life for themselves in Salem no less, my very own hometown? The people of Salem must be alerted at once to their falsity!"

"You will do no such thing, Lady Violet!" Sir Dexter's voice rose with the bravado of an opera singer depicting a tragedy.

"And why wouldn't you want me to?" Lady Violet asked with a snarl. "They've insulted you beyond reproach, Dexter!"

The veins of Sir Dexter's neck strained against his pale skin in undulations of blue as he exclaimed, "Because they have already paid their price and have suffered against all odds to attain their position. I don't seek to harm them any further. They have their life in Salem, and I shall have mine right here with you, my dear Miss Violet."

Lady Violet's piercing eyes became full of ill will. "Dexter Lund, I say you're still in love with the girl! Whom do you think you are fooling? Just look at the way you are mooning over her child, it's positively sickening! You love Emily so much you're even in love with her bastard son!" Lady Violet shouted in wild accusation.

"In love with Emily, nonsense, how could you say something so preposterous?"

"Why else would you seek to protect Emily if you didn't still have feelings for her? You can't fool me, I saw the way you looked at her baby, Dexter; it was as if you saw favor in the child." Lady Violet glared like a deranged gypsy about to put a curse on him.

"The baby is not to blame for the actions of his parents," Sir Dexter insisted magnanimously.

"Please stop lying to me, Dexter!" Lady Violet ranted wildly while her black hair flew in the air like venomous snakes ready to bite. "It's obvious you still love Emily!"

"I have never loved Emily. Why on earth should I now? It's you I love!" Dexter professed in a less than convincing tone as he surreptitiously glanced down at Lady Violet's impressive financial statement, strewn on his desk.

"I fear you only love yourself, Dexter!" Lady Violet snapped back.

"What kind of an awful thing is that to say, darling?"

"Well, just look at you! Emily has betrayed both you and your sister by her illicit affair with Lawrence. Then they run off and make a new life for themselves in Salem, very successfully I might add . . . As if the last article of Lawrence Gray's success in saving the 'Wood Twins,' in the December issue was not enough! Healer, phooey . . . fornicator, heartbreaker is a more accurate way to describe him! To think Lawrence has actually gained recognition in apothecary without having the proper schooling, and then ingratiated himself with the Salem society makes me sick!" Lady Violet shouted scathingly.

"Why let it bother you? It has nothing to do with us now," Sir Dexter retorted with a shrug of his shoulders.

"Dexter, if you are so emotionless to all this, then perhaps your feelings for me are equally as shallow . . . If there is one thing I detest it's a man without a backbone. Aren't you even angry, Dexter? I for one think it's abominable Emily and Lawrence should get away free of blame, when they have humiliated you!"

"What they do with their lives does not affect me now. You should know I'm not a vindictive person, Violet."

Lady Violet cut in disdainfully. "Well, that certainly surprises me! You seemed vindictive enough when they ran off, and jilted you and Mallory. You had plenty of derogatory things to say about them then! You might as well have stood on the pulpit, and made an announcement at The Old Church for all the people you told. So now, when it has come out Lawrence and Emily are the worst kind of social climbers, and are weaseling their way into the upper crust of Salem's society, you forget all about how they disgraced you. Flaunting their baby no less and you have no backlash!"

Lady Violet's dark eyes glared with malevolence larger than her ignorance to the truth. "That could not be humanly possible, Dexter, not unless you're still in love with Emily! I don't appreciate being taken on the rebound to begin a life with you, only to have this blatant display staring me in the face!"

Sir Dexter adjusted his starched collar. "Violet, let us get one thing straight. I've already told you agreeing to marry Emily was my parents' coaxing. Furthermore, I didn't ask for your hand in marriage on the rebound. I asked to marry you from my heart," Sir Dexter insisted.

"Well, I have it in my mind to call upon Emily the next time I'm in Salem," Lady Violet said with conviction.

"Lady Violet, promise me you will do no such thing! It will be of no earthly good to confront either Emily or Lawrence. What is done is done! Besides Emily has done me a favor since I would not have had the heart to turn her out, and would have been forced to honor my parents' match. But now we are free to marry, can't you see, what a blessing in disguise what she did has become?" Sir Dexter smiled crookedly.

"Are you always this selfish, Dexter?" asked Lady Violet with a scowl. "What about your poor sister Mallory? What good has she benefited by being jilted for the second time? She has barely even left the house since that day, and has become so thin and melancholy; no man will want her now! I will tell you one thing; I don't relish the idea of having your old maid sister come to live with us when your parents can no longer look after her. Mallory has become so pathetic; she is of no earthly use to anyone! We are ultimately going to be the one saddled with Mallory. Why should we have to make up for Lawrence's broken vow to her! Is there no justice to be had?"

Chapter Thirty

The Telegram

Lady Violet arrived in Salem on Friday morning of the Easter weekend. After a brief visit at her parents' house, she ventured over to the Gray's residence. Dressed in a somber black dress and an ostentatious black hat with peacock feathers, Lady Violet left her calling card with Miss Bethany.

Miss Bethany found Emily playing piano in the parlor. "Emily, there's a lady who is here to see you, and has left her card."

Emily curiously retrieved the flower-edged card from the silver tray when she set her unsuspecting sight upon the name of Violet Wexler written in calligraphy. "Miss Bethany," Emily whispered as her face contorted in displeasure. "Of all people, she is the 'Lady Violet' I've told you about!"

"Oh dear," Miss Bethany exclaimed. "I can tell her you're not accepting guests at the moment."

"Miss Bethany, although I hesitate to invite her in I fear the ramifications if I send her away. There is no choice but to show her into the parlor, and please bring in some hot tea at once."

Emily stopped playing her sentimental tune as Lady Violet entered with a pompous demeanor. Emily arose from her piano bench wearing a peach day dress appliquéd with gold trim with leg-o-mutton sleeves. Emily's face became strained as the very sight of Lady Violet showing up in her parlor made her jaw clench.

"Lady Violet," Emily enunciated her name as if it was a noxious weed to be plucked from her household.

"For what honor do I owe this unexpected visit?" Emily asked in a brusque tone.

"Well, are you going to invite me in, Mrs. Gray, or am I just going to stand here by the doorway?" Lady Violet asked with her head held up high, while the peacock feathers of her black hat menaced with ill will.

"By all means sit, and help yourself to tea," Emily tersely offered, avoiding her chilling stare.

Lady Violet removed her shawl, and filled herself a cup of tea from the teapot Miss Bethany had set down. Lady Violet lounged back, and took a sip with an air of superiority. "You don't mind if I smoke, do you, Emily?"

Lady Violet gave Emily no time to answer as she took out a cigarette, and struck it aflame. She inhaled a huge drag, and spoke with smoke filled words in a condescending tone.

"I see you and Lawrence have found a suitable house for yourselves, quite remarkable I may add."

"Yes we have. I'm glad to hear you recognize it as such," Emily said guardedly.

"I recognize a lot of things for what they are, Mrs. Gray." Lady Violet went inside her attaché to take something out. "This is a telegram Sir Dexter sent me last summer. I think perhaps I should read it to you, Emily. It's sort of unfinished business."

Emily trembled as Lady Violet began reading it, fearing the words it beheld.

"It is dated September 15, 1895, the telegram reads, "Dear Lady Violet, Miss Emily Reed has betrayed me, and Lawrence has deceived my sister Mallory. My engagement to her, as well as Lawrence's engagement to Mallory can no longer be honored. Emily has admitted she is carrying Lawrence Gray's child. It is imperative I see you at once, your friend, Sir Dexter Lund."

Lady Violet turned the telegram around to Emily to reveal its authenticity. "As you can see every word I have just read is there."

As soon as Emily digested the insidious lies, was as soon as Lady Violet neatly folded the telegram and placed it back inside her attaché.

Lady Violet's shrewd eyes focused on Emily like a vulture getting ready to devour its prey.

"So you see, Emily, I was figuring you might be interested in getting the telegram for your own safe keeping. After all, if I was to go to the Salem Record with this little tidbit, I'm certain Miss Lily Smith who writes Salem Town Talk would be most appreciative for my input."

Lady Violet chuckled maliciously. "I don't think the consequence would be favorable to your position in Salem society, Emily, and I'm sure you agree. Salem is a town of church-going citizens, to be assured." A ring of gray smoke smote Lady Violet's words with vengeance.

Emily became stunned at the prospect of being blackmailed to protect her from a lie. She shifted in her seat, and tried to maintain her composure while her blue eyes gleamed with rage.

"So you mean to tell me, Lady Violet, you have come here to blackmail me? It can't be money you're after. I'm quite certain you have your fair share of it. Pray tell, please make your intentions clear at once."

"Yes, you're quite correct, Mrs. Gray. It's not money I desire. Sir Dexter has sent me to retrieve the three-carat engagement ring he has given you. Since you're no longer associated with Sir Dexter, you shall have no more use of it."

Emily's blue eyes turned as cold as ice. "If Sir Dexter wanted the ring returned, why wouldn't he have come here and asked me for it himself?"

"Sir Dexter thought it would be more appropriate for me to broach the subject . . . After all since I am to be his future wife, Sir Dexter felt it was only fitting I should claim it. I must insist on the ring's safe return at once," Lady Violet vehemently demanded as she put out her cigarette on the saucer of her china cup, and remnants of ash flittered in the air.

"I find that most peculiar. When Lady Sarah gave me the ring she told me once you are given a Lund heirloom it belongs to you forever . . . I assure you there is no diamond shortage in the Lund family, Lady Violet," Emily quipped.

"Maybe not, but I'm beginning to suffer from a shortage of patience." Lady Violet's lips became terse as she snarled. "Lady Sarah might have said that to you, Emily, but it was before you betrayed Sir Dexter. I assure you she's presently in a different frame of mind. Let us be reasonable; we are both ladies of modern day ethics. Considering what has transpired between you and Sir Dexter, I am now the rightful heir of the wedding ring! It's only proper for you to return the ring at once!" Lady Violet demanded with annoyance.

"Mrs. Gray, I would not want to be forced to rehash an unpleasant circumstance that would upset your residence at Salem," Lady Violet declared in a threatening tone.

"And Sir Dexter knows you have brought his telegram with you for ammunition?" Emily asked with a stern brow.

"Emily, Sir Dexter is a lawyer, even if he did, do you think he would be naive enough to have me state something like that on his behalf? Please, Emily, I don't have all day to quip about this, I would like you to present the ring before I lose my patience, and bring the telegram over to the Salem Record, and then make a copy of it to pass around my parents' church on Sunday. After all, the town of Salem should be warned, especially Samuel Fulton. It would not be good for his business to have a man without character working for him. What would the customers at Fulton Apothecary say?" Lady Violet asked with a sneer.

"Excuse me, Lady Violet," Emily retorted in hesitation. "I will comply with your wishes, but only if you agree to be out of my life forever. Never will you be granted entry into my house again!"

Lady Violet grinned mockingly. "Be assured it's not often I travel to this side of town."

Emily excused herself to her chamber, and went inside a satin pouch inside her drawer where she had secured the diamond heirloom. She looked at it with deep remorse at having to forfeit it. Emily walked back into the parlor, and took the ring out of the pouch, just long enough to satisfy Lady Violet's acquisition. Without any further ceremony, Lady Violet opened up her attaché, and exchanged the incriminating telegram for the family heirloom.

Emily echoed in a terse tone as she turned her back, and her uninvited guest showed herself out. "I trust that should satisfy both you and Sir Dexter. If you have any plans on harassing me any further, I will counterattack. I warn both you and Sir Dexter; I will relinquish nothing more to keep my good name!"

Just then, the governess carried Jake into the parlor for his two o'clock feeding. Lady Violet glanced over at the baby with a keen eye as his shock of red hair beckoned attention. Emily took the baby from Fanny Ray, and held it close to her breast before beginning to nurse.

Emily felt traumatized by Lady Violet's confrontation. The sunlight gleamed in with fresh streams of honey, while inside all Emily saw was remorse and darkness. She counted the moments for Lawrence to come home from work as the day dragged on with unpleasantness.

By the time Lawrence arrived home from the apothecary, he found Emily sitting on the couch in the parlor staring blankly into space. Her complexion looked ashen, while her blue eyes were shadowed with gray circles beneath them.

"Emily, my sweetness," Lawrence walked over to kiss her hello. "Are you feeling all right? You look a little peaked."

"Look," she cried out, as she presented the telegram Lady Violet had brought in ill tidings.

Lawrence read it in horror. "Where ever did you get this?"

"Lady Violet paid me a visit today, and threatened me with this, saying she would go straight to the Salem Record if I didn't relinquish the engagement ring Sir Dexter had given me."

"You gave her back the ring I trust?" Lawrence asked in panic.

"Yes," wept Emily. "As much as I didn't want to return the ring, I was willing to do anything to be rid of Lady Violet, and the incriminating telegram forever. I had no choice, Lawrence. I cannot believe Sir Dexter would be low enough to send Lady Violet that telegram in the first place, and then send her to retrieve the ring after what happened . . . They have obviously learned of our whereabouts from all of the exposure we've been getting lately. I guess it must have killed Sir Dexter to see how well all has turned out for us . . . Lawrence, that was the most beautiful ring I have ever seen," Emily professed tearfully. "And I felt I deserved to keep it after how Sir Dexter compromised my honor, and then heartlessly turned us both out. Not to mention the ring was an heirloom, and they don't make rings like that anymore. It looked so perfect with my wedding band beneath it." Emily paused with a heavy heart.

Lawrence held her lovingly. "Emily, my dearest, thankfully things are getting better each day. I can well afford to buy you your own wedding ring. In fact, I was planning on it . . . They sell vintage rings in a shop right next to the apothecary. I will put a deposit on one at once to make up for this further insult. Not to mention it would not be fitting for you to be wearing an engagement ring I didn't buy you after what happened."

"That would be wonderful, Lawrence, but I don't expect you to squander your earnings on one as extravagant. A modest ring will suit me equally as well."

Emily regained her color when Lawrence took the telegram, and burned it in the fireplace. He let it burn into fiery flames. They watched as it became reduced to only ash before their satisfied sights.

"There, that should give you comfort, Emily. I'm proud you did what you did. It was the right thing. Let Lady Violet have the ring. The two of them deserve each other. Any man who would send a woman to retrieve an engagement ring after what he did is worse than a coward. And to resort to using blackmail as a route, we're both civil, reasonable people, Emily. Sir Dexter and Lady Violet are both detestable, and we don't need to incite anymore of their scandal . . . We have made a new beginning. I've worked very hard to make a good name for myself. So I'm happy you realized jewelry is only material." Lawrence kissed her tearstained cheek.

"It probably just killed Lady Violet that I should have even a piece of her inheritance. For a woman to be so heartless to one of her own is unconscionable. Lady Violet got what she wanted, and has no further business here. If she is ever to have the audacity to come here again, I have instructed Miss Bethany to send her straight away!

Chapter Thirty-One

Family Heirloom

Lawrence and Emily retired early into their perspective chambers. Emily surprised Lawrence by putting on the white satin gown from her trousseau with the tiny dove embossed on the shoulder. She knocked upon the door of his chamber feeling flushed with anticipation as a rosy glow enlivened her face.

Lawrence opened the door only to find Emily standing there, a demure vision in white. She radiated with an inner light. Her stomach had gone down considerably since Lawrence last saw her wear the gown on their wedding night. She now appeared as a sleek woman about to become his very own. Her blue eyes blazed against her porcelain skin like the sky at dawn.

Lawrence's eyes devoured her loveliness and sanctity with a tender expression. "My Emily, let me see how beautiful you look."

Lawrence tenderly kissed the nape of her neck before smothering her lips with his own. He hungrily skimmed his strong hands across the satin folds of her fabric. Emily submitted to his ardent desires, and molded to his passions.

"I love you, Emily, my sweet darling," Lawrence whispered in her ear while gently kissing her neck. He gave her sweet shivers of sensation, as silken as the satin she was about to shed.

"Thank you for being patient with me, Lawrence. I know you've waited for me to put this nightgown on again for eight months, but considering I just had Jake three months ago, it hasn't been that long at all. I finally feel myself again."

"I'm so glad to hear that. Come Emily, I want to lay with you and hold you in my arms." Lawrence's eyes burned blackly with ardor.

They reclined on his bed, and gazed into each other's eyes. Lawrence kissed her lips again as waves of sensation enfolded over them like the sea. They submitted to their desire in a delirium of pure delight. The summer air filtered in through the window, as they clutched onto one another in the heat of their passion.

Their moist flesh pressed against one another while their breath became the single flame of their lives entwined. They became encompassed in bliss, flesh to flesh, heart to heart; with no distinction between the two. Without boundaries, Lawrence's manliness, and Emily's femininity provided what the other lacked. They were at last lovers of each other, of the earth, of the night, and their future as well as their past. They nestled in the safety of each other's gift of intimacy. They were at last truly one.

Lawrence walked into Ralph's Jewelers to pay the last increment on the vintage wedding ring he had purchased for Emily. He counted the bills one by one. "Here you are, Mr. LaRose, it's all there."

The mustached jeweler went into his safe to retrieve the platinum engagement ring, of comparable size to the one Emily had been forced to forfeit.

Mr. LaRose opened the ring box to confirm the contents. "You got a good deal, Mr. Gray, this ring is worth three times what you paid for it . . . As I told you I fortunately got a good buy on it, that I was able to pass on to you."

Lawrence examined the flawless stone which looked fit for royalty. "It's a beauty; I wanted to surprise my wife with it. I came up with the balance just in time. Tonight is our one year wedding anniversary, and we'll be celebrating with a night out on the town."

That evening, Lawrence and Emily situated themselves upon the red velvet cushions at the Claremont Opera House before the show began. Lawrence looked dapper in his black satin tuxedo and white shirt. He had slicked his thick black hair beneath his combed-wool top hat. Emily was wearing a magenta velvet gown trimmed with silver paillettes and steel-bead appliqué. Her hair had been arranged in a festoon of curls, which enlivened her serene blue eyes. A single strand of cultured pearls adorned her swan throat.

Emily wiped her eyes with her handkerchief. "The opera always makes me cry. The singing and the costumes are so beautiful, Lawrence!"

Lawrence and Emily shared a loving glance, as the opulent atmosphere enveloped them. Lawrence placed her hand within the warmth of his own. "Those are good tears, my sweetheart. It shows you have a good heart." He lovingly kissed her gloved hand, as they luxuriated with the gleam of newlyweds.

During the intermission, the Grays partook in a bit of friendly conversation with Harrison and Victoria Clarion, upper class acquaintances.

"Emily and I are off to a French restaurant after the opera for a late dinner. Perhaps we can have a drink with you and Victoria at another time."

"French food, oh yes, crepes are my favorite. I definitely recommend Le Fleur in Boston for truly fine French cuisine. Perhaps Victoria and I will join you there one evening to dine. For now, it was nice to have a glass of champagne with you."

Lawrence and Harrison shook hands as Emily and Victoria gave each other a polite curtsy as they all departed to their seats.

After the opera ended, Lawrence chivalrously helped Emily on with her mink stole. He then ordered their driver. "You can take us to Cafe Du Village now, Edward, for our dinner reservation."

They drove off into the cool October night, reminiscent of their wedding night beneath the stars the year before. "I can hardly believe we have been married a whole year already, Lawrence. What a difference a year makes, now look at us, first we were off to the opera, and now we're going for French food at Cafe Du Village. We have to count our lucky stars."

"Emily, when I think of our wedding celebrants compared to our present acquaintances at the opera, I can't help but think the contrast is quite remarkable."

"Maybe so, but I would never trade our wedding day to be with the upper class society. Having ten minutes of conversation with Harrison and Victoria Clarion was more than enough for me." Emily giggled mischievously. "You know me, Lawrence; I never did care for formality. I shall never dine at Le Fleur for fear of running into the Clarions there.

You have to admit it, Lawrence, Joshua's friends really know how to have a good time . . . I hate to say it, but we'll never have another night like that with our present social circle."

"Are you thinking what I'm thinking?" Emily laughed.

"Just what are you thinking, dear wife?" Lawrence asked in amusement while his eyes twinkled.

"I'm thinking maybe we should have the driver take us to Joshua Martin's favorite haunt, Floes. Who knows maybe we'll even find him there." They both had a hearty laugh.

They soon arrived at the elegant French restaurant set alongside a quaint cobblestone street. "Emily, this restaurant is renowned for its impeccable service, rare vintage wines, and superb cuisine."

The maitre d' Andre greeted them with finesse. "Mademoiselle, Monsieur Gray, I have your table ready. Come right this way." With his head held high and proud, Andre led them to a cozy corner alongside a hearty plant which provided the ambiance of an outside garden.

Lawrence proceeded to order their fare. "We will begin with a bottle of Chateau Lafitte-Rothschild 1880, and then we will have two onion soups, two garden green salads with house dressing, and the bouillabaisse fish platter for two."

The white gloved waiter returned to pour them glasses of the fine bouquet. Before they drank the wine, Lawrence lifted his glass. "Emily, I would like to make a toast."

Lawrence gazed at Emily beneath the flame of a candle lit aglow on their circular table. Emily held her glass of wine in anticipation as Lawrence spoke in a honey-coated voice, rich with feeling. "In honor of our first wedding anniversary, I toast to you with all my love and devotion."

Lawrence clanked his glass to hers. "And here's to our future, my darling wife, this is just the beginning."

Lawrence went into his coat pocket, and took out the black velvet ring box. "Here Emily, this is a special anniversary present for you."

Emily's heart pounded with the excitement Lawrence had been anticipating ever since he first set his sights on the rare vintage piece. Emily opened the box and gasped in awe. "Lawrence, how did you get the ring back?" Her face became a portrait of shock.

"Get it back?" Lawrence asked in confusion.

"This is the very same ring Sir Dexter had given me!" Emily cried out.

"What are you talking about?" Lawrence sounded flabbergasted.

"Look at it! See this baguette, this is the one that had been replaced, it has a slightly different cast from the other. I remember that distinctly."

Lawrence studied the ring in wonder as it began to look more familiar than he had first thought. "Are you positive, Emily? I knew it looked similar, but what are the chances of it being the same ring?"

"I'm quite certain. I'd recognize this ring anywhere, Lawrence. It's exquisite and flawless! How in the world did you get it?" Emily asked as Lawrence placed it onto her slender finger.

"I purchased it fair and square at Ralph's Jewelers. It might have taken me six months to pay for it, but it's all yours now, Emily, fair and square. You shall have no fear of anyone coming to reclaim it now! Ralph told me a young widow in desperate need of money came in to sell it. That was how I was able to afford the ring. Otherwise it would have been too exorbitant to even consider."

"A young widow by the name of Lady Violet to be more accurate," Emily coolly retorted. "Come to think of it the day of her infamous visit, Lady Violet was out of synch with the season. Her black dress could have definitely been misconstrued for somber weeds, but obviously it matched her black heart!"

"Emily, I can't believe that Lady Violet would confiscate the ring from you only to sell it to Ralph's at a fraction of its worth. It's now become obvious she demanded it back more out of malice than anything else. We both know money is something she has far enough of already. How malicious can someone be, blackmailing you no less?"

"Talk about being malicious. Imagine Lady Violet claiming to be a widow . . . Poor Sir Dexter she has killed him off without even a proper burial, and then sold the profits already." Emily laughed triumphantly as she admired the prized heirloom.

"Well, we have outfoxed her now, Emily." Lawrence smiled in elation. "Emily, I have other good news. The portrait of you I entered into the contest at the New England Art League, Rosamond's Gallery told me about is one of the finalists. They will be making the final decision on the winner on Saturday, and I think I have a fair chance."

"That's wonderful news, Lawrence! Whether you win or not is immaterial. Being nominated as a finalist is enough of an honor."

"Well, let's not forget, Emily, you were my inspiration, and with a model like you, greatness naturally occurs." Lawrence beamed.

Lawrence picked up the telephone as soon as it rang on Saturday afternoon, waiting for the verdict. "Hello, may I speak to Mr. Gray, please."

"Speaking," Lawrence retorted.

"Hello, Mr. Gray, this is Mr. Kilmer, president of the New England Art League. I'm proud to inform you your portrait of Emily has won first place in our contest. As our prize stated, along with your cash reward, your painting will be on display at the Massachusetts Museum of Art, congratulations, Mr. Gray."

"Thank you so much, that's wonderful news!" Lawrence gushed with elation.

"Don't thank me; thank yourself for your excellent contribution to the art world. You are a remarkable artist, Mr. Gray," Mr. Kilmer continued in an enthusiastic tone. "In fact, the renowned Herbert Lustick was one of the judges. Mr. Lustick became so moved by your rendition of Emily he asked if he could paint a portrait of your wife himself. If it's all right with your wife, I can arrange for Mr. Lustick to start her portrait in the spring."

"The renowned Herbert Lustick," Lawrence exclaimed with awe. "My wife will no doubt be delighted! I'll tell her the good news at once, and then we can arrange for the sitting."

Lawrence exuded in a joy twofold as he found Emily sitting in the library with Jake on her lap, reading him Little Red Riding Hood. "And then the big bad wolf . . ."

"Emily, my beauty," Lawrence interrupted excitedly. "I have good news. Mr. Kilmer of the Art League just called, and I won first place, and along with a cash award, my portrait of you will be on display at the Massachusetts Museum of Art. Emily, I credit your beauty with my recognition."

"Congratulations, that's fantastic!" Emily exclaimed. "But don't be modest, Lawrence, it's your talent, not my beauty, be assured. I'm so proud of you, and so is Jake."

"Da Da," Jake shouted, as he outstretched his arms. Emily, and Lawrence giggled with amusement.

"There's more good news, Emily, that attests to your beauty. The renowned Herbert Lustick was one of the judges, and he desires to paint his own portrait of you this spring," Lawrence said jubilantly.

"Herbert Lustick, paint me? Are you serious?" Emily asked with surprise.

"Yes, we both know that's truly an honor, Emily. Think of all the others who are waiting in the wings to pay for his services, the Lunds for example, need I say more. And we don't have to pay one red cent for the privilege."

Chapter Thirty-Two

The Reception

Mr. Lustick's full head of white hair gave him a distinguished presence as he stood on the porch. "Please come in, Mr. Lustick. Mrs. Gray is in the parlor waiting for you." Miss Bethany led the way.

Mr. Lustick came upon Emily looking ethereal in an ecru lace dress, complimented by a cameo broach. "Hello, Mrs. Gray, as you might have guessed, I'm Herbert Lustick."

Emily got up from the couch to curtsy as Mr. Lustick tipped his top hat. "I must say, Mrs. Gray, you are even more enchanting than I envisioned. It's not often an artist has a subject as fair."

"Thank you, Mr. Lustick," Emily said blushingly. "I'm honored by your request to paint me, and to finally meet you after all the wonderful things I've heard about you."

"It's a delight to meet you as well, Mrs. Gray. When your housemaid told me you were waiting in the parlor for me, I was hoping you have not been waiting since last spring." With his smile, Mr. Lustick's face shrunk like the pleats of an accordion. "I know I promised to come last spring, but 1898 snuck up on me all too quickly. I apologize for the delay, so here I am a year behind schedule which is the usual."

"That's to your credit, Mr. Lustick. I hear your work is in high demand. If you don't mind my asking, did you ever get around to painting portraits of the Lund family?" Emily offhandedly inquired.

"Do you mean the Lund family of Newport, Rhode Island?" Herbert Lustick asked in surprise.

"Yes, that Lund family, I know of no other."

"Well yes, actually I have recently finished with the new addition to the Lund family, Miss Lady Violet." Herbert Lustick raised his brows in disapproval. "I shall say no more, other than painting you will be a welcome change, Mrs. Gray."

One year soon became another. Mr. Lustick cheerfully announced as he put his paintbrush aside. "Emily, I'm happy to tell you I just added my final stroke. Come, I'd like you and Lawrence to be the first ones to view the finished portrait."

"It's a masterpiece!" Emily felt awed to see herself materialize on canvas. Her freshness rivaled spring, set against peach damask walls with her flower adorned hat. Her blue eyes looked lifelike and full of spirit, while her dress encompassed her small frame in generous layers of femininity.

"What a remarkable likeness, Mr. Lustick. I cannot thank you enough for immortalizing my wife's beauty."

"Thank you both for allowing me the privilege. Having Emily as my subject was a great inspiration, and a portrait I felt moved to paint. That's the difference between being commissioned, and painting from your heart. By the way, Lawrence, I meant to ask you if you have spoken to Mr. Kilmer?"

"I haven't spoken to him since the contest. Why do you ask?"

"Well, I might as well tell you, you will be hearing from him shortly. Mr. Kilmer has planned a reception at the Massachusetts Museum of Art where both our portraits of Emily will be hung side by side, and we will all be the honorees of the evening. I trust you and Emily will both attend."

"That's wonderful news! We'd be delighted to be there, Mr. Lustick." Lawrence replied as he and Emily smiled in unison.

"It will be a big thing; people are expected to come from all over New England. In fact, Mr. Kilmer has intentions of asking if your portrait of Emily could become a part of the museum's permanent collection. From what I've heard, it has gotten a remarkable reception."

Lawrence's eyes lit up. "I would have no hesitation if he were to ask. An artist could have no greater aspiration than to have his work displayed in a museum, especially the Massachusetts Museum of Art."

Lawrence and Emily proudly entered the reception room at the Massachusetts Museum of Art. Refreshments had been set out while men in black tuxedos went around the room offering hors d'oeuvres. The cultured art devotees were dressed in their finery, sipping on wine, and conversing amongst themselves.

Emily whispered to the dapper-dressed Lawrence with pride, "There is nothing Sir Dexter or Lady Violet can say now to besmirch our reputation. Lawrence, you've proven yourself beyond reproach. Thankfully, the scandal of our Newport days has vanished into thin air. Just look at all these people who are here to honor you, Lawrence."

"And you too, Emily, remember there would be no portraits without you." Lawrence's dark eyes glistened as he looked at her with endearment.

"Lawrence, I will take no credit on your special night. All I did was sit and try to be still, and I know I wasn't always a pro at that."

They began surveying the room which was quickly becoming filled with newcomers, all dressed in the finest fashion. Lawrence and Emily's contrast of dark and light made them a striking pair while the years had matured them to ripeness.

"Look Emily," Lawrence cried out as he spotted a familiar manly form in the background. "That looks like my father over there! Could it be? Yes, it's him!" Lawrence exclaimed as the figure turned around and he recognized his father's weary face. William's hard work out in the fields had hunched his shoulders and gnarled his strong hands while deep furrows fanned out on his cheeks.

"I cannot believe my father has come all the way here!" Lawrence rushed over to William Gray with heated emotion as Emily became sidetracked by an admirer of her portraits.

William Gray's expression became filled with poignancy at seeing the majestic vision of his estranged son. "Lawrence, my boy," William cried out as he held Lawrence to his chest with heartfelt affection.

"It's so wonderful to see you again, son!" William said in an emotional exchange. "You have grown into a proper man. How proud I am of your accomplishments! When I heard word about the reception, I just had to take the trip to Massachusetts, to see you, and congratulate you after all these long years without word from you." William beamed with sentiment.

Lawrence clasped his father's work-weary chest close to his. "Oh, Father, it's been too long since I've seen you. You can't imagine how much I've wanted to contact you, but I was afraid it would cause trouble for you at Fairway, especially after the scandal that separated all of us . . . I want to forget those days!" Lawrence's eyebrows meshed together as Emily approached in her newly acquired womanly demeanor.

"William, what a pleasant surprise to see you!" Emily embraced Lawrence's father warmly. She then asked in a serious tone, "Are you still working for my father, William?"

"Yes, Emily, in fact I came here with your parents," William answered with a gleeful smile.

"You've come with my parents! I'll go look for them!" Emily excitedly echoed as she merged into the crowded reception while father and son caught up with each other.

Emily and her parents spotted each other by the alcove near the bar. They rushed toward each other in delirium. Philip Reed was the first to hold his daughter close to his heart while his eyes welled with feeling. "Emily, my dear daughter, just look at you, you've grown into such a beautiful woman, and now two beautiful portraits have immortalized you." Mr. Reed shook his head with feeling while the white-streaked hair along his temples highlighted the time-worn appearance of his face.

Emily reached for her mother who waited to embrace her. Her mother's matured face looked equally transformed by the rendering of time. Her stern demeanor had softened by their separation while her shape had become rounder.

Mother and daughter wept in a joyous reunion. "Emily, all I want is for us to be a family again," Mrs. Reed pleaded earnestly while her eyes beckoned regret. "Father and I didn't have the courage to contact you. We thought you must have hated us for trying to force you to marry a man you didn't love." Mrs. Reed sobbed through her words which fell from her lips with hope and heartache.

Mrs. Reed went on softly, "All that matters now is you are my daughter, and I love you, Emily. I have suffered so much because of my past ideals. Lawrence Gray has surpassed all doubt, and I have nothing but respect for him. I hear you are both the talk of the town."

"Oh, Mother, you have no idea what it means to hear you say that! I love you too. I've missed you and Father and the boys more than you will ever know. Those days at Fairway seem like a lifetime ago." Emily became besieged with emotion as she smiled wistfully, and tears warmed her iced-blue eyes.

"Lawrence," Mrs. Reed exclaimed as he approached with a reserved smile. "I know it's a little late, but welcome to the family!"

"Thank you, Mrs. Reed, I appreciate your warm welcome!" Lawrence said with a chivalrous bow.

"Also, Lawrence, I must congratulate you on your artistic recognition, and for your many accomplishments. Most of all, thank you for taking such good care of our Emily." Mrs. Reed gushed with sincerity and an undertone of apology for the past.

"Thank you so much, Mrs. Reed. I hope we can finally be a family again," Lawrence said hopefully as he cordially went on. "I have invited my father to come to our house in Salem to spend time with us and our son Jake. Perhaps you and Mr. Reed would like to pay us a visit as well. We would love to have you."

"Oh yes, Mother," beamed Emily. "It's high time all of you visited us. You are all grandparents! Our little Jake has been so deprived not to have had all of you in his life," Emily professed.

"We cannot wait to meet our grandson so we can spoil him!" Mrs. Reed beamed. "I'm so happy for the good fortune you and Lawrence have been blessed with. I mean just look at this, Lawrence and Herbert Lustick's portraits hanging side by side. This reception has been in all the papers."

Mr. Reed interjected, "I wanted to ask you something, Lawrence. Do you still have dreams of becoming a doctor?"

Lawrence answered proudly. "Actually, I have been working the evening shift at Fulton Apothecary and attending medical school during the day. I'm expected to graduate in 1905."

"That's truly commendable, Lawrence! That just goes to show when a man is motivated anything is possible." Mr. Reed patted Lawrence's shoulders with encouragement. "I give you a lot of credit for pursuing your dreams against all odds. I know you must be very busy with everything, but I do hope you can take time off so you can all come, and stay with us at Fairway."

Lawrence became enlivened. "I will tell you what, how about we come and stay for Memorial Day weekend, and then you can stay at our house in Salem for a visit. We have plenty of room for all of you. It would be wonderful for us all to be a family again! It means so much to me and Emily. We have suffered so from being estranged from you, and our little Jake will be so blessed to have all of you in his life."

Chapter Thirty-Three

The Jealous Wife

Emily's face was aglow beneath the brilliant light of day while her pink plume hat added a special crown. Her eyes began to tear with bittersweet sentiment as their driver approached Fairway. "Lawrence, I just can't believe we're back here again. I'm so excited I feel like I'm walking on a cloud."

"I'm so happy for you to be home again, Emily. This day has been long overdue."

Lawrence sounded on the brass knocker of Fairway. "Emily, it feels as if a day has not passed since I stood here with my father for the first time."

Mrs. Reed opened the door. Her eyes became filled with emotion at the sight of Jake. "Oh just look at the little fellow, please let me hold him in my arms at once! He's a little husky thing isn't he?"

Jake looked like quite the gentlemen dressed in knickers with suspenders and a crisp white shirt. His freckles were sprinkled generously over his nose and flushed cheeks. Mr. Reed promptly snatched him out of Mrs. Reed's grasp.

"Come to Grandfather little fellow," he gushed.

Emily's brothers appeared in the foyer. Emily's eyes widened. "You can't be the same scruffy boys I remember. I cannot believe how much you've changed! Come; let me take a good look at you."

Emily hugged them one by one. "Hal, you have grown as tall as father and both of you practically look like men."

"At eighteen I should look like a man, especially considering I have a nephew now," Hal retorted, looking over at Jake with pleasure.

"What about me, I'm an uncle at sixteen," Charles chimed in. "Now that's something to reckon with."

There was an affectionate interlude of hugging, and joyful sobbing. Emily scooped the overwhelmed Jake into her arms before pointing everyone out.

"Jake, this is your Grandma, and this is your Grandpa. This is your Uncle Hal, and this is your Uncle Charles."

Jake smiled broadly while his green eyes glistened. "And this is Jake." Everyone became charmed as Jake pointed to himself.

Mr. Reed looked Lawrence squarely in the eye with a bewildered expression. "So tell me, Lawrence, just where does Jake get his red hair from?"

Lawrence stammered for a moment, as Emily's face dropped. In the meantime Mrs. Reed peered at Jake with inquisitive eyes. "I can't say, I know it's a bit of a mystery," Lawrence replied offhandedly.

"It's a bit uncanny," Mrs. Reed commented with bafflement. "Just look at the two of you. Emily is as blonde as can be, and Lawrence's hair is as black as night. Here you have a baby with red hair and green eyes, it's most unusual."

Emily grabbed a hold of Jake. "I guess Jake is a mixture of ancestors we are not aware of." Emily paused with a smile. "I have good news for everyone that I have been saving for this opportune moment when all of us are together . . . I'm going to have another baby," Emily divulged with a bright smile.

"Another baby, Emily," Lawrence smiled in elation while Emily's blue eyes glimmered. "Why have you waited until now to tell me?"

"Lawrence, don't you realize the father is always the last to know." Philip Reed teased before embracing Emily warmly in acknowledgment along with Mrs. Reed. The excitement in the air was contagious. Soon Hal and Charles were celebrating the imminent birth as well, and taking turns hugging their sister.

"I'm hoping for another boy, so Jake will have a little brother. But mainly, I just hope for a healthy baby. That's the only blessing I ask for," Emily said thoughtfully.

After dinner, Emily retreated with her mother into the drawing room while Lawrence and Mr. Reed played cards in the study. Becoming a grandmother had brought a peaceful contentment to her mother's countenance.

"Emily dear, I don't mean to rehash the past or what your experience at Rosewood was like."

The mere mention of the Lund's Newport estate made Emily's mouth turn dry, and heart beat rapidly. She poured herself another cup of iced tea from a crystal pitcher set on the coffee table as her mother went on.

"When Lady Sarah first informed us that you and Lawrence had fled Newport together, it was quite a blow to Father and me. I'm sure you can understand how dreadful that news must have been for us, Emily." Mrs. Reed exhaled in bitter recall.

"Of course, Mother, but now all has worked out for the best," Emily said curtly, not anxious to rehash it.

"Not knowing where you were after you and Lawrence ran off was unbearable for us. I do wish you would have at least called to let us know you were all right," her mother said in a reprimanding tone.

"Those were hard times, Mother. Father had already warned me at my Debutante Ball, if I was to marry Lawrence I would be on my own . . . Thankfully, all turned out well," Emily reiterated curtly.

"That's not the point, Emily." Mrs. Reed cried out. "You were only a young girl then. What did you know about being away from home? When young people are not properly chaperoned inappropriate situations can occur . . . Not that I'm condoning what happened between you and Lawrence. It was inconceivable to me at first, that you could betray your fiancé with such deceit, and immorality."

Mrs. Reed turned up her nose. "Even so, Emily, we now have our little Jake, and I can see you and Lawrence are very happy. Maybe both Father and I are partly to blame for not respecting the genuine feelings you held for Lawrence. In retrospect, I'm ashamed for not taking you seriously."

"I told Father at my coming-out ball that I couldn't just turn off my feelings for Lawrence because of his status. I made myself quite clear from the start, but thankfully all that is of no consequence now," Emily reiterated impatiently.

"That's true, my dear Emily, but what baffles me more than anything was the fact it was Sir Dexter who asked Lawrence to work at Rosewood in the first place."

Mrs. Reed shook her head in bafflement. "Was Sir Dexter and his family so blind not to see the love between you and Lawrence? It was obvious to everyone else, although we tried to dismiss it. Lady Sarah told me how you and Lawrence were alone for hours at a time while he painted your portrait and how you walked alone along the Cliff Walk in the evening. The Lunds didn't act as proper chaperones to allow something like this to happen . . . It's become obvious the temptation of you being left alone with Lawrence was too great for the two of you to handle."

"It wasn't like that, Mother. Lawrence was always respectful," Emily said in a huff, wishing she could reveal the truth.

"Respectful?" Mrs. Reed interjected with a scowl. "Well, Emily, I suppose all it takes is just one time of losing yourselves to passion." She quieted to a hush. "Regardless, Emily, if Sir Dexter was truly a man of his word he could have covered up, and just raised the child as his own. It would have spared much scandal, and Sir Dexter is now no better off for the decision he made, mind you!"

"Just what has become of Sir Dexter?" Emily asked with curiosity and reservation.

"Oh, it's positively dreadful," her mother recounted. "He married that divorcee Lady Violet three summers ago. During the first year of marriage, Lady Violet claimed Sir Dexter was abusive to her when he drank. It's a known fact Sir Dexter drinks too much. I have witnessed his driver practically carry him to his carriage after the Stardust Ball." Mrs. Reed's judgmental face contorted in disgust. "Emily, their marriage was a complete disaster; Lady Violet ended up pressing charges that left Sir Dexter liable to go to jail for life."

"What in heaven's name happened?" Emily asked in alarm.

"All I can say is it's a good thing you got away from that monster," Mrs. Reed continued solemnly. "Just before Lady Violet and Sir Dexter left for her château in France they went to see her parents who happen to live in Salem. Well, Sir Dexter went out for a walk, and when he didn't return for afternoon tea, Lady Violet went out looking for him."

Mrs. Reed looked at Emily poignantly as her voice softened. "Emily, do you know where Lady Violet found Sir Dexter?"

Emily looked at her mother with a blank expression as her mother went on in a soft voice, "Lady Violet found Sir Dexter standing in front of your house, and peering into your yard, watching you play with Jake.

After witnessing that, Lady Violet became insanely jealous. She accused Sir Dexter of still being in love with you."

Mrs. Reed shook her head with pity. "Sir Dexter must have been in love with you, Emily, why else would he be standing there, mooning over you? It must have devastated Sir Dexter when you ran off with Lawrence."

"In love with me, I think not, Sir Dexter was probably just stealing a peek at Jake," Emily plainly said. "Let me ask you, Mother, how in the world do you know this?"

"Lady Violet's driver testified in court." Mrs. Reed's voice became husky as her face turned white. "Lady Violet claimed Sir Dexter tried to kill her."

"Kill Lady Violet!" Emily cried out in horror. "Sir Dexter has his shortcomings, but he is not a murderer! Even I will attest to that!"

"Emily, the two of them fought bitterly; and they were always at each other's throats."

"What happened?" Emily demanded in shock.

"Before she and Sir Dexter left to go to her château in France, Sir Dexter took out an insurance policy on each of them. If either of them had passed away, the survivor would have been left enormously wealthy . . . As it turned out Lady Violet claimed Sir Dexter set her château on fire after he had gone out fishing one morning while she was still asleep. Lady Violet had awoken just in time, and managed to descend to safety, but the entire right side of her château burnt down to the frame."

"Mother, I will admit Sir Dexter is a man who is capable of doing dreadful things," Emily attested. "But to try and burn Lady Violet alive, I cannot see him capable of doing that!"

"You can never be too sure about people, Emily. The French police found traces of kerosene. Lady Violet's testimony along with the evidence, and recent life insurance policies Sir Dexter had taken out, proved to be incriminating. Sir Dexter Lund was locked up in a French jail for over a year. It was in every French newspaper. They nearly threw away the key on him. Sir Dexter's family had a tough time getting him released. Granted they were a very wealthy family, but the lawyer fees, along with the settlement of millions that Lady Violet demanded for his release, devastated their assets . . . Well, Emily, Sir Dexter is a free man now, but a poor one indeed," Mrs. Reed revealed with a scowled brow.

"Mother, it's too much to envision Sir Dexter as a poor man. I'm sure he can regain his wealth again . . . After all he is a lawyer."

"After the scandal in France, Dexter's law license was revoked and he was blackballed from the Association of Lawyers." Mrs. Reed shook her head mournfully, as her eyes welled with tears of remorse and guilt alike.

"Emily, I will never forgive myself for insisting on you marrying such a monster. When I think of what might have happened had the wedding taken place, I shutter in terror. Who would have ever thought Sir Dexter had such an evil mind? All I can say is thank God you had gotten away from him. All of the Newport society who had originally shunned you now applauds you!"

Mr. Reed and Lawrence had just finished a friendly game of cards in the drawing room. Mr. Reed's expression softened as he looked over at his son-in-law. Lawrence appeared manly and regal in equal measure with intelligence burning in his dark eyes.

"Lawrence, I just want you to know how sorry I am for the way I treated you on the night of Emily's Debutante Ball. I have thought about it often, and have regretted it for the past few years. Things have since happened that have changed my way of thinking. I now realize a person's character and kindness is far more important than their status."

"Thank you, Mr. Reed, I appreciate your change of heart," Lawrence said with gratitude as their eyes met with mutual respect.

"I want you to call me Father from now on, and I wish to welcome you properly into our family." Mr. Reed shook his new son-in-law's hand warmly.

"Lawrence, I only regret I had been so blind not to realize what a special man you are. I feel humbled to have dismissed your aspirations. Here I set you out on the field to work amongst the illiterate farm help when you have achieved greatness." Mr. Reed bent his head in remorse as he went on. "I am so ashamed for my thoughtless deeds, and hope you can forgive me. I'm terribly sorry, Lawrence."

"Please, Mr. Reed; I mean, Father, don't be sorry. You were generous to my father and me. You took us in, gave us honest work, and fed us properly after we lost our farm. In retrospect, I can certainly understand how you found me an unsuitable match for Emily. Don't apologize, especially now that I myself am a father. I'm sure if the next baby is a girl, I would be equally selective."

"Don't be too selective, Lawrence. Sometimes parents' interference can be a matter of having your daughter, or losing her to a fate you cannot predict. It's far too steep a price to pay," Philip Reed warned with regret. "I have missed out on so much."

"I suppose that could be so," Lawrence pondered mindfully.

Philip Reed began to choke back his emotions. "Lawrence, I don't mean to bring up the scandal that forced you and Emily out of Newport. But I just wanted you to know that whole scenario is now viewed as merely child's play. What I am about to tell you will shock you."

Lawrence's dark eyes became enlivened with curiosity.

"Lawrence, while it was not a topic that was on the front page of American newspapers, it was all over the French papers. Sir Dexter Lund ended up marrying Lady Violet. Well, the story is, when they were vacationing at her château in France, she accused Sir Dexter of trying to kill her in her sleep, in order to receive a life insurance policy worth millions."

Lawrence's face became astonished as Mr. Reed elaborated on the sordid details. "Well, Father, I guess what really happened between them will remain a mystery. Lady Violet does not have the best reputation, and she milked her ex-husband dry with similar accusations."

"Yes, Lady Violet can be quite the charmer." Mr. Reed smirked. "I must admit with hesitation and please, not a word of this to Maggie, but she swept me off my tired, old feet to dance at the ball that night, and made me feel like a teenager. Had I been a single man perhaps I might have been her next victim."

Lawrence and Mr. Reed shared an inside laugh. Lawrence then raised a curious brow and casually asked, "Do you happen to know what became of his sister Mallory?"

"Oh, Mallory, what a pitiful creature she is." Mr. Reed rolled his eyes with pity. "The poor thing never married, and is forced to live in inferior conditions now that her family has lost close to everything. Mallory has had the worst luck, no fault of her own. Her life was once full of promise, but now it's full of regret . . . Don't feel too badly, Lawrence, for running off on her, agreeing to marry an old maid out of pity, is not a blessing for either. You and she were not a match. It's common knowledge Mallory has never gotten over the loss of her first fiancé, Sir Theodore Wellington, who deserted her after she fell off the horse. Mallory has had a most unlucky fate, to be jilted twice."

Later on in the evening, Lawrence and Emily met up in the library to reminisce over some poetry books they used to read together. However their agenda changed to an anxiousness to compare notes on Sir Dexter and Lady Violet. "Emily, let me just ask you, do you really think Sir Dexter is capable of murder?"

"Lawrence, I know firsthand how Sir Dexter gets when he drinks too much, but let's face it. Both you and I know this is probably a case of Lady Violet swindling another husband out of his riches."

Emily snickered knowingly. "My mother told me Lady Violet caught Sir Dexter watching Jake and me in our yard, and they had a huge fight over it. Of course, you and I know Sir Dexter was no doubt stealing a peek at Jake. But from Lady Violet's standpoint, she became insanely jealous, and accused Sir Dexter of still being in love with me. Lawrence, I believe Lady Violet's ill directed jealousy prompted her to set Sir Dexter up in revenge, even if it meant burning down her own château. I would not put it past her to have the kerosene on hand. What would Lady Violet care if her chateau burned down to the ground? Having Sir Dexter rot in jail, and then demanding millions for his release would obviously be more cost effective for her gold digging ways."

Lawrence whispered in spite of himself, "Let them all believe what they will. Now more than ever the stigma of Sir Dexter being Jake's real father must be silenced forever. Needless to say, the rumor of us being overcome by passion when compared to the guilt of Sir Dexter's attempted murder is the lesser of the two evils. Life sometimes gives back the evils you do to others tenfold, now Sir Dexter has been ostracized falsely, just as we had been. He has certainly got his own comeuppance."

"Yes, and we will not come to his defense, just as he did not come to ours," Emily added triumphantly.

Chapter Thirty-Four

Turn of the Century

The holiday spirit was upon the Gray's household. The Christmas tree shone out by the window while bountiful garlands draped the furniture and balusters. Emily sat quietly by the fireplace knitting a baby bunting with her nimble fingers. Lawrence walked in from the cold. His cheeks were enlivened from the wind while his black hair had a sprinkling of snow.

"Emily, I was wondering, would you like to go to the New Year's Ball at the castle tonight?" Lawrence asked as he sunk beside her on the couch.

"I'm sorry, Lawrence, but I don't feel up to it in my condition."

Emily unconsciously smoothed her hands over her extended belly. "I'm carrying much larger than I was with Jake. I'm afraid I would be quite ungraceful on the dance floor. Besides my feet are so swollen, even the thought of dancing makes them hurt." Emily sighed apologetically.

"Lawrence, you could go to the ball on your own if you'd like. I don't want to deprive you of a good time. After all, it's about to become the new century. Why should you sit at home when we are one of the elite couples to actually get an open invitation?"

"Never, are you crazy, Emily? I'll enjoy myself much more at home with you having a home-cooked dinner by Pierre than at the New Year's

Ball with a bunch of social climbers, be assured, my dear wife. It was merely a suggestion."

Lawrence and Emily sat at the dining room table with the merriment of the New Year in the air. Pierre carried in a festive fare of stewed tomatoes, roasted duck with a French flair, and mushroom crepes. He served Lawrence and Emily beneath the drama of candlelight while the winds rushed through the leafless trees in a hollow echo.

Emily looked rosy, bundled in her woolen shawl. Her hair cascaded to her shoulders in flaxen curls. Fatherhood agreed with Lawrence as manliness had overtaken his boyishness with charisma and style.

"Delicious," Lawrence raved as he tasted the delicately seasoned duck. "Pierre has outdone himself this time. I would have liked to have given him the night off, after all it is New Year's Eve, not to mention the turn of the century, but Pierre didn't seem to mind."

"Who would even want to venture out in this weather anyway, Lawrence? I'm more than content to be home. Once you've gone to one ball, the thrill is gone. All the stuffy people having superficial conversation about nothing, who can be bothered? I'm more of a family gal anyway. In fact how I wish Jake was still awake. When he goes to sleep early, I actually miss him. Isn't that odd?" Emily asked as maternal attachment softened her demeanor.

"Not for you, Emily, you have the devotion of ten mothers wrapped up into one. It's hard to believe Jake will turn four years old this spring. Where did all the time go?" Lawrence asked with a shrug of his shoulders that had grown broader and stronger with the passing years.

"It flies like the wind," Emily echoed as she reached for the photo of Jake on the bureau. "We are so fortunate Jake has such a wonderful disposition. He is full of kindness, and devotion. Not to mention what a sense of humor."

"Emily, he takes after you, my sweetheart." Nonetheless as they admired his photograph, Jake's red hair and freckles spoke of his inheritance without words.

Another New England winter claimed the season. Brisk snowfall settled heavily on the grounds, making travel difficult. Lawrence coddled Jake affectionately on his lap as they sat before the fire. Miss Bethany walked in with a tray of tea and pastries, and set it before them on the coffee table.

"Miss Bethany, at least there's one benefit of not being able to travel to school tonight. I can spend time with Jake. Not to mention it's cozy by the fireplace."

"Yes, and Emily is quite comfortable in her chamber. She is getting close, In fact she thought she felt her first contraction a half hour ago, but she hasn't had another one since, so maybe it was a false alarm."

There in the midst of the blizzard and peaceful hush of the house, Emily screamed out from her chamber. "Lawrence, hurry, come quickly!"

Lawrence darted to her chamber in expectation while his eyes glowed with the sacred light of their connection. "I just got my first contractions," Emily wailed as her face contorted with pain.

Lawrence placed a loving hand upon her brow. "Breathe and relax, Emily. It's a lucky thing I'm here at a time like this."

Before long the contractions were coming closer and closer. Emily moaned in distress as the pain became more intense. Emily shrieked in agonizing cries as Miss Bethany went to get the midwife.

"Tell her to bring the rags, and hot water, go quickly!" Lawrence demanded in frenzy.

Miss Dunn brought the items Lawrence had requested, and rushed in to assist in the delivery which was imminent. After a short labor, the perfectly rounded head of the infant emerged with a tuft of straight black hair on top. Then the olive complexion and well-formed features presented themselves.

Lawrence gently spanked the baby on the bottom as he proudly announced. "It's a boy!" The infant cried with powerful lungs as an encore.

"He's a handsome fellow, Emily, and what a strong pair of lungs!" Lawrence said joyfully.

Miss Dunn washed the baby before handing him over to Emily. Emily reached forward, and held the infant close to her breast. "He's so handsome, and such a big boy! Look at those strong legs!" Emily smiled with delight. "I can see it already; he looks just like you, Lawrence. He even has the same cleft in his chin. I think it's only appropriate we name him Lawrence Junior."

"Lawrence Junior it is, and if I'm to have the honor of choosing the middle name again . . ." Lawrence contemplated.

"Of course," Emily interjected. "Whatever name you choose will suit the baby."

"Very well, Philip on behalf of your father, Lawrence Philip Junior, the name has a nice ring to it." They both celebrated the moment with their love reaching a new height seen in the fine face of their newborn son.

Lawrence rushed off to phone Fairway right away. He announced to Mr. Reed as his father William waited to hear the particulars. "Emily has had a nine pound one ounce boy! We have named him Lawrence Philip Junior. You must all come to see the new baby as soon as possible," Lawrence said excitedly.

"Congratulations, how wonderful! I cannot wait to see him, and I'm touched by him having Philip for his middle name . . . We would love to come right now, but Mother Nature has put a stop to that. The roads are far too hazardous for travel, Lawrence. Unfortunately we will have to wait until the cold breaks, which I don't think will be anytime soon. The winter of 1900 is certainly one to remember for the birth of Lawrence Junior as well as for its fierce blizzards."

By the middle of March, Emily's parents finally arrived in Salem to meet their new grandson. Margaret Reed gushed as she held Lawrence Junior close to her chest in the first moment of kinship.

"Emily, the baby is just beautiful. He is perfect in every way!" Mrs. Reed melted to his presence as a devoted grandmother. Mr. Reed sat on the couch beside her, and patiently awaited his turn to hold the new infant. He looked the part of a doting grandfather with his blonde hair now dispersed with white.

Mr. Reed enjoyed his new grandson when Mrs. Reed finally handed him over. "Emily, I must say you and Lawrence do good work! Just look at this baby, Lawrence Junior is truly a prince!" Mr. Reed declared with certainty.

"Thank you." Emily smiled proudly. "Just look at the ensemble Miss Bethany has knit. It has a matching bonnet and booties. She also knit this blanket, it's so pretty." Emily draped the aqua, white, and pale pink blanket over the baby's shoulders as her father held him.

Her mother presented Emily with a baby gift wrapped in pale blue gift paper and decorated with tiny storks. Emily opened the box to find a white eyelet ensemble for Lawrence Junior to wear. "Mother, I'm so touched. It's so beautiful!" Emily swooned as Mrs. Reed unfolded the garment to show its fine detail.

"I got this outfit for the baby to wear for his baptism at the Saint James Church." Her mother smiled dreamily while twirling one of Emily's curls. "Emily, I can still remember when you had your baptism there as if it was yesterday."

"So now Father Dale will have the honor of baptizing my son." Emily tenderly caressed the white garment before she clutched it to her chest in reverence. "Mother, I will save it afterward as a family heirloom."

William Gray smiled proudly on the outskirts as he patiently waited his turn to hold his grandson. "Philip, who would have ever thought back in the old days we would one day become in-laws, with the same grandchildren. I tell you, life is full of curious surprises."

"Well, I'm glad it turned out the way it did, William," Philip Reed said with emotion. "We were best buddies back in the old days, and lifelong friends. It only makes sense our children should be drawn to each other as well. We should have known that from the start."

The following weekend the Grays went to the Saint James Church for the baby's baptism. Flanked by Lawrence, Emily proudly held their son on the pulpit. Lawrence Junior's white eyelet outfit contrasted strikingly with his dark complexion.

The priest stood regally in a white and gold gown as he blessed the infant in a sacred ceremony. An otherworldly light shone through the stained glass windows as biblical scenes in every color of the rainbow came to life. Gold statues of Christ and the Virgin Mary flanked the altar, while incense permeated the air with frankincense and sandalwood.

Father Dale immersed the crown of William Junior's head in holy water in supplication to the Holy Spirit. Sanctity filled the air as Emily and Lawrence gave each other an affectionate glance.

Afterward, guests and those in attendance of the Sunday mass all gathered around to see the blessed baby. Lawrence and Emily became overwhelmed by all the attention.

"Thank you so much for being here on our special day," Emily said repeatedly to all the congregants as her face lit up with joy.

"Congratulations, the baby has been blessed a Christian. Now let us all go back to Fairway to celebrate," Mr. Reed announced.

At Fairway, a bounty of home cooked specialties of Rock Cornish hen, meat pie, asparagus, sweet potatoes, and creamed spinach awaited them. Mr. Reed addressed Lawrence as they dined, "So Emily tells me all is going well at the apothecary, and your studies are progressing nicely."

"I have to admit, Mr. Reed. It's not easy juggling a job, and going to school, so it will take me longer to graduate than it would have ordinarily. I hate to sound immodest, but if I keep up my grades, I have a good chance of becoming the class valedictorian. I should be ready to start practicing medicine in five years. In addition, I will still earn a percentage from the apothecary, for the sale of my tinctures which is doing quite well. So that will supplement my income nicely until I become established."

"That's remarkable, Lawrence, best of luck! Where do you intend to set up your practice?"

"I plan on setting up an office in our house here in Salem with a private entrance. I've arranged to take over Dr. Kraus' practice, a well-known physician in Salem who will be ready for retirement by the time I'm ready to start my practice."

Chapter Thirty-Five

Act of Charity

White chairs were spread across the grounds of the Massachusetts Medical School for the graduating class of 1905. Emily exuded with pride for her husband's achievements. Jake looked like a true gentleman in his knickers and clean white shirt with five-year-old Lawrence Junior by his side. Ladies sat beneath their ruffled parasols dressed in their springtime finery while gentlemen wore formal attire.

A hush overtook the crowd as the distinguished dean, Mr. Devon, went up to the podium to speak. "I would like to commend everyone in the graduating class of 1905. It has been a difficult journey with all the demands on these young people nowadays. Nevertheless, they have come through with excellence. Without any further ado, I'd now like to acknowledge our class valedictorian, Mr. Lawrence Gray."

Everyone in the audience clapped enthusiastically as Lawrence took center stage. Dressed in a blue cap and gown, Lawrence looked the picture of success already. "Thank you, Mr. Devon, I would just like to say, it has been a long road, but I have stuck to my dreams. I used to work in the fields with the grit of my hands. If I can now use these same hands to help heal people, anything is possible. I would like to add, it's the love of my beautiful wife Emily, and my two loving sons, who have made it all possible. I would like to thank them for being there for me."

The audience clapped enthusiastically as Lawrence walked off with his diploma, and joined his family. Emily beamed. "Lawrence, that was so sweet of you to mention us, but it was you who accomplished your goals."

* * *

"I see retirement has put the sparkle back into your eyes, Dr. Kraus," Lawrence commented as they shook hands.

"Lawrence, it's you who is sparkling . . . I just stopped by on my way to play golf to tell you my former patients have been raving about my replacement."

"Thanks, Dr. Kraus, I try my best."

"Don't be modest, Lawrence." Dr. Kraus raised his willowy white brows. "I just read in the Salem Record how you were written up in the 1906 medical journal of *Unusual Recoveries* for curing Mrs. Janet Jenkins. I find that remarkable, and I wanted to congratulate you personally. Mrs. Jenkins had been coming to me for years with a mysterious illness no doctor could diagnose or treat. Her case study dates back to 1901. Then you come along and find a cure for the woman, when there was not even a name for what ailed her."

"It's all in the herbs, I just administered them, Dr. Kraus," Lawrence modestly retorted.

"Well, I suppose that explains why people call you, 'the man with the magic tincture.'"

After a long day at work, Lawrence relaxed in the parlor in his favorite chair. It granted him a view of the rustling leaves of the oak tree. Emily sat at the piano and entertained him with her sweet melodies and her pleasing voice.

"Lawrence, please come here at once!" Miss Bethany rushed in frantically.

"What is it, Miss Bethany; it's not like you to disturb me while I'm relaxing?"

"There is a woman by the name of Mrs. Renee Wilson, who is here to see you, it's urgent! Hurry come quick!" She demanded excitedly as Lawrence followed her.

Lawrence was greeted by the sight of a distraught mother in a bedraggled coat with unkempt brown hair. She stood out on the front doorstep shivering with a little girl in her arms. "Dr. Gray, please help me, my daughter Rachel can't breathe!" The broken-down mother pleaded.

"Please come in and let me examine the child," directed Lawrence.

The little girl's face was drained of color, and her lips were practically blue.

"Please." Mrs. Wilson cried. "No one has been able to do anything for the poor girl. I fear she'll die if someone doesn't help her!"

"She's having an acute asthma attack. I will stabilize her breathing at once with a custom blended respiratory combination I keep on hand for emergencies."

Lawrence administered the medicine, and within a matter of minutes, the little girl was able to breathe with less obstruction.

Mrs. Wilson smiled gratefully. "My daughter's asthma is so severe, I almost lost her several times this year." The exhausted mother murmured while slumping in her chair. "I'm a widow, and have been unable to work because of my daughter's illness."

"Where do you live, Mrs. Wilson?" Lawrence asked in concern.

"I rent a room in the boarding house on Grant Street," she muttered with discomfiture.

"So you have traveled quite a distance to come here." Lawrence placed a caring hand on Mrs. Wilson's dejected shoulders. "Don't worry about a thing, Mrs. Wilson. Your daughter will be fine. Due to your circumstance I will treat your child free of charge . . . I invite you and your daughter to stay in my office, while I nurse your daughter back to health. I'll bring in two cots for you. It looks like you could use some proper nutrition yourself, Mrs. Wilson. I will have my housemaid, Miss Bethany, bring you and Rachel something to eat."

Renee Wilson curtsied with gratitude as a look of relief transformed her face with hope. "Let me just say your generosity is a blessing to you, and your family, and it will never be forgotten, Mr. Gray."

"Thank you and I will return shortly, Mrs. Wilson, to check on you."

Lawrence left to go into the parlor. "Emily, a widow has just arrived with a very sick child. They will be staying for a couple of days until the little girl recuperates. They rent a room in a boarding house in the bad part of town. I was just thinking, you know the bag of clothes you gathered for goodwill, perhaps she could use them. She looks about the same size as you, and her clothing is so worn it's ready for the trash."

"I put them in the hall closet. By all means give the clothing to her if she can use it," Emily replied.

Lawrence carried the heavy bundles of clothing in to his office, and tapped lightly on the door. Miss Wilson soon appeared. "Miss Wilson, here is an assortment of my wife's dresses that she no longer wears, and we thought perhaps you could use them. I think they should fit you."

Mrs. Wilson's work-worn fingers opened the bags and touched the dresses in awe. "How can I ever repay you and your wife for your generosity, Dr. Gray? I'm eternally grateful for all you've done for us, strangers to you."

Health and vigor came back to the child at a rapid speed. By the third day, the child was as healthy as any ordinary three-year-old. "Dr. Gray," Renee Wilson said with tears in her eyes. "You have been benevolent beyond all expectations. It's nice to know there are people in the world as good as you are. May God bless you and your family, Dr. Gray."

"It's my pleasure to help, Mrs. Wilson. I have devised a custom-made tincture for your daughter I would like you to take it with you when you leave. It contains ephedrine and lobelia, which are powerful herbs, and must be used sparingly, one or two drops at most. If you hear her wheezing, the tincture should open up her airways immediately to prevent any further attacks."

"Thank you so much for that, Dr. Gray, and for the clothing. This new wardrobe you and your wife have been kind enough to give me will allow me to go back to my job as a milliner. Rachel can go back to nursery school again, and we will be able to find a better place to rent in the future."

"Mrs. Wilson, I wish you and your daughter all the best, only good things, health, happiness, and prosperity." Lawrence bid them farewell only to be greeted by another desperado in need of his charitable treatments.

Chapter Thirty-Six

The Children

Caramelized leaves sweetened the earth as the last of summer's flowers shed their petals while the autumn winds refreshed the air. Emily sat in the yard dressed in a mustard dress with a matching shawl wrapped over her shoulders. She watched her children play in the sunlight, bundled in their woolen sweaters.

Lawrence came into the yard holding a bunch of Indian corn. "Emily, I'll put these on the front door to welcome autumn."

"Don't forget the wreath of dried leaves and acorns the boys made last year. It's down in the basement. We'll need a pumpkin or two; the boys just love making jack-o'-lanterns," Emily said with a sentimental smile.

"Farmer Bill is selling them down the block. I'll pick up an extra one for Pierre's famous pumpkin pie," Lawrence retorted.

The crisp winds rustled Lawrence's ebony hair as the sun accentuated the first glints of gray. Lawrence sat on the wrought iron chair beside Emily, and looked over at her wistfully.

"I still can't believe how the young girl I married has become a fine woman of thirty, and you're every bit as beautiful as ever, my Emily." Lawrence's dark eyes melted with favor upon her face.

"Lawrence, that's so sweet of you to say." Emily smiled devotedly. "The years seem to have just flown by. It's hard to believe Jake is eleven already, and Lawrence Junior. will be turning eight this winter. Just look at them, what big boys they have become. We're so fortunate to have two wonderful children who get along so well."

Emily's eyes became filled with emotion. "Lawrence, now that the boys are becoming more self-sufficient, I'm beginning to think about having another child. I'd love to have a daughter to complete our family. How do you feel about having another baby?" Emily studied his reply with a look of yearning on her still girlish face.

"I would love to have a new addition to our family if you're up to it. Of course, if we did have a girl, she would be Daddy's little girl." Lawrence mused.

"I guess that's only fair since I already have two Mommy's little boys." Emily smiled proudly as Larry Junior called out, "Mommy, Mommy hurry come quick."

"Lawrence, see what I mean. I better go see what he wants."

Before long Emily sat in the yard with her feet stretched out upon the lounge. Her face had a listless expression. Lawrence looked at Emily with concern. "Are you still feeling nauseous?"

"Yes, and I can smile about it, Lawrence, because I'm certain I'm going to have a baby. I know the symptoms quite by heart," Emily divulged with a radiant smile.

"That's wonderful news, Emily, my darling!" Lawrence took a break from planting pansies to place a loving hand upon her abdomen. "At least this time you told me first." Lawrence embraced Emily close to his heart as a fringe of yellow and magenta pansies in the flowerbed added a picturesque backdrop.

Emily's growing stomach soon became apparent from beneath her floral dress. Larry Junior touched her belly. "Hello my little brother or sister, this is your big brother Larry speaking." He then looked up at Emily, "Mom, do you think the baby will remember me by my voice after it's born?"

"Possibly, Junior, but don't expect the baby to call you by your name," teased Emily.

Jake entered the parlor with his red hair glaring out against his fair complexion, all too reminiscent of Sir Dexter Lund. "Are you excited about your new brother or sister, Jake?" Emily asked.

"If it's a boy I suppose that would be nice," Jake replied offhandedly. "Do you think, if the baby is a boy, he will like to play with trains as much as I do?"

"If it's a boy, he will probably grow up to be a conductor," Emily quipped. "But what about if it's a girl, don't you think you would enjoy having a baby sister, Jake?"

"No, girls are silly with their little fluffy dresses and hair bows. I would much rather have another brother."

"Unfortunately, Jake, we have no choice on the sex of the baby. We can both hope and wish for what we want, but nature will deliver on her terms. Most importantly is for me to have a healthy child."

Larry Junior chimed in. "Mommy, why do we have to worry about such things? We have Daddy to make the baby better if it gets sick."

"Larry, I know you might think that, but Daddy is only a human being, who happens to be a doctor. That's why it's important for us to take care of our health. Medicine can't make up for good nutrition and proper rest. A doctor, even a great one like Daddy, is not God."

The boys followed Emily into the parlor where she began playing the piano. The children sat on a loveseat adjacent to her, and listened with wide-eyed wonder as Emily's lovely melody reverberated throughout the house. Together they all sang, "Last Rose of Summer," and "Home Sweet Home."

The music drew Lawrence into the parlor, and as usual they all spent the night singing, and chatting quietly, while Emily played her vast repertoire. Miss Bethany walked in with her usual tray of tea and croissants, along with cookies and milk for the boys. The music shrouded the night in melodious calm.

Out of the peacefulness within, came the intruding sound of the doorbell of Lawrence's office, with the all too familiar sequence of chimes, "At this hour of the evening!" Emily frowned with disapproval as she stopped playing the piano.

"The ill cannot always wait out the night," Lawrence dutifully interjected before he rushed over to the door.

Behind it stood a desperate woman, clutching her young son to her breast. The poor child had such a deep cough he was breathing in shallow wisps of air. "Dr. Gray, I'm sorry to intrude on you at this hour, but a friend, Miss Wilson, recommended I see you. Allow me to introduce myself, I'm Mrs. Rand. My little Daniel can't sleep through the night. His cough gets worse in the evening, and now his fever has gone up."

"Please come in, Mrs. Rand, and let me take a look at him."

Lawrence examined the three-year-old boy. "Your son Daniel is severely dehydrated and has a high fever. He will do best to stay the night; the temperatures are expected to go way down. You may stay as well, as any further travel would be inadvisable at this time."

Lawrence administered medicine to the child, and took all the necessary precautions for his recovery.

Within a course of two days, the little boy was able to sleep through the night, cough, and fever-free. The grateful mother, Mrs. Rand addressed Lawrence, "Dr. Gray, I was hoping you'd be reasonable with your fee. My husband has been out of work for the past year with back troubles, and times are hard."

"You owe me nothing, Mrs. Rand. Your son's renewed health is all I need at present," Lawrence said with a caring smile. The mother bowed her head graciously as Lawrence tipped his hat, and bid her adieu.

Afterward, Emily looked at Lawrence in concern. "Don't you think you should put boundaries between your profession and your family life? I worry you are working yourself too hard; you look exhausted."

"Being a doctor isn't easy, Emily. Being sick is not always at a doctor's convenience, we both know that."

"Yes, but you're just a one-man office, and after running around all day on house calls, you come home only to be bombarded by patients at all hours of the night. It's too much for one man to bear, Lawrence. I fear your benevolence is becoming far too demanding!"

Lawrence looked at her through the heavy lids of exhaustion. "I'm fine, Emily. I can handle anything that comes my way. I know what it's like not to have money. It's my divine responsibility to care for the sick. I cannot very well send them away, Emily."

Emily had been in labor for over twelve grueling hours. She contorted her sweat-drenched face as she bore down with all the might her exhausted body could muster. Miss Dunn watched as the infant emerged into the world with a healthy cry.

"It's a girl, Emily! I'll go tell Lawrence the good news as soon as I wash her."

"A girl," Emily weakly echoed. "I couldn't ask for more."

Miss Dunn rushed to Lawrence's quarters, and knocked loudly on his door. "Lawrence, Emily has given birth to a beautiful baby girl. Congratulations on your first daughter, Lawrence!"

Lawrence rushed into Emily's chamber, and found the infant lying beside her on the bed. He bent downward to look at the newborn, becoming greeted by the most beautiful face with Emily's delicate features, blue eyes with dark eyelashes and a head full of platinum curls.

"Emily, we finally got our little girl, and what a beautiful angel she is!" Lawrence smiled joyously.

"We will call her Maggie Beth, after my mother, and Miss Bethany," Emily announced wearily yet excitedly.

"It has a wonderful ring, Emily. Maggie Beth it is!" Lawrence lifted the precious infant to his husky chest. "Maggie Beth will be a wonderful addition to our family. We must tell the boys to treat her as gently as if she was a porcelain doll. I know they will both grow to cherish their new sister in spite of the fact Jake would have preferred a brother."

Chapter Thirty-Seven

Maggie's Wish

By the time Maggie Beth could speak, she pleaded to Emily, with her big blue eyes filled with yearning, "Mommy, I want a baby sister so badly."

"But you have your brothers to play with, Maggie."

The curly headed child pouted inconsolably. "My brothers don't like to play dolls like me."

"If I have another baby it might be a boy."

"I don't care; at least the baby will want to play with me."

"Only time will tell, Maggie," Emily answered as she went to talk to Lawrence.

"What is it, Emily, is everything all right?" Lawrence looked up from his paperwork. "You look upset."

Emily sighed despondently. "Maggie Beth keeps telling me how badly she wants to have a little brother or a sister. I feel badly for her. After all Jake is sixteen, Junior is already twelve; they're not interested in playing dolls with her."

Lawrence looked into Emily's eyes with the devotion time had bestowed.

"Emily, you have given me three beautiful children and such happiness. Sometimes I think it would be selfish to hope for another. How much happiness and good fortune should people expect to receive? God has been good, terribly good. Is it right for us to hope and ask for even more?" Lawrence asked with a humble voice.

"Lawrence darling," Emily reassured. "We will not ask. Let us be patient and hopeful. If God wants us to have another addition to our family, we will be granted. We will leave it entirely to God, and we shall praise the Lord for all the blessings we have been provided. The Lord has been merciful."

They kissed ardently, unaware both Jake and Larry Junior were watching them at the foot of the stairs in adolescent wonder. "Hurry, Maggie," Larry whispered. "Mommy and Daddy are kissing."

The little cherub joined them at the foot of the stairs, "One day I want to be in love like them."

One year became another, and once again Maggie complained, "It's not fair Jake and Larry have each other. Am I to play by myself forever?"

"I'm sorry, Maggie," Emily sighed in anguish. "Time has not provided me with another baby. I'm afraid you will have to be content with your two brothers. It seems my belly is closed forever."

"That's not fair! All of my friends have baby sisters and brothers." Maggie Beth's mouth quivered while her saucer eyes welled with tears.

"We're not always in control of what we want, Maggie. At least Uncle Hal has given you a cousin, and you and Mona are more like sisters than cousins."

"But Mona doesn't live with us; it's not the same thing." Seven-year-old Maggie Beth sulked.

The years continued to pass fruitless when suddenly, two months after Emily's forty-second birthday, the telltale symptoms of motherhood emerged.

"Miss Bethany, please get me another cup of peppermint tea," Emily muttered weakly.

"Are you still feeling nauseous, Emily?" Miss Bethany asked in concern.

"Yes, and this time I'm afraid to tell Lawrence what I think it is. I fear I'm too old to have another child."

"Nonsense, Emily, God doesn't give us what we can't handle."

Emily found Lawrence in the library doing research on South American herbs. She sat across from him finding it hard to utter the words while Lawrence remained too engrossed to even look up. Lawrence murmured beneath his breath, "Emily, we can read poetry together in around an hour."

"I'm not here to read poetry with you, Lawrence . . . I have something important to tell you," Emily announced with a worried tone.

"What is it, Emily?" Lawrence glanced over his reading glasses, looking too mature to be an expectant father.

"I'm glad you're sitting, because what I'm about to tell you will no doubt come as a shock."

Lawrence removed his spectacles with a look of queer interest. "Tell me whatever it is you intend to."

"I wouldn't tell you unless I was certain." Emily smiled before she laughed nervously. "Believe it or not, I am going to have a baby."

Lawrence's dark eyes became dazed while his mouth dropped open and stayed that way. It seemed as if speech would not be forthcoming as he slowly got his bearing.

"Emily, you just turned forty-two, women your age sometimes go through an early change of life. Perhaps that's all it is. After all, we have been trying for all these years to have another child. It seems unlikely it should happen now," Lawrence said skeptically.

"Lawrence, I'm not going through my change of life overnight. I know my body, trust me." Emily smiled knowingly.

"Come here, let me take a look at you."

After examining her, Lawrence agreed. "Emily, you are at least three months along . . . Maggie has just turned eleven, and my hair is turning gray, but she will have her baby brother or sister after all!" Lawrence joyously exclaimed while they giggled merrily at the scenario.

"Your hair is not gray, it's salt and pepper, and it makes you look distinguished. What about me, how will I be able to handle having a baby at my age?"

"Emily, sweetheart, you are still a youthful, healthy woman. The body does only what it's capable of. You will have to take it easier with this pregnancy than with the others. You're obviously not a kid anymore, and we will have to be vigilant and very careful, but you'll be fine," Lawrence reassured.

"It will be no problem for me to slow down. After all we have grown children already. By the time I give birth Jake will be twenty-three, Maggie will be almost twelve, and Larry will be nineteen. Can you imagine that?"

"Emily, we've been blessed. This baby will keep us busy in our older years. Maggie Beth will be a teenager before we know it. Larry Junior will soon be in medical school. Jake will be a lawyer before long. And you, my dear wife, are going to have a baby." They both shared a hearty laugh.

Jake appeared by the doorway looking tall and thin, holding his law books. "Laughing again you two, after being married for a hundred years, I would think you would finally become sober."

Lawrence and Emily chuckled at Jake's sarcastic wit. "Actually," Emily burst out. "I'm going to have a baby."

"You cannot be serious, Mother!" Jake's green eyes opened wide, and glowed like a cat in the dark.

"She's telling you the truth, Jake." Lawrence chimed in. "You'll be old enough to be the father, and I'll be old enough to be the grandfather, and . . ."

Emily interjected in a gleeful spirit, "Please, whatever you say, don't say I will be old enough to be the grandmother!"

Jake laughed. "No, I'll give you a break, Mother, but now that you're having another baby, you might as well finally tell me just where I got my red hair from. Was it really the milkman?" Lawrence and Emily chuckled at what had become a standard joke in the family.

Chapter Thirty-Eight

The Bad Penny

Winter was upon the Gray's New England house once again. The family huddled together by the fireside in the aftermath of Christmas, with the holiday spirit of the New Year still fresh upon them.

Emily thumbed through the January 1920 issue of Harper's Bazaar. "Miss Bethany, I love these flapper styles, but at seven months pregnant I regret I won't be able to wear these dresses for a long time to come."

"Don't feel too bad, Emily, neither can I, and I have no excuse aside from having too hearty an appetite, and I'm not eating for two." They both shared a laugh.

Maggie Beth sat beside the decked out Christmas tree knitting a yellow and white blanket for the baby. "Mother, I still can't believe I'm finally getting my baby brother or sister after all these years. Let's hope history doesn't repeat itself, and the baby doesn't beg for a little brother or sister like I did. At this rate you'll still be having babies when Jake and Larry Junior are ready to start their families."

Emily laughed. "I guess if I could become a mother again at my age I wouldn't doubt anything is possible."

"Let's not jump the gun, Maggie! I still have to finish law school before I can even think of marriage," Jake retorted with a distasteful expression.

"But you will be married to Ella Winning before you graduate." Maggie instigated in a teasing tone.

Larry Junior interjected laughingly, "Ella has already told you she wants to have five children, hasn't she Jake? She has told everybody else."

"What about you, little brother, don't sell yourself short?" Jake quipped. "Let's not forget you have been courting Celia Stanton for over a year now. I hear wedding bells; who knows maybe you'll be the first to tie the knot?" Jake smiled triumphantly as Junior's face turned red by the mere mention of their association.

"I first have to finish medical school before I can even consider marriage," Junior stammered.

"Who knows, maybe you will be the one to get married before you graduate?" Maggie laughed as Junior sunk further into his seat.

Grandfather William, engrossed in a book on the other side of the room, picked up his tired, gray head. "Boys, I hear wedding bells for both of you. I only hope I will live long enough to be a great grandfather."

The driver loaded the last trunk onto the carriage as Jake and Larry Junior piled in. Lawrence and Emily bid their sons farewell as Maggie hurriedly rushed into the stagecoach.

"Hey wait for me! Don't forget I'm going to stay with Cousin Mona for the rest of the Easter vacation," she said breathlessly.

Lawrence and Emily hugged their children one by one. "We love you! Have a safe trip," they echoed.

Lawrence smiled lovingly at Emily as the carriage disappeared behind the horizon of winter's sterile landscape. "It will be good for you to have a little solitude for a change. The boys will be off at school until the summer, and by the time Maggie returns you'll feel refreshed, Emily."

Emily looked over at the hollows beneath Lawrence's heavy lidded eyes. "It would do you good to relax a little yourself, and take some time off for solitude of your own. You look exhausted, Lawrence."

"Winter is a difficult time of year, Emily. The flu has practically become an epidemic this season. Once the springtime comes, I'm sure I will get a break," Lawrence said with unstoppable determination.

"I worry for you, Lawrence; you're working yourself too hard. And with a new baby on the way, I fear you will burn yourself out before the first flower of spring."

The following evening Emily relaxed by the fireside after Lawrence had fallen asleep in his chamber. Her overblown pregnancy made her feel encumbered, and content just to huddle beneath layers of blankets. The flames of the fireplace mesmerized her as they danced before her sights. Out of the silence of the night intruded the chimes of Lawrence's office. The melody blared ominously, and broke the peace of late evening.

Emily hurried down to the servants' quarters and knocked on Miss Bethany's door. "Miss Bethany, someone is at the door of Lawrence's office. Please see who it is at once, before they disturb the whole house," Emily commanded in agitation.

Miss Bethany dutifully stumbled out of bed. "Yes, Emily, I will go right away." Miss Bethany hurriedly put a black velvet robe over her nightdress. She looked flustered by the intrusion as she rushed upstairs to the door.

Moments later, Miss Bethany came into the living room with a grave look on her face. "What is it, Miss Bethany?" Emily asked in apprehension.

"A very sick man has arrived," Miss Bethany stammered. "And he has asked to see you."

"Asked to see me?" Emily echoed in queer surprise. "That is most unusual, especially at this ungodly hour. Has he left you with a name?"

"No he hasn't," Miss Bethany replied apologetically. "Do you want me to wake Lawrence up?"

"No," Emily insisted emphatically. "It's inhuman how Lawrence is constantly bombarded at all hours of the night. Let me see who it is."

Emily slowly walked into the waiting room of Lawrence's office. There she found a bedraggled man sitting with slumped shoulders. The light of a single lamp shone upon his gaunt countenance. He was thin, frail, and unshaven. He appeared to be deprived of food and sleep while his pale complexion and facial features looked drawn.

Dressed in a shabby black overcoat, barely warm enough for the night, his untimely arrival had brought in the bitter chill of the outside air. Emily studied the man in puzzlement, not recalling ever seeing him before.

It was then the mysterious man lifted his seedy black hat, and tipped it in respect. It all came rushing back to Emily. Like a bad penny from the past, beneath the hat hid the remnants of red hair as Sir Dexter Lund's identity emerged, now the ruin of a lost man, with his hair grayed to the same ghastly shade as his father Hector.

A chill of terror ran through Emily's entire body as her expression changed from concern to alarm.

"Hello Emily," Sir Dexter said in a weakened voice.

Emily nodded her head in grave acknowledgment, caught too off guard to even utter a word.

"I'm so sorry to intrude on you, Emily, but when your housekeeper told me Dr. Gray was asleep, I inquired of you." Sir Dexter turned his head over in the direction of Miss Bethany. "She informed me you were still awake and sitting by the fire. I hope I haven't disturbed you, Emily," Sir Dexter said weakly, but with the same aristocratic intonation she remembered, and detested.

Stone-faced, Emily nodded neither yes nor no as the silence of a trance left her motionless. At that juncture, Miss Bethany went into the linen closet for a thick woolen blanket, and carried it into him. Sir Dexter gratefully took the blanket with feeble fingers, and covered his frail body.

"Thank you, Miss," Sir Dexter added respectfully.

"Please call me Miss Bethany, would you like me to bring you some hot tea?"

Sir Dexter nodded his head in due appreciation as his bleary eyes closed slightly, making it obvious he could not keep them open for much longer. Sir Dexter then whispered beneath his breath, "A warm blanket will be quite enough, Miss Bethany. There is no need to fuss with tea at this hour."

"Very well then," Miss Bethany curtsied as she departed to go back to her chamber.

Sir Dexter continued feebly. "Emily, I have not come under any ill tidings. I have come only to see Dr. Gray. As you can see I've grown quite ill."

He slowed down, breathing in a rasp, as a deep cough intruded. "I have traveled far to arrive here, and this is clearly my last hope." Sir Dexter looked down solemnly as Emily cringed inside.

"I'm dying, Emily," Sir Dexter said softly in resignation.

"Dying?" Emily repeated in alarm.

"The doctors have not been able to help me, and I have already seen many. I've heard of Dr. Gray's many miracles." Sir Dexter sighed desperately. "I was hoping perhaps he would be kind enough to provide one of his miracles for me . . . I hope my coming here doesn't disturb you too much, Emily. I come only for medical treatment, that's all, I assure you."

"I see," Emily said in bittersweet triumph, musing how the situation had been reversed.

Sir Dexter looked up at her poignantly, as he implored. "Emily, if you'd just allow me to sit here quietly out of the cold, and wait until morning to see Dr. Gray, I would be very grateful . . . Again I apologize if I've disturbed you, Emily."

"Very well," Emily said indifferently, as she retreated back into the living room in a state of stupefaction.

It had all happened so suddenly. She felt stunned how, after all the years that had passed, nearly twenty-five in total, Sir Dexter Lund had come back into her life again under such a dire circumstance. Emily could not fathom how the singular presence of a man, now far removed from her sight could intrude on her peace.

The truth was she loathed having Sir Dexter beneath the same roof, and intruding in her space, even considering his ill condition. The rest of the night brought Emily much discomfort, as she dozed off here and there in a state of disorientation.

Come morning, Miss Bethany knocked on Lawrence's chamber. "Lawrence, there is a very sick man who arrived in the middle of the night waiting for you in your office. Pierre is preparing a breakfast tray for him."

"Very well, Miss Bethany, I will tend to him right away." Lawrence rushed downstairs to find the frail, miserably sick man. At forty-seven years old, Sir Dexter passed for far older.

Upon seeing Lawrence's entry, Sir Dexter came out of his semi-slumber. "Dr. Gray." Sir Dexter sat up slightly. "Mrs. Gray has been kind enough to allow me to wait here until morning to see you. As you can see with your own eyes I'm a gravely ill man," Sir Dexter murmured.

The voice, the mannerisms, and suddenly Sir Dexter reached to shake Lawrence's hand when it began to all come back to Lawrence, though he still did not recognize him just yet.

Lawrence instructed him to come into his examining room. Sir Dexter did so; with a weakened step, as if it was a burden to merely stand. Without the blanket shielding his form, Lawrence took note how his new patient was undernourished and emaciated.

Then, with the light of the office, and the morning sunlight reflecting the white-light of winter, Lawrence finally realized the unfathomable man looked oddly familiar. Sir Dexter then took off his shoddy hat, and the unmistakable trademark of his faded red hair blared out in the light of day.

"Sir Dexter Lund, is that really you?" Lawrence asked in shock, feeling like he had seen a ghost, as everything came flooding back to him again.

"Yes, it is I, Dexter Lund," he said simply with the paradox of the past humbling him.

"What in the world has happened to you, Dexter?" Lawrence inquired in incomprehension.

"Lawrence, I have lost everything, everything! I cannot pay you, and I'm counting on your benevolence, if you would be so kind as to help a dying man in spite of our past connection, which I regret. I would be eternally grateful." Sir Dexter swallowed weakly as his voice faded into oblivion.

"The past has no bearing now, Sir Dexter. I treat anyone who calls upon my services charitably. Come with me at once; let me take a look at you, Dexter."

"Dr. Gray, I'm indeed dying in a self-fulfilling prophecy of drinking myself into an early grave," Sir Dexter confessed in a weak voice.

"Sir Dexter, if you want to live, you will have to sober up, and dry out. Then you will get your appetite back, and good nutrition will make you strong again," advised Lawrence.

"My appetite has become so poor. All I have been ingesting is spirits, and I haven't had a good night's sleep in God knows how long," Sir Dexter admitted as if he was bearing his soul to a priest at the confessional. He then went into his tattered coat pocket and handed Lawrence a silver flask of liquor. "Here, Dr. Gray, maybe it would be best if you would take this from me, otherwise I will surely drink it."

Lawrence did so with authority. "Sir Dexter, you will need to take a tonic specifically designed to aid your overworked liver, and to help alleviate your craving for alcohol. I will formulate one right away. I have the specific cleansing herbs in mind already. I will start in the preparation of my tincture while Miss Bethany brings you in a breakfast tray. Please try to eat a little," Lawrence encouraged with a kind look.

"Thank you so much, Dr. Gray," Sir Dexter said with gratitude.

Lawrence walked back into the center hallway before going downstairs to the basement to devise the formula. Emily stirred in the living room with a distraught expression.

"Lawrence, is he still here?" Emily muttered beneath her breath.

"Yes, Sir Dexter is in my office. He is a gravely ill man, and will die without proper treatment, Emily."

"Oh yes, even I can attest to his grave condition," retorted Emily with a snarl. "Of that I saw last night. Let me ask you, Lawrence, what business does Sir Dexter have bringing his illness here?"

"Emily," Lawrence spoke sympathetically. "The poor man has lost everything; Sir Dexter is in desperate need of help. I cannot worry about past grudges at a time like this!"

"Past grudges, is that what his cruelty has been reduced to?" Emily asked with a grimace. "What right does Sir Dexter have to come to us after all the harm he has done?"

"Emily, my sweetheart, people change and mature. Sir Dexter is not the same young man we once knew . . . It's such a shock to see him in such a grim condition. The man has literally drunk himself into his own undoing. He has one foot in the grave already," Lawrence said solemnly.

"So we aren't the Salvation Army, let him go there!" Emily shouted resentfully. "We already know Sir Dexter has a tendency for overindulgence in alcohol, and I'm a living proof of it! God only knows the damage he's done throughout the years with his binging."

"Emily, that's all in the past and Sir Dexter has already expressed his regret."

"Of course," Emily blurted out. "Sir Dexter regrets the tables have turned and he has been humbled enough to now have to call upon you for his very survival! The Lord has punished Sir Dexter, and there has been justice!" Emily exclaimed victoriously. "He doesn't deserve your mercy after what he has done to us!"

"Sir Dexter has chosen to come here, and I won't send him away to die! I intend to treat Sir Dexter just as humanely as I would treat any other man. I'm a professional, one hundred percent. Here, Sir Dexter can recover, and be on his way after he does. It's my duty to help all who come to my door, regardless! I have not sent anyone away yet, and I'm not planning on it now, Emily."

"Lawrence, can't you see what a degraded individual Sir Dexter has become? He of all people doesn't belong in our household in any shape or form! If not for the passing of the eighteenth amendment, Sir Dexter would have no doubt just gone on with his excessive drinking and merrymaking. He has probably been consorting with bootleggers as it is. I cannot believe the change in him; he looks like the lowest dregs of society!"

"Emily, the prohibition isn't stopping people from drinking. I believe Sir Dexter's wanting to stop is more than that. He wants to live, and there is no fear of him harming us anymore, my sweetheart."

Emily clenched her jaw. "I don't care how harmless Sir Dexter might have become with time, his proximity has overtaken our happy home, and I want no part of the man after what he has done to me!" Emily cried out inconsolably.

Chapter Thirty-Nine

The Bitter Dispute

Emily raged her battle relentlessly. "Lawrence, can't you see how devious Sir Dexter is? His resurfacing in our lives has been the catalyst of an irreconcilable difference! For twenty-four years of marriage we've been congenial, and now Sir Dexter's mere presence has ruined our tranquility."

"Emily, please be reasonable, Sir Dexter is doing nothing other than recuperating quietly in my office!" Lawrence insisted.

"He is quiet only because of his condition. Let's not forget Lady Violet accused Sir Dexter of attempted murder. The only reason he was even let out of the French prison was because his family paid his way out, millions I may add. It's no wonder he has nothing. That was the price he had to pay to merely be a free man."

"Both you and I know Lady Violet would go to any extreme to get money and cause misery. We both agreed how that whole scandal was a farce!" Lawrence retorted impatiently.

"We are not in the position to attest to Sir Dexter's innocence," Emily shouted vehemently. "Sir Dexter was freed from jail only because his parents hired high-powered attorneys. They would have thrown out the key on him if not for his family's money!"

"Emily, you are talking nonsense. I know Sir Dexter has been far from perfect, but I can assure you he poses no threat to us whatsoever. Relax, my darling, he's just a patient of mine like any other."

"I cannot relax!" Emily cried out. "Sir Dexter is pathetic in every way. What about him sending Lady Violet here to blackmail me into returning the engagement ring? I choose not to be around a lowlife like him!" Emily seethed through clenched teeth.

"Emily dearest, you have gotten the ring back years ago. Let's not forget Lady Violet sold the ring to Ralph's for a fraction of its value. It was clearly not money she was after, the whole thing could have been fabricated for all we know."

"Lady Violet might have received only a fraction of the ring's value, but she still received instant cash. Sometimes impatience to attain money can make one a bit hasty."

"Emily, Lady Violet disposed of the ring so quickly it has become obvious to me; she stole it away from you and Sir Dexter alike for her own selfish motives. I guarantee Lady Violet's vengeance was more to her liking than the cash. We both know she was so jealous of you, Emily. After all she is ignorant to the truth, and believed Sir Dexter was in love with you."

"Emily, sweetheart," Lawrence said her name with endearment. "Sir Dexter has come to me as a patient. Pretend he's merely a stranger. I choose not to pry open the past. It's gone! I prefer to live in the present moment," Lawrence said magnanimously.

"In that aspect I agree, but it still doesn't change my feelings. I want him out!" Emily raised her voice inconsolably. "I can never forget the personal grief that man put me through. Of that I have witnessed, and I know firsthand of Sir Dexter's brutality! He is a man of miserable character, and a drunkard to boot! He always was, and I'm sure he will always be a lush! Even if you manage to sober him up, who is to prevent him from going back to his lack of self restraint?"

"Emily, I still must do my best to help the man. The rest is up to him. I believe if Sir Dexter truly wants to recover from his addiction to alcohol, he can. As good Christians, we have to forgive people, Emily. You know as well as I, it's the way of the Lord. We've taught that motto to our children, and give praise to forgiveness when we're at church on Sunday."

"Lawrence, I wish with all my heart I could be a bigger person and forgive Sir Dexter, but remember it's far easier for you than for me. This man forced himself on me, and then sent me away as if I was no more than a trollop! Sir Dexter humiliated me, and for that I can never forgive him!" Emily began to weep on recall as her face contorted with long suppressed ire.

"Well then, my darling." Lawrence tenderly wiped her tears away. "Maybe that's why Sir Dexter has come back into your life again. Everything happens for a reason, and maybe this is God's test of you. Emily, I guarantee it will be a big relief if you could finally release the anger you have held onto for so long . . . Anger is poison for the soul. I have faith you can finally let it go if you really tried. Now is the proper time, Emily, release it, and it will set you free."

"When he leaves I will be free!" Emily cried in despair. "As far as I'm concerned Sir Dexter does not deserve your compassion, and to be a part of your clientele. It's just not appropriate. You are not the only doctor on earth for heaven's sake!"

"Emily, you're getting carried away. Sir Dexter will only be here for three days at the most. If I was to send him away now, he will surely die. I couldn't have that on my conscience. The days will pass quickly, please, sweetheart, pay no mind to what you cannot see. I never let my patients interfere in our household, and I don't intend to now. Sir Dexter will be out of sight just like all the others."

Emily's eyes beamed with venom as her face reddened. "Lawrence, you speak as if we live in a fairytale and people can be removed from their sins by our forgiveness! Whatever anyone does in their lifetime becomes a part of them forever! Even if I could forgive Sir Dexter, it can never change what happened." Emily stormed off in tears.

"Emily, today is a new day, please let us not continue this folly. It's beyond my comprehension how the mere presence of a man could disturb you so. You haven't even laid eyes on Sir Dexter since the night he arrived. I cannot fathom how his presence can prey so heavily upon you."

Emily reprimanded angrily, "Lawrence, are you so blind not to see what Sir Dexter is doing to us? He is turning us against each other. Is that what you want? Hasn't the man done enough harm to us already?"

"He is doing nothing to us! You're doing it all to yourself, Emily. As a doctor I must be professional, it's my duty!" Lawrence argued adamantly.

"And what about your duty to your wife, and her happiness, don't you have responsibility for my feelings? I'm eight months pregnant, Lawrence. I certainly don't need this added aggravation at such a delicate time!" Emily shouted.

"But you're the one who is aggravating yourself, Emily. Can't you see that, dearest? Please do try and be reasonable," Lawrence pleaded tenderly as he touched her shoulders.

Emily flinched away, and shouted in rage with a face no longer her own. "I don't want to be reasonable! I want closure from this man. Let Sir Dexter go elsewhere for charity."

"Emily, I realize how emotional women can be in your condition, you're overreacting; it's no doubt your hormones. I've never seen you like this before. Please let me make you a tonic to calm your nerves." Lawrence smoothed his hand tenderly over her extended belly.

"Don't you touch me! Not until you do the right thing, and send him away. Sir Dexter doesn't deserve your compassion. I'm your wife; I'm the one who deserves some understanding. Look how you treat my feelings!" Emily shouted.

"Emily, your inability to forgive is not appropriate. I cannot fathom how you could have such a lack of empathy! It's not like you!"

"And it's not like you to allow a man who has violated my honor to stay beneath our roof! Have you no heart for my feelings, Lawrence?" Emily blasted.

Chapter Forty

Head Over Heels

Sir Dexter insisted, as he looked Lawrence straight in the face, "I will never go back to the bottle again, Mr. Gray. My life has been grim for the past twenty-five years, and I have learned the hard way drinking is not the solution."

"Drinking does havoc to the body, especially in large quantities," Lawrence warned with a solemn expression.

"Yes, thankfully, I feel much better now after your tonic. These past years have been difficult, and drinking helped to alleviate my stress . . . After my divorce from Lady Violet, I lost everything, and shortly afterward, both of my parents died within a year apart from each other. That left me to look after Mallory, who has never married." Sir Dexter's raspy voice was tinged with regret.

"Where do you and Mallory live?" Lawrence inquired.

"We live together in a modest apartment in Westwood, Connecticut. It has been hard for Mallory to adjust to our circumstance. Unfortunately, I'm no longer a practicing lawyer." Sir Dexter looked downward in shame. "I've held some odd jobs around town since, but money is scarce. If things turn around, I will repay you for your services, Dr. Gray."

"That won't be necessary, Sir Dexter. The only payment I ask for is your sobriety."

Lawrence found Emily in the parlor drinking a cup of tea. "I'm going out on my rounds of house calls. I just want you to know Sir Dexter will be gone by this evening, so you can be assured everything will be just as before. He will be out of our life, not to worry, sweetheart, and things will be like they were before."

Emily glared furiously. "And how can you be sure Sir Dexter won't come knocking on your office again?"

"I can never be sure of that, but I'll hope for the best."

"Being hopeful cannot cure a man from evil! Once he's gone, that had better be the last of him! If there is a next time, and I answer the door first, be assured Sir Dexter will not be granted entry!" Emily shouted with vehemence.

"I must go, Emily, I have patients who are waiting to see me," Lawrence said with annoyance. "Emily, this entire discussion is counterproductive. We have gotten to the point where we are unable to even discuss this topic without getting into a full-blown argument, and I can't go through this again." Emily turned her back as Lawrence went to kiss her goodbye.

Emily headed toward the drawing room to write letters. When she had completed her correspondences, Emily proceeded to go up the stairs when a voice urged her back.

"Emily." She turned an inquisitive eye to see Sir Dexter Lund standing in the center hallway looking much improved.

Emily wondered how he could have the audacity to enter the family quarters, and address her in such a forward manner. Sir Dexter broke her incriminating stare and looked downward in shame as his voice became tender.

"Emily, I hope you don't mind me taking the liberty of speaking to you like this, but Lawrence told me I will be well enough to leave tonight." His voice softened. "I just wanted to apologize to you once and for all, and to let you know how sorry I am for the indiscretion of my youth, and the wrong I have done to you. I have lived with the guilt everyday since then, and things have not turned out well for me."

His pitiful expression and heartfelt apology made Emily realize Lawrence had been right after all! Sir Dexter was not the same villain he had been twenty-five years ago. Emily's anger drained out of her body as forgiveness replaced it.

"I appreciate your apology, Sir Dexter, you need say no more," Emily offered in earnest.

"Emily." Sir Dexter went to reach for her hand, but held back the inclination. His book-smart eyes looked at her with a spark of humanity. "What a fool I was to have sent you away, Emily. I have thought about you every single day since then. When I sent you off in such haste . . . I sent away my own unborn child." Sir Dexter lamented. "And I have had to live with my poor judgment for all of my days. I have drunk myself into a stupor over my misery."

Sir Dexter's face contorted in deep regret as tears of emotion filled Emily's eyes as well.

"The boy, Emily, please tell me about our son," Sir Dexter urged as his downcast lips quivered.

Emily looked at the blank expression in Sir Dexter's eyes. It looked like crosses were drawn over his irises, obliterating their green color to murky gray. She remembered with clarity the one fact she had tried to forget all these years, Sir Dexter Lund was the flesh and blood father of Jake.

Emily inhaled deeply as the words were difficult to find. She looked at Sir Dexter standing there, a remnant of what he used to represent as mercy set her free.

"Jake has always been a wonderful child, and now he's grown into a fine young man. He has plans to marry a lovely, young lady by the name of Ella Winning from a well-respected family, and they have decided to live in Salem. Jake will turn twenty-four on March 14. He is currently away at law school in Pittsburgh, Pennsylvania."

"That's wonderful news; I'm delighted to learn he is studying law. Isn't that something?" Sir Dexter's eyes looked distant, but oddly at peace for the moment.

"I have never had another child, Emily," Sir Dexter said soberly as their eyes locked. "I guess that was God's way of punishing me for what I've done. I have always believed that Emily." Sir Dexter looked down painfully. The sunken contours of his face made him look even more pathetic.

Emily's heart melted at his remorse. "I will admit to you, Sir Dexter, when you showed up at Lawrence's office, it brought back a lot of old anger, but now I feel sad that you have never had another child. Jake is the spitting image of you. He has red hair and freckles, and could easily be your twin."

"How do you like that?" Sir Dexter smiled affectionately while his eyes reflected his inner torment.

"Wait right here, Dexter, I'll go upstairs and get you a recent photo of him from his college graduation, and then you will see what I mean." Emily animated with enthusiasm.

Emily proceeded to walk up the long winding staircase in the haste of heavy emotion. Just before she reached the top step, the heel of her boot became entangled on the bottom of her hem. She tried to steady her footing, but the pregnancy made her unbalanced. Without warning, Emily lost her foothold and began to tumble down the long, steep staircase headfirst.

As she plunged from the heights, Sir Dexter lunged forward to thwart her fall. It all happened so fast there was no way for him to intercept her descent. Sprawled out at the base of the stairs, Emily lay like a rag doll.

Sir Dexter frantically screamed as Miss Bethany and Miss Haskell, the midwife, became alerted and quickly came forth. The women shrieked at the sight of Emily sprawled at the base of the stairs.

"What happened?" Miss Bethany cried out while Miss Haskell bent over to aid her.

"Emily lost her footing, and fell down the stairs!" Sir Dexter relayed like a zombie in a state of shock and guilt alike.

Sir Dexter lifted Emily in his own weakened condition, with the help of Miss Bethany and the midwife. The three of them carried her with great difficulty, and laid her down upon the four-poster bed in the guestroom adjacent to the drawing room.

Sir Dexter was promptly booted out as Miss Bethany and Miss Haskell did everything they could to bring Emily back to awareness. Nonetheless, Emily's eyes stayed tightly closed, and her breathing remained shallow, even after the smelling salts. The women put a cool cloth upon her head while her blue eyes rested beneath their quivering lids, and Emily began to sporadically open and close them.

Miss Haskell cried out with worry, "From the way her eyes are rolling around, she probably has a concussion."

For a moment Emily became cognizant as she frantically called out, "Lawrence, Lawrence, where is Lawrence? I must speak to Lawrence at once!"

"He is at a patient's house, and should return soon, Emily." Miss Bethany tried to console her, as she reached to hold Emily's hand.

It gave little comfort to Emily's spinning thoughts. Coming in and out of consciousness, at last Emily saw eye to eye with Lawrence about Sir

Dexter. She desperately wanted Lawrence to know her change of heart, and to apologize for their dispute.

"Lawrence, Lawrence," again Emily cried out in agitation. "I need to see Lawrence right away!"

Suddenly in a frenzy of torment and disorientation alike, Emily shrieked as a labor pain took over the tranquility of her womb. Then another one came a few minutes later, causing Emily intense discomfort. Before long, the labor pains were coming closer and closer together.

Miss Haskell nervously announced, "The baby is coming prematurely, and there's no way to prevent it!"

Emily began going in and out of coherency as the pain became excruciating. Miss Haskell felt for Emily's pulse intermittently. "She is falling in and out of consciousness, and her heartbeat is weakened. Miss Bethany, I certainly could use Lawrence's input on stabilizing her, I have no experience with premature deliveries," Miss Haskell said in panic.

"Do the best you can!" Miss Bethany frantically yelled out. "Lawrence is not expected home until late afternoon, and there is no saying where he might be!"

The baby began to emerge as Emily became fully dilated. With all the trauma of Emily falling down the stairs, and her rampage of emotions, the birth of one life, became the termination of another.

Miss Haskell shrieked as she held Emily's lifeless pulse. The newborn cried faintly, as Emily became lost to the land of the dead. Miss Haskell tried desperately to revive Emily with smelling salts, as Miss Bethany wiped Emily's forehead with a cool cloth.

"Emily, it's me Miss Bethany." The housemaid wailed with more fervor than the infant.

"It's no use, Miss Bethany, Emily has left us, and there is no bringing her back," Miss Haskell cried out as Miss Bethany shrieked.

"Thankfully, the infant is close enough to full term to survive with the help of a wet nurse. Otherwise the infant shall perish as well. I will make the arrangements at once . . ." Miss Haskell tearfully said, as Miss Bethany sobbed inconsolably.

The wet nurse, Mrs. Elsa Cooper, arrived shortly afterward. "Thank goodness you have arrived, what an angel of mercy you look like, please follow me, Mrs. Cooper." Miss Haskell led her to the nursery.

"Oh, what a beautiful baby," Miss Cooper said as she scooped her up. "And what a shame about the mother, my heart goes out to all of you."

Miss Haskell and Miss Bethany became crazed upon hearing Lawrence open the front door. The two desperate women rushed over to him as he innocently returned home from work. Lawrence walked in carrying a box of Valentine candy and a card with cupids and tender endearments for Emily with a hopeful look upon his lovelorn face.

Upon seeing the distraught demeanor of both Miss Bethany and Miss Haskell, Lawrence became alarmed. "Is Sir Dexter all right?" He asked in panic.

Miss Haskell wailed with her head bowed, "We lost her!"

"Lost who?" Lawrence shouted in confusion. "Where's Emily?"

Like twin angels of death, the two women stood there as Miss Haskell answered his question with immeasurable dread, "I have done my best, Lawrence. I'm so sorry, but I have lost Emily."

"Lost Emily," Lawrence cried in frenzy. "What are you talking about?"

"She had a bad fall," Miss Bethany divulged as they led him into the room where on a small bed the remnants of Emily's womanhood lay motionless with the grief of hell upon Lawrence's disbelieving sights.

Lawrence bent down to feel for her stilled pulse. He looked at her closed eyes, and touched her cold face, as he bowed his head in agony, and fell upon her chest, and wept like a child.

The two women left Lawrence alone with his grief. He moaned with the misery and loss he could not fathom all at once. He had left just hours ago, and now upon his return, his beloved wife, his soul, his dear Emily Grace Gray had vanished forever.

Miss Haskell explained to Lawrence when he left her chamber over an hour later. "Emily must have gone into premature labor as a result of the fall. She had a head injury, and I did the very best I could to stabilize her. Sir Dexter Lund must have heard her bloodcurdling screams, because when I found her sprawled out at the base of the stairs, he was standing over her, trying to save her. In his weakened condition, Sir Dexter helped us carry Emily into the guestroom. That man is a saint!"

Miss Bethany brought the newborn in, swathed in a pink blanket, and made motion to hand her over to Lawrence. Emotionless to the joy of the new life, Lawrence barely even glanced at the infant as he paced about deliriously, wailing aloud in a hysterical frenzy.

Sir Dexter became alerted by all the commotion, and gravitated from Lawrence's office into the hallway. Miss Haskell rushed over to him in grief and gratitude for his help. "Thank you so much for helping Emily, but I have some bad news."

Miss Haskell's voice became strained. "Emily has gone into premature labor . . . and has died in childbirth."

Sir Dexter looked over at Lawrence who stood still for a moment, and they just stared at each other. Their mutual tragedy concerning Emily bonded them with an intangible thread. Sir Dexter cried out inconsolably, as he approached Lawrence and held him close to his chest.

"No it can't be!" Sir Dexter screamed in mortification. "That can't be true!" Tears filled his eyes as Miss Bethany intercepted and embraced Sir Dexter.

"Thank you so much for rushing in to help Emily after she fell, and for helping to carry her into the guestroom when you should be resting yourself," Miss Bethany said in due appreciation.

"There is no need for thanks at a time like this. Dr. Gray, I insist on helping you in any way I can," Sir Dexter offered with a solemn expression tinged with guilt.

"Thank you, I could use all the help I could get right now. Miss Bethany will tell you who to call, and help you make the arrangements."

Lawrence grieved with a vacant expression, his head bowed in mortification. "I blame myself, Miss Bethany. Emily and I had an argument before I left, perhaps if I hadn't upset her so with our quarrelling, she would not have fallen," Lawrence berated inconsolably.

"No, Lawrence, it wasn't your fault, it was an accident."

"If I had any inclination Emily was going to go into premature labor, I would have never left the house, but how was I to know?" Lawrence asked despondently.

"Emily was calling out to you, Lawrence, she wanted to see you," Miss Bethany revealed with a poignant smile.

"If I was there, she would have probably just blasted me for my insensitivity." Lawrence frowned. "How can I live with myself after what has happened? There is no way to make peace with my Emily now, other than to smother her grave with red roses!" Lawrence professed as his vacant eyes became alive with purpose.

Chapter Forty-One

Church on the Hill

Sitting like bookends at Emily's wake, Lawrence and Sir Dexter looked on as Mrs. Reed, dressed in her mourning attire knelt beside her daughter's open casket and wept pitifully. A bounty of funeral flowers bloomed around the outskirts, flirting with death.

Lawrence could not bear to look at Emily's sleeping face any longer. He believed she now belonged to the heavens, while his conscience belonged to hell.

Emily's mother approached Lawrence sorrowfully. "My baby is in heaven with all the angels," Mrs. Reed wailed. "I want her back here on earth with us where she belongs." Then recognizing Sir Dexter Lund inspired the same look of disdain Mrs. Reed used to reserve for Lawrence when he worked the fields.

"Come," Mr. Reed grabbed a hold of his wife's arm, to lead her away. "We have had quite enough for today." Mr. Reed shot Sir Dexter a cold glance.

William Gray bent down to embrace his son with a mournful countenance. "Lawrence, hang in there, and be strong for the children. They need you, and you'll see they will give you comfort as well."

"Thanks, Father." Lawrence's voice faded into silence.

The time had come to bury Emily beneath the chill of winter's earth at the Saint James Cemetery. Against the white shroud of snow turned ice, a sea of lost souls stood swathed in black. Grayed embers of light spilled down from the sky, as all became stilled before the sunless dawn.

The priest, a young Father Dale spoke solemnly, "Emily Grace Gray was a special someone to everyone. She was a devoted daughter to her parents, Philip and Margaret Reed, a caring sister to her brothers, Hal and Charles, a loving wife to her beloved husband, Lawrence Gray, and a dedicated mother to her dear children, Jake, Lawrence Junior, Maggie Beth, and Emma Grace, who was named in remembrance of Emily. Emily would have been devoted to her newborn Emma as well." Sounds of sobbing reverberated through the air like a flock of mourning doves.

Father Dale became choked with emotion as his blue eyes melded with the winter sky. "Emma never got to know her mother, but Emily gave her the gift of life. Emma was the last gift Emily has given to us . . . it was Emily's sacrifice, and now it will be part of her legacy. I have had the honor of baptizing Emily, and I have faith Emily will live on through the love she has selflessly given, and received in the name of our Lord Jesus Christ."

Father Dale opened his bible, to recite a prayer for the deceased. The words fell coldly from his lips as the pallbearers lowered Emily's coffin into the waiting abyss of earth.

"'May their souls of all the faithful departed, through the mercy of God, rest in peace. Amen.'"

Emily's children clutched each other in doleful sequence. Jake tried to shield the others by being the bravest. However, in the crowd of black weeds sounded mournful cries of bereavement. Lawrence had his torso bent to the grindstone already. It looked as if he wished he could merge himself right beside Emily's coffin, even if the price meant his own earthly annihilation.

If there was ever a myth—grown men do not cry, it was dispelled on the solemn morning of Emily's burial. Lawrence's weeping sounded in a macabre melody, pitched low, from the pit of his soul, where his spirit dwelled.

All was still for a moment as the men covered Emily's coffin with snowed soil. Each shovel full of earth sounded like the ominous smashing of life into the smithereens of nothingness. Black and barren, emotions heaved up, and then ran out of Lawrence Gray. His blood became stilled within his veins, turning his face as white as the snow, and his flesh as cold.

"Emily, my Emily," Lawrence shrieked. "Please don't leave me! I want you to haunt me forever, my sweet angel. I will look over my shoulder for you always!" He shouted wildly, bending his head downward, conspiring with the devil, and detesting God for taking away his soul.

On the horizon of the dismal sky, chilled with the frost of morning, Lawrence envisioned the last glimpse of Emily's deathbed countenance. The memory of her once beautiful face appeared as if she was in the midst of a peaceful dream where she would be taken to the land of angels.

Lawrence looked up toward heaven, and envisioned Emily transcending beyond the skies to fields of emerald green, to a paradise, where songbirds bless the air with heavenly tune. Lawrence believed Emily's spirit was already half in heaven, half on earth, hovering in-between, for one final, blessed moment. Now with the last sweep of earth, came the woeful momentum of losing Emily forever.

Lawrence's lips trembled. "Father, Emma Grace is a bittersweet baby, for she has brought joy and taken joy in equal measure."

"It's not Emma's fault," William said kindly. "We don't know why these things happen, but we have to trust in the Lord. You will see one day Emma will bring you much joy."

Lawrence took one last glance at Emily's resting place as Jake intercepted, "Father, I think it's best we head back to the limousine now. Come, let us go." Jake put a comforting arm around Lawrence's slumped shoulders, and led him away from where half of his life would remain.

The sorrowful clan went back to Fairway. Lawrence could barely touch a morsel of food to his mouth. Flavorless was the fare as black thoughts spun around Lawrence's head, oblivious to all the people conversing around him.

By the next morning, Lawrence was anxious to leave Fairway. He stood in the center hallway envisioning the first time he had set eyes on Emily as if it was only yesterday. He remembered her golden curls, and her laughing blue eyes, and the way she bestowed grace upon his weary countenance without judgment.

Emily's father stood by the door, to bid Lawrence and his grandchildren farewell. Lawrence's eyes met Mr. Reed's in despondency as Philip Reed reached forward and patted Lawrence on the shoulders just as he had done the first time Lawrence met him. Emily's death had taken a toll upon Philip Reed's countenance. He looked pale and exhausted, and his eyes were glazed and disoriented.

"Lawrence, we have lost our princess," Philip Reed murmured with the tender emotion a father has for a daughter.

"Yes, we have lost our angel, and I have lost my heart," Lawrence echoed dolefully while his children hugged their grandfathers, William and Philip, goodbye.

Lawrence tried to get his bearing back to the real world as he told Jake in a matter-of-fact manner, "We will have to get a proper governess for Emma and Maggie Beth. Miss Bethany will do what she can for now, but the girls need someone to look after them."

Maggie Beth cried out, "I don't want a governess! I want my mother back!"

Maggie began to outburst hysterically. "It's all my fault! It was my idea for her to have another baby in the first place. Now I have my little sister, but I don't have Mom." Tears besmirched Maggie's reddened eyes as she chastised herself.

Larry Junior reached over to comfort his distraught sister. "Maggie, it's not your fault. Let's try to be positive, at least we have the baby, Emma is part of Mom, and we'll love her just as we loved Mom. And she will love us just as Mom did."

Maggie Beth shouted obstinately, "I will never love Emma the way I loved Mom, never! If not for Emma we would still have Mom, can't you see?"

"Maggie," Lawrence said consolingly. "We love each family member in a special way, different but equal."

Sunday mornings became a day reserved for Lawrence to honor Emily. Jake looked over at Lawrence who was leaving with a bouquet of red roses in hand. "Father, don't tell me you're taking the long drive to Clinton again. You just went to Mom's gravesite last Sunday."

Stone-faced Lawrence replied, "And I will go there each and every Sunday. If no one else in this house wants to accompany me, that's all right with me. I want to be with Emily. She depends on my visits." Lawrence's face looked crazed with conviction.

Maggie Beth said with concern, "But Father, Mom isn't there, she has gone to heaven to be with Jesus. Your devotion to Mom will bring you nothing but sorrow. Why don't you come to church with us, and pray."

Lawrence's lips pressed tightly together as he vowed. "I don't care if I ever go to church again! Not all the prayers in the world could have saved Emily from her demise. What is the good of prayer now that she's gone, if it can't bring her back? Your mother used to pray at church every Sunday and now look at her!"

Chapter Forty-Two

The Easter Bonnet

Lawrence arrived for his usual Sunday morning of devotion at the Saint James Cemetery. There, set amidst a backdrop of old headstones, the monument of Emily Grace Gray stood as a tribute in steel-gray against the springtime sky. Lawrence read her inscription with a heavy heart, feeling like she had just died all over again when it had been a year ago.

> Emily Grace Gray
> April 12, 1877—January 28, 1920
> Beloved Wife
> Devoted Mother
> Loving Daughter and Sister
> Budded on earth to bloom in heaven

On Easter Sunday, Maggie pleaded with a helpless expression as Lawrence stood by the doorway with a bouquet of red roses in hand. "Father, please don't tell me you're going to the cemetery today. I thought we could all celebrate the holiday together. Pierre is roasting a turkey with all the trimmings."

"I will be home for dinner, Maggie, be assured, and we will have a nice evening together. But I must visit Emily; she cannot spend Easter alone."

"But Father, it's been over a year since Mother has passed away. How long are you going to continue with this driving back and forth such a long distance?"

"I've already told you, I have made a vow to myself. I will continue to visit Emily every Sunday for as long as I dwell on earth! I would visit her everyday if not for the distance," Lawrence said with dedication as Maggie sighed in disapproval.

Lawrence arrived at the cemetery with his usual dozen red roses. In approaching the vicinity of Emily's gravesite, Lawrence noticed a darkly clad woman bending over Emily's tombstone. Lawrence curiously approached thinking the woman had mistakenly situated herself by the wrong graveside.

The spirit of Easter brightened the cemetery. Colorful bouquets were placed upon many of the graves. In contrast, the woman's black hat, with brooding net, obscured her face. Lawrence gazed at her in deliberation, and surmised by her black weeds she must have been in mourning. He managed to catch a glimpse of the woman's face from beneath her veil seeing her features were contorted in grief. The crying woman then lifted her head, as she noticed him only to wail out in anguish.

"Lawrence, Lawrence," the woman cried out. "I loved Emily too! It's so unfair for her to have died!"

Lawrence heard the voice, and looked over at the face seeing a woman older than he, who appeared to be in her mid to late forties. All at once the past lifted its veil to the present, and the face of Mallory Lund stood out with the certainty of a coin's portrait, on the flip side of fate.

"Oh, Lawrence, I am so sorry." Mallory reached her frail arms around Lawrence's shoulders, and cried with remorse. "Emily was like a sister to me. I have been so crushed all these years over what has happened between us all, and now this!" Mallory clutched Lawrence tightly to her chest in overflowing emotion.

Yesteryear flooded back to Lawrence in a tragic reminder.

"Mallory, I cannot believe it's really you! It has been so many years since I last saw you. It seems a lifetime ago."

Lawrence zeroed in on her face, worn by time, and surmised her life had been as miserable as his had been for the past year. Mallory clung to his chest and cried bitterly.

Lawrence broke her embrace. "Mallory, come, let us get a cup of afternoon tea, and a bite to eat. It's almost noon. Let's go away from here where we can sit quietly and chat. It has been such a long time."

Lawrence led Mallory by the arm amidst the sea of sepulchers into the spring air. Arm in arm they walked down the block to Truffles, a quaint restaurant where off in the far corner, adjacent to a piano bar they became situated. The dimness of the restaurant made it seem more like evening than midday. Lovely crimson cloths covered the tables with vases of freshly cut lilacs placed in the center. They ordered tea and sandwiches with the intimacy of their prior connection bringing them back to the beginning.

Mallory spoke with poignancy, "Lawrence, I have never gotten over what happened between all of us. I've suffered from the loss of Emily's friendship even before she was laid out at Saint James. We were going to be such a happy family, living side by side, in the East and West wings of my father's estate. I had such hopes for the future back then."

Mallory spoke through a rampage of tears, "Then out of the blue everything became destroyed. I believed Sir Dexter when he told me you and Emily had betrayed us . . . When Sir Dexter finally admitted the truth to me years later, it tormented me all the more, and it remains to be the misfortune of my life, Lawrence. I had not only lost my future husband, but I had also lost my future sister-in-law as well."

Mallory dried her weeping eyes with her handkerchief. "It tormented me day and night when Sir Dexter admitted to me one night when he was drinking, that it was he who had ruined everything, and at my expense as well."

Lawrence tried to comfort the distraught Mallory. "Please don't fret so much, Mallory, the past is gone, why look back?"

Nonetheless, Mallory's eyes wept a steady stream of tears. "All I have is the past, Lawrence! It held my chance for happiness. I have lost my future as well. Sir Dexter's marriage to Lady Violet and their scandal was the ruination of my entire family. We've been destitute ever since. I have never married," Mallory said in deep lament. "Two broken engagements are more than enough for one woman to bear."

"I'm so sorry," Lawrence softly said. "I know I gave you my word of promising to marry you, but it was out of my hands when Sir Dexter sent Emily and me away. I'm so sorry for any heartache my actions have caused you, but I could not fight the power Sir Dexter had over us."

"Thank you for your apology, Lawrence." Mallory shook her head grievously. "Lawrence, I know you're not to blame. Sir Dexter told me how you stood little chance of defending yourself when he accused you of being the baby's father."

Mallory's lips began to quiver. "Lawrence, I will never forgive myself for the way I treated you and Emily that morning after church when James was bandaging the horse's shin. I said dreadful things, and my family treated you and Emily abominably. When Sir Dexter admitted the truth, it haunted me to know I sent off my two closest friends on such an ill note. It is I who is sorry for believing Sir Dexter's lie."

"It was not your fault, Mallory," Lawrence comforted. "Everything happened so quickly."

"I know, but the aftereffects have lingered. I have no life . . . To think you have taken the blame for Sir Dexter's violation of Emily and then raised Sir Dexter's son as your own shows me just how flawless your character is, Lawrence. It was extremely gallant of you to put Emily and the baby before your own reputation."

Mallory looked deep inside Lawrence's dark eyes. "Lawrence, I have no one, nothing. Now that my parents are both gone, Sir Dexter has been a wretched companion with his binges of alcohol. He has a dark and ugly side, and I have been dependent on him, and at his mercy. If you saw the miserable hovel I'm forced to live in, you would be aghast. It's in the basement of a dilapidated boarding house in Westwood. Life has not been kind to us. Sir Dexter has been sober for the past year, but I fear he is a time bomb waiting to explode."

"Mallory, for the first time in over a year, I can finally feel for someone else's grief aside from my own," Lawrence said with guilt. "I know it was a long time ago, but I feel partly to blame for your circumstance. After all I didn't fight Sir Dexter when in retrospect perhaps that might have been the right thing to do."

"Nonsense, Lawrence, and leave Emily to face the ramifications of Sir Dexter's depraved actions alone! You and Emily have had twenty-four years of marriage to show for your choice, and three children of your own. You were lucky, but for Emily to die so young just isn't fair! It killed me the way I never had the chance to make amends with you and Emily for the way you were wrongly ostracized. Sir Dexter forbade me from ever contacting Emily again, saying he would disown me if I had. Like an obedient sister I listened, and now it's too late!" Mallory's voice became breathy and spirit like.

"Sir Dexter's son, Jake, is twenty-five already, and looks just like him. As a matter-of-fact, his friends call him Red," Lawrence said with affection.

Mallory began to weep sentimentally. "My poor parents died never knowing they even had a grandchild. It was a tragedy for our entire family, but a blessing for Emily to have gotten away from Sir Dexter. He is my brother, my own flesh and blood, but he would not have been a fit husband for any woman . . . How are your children handling everything, Lawrence?" Mallory asked with a sorrowful countenance.

"It has been very difficult for them. My sons are taking it better since they're older and away at school. It's especially hard for little Emma. She never even knew her mother . . . It's very difficult to find a caring governess. I had to let the last one go, so my housemaid, Miss Bethany, has been doing all she can until I find a new governess." Lawrence sighed in distress.

Mallory's face softened with understanding. "I can sympathize with you, Lawrence. I worked as a governess for a few years, and it's difficult for the children to adjust to death."

Lawrence's face lit up. "Mallory, would you consider coming to Salem with me, and being a governess for Emma and Maggie Beth? If you agree, I will have no need to look for another governess now that I know you're experienced with children."

"You have no idea what a Godsend that would be. Yes. Lawrence, I will gladly be their governess, thank you." Mallory bowed her head in gratitude as her face beamed with immeasurable joy. This in effect gave Lawrence the first spark of cheer he had experienced since losing Emily.

Chapter Forty-Three

The Governess

"Hello I'm Miss Bethany, you must be the new governess, Miss Mallory Lund. Lawrence has left word you would be arriving this morning. Please leave your bags by the front door, and Lawrence will carry them down for you."

"Thank you, Miss Bethany. It's a pleasure to meet you," Mallory said with a curtsy.

Mallory looked appropriate for the position of governess, dressed in a high-collared gray dress, cinched at the waist. Her brown hair was smoothed into a bun at the nape of her neck, and topped with a somber hat. Her spectacles had gotten larger and thicker with time.

Maggie Beth rushed in with her flaxen curls looking as pale as husks of corn. "You must be the new governess. I'm . . ."

"Don't tell me, let me guess . . . You must be Maggie Beth." Mallory illuminated in a smile.

"I am. What is your name?" Maggie Beth's expression lit up.

"Maggie, your new governess' name is Miss Mallory," interjected Miss Bethany.

Mallory smiled intimately, as she leaned down and twirled one of Maggie's platinum curls. "There is no need for formality with me. You can call me Mallory, and for short you can call me Mah."

It was clear Mallory had already won Maggie Beth over by her down-to-earth manner. Two-year-old Emma appeared who was a gem of another color. Mallory lifted the golden haired cherub to her chest in sympathy for her never having a mother. Their connection was instant and intense, each provided what the other lacked, and desperately desired.

"Emma, this is our new governess. You can call her Mah," Maggie Beth told her baby sister.

Emma's large blue eyes illuminated as she shouted out, "Ma Ma." They all laughed while Mallory found the pet name endearing.

Lawrence emerged from his study. "Hello, I see you have already met my little darlings, Mallory."

"I have, and they are charming children," Mallory exclaimed as her face became lit with light and life.

It brought comfort to Lawrence's forlorn heart to watch Mallory lovingly feed Emma mashed bananas.

"Mallory, I'm so happy we have found each other again. I just want you to know, your presence has brightened up the house. It's obvious you have a way with children."

"Thank you, Lawrence, I'm so grateful for the opportunity you've generously offered me. I have always loved children, and regretted never having any of my own. That's why I used to work as a governess. But it's difficult because I grew to love the children, and they grew to love me, but when the little ones became school age, I was let go. But life goes on, and babies grow up. It's only a job, although when you're living it, it feels like much more."

"It's much more than a job, Mallory. You're like a mother to the girls. Not to mention Emma has never known another mother."

Mallory smiled sweetly. "I love them both just as if they were my very own. What lovely girls they are. You should be very proud, Lawrence."

"And you as well, Mallory. You have taught them so much, good manners, good hygiene, how to play the piano, voice lessons, Italian among countless other things. They have really blossomed under your care."

Mallory sat at the piano, playing a tuneful melody while Maggie and Emma gathered around her singing. Lawrence watched their joy, and listened to how their beautiful voices harmonized with tears in his eyes.

Lawrence and Mallory sat beside the fireplace afterward while Emma played with her dolls. Emma came rushing over to Mallory holding onto a porcelain doll with brown curly hair. "Look, Ma, this doll has hair just like you."

"She does, I can see that, Emma." Emma kissed the doll. "And I love her like I love you, Ma. See she is a mommy too, look at her baby." Emma pointed to her infant doll, tucked into a tiny crib.

"And I'm sure her baby must be hungry, why don't you give her a bottle. It's in the toy chest." Emma rushed over to feed her doll while Lawrence looked on lovingly.

"Mallory, I realize Emma will soon be old enough to go to school, but to dismiss you from our household would be a trauma for the entire family. I cannot turn you out, Mallory."

Mallory smiled shyly with her plain demeanor, beaming with goodness as Lawrence bent on one knee. "Mallory, you have become more than a governess to us. You have become a part of our family. It would be a great honor if you would accept my hand in marriage, and become a wife to me, and a mother to the children."

Mallory's eyes welled with joyful tears. "Lawrence, I would be honored and moved to accept your offer."

Lawrence went into his pocket to take out her great grandmother's engagement ring.

"Oh, Lawrence, I cannot believe you've saved my great grandmother's ring for all these years! My parents were forced to sell all the family heirlooms, how nice to have a memento of my past."

"Mallory, we have developed an attachment of respect, trust, and duty. I want you to know I value our friendship," Lawrence said in a matter-of-fact manner as he slid the ring onto her delicate finger.

"Mallory, when we first became engaged, we didn't pretend to be in love, so I will not talk false flattery and shower you with romance. We are mature adults who can make a life together."

Mallory glowed just the same. Her beady brown eyes became enlivened with expectation. "That's more than many couples can boast. To think at fifty years old, I will at last become a bride means the world to me. You have kept your word to marry me after all!" Mallory exclaimed gleefully.

Emma walked over with her rag doll. "Emma, you will be the first to know. Mah and I are getting married, and she will be a real mother to you, and the boys," announced Lawrence.

"Ma has always been my mommy whether you marry her or not, but I'm glad," Emma artlessly replied with a grin.

The spring day of Lawrence and Mallory's wedding glistened with golden sunlight. Beautiful peach and pink roses filled The Lady of Our Lord Church. The stained glass windows reflected prisms of jeweled tones, which shimmered in the light.

Mallory wore a white bridal gown with all the trimmings of a young bride. Her hair was arranged in cascading tendrils, crowned by a delicate veil, in contradiction to her age, but in accordance to her purity. Holding a bouquet of dusty pink roses, Mallory's happiness made her look youthful.

In fact, from never having children, her figure was now extraordinary as her petite frame had matured into womanhood with a waist as tiny as a teenager's. Even her lame gait seemed to have improved, or perhaps Lawrence had merely gotten used to it. In fact, he began to find her defect endearing.

Lawrence looked regal in his black tuxedo, stark white shirt, and satin bow tie. However, his salt and pepper hair made him look more like the father of the bride, than the groom.

It was a tender moment for Sir Dexter, dressed in his Sunday finery, to accompany Mallory down the aisle with all past grudges put aside. Sir Dexter looked rather well compared to how he had looked the night he had arrived at Lawrence's office.

Lawrence approached Sir Dexter. "I would like you to meet Jake, but out of respect to Emily, you must promise me the truth of your connection will never come out."

"Lawrence, you have my word! I would never disrespect Emily's memory."

"Come, Jake is waiting for the wedding procession to begin."

"Jake, I would like to introduce you to Mallory's brother, Sir Dexter Lund."

Jake reached forward to shake Sir Dexter's hand which clasped onto his tightly. "I'm so pleased to finally meet you, Jake." Sir Dexter beamed with a sentimental smile. "My sister has told me many wonderful things about you and your aspirations. I hear you have graduated from school and have become a lawyer. I used to be a lawyer myself way back when."

"You're not a lawyer anymore, Mr. Lund?" Jake asked.

"Please, if you can call my sister Mah, then you can call me Dexter. In answer to your question, I'm no longer a practicing lawyer."

Jake looked puzzled. "You can't be retired, you're far too young."

Sir Dexter's face reddened. "Well, I'm not exactly retired."

Just then, Mallory grabbed a hold of Sir Dexter's arm. "Come, the ceremony is just about to begin."

Sir Dexter led Mallory down the petal-strewn aisle while wedding music accompanied their steps. Amidst the glory of garlands, Lawrence and Mallory exchanged their wedding vows, and professed their commitment to one another.

At the end of the ceremony, Father Dunn joyfully announced while the family looked on, "You may now kiss the bride."

Lawrence met Mallory's lips, not with repugnance as he had once felt, but with maturity, and appreciation for her companionship. Afterward Mallory smiled with the mirth of a schoolgirl looking forward to their wedding night.

"Lawrence, all is well that ends well, isn't that right?" Mallory beamed.

"Thanks for being here for me Mallory and making my home complete, I guess it was our destiny to marry each other after all," Lawrence said with a half smile as they both chuckled.

They went back to the house for a small reception. Sir Dexter and Jake sat together on the sofa, enthusiastically discussing law. Sir Dexter looked ecstatic to be a part of his son's life in spite of the secrecy. It became apparent their resemblance was more than skin deep, as they had barely left each other's side since they had met.

The following morning Miss Bethany asked Lawrence, as he stood by the door holding a bouquet of red roses, "So you and Mallory must be getting ready to leave for your honeymoon?"

Lawrence smirked. "I'm too old to go on a honeymoon."

"Then why the red roses?" asked Miss Bethany in puzzlement.

"They're for Emily's grave. You know I always bring her roses on Sunday," Lawrence echoed as Mallory walked downstairs.

"Good morning, Mallory. You can take the girls to church as usual if you would like. It's a long drive to Saint James, and I'll be gone for hours," Lawrence announced half out the door.

"No, Miss Bethany will take the girls to church. I'd rather go with you, Lawrence. I would like to visit Emily as well. Please wait for me to gather some flowers from the garden."

Mallory devised her own bouquet of wild flowers, and in her tender heart were genuine tears for her sweet friend, Emily Grace Gray.

Chapter Forty-Four

Spring of 1959

The priest, Father Benedict, began his eulogy. "You can be assured Mallory Gray will be granted wings in heaven. She was loved by her family, and all who knew her. She might not have given birth to her loving stepchildren Jake, Larry Junior, Maggie Beth, or Emma, but she had the devotion as if they were her own blood. Mallory was a kind and gracious soul, who brought the girls to church on Sunday when they were young. We will always remember Mallory's enchanting piano playing, and her melodic voice. She sang like an angel for the simple reason she was one. She will be singing up in heaven."

Lawrence stood solemnly awaiting for Mallory's coffin to be lowered into the waiting abyss. The priest put a caring hand on Lawrence's shoulders as he looked down at the cavity of earth that was now taking away his long time companion.

"I'm so sorry, Lawrence, but Mallory is at peace. Please feel free to come speak to me if you need anything. I will always be here for you."

"Thank you, Father Benedict, perhaps I will," Lawrence said mournfully.

Lawrence addressed Father Benedict as they sat together in the church office. "As you know, Mallory and I had been married for thirty-four years Father, but now that she is gone, I have an overwhelming desire to move to Clinton to be near where my first wife Emily is buried. I hate to admit it, while I gave Mallory my all when we were married; in death they are not equal."

"Give yourself time, Lawrence, and you will heal. It's not good to jump to any rash decisions after such a loss."

"I'm an old man, Father Benedict, and I might not have much longer to do as I please. I know it might seem strange for me to still be holding a torch for Emily, but the truth is I've never gotten over losing her. Mallory was a diversion, but now that she has passed away, I'm right back where I started. I'm mourning my Emily as if it was just yesterday that I lost her, when she died so tragically, I had been robbed."

"Perhaps counseling will help, have you considered that? Maybe you have certain unresolved issues you'd like to discuss with a professional," Father Benedict mindfully advised.

"You don't understand, Father Benedict! I don't want to get over my grief; it keeps my love for Emily alive," Lawrence vowed with gleaming eyes.

Thirty-nine year old Emma chastised Lawrence. "Father, how can you just pick up and move to Clinton, it's ridiculous? All my memories are here in this house, and you're just going to sell it for what? To be near your first wife's grave, that's morbid, Father!"

"You say my first wife as if she has no connection to you. For goodness sake, Emma, Emily was your real mother. You were too young to understand because you never knew her, but I feel moving near Emily is my calling. I owe it to her."

"But what about Ma, you plan on showering Emily's grave with roses, and just leaving Ma's grave barren after all she has meant to us. You were married to her for thirty-four years, and she was good to us! Ma was the only mother I've ever known, and I loved her just as much as any daughter could ever love a mother, if not more!" Emma Grace cried out with devotion.

"I have already paid my dues to Mallory. I've given her a life in spite of losing my own, and now it's time for me to do what I must for myself," Lawrence stoically attested. "I have found a beautiful Tudor in Clinton, within walking distance to the Saint James Cemetery."

"Walking distance, after breaking your leg you should not be going to cemeteries unescorted in the first place. It's very easy to stumble on your way in or out." Emma warned.

"I'll be fine with my cane. I've already made plans to move there. There's no stopping me now that all of you are grown with families of your own. There will be plenty of room for all of you to come visit."

* * *

Meg Bailey looked outside her kitchen window as the frail Lawrence Gray bestowed another bouquet of red roses upon Emily's grave. At eighty-three years old, time had grayed his hair, and stooped his shoulders. It had weathered his skin, and robbed his spirit, but time had only enhanced Lawrence's love and attachment for Emily.

When Lawrence Gray did not show up at the cemetery for three days, Meg Bailey feared something must have happened to the old man. The snow obliterated her vision as she trudged on a mission of kindness toward Lawrence Gray's Tudor, isolated behind a hedge of tall bushes.

Meg apprehensively rang his bell; a symphony of chimes beckoned her. Lawrence Gray's baritone voice resonated powerfully. "Who's there?"

"It's Meg Bailey, a neighbor."

Lawrence unfastened the door with the absence of light distorting his face. Like the composition of a negative, his skin had a gray undertone, while his hair appeared as a shock of silver. "Meg Bailey?" Lawrence echoed as if it was a question, eyeing her out on his porch with scrutiny. Seeing Meg's quiet beauty of dark hair and almond eyes lifted his melancholy expression.

"I hope you don't mind me intruding, Mr. Gray," Meg stammered. "I live in the old stone house next to Saint James, and I was worried when I didn't see you for the past few days." A blustery wind whipped between their words.

Lawrence Gray reached forward to shake Meg's glove clad hand as her teeth began to chatter. "Do come in out of the cold, Miss Bailey. Here you are worrying about me, and you shall catch your own death out there in this storm."

Standing five-foot-ten, Lawrence still had a considerable frame, in spite of the falter of his gait. He motioned for her to sit beside him on a couch facing the heat of the fireplace. Meg became mesmerized how

Lawrence's silhouette looked against the fire, and the warming effect it had on his features.

"I was just about to have my afternoon tea, please join me. Meg, I thank you for your concern. As you can see I'm quite fine, I just didn't want to push my luck in the storm." Lawrence paused pensively. "I must say it's nice to have the company of a neighbor. Do you know ever since I moved here last year, you're the only neighbor to befriend me, Meg?"

"That surprises me. I always thought of Clinton as a friendly town."

"Let's face it," Lawrence grumbled. "If you're not a church member, you're on the fringe in this town. I hate to say it, but the church elders are the worst hypocrites of all! I can see the way they look at me, and hear them talking behind my back. Just because I'm an old man, doesn't mean I'm oblivious to their whispering. They judge me because the only time I go near a church is to put flowers on Emily's grave . . . Meg, my sweet wife Emily has been laid out at Saint James for forty years now, rest her soul. And I blame myself," Lawrence professed as the edges of his face became as hard as bronze.

"Don't blame yourself, Mr. Gray. I'm sure your wife Emily is at peace." Meg smiled in false cheer. "After all she receives more flowers than any woman in town."

"Believe me the roses are more to appease my own guilt," Lawrence protested.

"Death is blameless," Meg reassured. "People always look back and think if only I would have done this or that, but you can't think like that."

"Maybe so, Meg, but the circumstance of Emily's death will never leave my mind for as long as I shall dwell upon this earth, never!" Lawrence vowed grievously.

"True love makes amends for everything!" Meg exclaimed with conviction.

"You know you remind me of Emily, she was just like you with her head in the clouds." Lawrence laughed with a grimace.

"I should only be as lucky as Emily to have someone love me the way you love her," Meg professed with awe.

"Meg, sometimes love finds us when we least expect it. It's obvious love has really taken a hold of me. To still be able to bring Emily roses gives me such pleasure."

Meg looked at him with a dreamy expression. "I'm sure Emily receives pleasure as well. She is in heaven smiling at you. I believe love is eternal."

"Do you, Meg?" Lawrence's expression turned peaceful as Meg nodded her head with certainty.

"You know, Meg, I have a handsome, twenty-one-year-old grandson who lives in Essex. Would you be interested in meeting him?"

"I would chance it." Meg shook her head affirmatively.

"Very well, then I will arrange it. He is my daughter Emma's son, and his name is Wade Stephens... Who knows, maybe your children will become descendants of the Grays?"

Meg smiled at her possible entry into the Gray legacy Fanny Brund had divulged.

The springtime day greeted Meg with dual joy since Lawrence had invited her to meet his grandson, Wade Stephens, in his yard for lunch. Meg put on a red plaid, pleated skirt with the modern touch of black leather closures in the front, paired with a formfitting black tank top with a white blouse underneath.

The first glimmer of spring welcomed Meg as she walked down the block to Lawrence Gray's stately residence, while golden sunlight brought out the fiery highlights of her long, auburn hair.

Meg could barely contain her smile when Lawrence opened the door. "Good afternoon, Meg," he greeted as he invited her in. "Why just look at you, Meg, aren't you a vision of loveliness."

"Really?" Meg retorted in a questioning tone.

"If I say you're a pretty girl, you can be assured it's true. I'm an artist who used to paint portraits. I haven't painted in a great many years, but I tell you, Meg, you tempt me to pick up my paint brush again."

"Thanks," Meg said shyly. "I'd be honored to pose for you."

"Would you, Meg?" Lawrence's ancient eyes became enlivened. "I just might take you up on it... Come, my grandson will be meeting us in the yard shortly."

Lawrence had set the wrought iron table with burgundy placemats and the white china with pink roses Emily had purchased at the turn of the century. Tulips bordered the garden in multicolored delight, while the blossoming trees fanned their white and pink petals in the breeze.

"Take a seat, Meg, and have some tea."

"Thank you," Meg murmured as she filled a cup with Lawrence's aromatic blend.

"You know when I asked if I could paint you before I wasn't just saying it. I mean it, Meg. If you would oblige me, in fact . . . you're pretty as a picture just as you are right now, holding onto your teacup."

"It would be my pleasure to sit for you," Meg warmly replied.

"Now that you've inspired me, I'd like to start right away, but I have a feeling my grandson will have his own ideas on monopolizing your time once he sets his eyes on you." Lawrence chuckled, as the sunlight momentarily obscured the face of a tall, broad male form approaching, dressed in khaki pants and a white shirt.

"Hello, Wade, come take a seat," Lawrence exclaimed as he stood to make the introductions. "This is my neighbor, Meg Bailey. Meg Bailey, this is my grandson, Wade Stephens."

"I'm pleased to meet you, Meg." Wade reached forward to encompass her hand beneath the warmth of his own, while Meg met his hypnotic eyes.

"I'll let you two become acquainted while I go to get the sandwiches," Lawrence said as Wade sat on the chair across from Meg, and dazzled her with his chiseled features, made striking by his swarthy coloring and jet black hair, reminiscent of how Lawrence looked in his youth.

Meg poured Wade a cup of tea with her dainty hands. "Afternoon tea is your grandfather's specialty," Meg said as they took a sip in unison.

Wade's burly eyebrows lifted. "I thought my grandfather's specialty was his tea as well until he introduced me to you, Meg. I don't mean to be forward or embarrass you, but when my grandfather told me what a charming young lady you were, I didn't expect you to be so beautiful."

"I appreciate your flattery," Meg blushed.

"It's not flattery; it's the truth." Wade smiled a flash of white teeth as he half laughed. "Who would have ever thought my grandfather's going to Saint James every day would have been instrumental in meeting you. You know, I must admit I was worried when my grandfather told me he had a girl for me to meet, but now I see he knows me better than I thought . . ."

Lawrence appeared with a platter of turkey sandwiches, which he placed in the center of the table. "You know, Meg has agreed to let me paint her portrait, Wade. I was thinking the flowerbed would be a perfect backdrop."

"That's wonderful news, Grandfather. I can understand how Meg could inspire you to pick up a paint brush again, but be forewarned, Meg, anyone who my grandfather paints ends up being in a museum. Maybe your portrait will one day be hanging in the Massachusetts Museum of Art, beside the portrait of my grandmother, Emily Gray, who I've heard such wonderful things about." Meg peered into Wade's dark eyes, and as she did, she saw her destiny within them.

Out from the shadows of a new dawn, Meg heard the melody of the songbirds, and then a faint murmur of where the spirit of Emily Grace Gray dwelled upon the hill, waiting for her beloved Lawrence. The sun shined brightly overhead as a Robin redbreast perched on a tree outside her kitchen window, and serenaded her with the song of love. The bird flew away and ascended upward, but the enchanting melody continued. The breeze rustled carrying the sweet murmur of a voice whispering in the shadows.

When the wind over the Saint James Cemetery gets strong, it whips over the treetops with a vengeance equal to all mortal unrest. Out of the shadows, betwixt the other side, connected through prayer and longing for the past. Lawrence Gray listens closely to the silence of earth.

He can hear the murmur of the sweet, stirring of Emily's spirit grace above him. Bathing him in the mystery of eternal life, where one day he will shed his mortal woe, and mesh his essence beside Emily's. Where dispersed beyond life and worldly reason they will both roam with the wind, atop of the hill, free together at last!

Bibliography of Afternoon Tea by J. R. LaGreca

Arbor, Marilyn. *Tools & Trades of America's Past: The Mercer Museum Collection,* Pennsylvania: Tower Hill Press, first edition, 1981

Brown, Hablot. *All About Kisses.* London: Charles Henry Clark, rare 1800s Victorian book

Gavan, Terrence. *The Barons of Newport.* Rhode Island: Pineapple Publications, 1988

Harper's Round Table, 1895. New York: Harper and Brothers Publishers, 1895

Lochhead, Marion. *The Victorian Household.* London: John Murray, 1964

Mrs. Humphry. *Mrs. Manners for Men.* London: James Bowden, first edition, 1897

Mrs. Humphry. *Mrs. Manners for Women.* London: Ward, Lock & Co., Limited, first edition, 1897

The Mystery of Love, Courtship, and Marriage Explained. New York: Wehman Bros. 1890

The 1900 House. Video recording, London: PBS, Home Video, 2000

Priestly, J.B. *Victoria's Heyday.* New York: Harper& Row, Publishers, 1972

Washington, George. *George Washington's Rules of Civility & Decent Behavior In Company and Conversation.* Massachusetts: Applewood Books, 1988

In memory of my sister, Wendy Ellen Lehrer

A GRAIN OF SAND

A grain of sand,
A glimmer of hope
Held tenuously in the hand.
Pressed between the flesh
And the beach, infinitesimal.
Though on second glance, grand!

A part of earth, undivided,
An entity, a prism of glass.
I look inside my fleeting grasp,
Escaping quick and fast.

A grain of sand,
A shadow of summer,
Swept away with the sun.
A shadowed thought
Sifted through the soul.

A single thought, a single grain,
Together in triumph twist.
In the smallest part of the whole,
Whereas humanity shall exist.

I grasp the grain
I hold onto the thought,
As both blow away in vain.

I cannot capture the essence
Of either, for both,
Are one and the same.

By: Jody Riva LaGreca